PRAISE FOR CAROLE NELSON DOUGLAS AND THE IRENE ADLER SERIES:

IRENE AT LARGE

"An absolutely ripping adventure."
—Anne Perry, author of BELGRAVE SQUARE

"Fresh and amusing...the action never loses its jaunty, high-heeled pace."
—*The New York Times*

"A perfect Chinese puzzle of a book, with layers of mystery, history, romance, and intrigue. An irresistible read."
—Mary Jo Putney, author of SILK AND SECRETS

GOOD MORNING IRENE

"A carefree, romantic romp."
—*The New York Times*

"A rollicking and complex story brimming with Victorian atmosphere and details."
—*Publisher's Weekly*

"Carole Nelson Douglas does it again! GOOD MORNING IRENE leaves no doubt that Ms. Douglas is destined to become one of the first ladies of the mystery scene."
—*Romantic Times*

"Douglas has given us a woman worthy of Holmes' attention."
—Phyllis A. Whitney, Mystery Writers of America Grand Master

Tor/Forge books by Carole Nelson Douglas

MYSTERY

IRENE ADLER ADVENTURES:
Good Night, Mr. Holmes
Good Morning, Irene
Irene at Large

MIDNIGHT LOUIE MYSTERIES:
Catnap
Pussyfoot

HISTORICAL ROMANCE

*Amberleigh**
*Lady Rogue**
Fair Wind, Fiery Star

SCIENCE FICTION

*Probe**
*Counterprobe**

FANTASY

TALISWOMAN:
Cup of Clay
Seed Upon the Wind

SWORD AND CIRCLET:
Keepers of Edanvant
Heir of Rengarth
Seven of Swords

*also mystery

IRENE'S LAST WALTZ

CAROLE NELSON DOUGLAS

A TOM DOHERTY ASSOCIATES BOOK
NEW YORK

This is a work of fiction. All the characters and events portrayed in this book are fictitious, and any resemblance to real people or events is purely coincidental.

IRENE'S LAST WALTZ

Copyright © 1994 by Carole Nelson Douglas

Cover art by George Bush

A Tor Book
Published by Tom Doherty Associates, Inc.
175 Fifth Avenue
New York, NY 10010

Tor® is a registered trademark of Tom Doherty Associates, Inc.

ISBN: 0-812-51703-2
Library of Congress Catalog Card Number: 93-43825

First edition: February 1994
First mass market edition: November 1994

Printed in the United States of America

0 9 8 7 6 5 4 3 2 1

For Sam,
the wind beneath my wings

ST. VITUS'
CATHEDRAL

HRADCANY
CASTLE

CHARLES
BRIDGE

NATIONAL THEATRE

OLD JEWISH
CEMETERY

OLD-NEW
SYNAGOGUE

OLD
TOWN HALL

CITY OF

PRAGUE

CONTENTS

Chapter One

GIVE HER LIBERTY OR DEATH

Irene lifted the cream parchment envelope on her joined palms like an offering to a pagan god.

"It has arrived!" she declared rapturously. "I have obtained at last one of my dearest ambitions."

I tilted my head to better survey the missive. "No doubt another scandalous invitation from that Bernhardt woman."

"Better!" she answered without hesitation.

I was not optimistic. In certain matters, Irene's and my estimations of worthiness were worlds apart.

"But I am being selfish," she admonished herself, glancing from the hypnotic envelope to the stitchery work dropped to my lap. The cat, Lucifer, had already pawed my ball of thread to the ground and was proceeding to claw it into a snarl. "We must open the *package*, of course, first."

The same post had also brought to our rural cottage at Neuilly, near Paris, a massive parcel wrapped in brown paper that now squatted on our parlor carpet. I had noticed the letter's Paris postmark, but the intriguing parcel bore London markings. Given our recent adventures in that city, I was far more curious about its contents.

With great care, Irene laid the unopened envelope atop

the marble-topped occasional table, then rushed over to seize my small scissors. She cast herself at once onto the carpet to worry the parcel wrappings with a savagery as intense as Lucifer's attacks on my hapless ball of thread.

"Irene!" I remonstrated. "You will dull my finest German embroidery scissors."

"Oh." She eyed their dainty, curved gold tips before casting them down. "No wonder they're so ineffective!" she complained, tearing away great ragged swaths of wrapping paper with her bare fingers.

"What can have you in such a frenzy to unveil it?" I wondered aloud.

"Liberty silk! Our Liberty silk gowns have arrived."

"Our?"

She threw me a quick glance. "Of course 'our.' You don't imagine for a moment that I would indulge myself without ordering something for you."

"But you refused my company to Liberty's when we were in London. I remember most clearly. You said that I abhorred the fashion for aesthetic dress, and furthermore that we were incompatible shopping partners. You planned to order some gowns for yourself and a . . . gift for Sarah Bernhardt."

"And so I did," Irene said cheerfully, frowning as she struggled to untie lengths of string. "And two for you as well."

"For me!?"

"Indeed."

"I cannot see why, since I am such an unpleasant shopping companion."

"Nell, don't be such a goose. Of course I didn't *mean* any of those things I said. At the time, I needed to discourage your company, since I planned to follow my visit to Liberty's with activities that you could not know about."

"Then you lied."

"Exaggerated for good cause."

"Lied."

"Embroidered for effect."

"Lied."

"Extrapolated for your own good."

"I can consult my diaries for your exact words."

"Oh, a pox on your diaries!"

"At times you find them useful," I pointed out.

Irene sat back upon her heels, no very fine way to treat a pleated silk morning costume. Huge leaves of brown paper surrounded her like jungle foliage, and made her resemble an elegant fashion doll abandoned among the fish-and-chip wrappings.

"A small deception," she conceded at last, "necessary for the greater good."

"The 'greater good' being that you and Quentin deceived me so that you could have a personal look at the lodgings of that dreadful detective."

"Quentin had no choice, since I insisted, and I only deceived you because you might have given away the game. Whatever you may think of Sherlock Holmes, I should not like to be caught by him in a deception."

"I am not so sure that you *did* deceive him."

"What?"

I shrugged and contested Lucifer for my poor mangled ball of thread. "Mr. Holmes, however odious, is clever enough to have *appeared* to accept you in the ludicrous role of Quentin's aged mama. It was not one of your more likely impersonations."

"Ah. So acting criticism is the thanks I get for rushing to Liberty's to purchase gowns for my friends when I had weightier matters on my mind."

Despite myself, my severe expression lapsed into a smile. "Only think how critical the Divine Sarah would have been had she witnessed the scene instead of me."

That thought gave Irene pause; the Divine One tolerated no rivals in her art. At length Irene smiled and flourished the cover free of the box.

"At least no poisonous serpents inhabit this case, only rare silks. Do stop pouting and come see!"

Of course I was too curious to hold back any longer, especially when a riot of rich colors foamed over the carton edge. I joined Irene's undignified seat on the carpeting as she rooted among pale tissues, throwing them hither and yon to the great entertainment of Lucifer.

The huge black Persian cat pounced with serial crackling sounds while, from his cage, the parrot Casanova urged the cat on with hoarse cries of "*Avanti! Avanti!*"

I was distressed by the bird's apparent ease in yet another language, Italian—no doubt due to Irene's operatic origins—but restrained myself from responding with my one Italian word, "*Basta!*" Enough.

Lengths of patterned silk spilled over the cardboard rim, a shimmering, exotic, rainbow river on which a Marco Polo might have sailed to China.

"Here. This is yours, Nell. The wedgwood blue and ivory."

"How could you order for others? The size—"

"Size does not matter in this uncorseted, loose-flowing style. You must think of these as draperies."

Indeed, when I had untangled the roil of color and sheen that Irene had called mine, I held a high-waisted gown of a celestial shade of blue. A darker blue silk overgown had huge cuffs and collar of ivory and blue brocade in a sinuous pattern.

"This is a . . . nightgown," I murmured, pressing the voluminous, soft folds to my well-corseted bodice. "Not for public wear."

"That is the point; the more public the better. No more whale-ribbed corsets, simply the soft fall of fabric. And the hair must be styled more loosely as well." Irene eyed me critically. "Perhaps half-down."

"I have not worn my hair down since a girl of sixteen!" I protested.

"Hmm," Irene agreed with absent disapproval. She continued drawing silken lengths from the box, a magician concentrating on an endless illusion.

I could not see how these untucked, unstitched, unberibboned lengths could pass as afternoon gowns, but Irene was untroubled by their unconstructed grace.

"Green for Sarah, naturally, given that incendiary hair of hers, with touches of imperial purple and red. Gold and crimson for me, and the silver and black. A pink for you. How do you like your blue?"

"Very . . . discreet." I eyed the clashing colors that bedecked the other gowns. "I suppose that items Moorish and Saracen are in fashion at the moment, though I shall likely never wear mine."

"Oh, everything from the exotic East is à la mode nowadays," Irene assured me, adding, "as are personages from the same quarter." A wicked gleam warmed her tiger-brown eyes.

I knew precisely to whom she referred and blanched to think of Quentin Stanhope seeing me in such unconventional garb, even as I wondered if my wearing it might surprise, or intrigue, him. I found my fingers clutching the smooth silk as if it were a blanket and I was cold.

"What is this?" came Godfrey's liquid baritone from the threshold. "Have you two curiosity-seekers discovered a body in a box? Or rather, a missing person represented only by yards of silk? Some sybaritic mummy, perhaps, Irene, that you have unwound to nothingness?"

"Darling!" she cried, springing up to greet him, her arms full of Liberty silk. Godfrey was used to saluting her over such fashionable barriers, and managed to brush her cheek with his lips. "You are in the nick of time for a celebration. Do pour something amusing before I open the letter that arrived today."

Godfrey had divested himself of stick and top hat in the hall, but he still looked very much the British gentleman abroad in his black frock coat and pin-striped gray trousers as he crossed the threshold into our furbelow-occupied lair. He stepped over the paper-trouncing Lucifer to the wine decanter.

"Liberty silks," I explained.

He nodded cautiously, as incurious as only men can be about the mysteries of female fripperies. "Most colorful and . . . prolific. Will sherry do?" he asked Irene.

"Whatever." She was draping her booty over the back of the bergère before reverently lifting the envelope from the tabletop. "I have been waiting for this for . . . months."

Godfrey brought me a dainty-stemmed glass of Vichy water, which I accepted. My mind remained on Quentin Stanhope and the cruel manner of our parting only weeks before, when I thought him dead from a fatal plunge into the Thames in the murderous grasp of the villainous Colonel Moran. Oddly, I found the notion that Quentin might still live even more disquieting.

Godfrey handed Irene her glass, and gently abstracted the precious envelope from her other hand before she could object, just as she was about to rip it open.

He stepped into the hall, leaving her openmouthed, and returned a moment later bearing the console table's gilt letter opener with the dolphin's-head handle.

"If you have been waiting that long," he said, slitting the creamy parchment, "you can wait a bit longer to open it neatly."

Reproved, Irene demurely sipped her sherry, then handed him the glass in exchange for the envelope. Her husband's calming presence had quenched her immoderate spirits, for she drew the folded paper from its sheath as delicately as a wine steward decanting a rare vintage.

I held my breath. Irene adored dramatic moments, but she also had a genius for attracting to herself the outré, the deadly and the puzzling. Perhaps the missive held news of Quentin's survival, his whereabouts . . . How like Irene to inquire into the matter privately, and surprise me—us— with the results!

Her face was a study in still, perfect beauty poised upon

the brink of expression as her eyes darted back and forth to read, or, rather, consume in quick visual gulps, the contents of the page. Joy, dawning on that still perfection, flooded it with bright relief.

"As I thought," she announced. "My carefully laid plans have come to fruition. My dears"—her triumphant eyes sparkled in each of our directions in turn, indeed, encompassed even cat and parrot, both of whom grew eerily quiet—"I have an appointment on twelve September on the rue de le Paix with the maestro himself."

"Maestro?" The operatic term confused me. Surely Irene could not be contemplating a return to the stage?

"The rue de la Paix?" Godfrey echoed with lawyerly precision, his handsome face puckering as he mentally envisioned the addresses to be found along that highly fashionable street, which began at the place de l'Opéra and swept like a red carpet of luxury to the old royal promenade of the Tuileries via the rue Castiglione.

"I am to see Charles Frederick Worth himself," Irene elucidated. "I have a personal fitting with the king of couture. I am truly Parisienne. I have joined the aristocracy of artifice. I shall be dressed by Worth himself at last!"

Godfrey and I exchanged a polite but puzzled glance of mutual mystification. Irene, clasping the stiff parchment to her bosom like a debutante's first bouquet, noticed nothing.

Over dinner, Godfrey and I were educated on the subject of Charles Frederick Worth far more than we wished to be.

"Have you not several things already from the House of Worth," Godfrey asked quite innocently, and unleashed what became a cataract of retort.

"Nothing from the mind of Worth himself."

"Who is he?" I asked.

"Who is he?" Irene railed. "What a question! Only the architect of the world's finest gowns, a monarch of material, a king of cut, a prince of profile—for it was he who

invented the princesse line—the man for whom the word
couturier was coined in the masculine gender, a master who
dresses queens and empresses from the tundra of Russia to
the castles of Austria as well as queens of society from St.
James to Newport.''

Godfrey's dinner fork dissected an odd arrangement of
asparagus and chestnuts created by our cook, the maid
Sophie's aunt Nathalie. "I suppose that such exceptional
concoctions of the maestro himself are exceptionally . . .
expensive.''

Irene looked insulted. "Cost is no consideration. Genius
does not come cheap.'' She reconsidered. "Or it should
not, in a perfect world.''

"In a perfect world,'' he pursued wryly, "to how many
works of the genius Worth should an incognito opera
singer aspire?''

"I had not considered. His evening gowns are sublime,
but then so are his visiting ensembles. I do not wish to
appear . . . tightfisted. And then, as long as one is ordering,
one might as well order a season's worth of gowns.''

"As long as one is paying, what will so many Worths be
worth?'' he asked.

"More than enough,'' she admitted, laughing, "but this
is the opportunity of a lifetime. Worth at this stage in his
career does not accept just anyone as a client, and seldom
sees them in person. Besides, we have plenty of money left
from the sale of the Zone of Diamonds.''

"No doubt,'' I said, "Sarah Bernhardt put in a good
word for you with this man-milliner.''

"I hope not! When she was still with the Comédie Fran-
çaise years ago, Sarah insulted him by ordering five of his
gowns for a play, then using only one and filling in with
dresses by designers he considered lesser. Worth was livid,
as Sarah told me. He is a tyrant in the fitting room who
tolerates no rivals. No, I have won this coup on my own,
by a careful campaign of dropping a word in the right ears.''

Godfrey shook his head, smiling. "It is your money,

Irene; you may spend it as you wish. I can't help thinking that an idle mind is the couturier's workshop, though. I have seen your boredom rise at the quiet life in France after our latest adventure. You must do what you will to occupy yourself. Nell and I will have to take your word that this is 'Worth' it."

"Do not include me in your approval," I told Godfrey. "I am not convinced that it is proper for a man to involve himself in the intimacies of women's dress."

Irene tossed her crumpled napkin to the tablecloth. "Your respectable reservations are thirty years behind the times, Nell. That issue was decided in Mr. Worth's favor when he first began dressing the Empress Eugénie in the sixties. Now she is in exile, empires have toppled, but Worth still reigns supreme. Besides, he is an Englishman born and reared; how can he even dream of being improper? Such old-fogeyism is old hat."

"No," said Godfrey, installing peace, "it is new hat. I suspect that we will see a good deal of those as well."

"And gloves and parasols, boots and slippers, and jewelry," Irene enumerated happily. "Worth dresses the whole woman."

"Until she has a hole in her pocket," I mumbled to my own mutilated asparagus.

"Wait to judge, Nell, until you see number seven, rue de la Paix," Irene said.

"I? I never intend to view such a place."

"But you must!"

"Why?"

"Godfrey has no interest in the rituals of commissioning gowns, and I can hardly be expected to make up my mind on such vital matters alone. Worth gowns cost a king's ransom, after all."

Irene's husband and I stared at each other in the face of this sudden confession from a woman who recently had faced down a murderous heavy-game hunter and hooded cobras.

"Please, Nell," she pleaded very prettily indeed. "You can't allow me unchaperoned into such a den of mousseline and man-milliners. Godfrey is right; boredom is fatal to me. I must make my forays into something new, even if it is only as frivolous as fashion. I require a witness, a supporter, a recording angel. You cannot deny me, dearest Nell."

As usual, she was quite correct. I could no more resist an appeal to my governess instincts than Irene could resist the siren calls of imagined luxury and calculated risk.

Godfrey had done with dinner and laid down his fork. He regarded Irene, an indefinable glint in his silver-gray eyes. "As for your rash assertion that it is impossible for an Englishman to be improper, I will be forced to put your theory to the test."

"I will take a great deal of convincing," she suggested.

"I do hope so," he responded in a baritone purr.

I, of course, could make no more head or tail of this last exchange than I could discern front from back on a Liberty silk gown.

Pleading headache, I excused myself immediately after dinner to withdraw to my room with my peculiar new gowns. Neither Irene nor Godfrey seemed discernibly bereft by my absence.

Chapter Two

ENTER MADAME X

❧

Even the weather cooperated with Irene's desire to make a grand entrance the day our carriage drew up before No. 7, rue de la Paix. Silken swaths of dove gray cloud shrouded the Parisian skies. Some somber sprite had draped the same dull veil over the stone streets and building facades, turning them into a dreary blank canvas awaiting a splash of pigment.

Despite ground-floor display windows flaunting fine fabrics and costly accessories, Maison Worth was the usual five-story edifice that lines the rue de la Paix. Such buildings are pierced by narrow, long windows stretching from floor to ceiling behind fences of wrought iron and crowned with a rickrack of gables and a grim, charred forest of chimney pots. The single word WORTH was blazoned in gilt letters above the double entry doors.

When our driver André helped Irene alight before the central archway, her crimson and gold Liberty silk gown flamed like an illustration from a medieval book on a dirty page.

Heads all along the thoroughfare turned to see Irene in the high-waisted gown, her dark hair drawn into smooth wings that covered her ears and gathered into a loose chignon low on her head beneath a red velvet bonnet.

I, of course, would never dream of wearing a Liberty silk gown on the street for all to gawk at.

"Such unconventional dress may annoy Mr. Worth," I warned Irene in a whisper as we were ushered through the portal by a white-gloved page boy.

"Quite true," she surprised me by admitting, "but far better to beard a fashion lion wearing exquisite unorthodoxy than inferior conventionality."

"Since I am the picture of such inferior conventionality," I protested, "I will wait outside."

"Nonsense. Exquisiteness requires contrast to set it off; your ordinariness is absolute perfection."

By then we—she—had glided into a richly upholstered salon in which fashionable ladies sat and strolled like figures from *La Mode Illustrée* come to life.

Even Irene paused at such intimidating perfection as was reflected in the gilt-framed mirrors. One of the strolling women approached us, her gown a triumph fashioned of gathered tulle frosted with beads and lace.

"*Mesdames* require a *vendeuse?*" she inquired in an odd blend of English and French.

Irene flushed, as I had not seen her do since Bohemia.

"I have an appointment with Monsieur Worth for half past three. My name is Madame Norton. My companion is Miss Huxleigh."

"You are early, Madame Norton, and Monsieur Worth is a bit behind. One of his migraines. Please observe the mannequins. If a particular gown strikes your fancy, it can be made for you in a manner to suit. Meanwhile, you and Miss Huxleigh may stroll or sit, as it pleases you."

The woman wafted off in her sparkling cloud while Irene's inquisitive expression consulted me.

"Please let us sit," I suggested. "I need to absorb the surroundings."

She did not argue, perching quickly on a huge tufted

ottoman, her reticule centered on her lap, as mine invariably was when I was nervous. In fact, as my reticule was always placed when I sat, just as my feet stayed as closely paired as empty shoes.

We sat there, silent and side by side, for several minutes while unknown women—elegant, exquisitely attired women—swirled around us in a grande promenade, twitching their trains and plucking at the airy sleeves that thrust above their shoulders like butterfly wings.

At last Irene leaned toward me to employ a genteel whisper in English. "Some of these women are mannequins employed by the house to model dresses; some are *vendeuses*—shop assistants who sell the gowns. The rest are clients like ourselves."

"Speak for yourself! I am no client. And you are the only woman present dressed in the aesthetic style. No doubt 'Monsieur' Worth abhors such unorthodoxy. What kind of Englishman would allow himself to be bowed to as 'Monsieur this' and 'Monsieur that,' at any rate? It smacks of Frenchification."

"Worth has lived in France for some decades, Nell. His wife is French. His sons are named Gaston and Jean Phillipe."

"Oh, dear; he *has* been thoroughly corrupted, then," I began, only to stop short as our greeting angel rustled toward us again.

"Monsieur Worth will receive you in the salon above," she announced with a pleasure that I did not share. "Come this way."

We followed in her wake, a meringue-like froth of lace and tulle that reminded me all too well that the prized black silk "surprise" dress I wore made me a crow among birds-of-paradise, despite its embroidered old-rose revers and the overskirt coyly caught up on one side to reveal more old-rose embroidery.

On the other hand, I did not attract the untoward attention that Irene did. Every eye in that room glittered like a

furtive jewel behind downcast lashes, watching Irene's fla-
grant Liberty gown retreat up the carpeted stairs to the lair
of the master of Maison Worth.

The private rooms above were as grandly furnished, if
less populated, than the imposing salon. Our guide led us
to a chaise longue on which a gentleman reclined, a compress clinging damply to his temples.

At the sight of Irene, he leaped up, flinging the compress
aside, where it landed wetly on the wine-colored brocade
upholstery. His sofa partner, a large spaniel, lowered its
black muzzle to the castoff.

Monsieur Worth stared at Irene (I doubt that he even
noticed me, at least not until later in our encounter) and
Irene stared right back with her brand of distilled American
forthrightness. And well she might.

This so-called Englishman born was a man of ordinary
stature attired in a velvet beret of excessive dimension. He
also wore a "poet's" shirt, which is to say a sloppy one; a
soft tie of spotted silk; a reasonably respectable buttoned
vest and some silly shapeless brocade jacket banded in
black velvet. No wonder the man's head pained him.

Beyond his manner of dress, he was unprepossessing. In
an uncharitable mood, I should have called him uncomely.
Certainly, compared to Godfrey, he left much to be desired. I could have pitied him for his lack of attractions had
he not chosen to surmount an insufficient chin with a great,
bristling, overhanging eave of rusty mustache, much resembling a walrus's.

Irene was not in the slightest taken aback by this bizarre
appearance. The man eyed her up and down, then lifted a
pudgy hand, let the forefinger droop down and twirled it.

"Turn," he ordered in English.

Irene lifted one eyebrow, at which she was most adept,
then spun away from the man-milliner in a shimmering
sweep of red-and-gold silk that echoed the highlights in her
hair.

"Ah!" Monsieur Worth clapped his palms together in an

irritatingly French fashion, although he had spoken thus far in English. "Marie must see."

This last phrase, in French, was directed to our guide. She rustled away while Monsieur Worth cast himself to the chaise, nearly sitting on the damp compress.

"Walk," he instructed, again in English. Irene paraded back and forth a few times before coming to a stop before this would-be Napoleon of costume.

"Her Soon-to-be Serene Highness, Princess Alice," he said in the same high, slightly strained voice, "speaks well of you, Madame Norton. I have no favorite clients, but some are more likable than others, and she is among the most charming."

Irene curtsied silent thanks for the compliment to her friend. The motion made her gown hem pool on the carpet in liquid metal rivers of red and gold.

"Liberty of London," Monsieur Worth noted approvingly. "I have a great affection for the aesthetic dress, but most women are too timid to wear it. Her Serene Highness assures me that you are not timid, and I see that she is right."

I did not miss the triumphant look Irene shot me from under her veiling eyelashes.

"What kind of gown do you require?" he demanded next.

"I require nothing. I desire only." Irene's supple voice had a husky tone all the more arresting, that commanded the attention as imperiously as a low, trembling chord on a cello. Monsieur Worth (he was English in surname only now, I saw) nodded again, as if further pleased. "What I desire is a gown of your own special design," Irene said, "perhaps an evening gown, since that is your specialty, and mine."

Returning rustles announced the advent of the angelic model and the mysterious "Marie." This personage, I am happy to report, was clad almost entirely in dignified black—a solid, maternal figure of sixty-some years. Despite this, her hair was as dark as her dress and drawn tightly from a center part into a curled chignon at the back of her head. She possessed a Gallic nose (no doubt for endless sniffing of wine "bouquets"), long and strong. Her eyes and brows were almost black, and all of these sternly handsome features were inlaid into a placid moon of face that cast its own soft radiance no matter the hour.

"My wife," the miserable martinet announced, enough proud fondness in his voice to redeem him somewhat in my eyes.

Irene's curtsy was deeper and yet more playful this time. She reminded me of a schoolgirl on her best company manners. "All Paris knows of Madame Marie, who was the first and most fortunate woman to model a Worth creation."

I had never heard of the woman, nor that she was the first of these scandalous walking fashion dolls.

"We were poor," Madame Worth said with a nostalgic smile. "Almost thirty years ago, I took my courage in hand and approached the Austrian ambassador's wife with some of my husband's sketches. Princess von Metternich almost refused to see me—until her waiting woman persuaded her to glance at the designs. Yet I must admit"—she glanced at her husband—"that it took more courage to wear Charles's early creations to the races at Longchamps when he dispensed with shrouding shawls and deep-brimmed bonnets. Had I not been a respectable married woman, I wonder what would have been said about such unprecedented exposure."

"You *are* a wonder," he replied, "and went among the great ladies on your own terms, just as I clothe them on mine. As for my early innovations, they are as nothing today."

Madame Worth shrugged her broad shoulders, removed the abandoned compress from the sofa, shooed the spaniel and sat in its place. Here indeed was a formidable woman.

I detected the power behind the throne, or, in this case, the pincushion and the poppycock.

"This is Madame Norton," he went on, "whom dear Alice recommended. Would you walk again, my dear? For my wife."

I noticed that his orders softened in the presence of that lady.

Irene obliged. Her theatrical training had made her docile in only one area: that of heeding a maestro, a stage director, or a composer like Antonín Dvořák—and perhaps a world-renowned composer of ladies' toilettes like Worth.

He shook his head as she paraded, not in disapproval but in wonder. "I have not seen such fine carriage since yours," he commented to his wife. He then waved Irene to a halt. "You are American, no?"

She nodded.

"Ah, my American clients. Such women! Goddesses of liberty with three divine attributes: faith, figures and francs. Between them and the Russian grand duchesses I am kept in seventh heaven . . . and caviar."

"Thank you, Monsieur," Irene said, "but I fear that I somewhat lack the third element in your dressmaking equation."

"That may not be fatal, my dear," Madame Worth put in quickly. "My husband is aware that the times change as we near the twentieth century. We have seen royal houses fall, empires dissolve and aristocrats flee. Commerce remains. I have long passed the time when I could introduce my husband's more daring inventions. He seeks a substitute."

"But—" Irene appeared bemused. "The mannequins below. Among them I recognized a duplicate of Alice Heine, and of Maria Feodorovna, the Empress of Russia. You shrewdly employ living dressmaker's dummies, 'doubles' of your most famous patrons, Monsieur, but I do not resemble anyone famous."

"Exactly!" The silly man clapped his hands again, his ludicrous beret trembling like a blancmange. He glanced at his stolid wife. "I believe that we have found here our own Madame X, our *mannequin de ville*."

She nodded at this mysterious statement, and even Irene allowed herself to look a trifle blank.

"But first I must see more!" he declared. "You must repair below and allow yourself to be laced into a more fitted gown. Aesthetic dress is all very well for effect, but most of my clients prefer to exhibit their small waists. I trust that you are as accomplished, Madame."

"The cruel schoolmistress Corsetry has long since made hourglasses of us all," Irene answered, unruffled.

"True!" Marie Worth's hands patted her broad midsection with a laugh. "One of the comforts of old age is . . . comfort."

"I will do as you suggest," Irene said, turning to leave. I began to follow her.

"Wait!" came Worth's command. We stopped as one and looked back. The odious man-milliner was glaring at me through narrowed eyes. "This other lady. She is to be clothed as well?"

I froze in blind umbrage, as speechless as a rabbit.

"Miss Huxleigh," Irene answered swiftly on my behalf, "is too sensible to follow fashion. She is Shropshire born."

"Ah." Monsieur Worth nodded soberly under his frivolous beret. "I myself was a Lincolnshire lad until I went to London at twelve to make my fortune." He frowned at me. "It is for the best. Even I could not do much for her." A plump hand waved us on.

So I was allowed to escape that interview unmolested.

Chapter Three

A GOOD DRESSING-DOWN

We were escorted below by the waiting mannequin through the crowded salon and ensconced in one of several dressing rooms. These private chambers were paneled and gilded as lavishly as the main salon, with hooks for gowns ringing the perimeter.

"A shame to drive so much hardware into such splendid woodwork," I commented after our guide left us.

"Forget the woodwork!" Irene's voice was hushed as in a church, but her excitement was hardly religious. "Do you realize what good fortune I may have? Maison Worth is seeking a discreet but public mannequin for its most forward designs. 'A model of the city.' I may possibly acquire more gowns than I can afford for a discounted price!"

"I should think that Monsieur Worth would pay *you* for acting as his experiment, if so."

"You do not seem to comprehend the honor. His wife was key in his early career; he apparently hunts a modern substitute, and I am a candidate."

"Honor, like beauty, is often in the eye of the beholder."

Irene sighed hugely. Her cheeks were fervid and her eyes glowed as if glossed by fever. "This is a fabulous piece of luck, Nell! Monsieur Worth is not merely considering another in-house mannequin, but an . . . ambassadress of dress, as it were, someone who will move in the larger society and command attention for his gowns.''

"I should think he has achieved all the attention necessary and indeed healthy by now, Irene.''

"A genius like Worth never stops innovating; that is his brilliance.''

"He has made a lot of money from vain and foolish women. That is his true genius. You will be both of those if you allow yourself to become a fashion advertisement.''

"Wait until you see a Worth gown in detail. Even a Shropshire lass will be impressed.''

At that moment a knock tapped lightly at our door. A *vendeuse* swept in with an armful of violet velvet sparkled with an entire firmament of ornament: jet-spangled black lace splashed with silver, peacock blue and green beadwork.

Irene's sigh escaped with the ecstatic control of an aria: a long sustained exhalation of utter bliss.

The *vendeuse* smiled as she hung this theatrical curtain of a gown on a gilt hook. "I will let Madame's maid assist her,'' she said, preparing to withdraw.

I remained mystified, but Irene merely reached up to unpin her bonnet. "Huxleigh will consider it an honor to fit a Worth gown,'' she murmured wickedly.

No sighs for me. I gasped my indignation, too late. The *vendeuse* had bowed herself and her full skirts out of the chamber and shut the door.

"Irene! I am not your personal maid. How could you let her think so?''

"You do aid me now and again with my corsetry, when Godfrey is not available, as I aid you in turn.''

"Yes. But—''

Irene ignored my sputterings. Instead she was circling the dress—yes, like a hunter circuitously approaching a rare and dangerous beast. She avoided coming too near too soon, only to draw out the moment of capture.

I shook my head, took her bonnet and laid it on a small table, then marched up to the garment in question.

"Silk velvet," I pronounced from my ancient few days in Whiteley's drapery department. "Probably French," I added, crushingly.

"Lyons silk," Irene speculated dreamily. "Worth has made the Lyons looms and their products famous."

"This is most oddly constructed," I said, ignoring her indrawn breath as I reached to examine the gown. "Many panels make up the skirt, but the bodice, the corsage, is all of one piece."

"Cut on the bias," Irene explained, as though discussing a work of art. "Worth is noted for it."

"No doubt to save fabric."

"He is also famed for asymmetrical decoration. He does not wish a dress to be predictable, to be anticipated. A woman wearing a Worth is a living sculpture, imbued with the capacity to surprise from every angle."

"Oh, really, Irene! Will you stop mooning over this overdone piece of dressmaking? I will at least help you to disrobe."

I did indeed play lady's maid, for Irene was so enraptured by the sight of the gown that she stood as leaden-armed as a sleepy schoolgirl while I worked. Fortunately, the shapeless Liberty silk gown was child's play to unfasten. I soon had it hung on an opposite hook and turned to regard its monstrous replacement. This gown's drama, sheer yardage and glittering trellis of ornament made it a kind of feminine suit of armor, and a far more rambunctious garment to don or discard than the Liberty.

Irene remained frozen in dreamy contemplation of the violet gown, looking quite charming in her silk-and-cotton combinations, lace-trimmed at shoulder and knee, and very like an abbreviated bathing costume, in that her pale silk stockings were her only covering from knee to slipper.

"You are wearing no petticoats!" I observed.

She answered me without taking her eyes from the gown.

"That is the entire idea of aesthetic dress: to dispense with excess yardage and poundage. The silk must fall unimpeded."

"But—" I began, for I had never left home without a petticoat, and usually several, under the plainest of day dresses.

Irene frowned as if hearing a sour note. She waved me silent with the same imperious gesture that Monsieur Worth had used, save that hers indicated mental abstraction rather than arrogance. "Shhh. I hear something," she whispered.

Of course she heard something. The women in the salon, in the other dressing rooms, were chattering like chickens. We had simply ignored them as we would an out-of-tune chorus at the opera.

Now Irene did not ignore those nearby voices. Now she cocked her head to listen.

I couldn't help following her lead, though I abhor eavesdropping. The first familiar word I heard struck my composure with icewater shock.

"Of course he is divinely handsome," a languid, viola-like voice was pronouncing in oddly accented French. "If I deigned to take a lover of no consequence, I would insure that his personal attractions made up for his lack of social ones."

"But to wed such a man, Serafina!" another voice broke in, merry as a flute. "A mere barrister. To end all opportunity of marrying well! Or at least of mistressing well."

"And have you seen her jewels?" a deeper, crueler bassoon voice intoned. "No, of course not. She has none, save for a few sorry trinkets."

"Still," the more charitable flute trilled, "she has powerful friends."

"La Bernhardt?" mocked the bassoon. "That upstart broomstick. I am surprised that she does not desert Paris for good one day and fly off on one. Even Alice Heine is only American-born, after all, and connected to those Ger-

man bankers, and you know what they are. Vulgar par-
venus. Money men. Like the Rothschilds.''

"She *is* beautiful," declared the viola, entering the fray,
"and is said to sing like an angel. I hear that she quieted
some scandal involving Alice Heine that paved her way to
marrying the Prince of Monaco this autumn. Some say that
this Norton woman is terribly clever."

"Not clever enough," the bassoon retorted, coughing as
if from cigarette smoke. "A truly clever woman would
cease pushing her nose into other people's affairs and pursue her own. She shouldn't have to sing for her supper.
With her looks she could snag a grand duke, even a prince
or a king, if she played her cards correctly. She could
collect jewels enough to make even Monsieur Worth's
spaniels sit up and take notice. Clever? Oh no, my dears.
She is an utter fool, with enough pathetic pretensions,
mind you, to show up here. I cannot think what came over
Monsieur Worth to allow her in."

I had clutched a hand to my mouth, and found my other
hand was fanned upon my breast, as if to hold my jumping
heart inside my corset.

Irene had moved. I turned to look. She was marching
toward the dressing-room door, her face as white as cam-
bric. I hurled myself into her path, and found myself, back
to the door, facing a whirlwind of ice.

"Irene! You mustn't. You cannot."

She reached beyond me for the door lever even as I
inched in front of it. "No, Irene. Confronting them will
serve nothing but make a scene and make them happy—
please!"

"Step aside," she bid me in the most polite, stony tone
I had ever heard. Her eyes were agate, and her lips were
carved coral.

"Irene—" I inched away from that terrible gaze. In my
instant of retreat, she seized the lever.

"You cannot!" I repeated in the same forced whisper I
had used throughout our battle of wills.

"Why not, Nell?" she asked me calmly, coldly.

She pulled the door inward and, stunned, I gave with it, only mustering my final argument when she was already over the threshold.

"Irene!" I cried raggedly. "You are not fully dressed."

She glanced over her implacable shoulder, over the lace and blue satin ribbon that edged her camisole like tiny angel wings. "I am fully indignant, Nell, and adequately attired to administer a dressing-down." Then she marched into the hall toward the lightly laughing voices.

Never had my duty been so painful: I must follow, witness and pick up the pieces.

As I scurried after her, there was no mistaking the proper door. Irene had paused, looking like a vengeful undergarment advertisement, and thrust open a door without knocking. Laughter choked and stopped.

I rushed to follow in her footsteps before I was shut out, and skittered over the threshold to find her momentarily facing me as she had turned to shut it behind her . . . quite softly.

She said not a word to me, but twirled to confront the five or six women in the room. I was too agitated to count precisely. Most sat on a pair of brocade sofas at right angles in the corner. Two, I noted with relief, were in equal déshabillé to Irene, though they had not deserted their private rooms to parade in the passage as she had.

One stood by the long mirror in a hunter's green riding habit, her auburn hair filling a net snood beneath a jaunty riding derby.

"Forgive the intrusion," Irene began in a tone that asked no such thing. "I am helpless to resist a good round of gossip, especially when I am the subject of it."

A worried looking woman with light brown hair spoke up. "You are m-mistaken. Madame—?" In the interrogative lilt, I recognized the flute, as well as the false note in her current performance.

"Norton," the woman in green at the mirror finished for her—and for Irene—without turning. The bassoon. Her sharp-featured face wore the icy indifference of the hunter as she looked Irene up and down even more narrowly than Monsieur Worth had. She won no advantage there: Irene wore only the most exquisite underclothes. Much as I disapproved of their public debut, I had to admit that Irene's undergarments were as imposing as most women's outerwear.

Besides, unlike most women, Irene was never one to let whatever she wore—or did not wear—put her at a social disadvantage.

"You have the advantage of me," Irene told the woman by the mirror, "but please do not bother to introduce yourself. That will save me the momentary effort of forgetting you. I must, however, correct your misapprehensions."

The woman at the mirror whirled to face us. "We need take nothing from you, including correction. Now get out."

"I think not . . . yet." Irene smiled, her voice adding a fourth and dominant instrument to the chamber orchestra here gathered. She was the cello—rich as chocolate brown velvet, deep and overpowering.

She began to prowl back and forth like a wolf in deceptively frilly grandmother's garb.

"You suffer from certain delusions," she announced. "I do not complain about your attacks on my cleverness. Cleverness is most effective when it is underrated. Nor do I object to your debates about my talent and my physical attractions. These qualities are often the stuff of debates, and I have rather firm opinions of your failings in these areas myself, now that I have seen you all."

A joint indignant sigh escaped several well-laced sets of lungs. One woman, partridge-plump with jet black hair and rice-powder skin, half-rose.

"We need not stay to be insulted," she said.

The other seated women stirred, even the unclothed ones, as a mass exodus threatened.

"I differ," Irene said. "You definitely must stay. I insist."

"Who will make us?" demanded the woman at the mirror. In her stern riding habit, she appeared most formidable. I shrank behind Irene as she stepped toward us.

Irene snatched something off the fragile Louis XV table by the door and held it up. At first I took it for a parasol.

"Sit!" Irene commanded the bestirring ladies on the sofa. She brandished her new accessory like a pointer—a riding crop, I saw, its base trimmed with a green plaid taffeta ribbon. The effect was akin to seeing an organdy bow gracing the neck of a bulldog.

Five ladies eased back obediently with a sighing rustle of dressmaking goods. The one at the mirror paused, then moved forward.

Snap! The crop licked at the charged atmosphere of the crowded room; it whipped like a long, thin snake-tail toward the red-haired woman, driving her back into her own reflection.

"As you were. You may stand," Irene gave the redhead elaborate permission, "but you may not move."

"This is intolerable, Madame," the viola throbbed indignantly from a sofa.

"Undoubtably, but I assure you that it is most satisfying to me. Now." She resumed pacing, the riding crop striking softly across the palm of one hand.

One of the seated women whimpered. Irene had proved at least that they were easy to intimidate. And she craved any sort of audience, even—or perhaps especially—a captive one.

"No, I must admit that my voice, my mind, my face are fair game," she resumed. "What else are the idle to talk about but others?" she inquired cuttingly, then stood still. "But you began by insulting my bourgeois flaw of marrying—and marrying so unexceptional a man as an English barrister, although you admit that the wrappings are attractive. You have erred grievously."

"Oh?" the woman at the mirror inquired archly. "Does Monsieur Norton wear a toupee?"

Irene paused to smile sweetly. "I meant that you err in assuming that he is unexceptional. You ladies all suffer from shortsightedness. I, on the other hand, take the long view. It is true that I have few jewels, only those earned by my own work, or given to me by persons grateful for the exercise of any small wit I may possess. This gives me an advantage beyond price, one that may not be immediately evident to such eager acquirers as yourselves. My sorry trinkets may be modest and few, but no emerald's sparkle is tainted by memories of the fools or indignities suffered in its pursuit. No diamond necklace's blue fire is dimmed by the number of the ceilings contemplated in boredom to earn each stone in the endless string. No ruby's gleam is bought at the cost of self-respect or dishonesty.

"As for my marrying, and marrying so modestly, I console myself by regarding the husbands and lovers of women such as yourselves. They leave much to be desired, as you have noted yourselves by observing my husband. I shall never have to embrace some overstuffed sofa of a self-satisfied duke, or kowtow to a prince of industry for the reward of a few costly baubles. I shall never have to contemplate the ceiling—or anything else—in boredom. In truth, I have chosen the better part, which is why I am a subject of such fervid interest to your gossiping circle. I have no pretensions of any sort, which is what offends you. And you are quite right. I am a dangerous sort of woman.

"Now," Irene finished grandly, flourishing her borrowed crop like a wand, or a scepter, "you may resume your petty discussions. It will amuse me to overhear what you have to say on my withdrawal. I will even have Miss Huxleigh take notes. Perhaps you will be worth a paragraph in my memoirs."

They looked as one toward me for the first time, and

scowled horribly. Had Irene and her whip not been present, I do believe that they would have done me some bodily harm. Witnesses are never cherished.

Only the sounds of whispers and rustling clothing penetrated our dressing room after our return.

Irene perched on the edge of the Empire sofa in her frilly combinations, looking like a chastened schoolgirl required to sit through a lecture, rather than like someone who only moments before had wielded the whip hand.

I was trembling, in shock and—now—with righteous anger.

"You have caused a scene!" I charged in a hoarse whisper.

She nodded.

"You have paraded yourself in your unmentionables."

She said nothing.

"You have . . . destroyed your so-called opportunity to become Monsieur Worth's experimental *mannequin de ville.*"

She looked meekly up at me with enormous bronze-colored eyes. "Probably." She sighed.

"It is your own fault."

"I know."

"Such irresponsible gossip is best left undignified by an answer."

"True."

"You have gained nothing and lost everything."

"I cannot argue, Nell."

"Well?"

"Well what?"

"What are you going to do about it?"

Irene rose slowly, subdued. She looked around the frivolous little room for her Liberty silk.

"Very wise," I said. "The best thing is to go quietly home and forget the entire episode."

She moved toward the hook.

The hook holding the violet velvet gown.

"Irene—?"

She lifted it down, then cast the hanger onto the sofa seat. "Will you help me don it, Nell? Or shall I call the *vendeuse?*"

"You will persist in this madness?"

"Since I have already made a scene, I might as well make another, only with a better costume." Her lips quirked with rue. "It would be rude to leave without showing the Worths what they wished to see. I believe you'll have to tighten my corset strings, Nell; I wore them quite loose for the Liberty."

I would not waste my breath in arguing. I approached her and pulled the corset strings very tight indeed.

Shortly after, I was trailing the violet gown, watching the bejeweled train dragging down the hall ahead of me like a gaudy lizard's tail.

Where Irene passed, voices choked and stopped in midsentence. Eyes fixed on her, not with the sly glances of an hour before, but with bald, hostile curiosity. A subdued *vendeuse* intercepted us at the bottom of the stairs to the Worth quarters. I braced myself for a public rebuff.

Irene paused, on her face the same stiff, slight smile that she had shown the King of Bohemia when he had revealed himself to be without honor.

Of course she looked magnificent in the Worth gown, like a queen, and worth ten of the women in the salon put together, be they patron or mannequin or "double" of a world-famous beauty.

The *vendeuse* stepped aside without a word, and Irene's heavy velvet skirt swayed up the stairs, myself in its wake. At the top we heard chitters and laughter break out behind us. Or at least I did; Irene gave no indication of apprehending anything.

The old spaniel greeted us at the salon door and waddled

away. Mr. and Mrs. Worth still sat—or sat again—on the chaise with grave faces. Irene paraded before them without being asked, ending in a breathtaking swirl.

"I have no accessories, of course," she said without preamble. "No gloves, no hair ornaments—"

"No jewels," Monsieur Worth barked out suddenly.

They knew. Of course they knew. A man who catered to the aristocracy would be sensitive to every undercurrent of his business. A public scene in a dressing room would affect such a genteel enterprise like a tidal wave.

My cheeks flamed, but Irene's remained cool and pale as vanilla ice. Only one word described such an incident: *scandal.*

Monsieur Worth looked at his wife. A severe expression made her heavy features seem implacable.

"Few jewels," Irene corrected modestly.

"What do you think?" Monsieur Worth asked his wife, who could have been a pillar of disapproving salt.

"No jewels," she said slowly, as if reading a verdict.

Irene had told the women in the dressing room that jewels did not matter, that rich men did not matter. Yet they did, they both did indeed matter in this artificial world of the rue de la Paix and Paris and France and Society with a capital "s" everywhere. . . . Now she would discover again the power of that terrible truth, as she had on a darker day at Prague Castle more than two years before.

I wrung my gloved hands, unable to prevent the bitter lesson, and bit my lower lip.

Madame Worth glanced at me, attracted by my gesture (Irene remained as still as an elegant statue). Amusement tickled her stern features.

"You are right," her husband told her. "I want nothing to distract from my work. I will *create* jewels. A waterfall of jet beads. And emerald satin gloves, I think. A dash of the unexpected." He glanced at Irene as if remembering that she was alive. "This gown is destined for the Queen of

Italy, but I will make a duplicate for you, and another gown for you alone."

"I wanted only a single gown to begin with—" Irene said.

"Two." Worth held up one imperious, and inaccurate, finger. His bulging eyes narrowed, a trick that did not flatter them. "I see feathers, many feathers."

"Like your peacock gowns," Madame Worth prompted.

"Peacock feathers!" Irene repeated in the same tone she had used while she stood dreaming before this dress when it was presented. "I adore those colors—"

He nodded. "I have done this twice. Once, long ago, when crinolines made skirts into canvases for the dress-maker's art. A complete gown of peacock feathers, and more recently, for Lady Curzon, a gown beaded overall in the likeness of individual feathers."

"With iridescent green beetle shells as the eye of each feather," his wife added.

"Oh, yes," Irene cried rapturously, extending her clasped hands like an ingenue in an opera viewing her beloved for the first time. "Wonderful."

"No. Not for you," Monsieur Worth pronounced.

Now it would come. The denouncement. The end.

"Too gaudy for you," he went on. "Something . . . different. Come back Wednesday and you will see."

"Wednesday? That soon?" Irene was too amazed to argue. I was astounded by the mature grace with which she had relinquished the cherished peacock feathers.

"I waste no time," he said. "Now we must discuss a less pleasant matter: your performance in my dressing room."

"I thought you would refuse to dress me," Irene admitted.

"So I should have, yet you still came up."

She shrugged with a soubrette's charm. "The gown was too tempting not to try on."

Monsieur Worth stood up, which frankly did not add much dignity to his figure.

"I am English," he said, "yet I have become French, as my custom, my family and my fame lie in this land I have adopted. You are American and have adopted other lands. I am a genius. I have changed the facade of fashion for over three decades, until empresses bow to my wishes, but only because in matters of the toilette, I am always right. You are a performer, and something of a genius at solving human mysteries, I have heard. I am a tradesman. No matter how the world echoes my name, I am never, and never will be, on an equal footing to my patrons. I am both their inferior and their superior, and I understand that position well."

He smiled suddenly, though it was hard to detect the change of expression under the cover of his enormous mustache. (Thank heavens that Godfrey—and Quentin Stanhope—restrained themselves, and their mustaches, in this regard.)

"I mentioned that I do not always like my clients," he went on, "and that some I like quite well. It is your vast good fortune, Madame Norton, to have irritated those whom I do not like, and to have intrigued one of whom I"—he glanced at his wife with a smile—"we, are quite fond.

"When you have donned your own clothes, I would like you to call in my chambers upon a personage who urgently requests your confidential attendance. The Queen of Bohemia."

Chapter Four

THE QUEEN'S CONFESSION

❧

"**I cannot** withstand so many rapid changes of fortune in one afternoon," I complained in the dressing room as I unhooked the line of rear fastenings that closed Irene's velvet bodice.

"Two," Irene repeated in muted glee. "Two Worth gowns. And now this!" She whirled on me before I was done, her face aflame with twin triumphs. "Do you remember her, Nell?"

"You speak as if we had met. I remember seeing her portrait in the newspapers. Rather unflattering."

Irene began to pace, despite the gown that was ebbing farther down her shoulders at every step.

"Clotilde Lothman von Saxe-Meningen." The long foreign name tripped off of Irene's tongue like the syllables of an aria sung about a bitter enemy. "The King of Scandinavia's second daughter, whom His Royal Highness, Wilhelm Gottsreich Sigismond von Ormstein, felt himself compelled to wed by virtue of becoming King of Bohemia."

"Which title he assumed," I reminded her, "on the death of his father, whose murder you proved."

"That was a mere chamber murder, Nell, solved in private in the late king's own bedroom. No one knows what happened but the family circle and we two—and the poor, deluded servant girl who was the victim of rebel and royalist alike in that affair. I wonder what ever became of her?"

I captured Irene during a restless swing past and firmly resumed my unhooking. Sometimes it was best to treat Irene as an errant schoolroom charge.

"Nor," said I, "can I keep up with your change of subject. Surely you will not see this Scandinavian woman?"

"If you mean the Queen of Bohemia," she intoned with relish, "how can I refuse the royal command?"

"Easily. Say no."

She sighed, drawing several still-fastened hooks all the tighter. "I cannot disappoint Monsieur Worth twice in one day. I will have to go through with it."

"But you . . . you loathe this woman, Irene! Because of her, the King spurned you. You should have been Queen; even he admitted it, to the very last, in front of myself and Sherlock Holmes and Dr. Watson."

"The road to hell is paved with 'shoulds,' Nell." She shrugged out of the bodice, then raised her bare white arms while I lofted the gown over her head.

Irene soon had inserted the hanger and installed the dress on its hook. She patted the velvet skirt in farewell, then turned toward the Liberty silk at last.

This unconventional gown required no help in donning; in moments Irene was her respectable, clothed self. I had never expected to regard the aethestic mode of dress as a kind of return to sanity, but so I did now.

She resumed pacing. "I suppose I must not light a cigarette in Monsieur Worth's environs; how frustrating. At any rate, the question is not how I feel toward this usurping princess, for Willie was himself at fault for not telling me that his fate was locked into a royal marriage. The question is, what does this woman want of me?"

I shook my head. "I cannot begin to guess."

"Then we must see her."

"No treat, that," I said stoutly. "From her sketch, she was a long-nosed creature as bland as milk."

"Yes." Irene sighed happily at the remembrance. "And just think! Sketches can be—and usually are—*enhanced* by the artist." She turned to survey herself critically in the mirror from toe to topknot, ending with a satisfied smile. "Let us go and pay our disrespects to another royal personage, my dear Nell. We are becoming rather good at it."

Monsieur Worth—along with his spaniel and compress—no longer occupied the upstairs salon, but Madame Worth was present. She led us with soundless steps down a thick hall carpet to a closed mahogany door.

"Her Majesty wished to see you alone," Madame Worth noted, favoring me with a glance.

"Miss Huxleigh is more discreet than a church mouse," Irene said quickly. "I am sure that the Queen will not object when I explain Miss Huxleigh's vital role in my . . . enterprises."

Madame Worth looked dubious, but opened the door for us herself. Evidently no servant was to know of the meeting, an ominous sign.

The parlor within was papered in green velvet flocking and furnished with many polished wood pieces, so it seemed very English, after all.

A tea table glittered between a matching pair of sofas upholstered in shiny sable horsehair. On the farther sofa sat a figure wearing a lightweight steel-blue cloak, the hems of its floor-length skirt and waist-length overcloak edged in gray ostrich feathers. A gray felt bonnet brim trembled with more of the simpering feathers, and pink velvet roses massed against the wearer's hair and cheek on one, coy side.

Altogether an insipid ensemble for one whose coloring was as pallid as whey, I thought uncharitably. Queen of Bohemia or not, Clotilde Lothman von Saxe-Meningen had far to go if she·was to make me forget her role in destroying Irene's fondest expectations, if not in breaking her heart.

This so-called Queen was self-conscious enough to start at our entrance and move as if to rise. Irene restored the situation to its proper tone by executing a small curtsy. I managed an uncivil bob, but the Queen seemed little interested in social courtesies.

"Madame Norton." She looked unerringly toward Irene. "Please be seated, but your companion, I fear—"

"No one fears Miss Huxleigh," Irene said, stepping around the sofa to take the indicated seat. "I never consult without her; she is the soul of Prudence, even though her Christian name is the classical Penelope. Besides, who is to pour if we have urgent matters to discuss? I cannot manage teapots and think at the same time."

"Oh, I as well!" the Queen exclaimed in a tone of pathetic relief. Her French had a slight, Scandinavian singsong, and she eyed me nervously. "Miss . . . Hussey may stay if she will swear to say nothing of what we discuss."

Irene smothered a hoot at this latest corruption of my surname. "Oh, she will be as silent as the grave, our Miss Hussey. Depend upon it. I do, however, ask her to take notes on occasion. You must warn her if any matter is of such sensitivity that she dare not write it down."

The Queen slid me another uneasy glance from dismal gray-green eyes. "Miss Hussey will recognize such a juncture, I fear, only too well."

Her nod admitted me to the society of the sofa. I came around the one Irene occupied and found myself neatly finessed into position behind the Georgian silver teapot that I would command.

Now that I was seated, and virtually ignored as the two women warily examined one another, I could examine the Queen's appearance. When Irene and I had studied her likeness in the newspapers at the time of her engagement to the King of Bohemia—and "studied" is too scholarly a word; we had dissected her like a biological curiosity—our verdict had been unflattering.

I saw nothing before me to change it. Queen Clotilde was a vapid blond woman, a sort of human daisy who looked as if she would shed her petals at the mildest breeze. Her pale hair, so fine it shone like wet satin, made her oval face seem browless and lacking eyelashes. True, this gave her large, limpid eyes a certain sad prominence, like a spaniel's, for they drooped at the corners.

And her nose! This was a long, unlovely feature that ended at too short a distance from her upper lip. She had one of those overpraised rosebud mouths, small and bowed, but with little natural color. Apparently she lacked the artifice to enhance a single one of her unfortunate features. I am not in favor of artifice, but could see its need in this case. Her eyes were rimmed with the red that should have warmed her cold lips and cheeks, not from weeping, but by virtue of her almost-albino nature. Even her hidden ears, I suspected, would be awkward in some way.

I made my observations, all the while fussing with the tea things. Most domestic chores are a perfect disguise for a wandering mind or eye. I couldn't help clattering spout to cup and spoon to dish; did the Queen know of Irene's former connection to the King? As soon as I offered a cup of tea to her gloved hand, the Queen, in fact, seemed to forget me, and saved her nervous glances for Irene. What did Clotilde know?

My friend suddenly took the conversational reins that had lain slack for far too long.

"And how may I assist Your Majesty?" she asked outright. "Monsieur and Madame Worth said that you wished to consult me."

"Consult you," the Queen repeated. "You make it sound like a transaction. Perhaps I do. I could not help overhearing you . . . admonish the ladies in the dressing room."

"Ah. The flaws of theatrical training. My voice, I am told, carries well."

"Superbly, Madame, but so did their voices beforehand. I am curious about these puzzling affairs they mentioned, in which you take an interest, and about your cleverness. These women implied that you had aided the soon-to-be Princess of Monaco in avoiding a scandal before her forthcoming marriage."

"That is true." Irene leaned forward to take the Meissen cup, thin as a butterfly wing, that I offered her. "I of course cannot tell you the exact nature of her difficulty—"

"Of course not!" The Queen seemed ready to press her palms to her ears at the very thought. "But the matter was of a personal and delicate nature?"

"Of the *most* personal and delicate nature," Irene said complacently, sipping what I had discovered to be a delicious cinnamon-flavored tea.

"I see. But I do not understand how you undertake such matters."

"For friends," Irene replied, "and for fees. I acted as an inquiry agent in my youth for the Pinkertons in America and later for private parties abroad. Some were American themselves, such as Charles Lewis Tiffany; others were English, such as Oscar Wilde."

"Oh. Oh, my, Madame. You have indeed aided some prominent individuals, and I doubt that your youth can be spoken of in the past tense." Queen Clotilde smiled as she sighed, her breath agitating the curling feathers at her neck and bosom. She herself, I saw with some surprise, was a mere girl, perhaps of twenty or so.

Yet she was an aristocratic ghost, this woman, a pale specter who frightened even herself. She had sipped the tea but once. Now it sat cooling within the exquisite rim of her cup while she sat before us nursing cold, aristocratic feet.

"How may I aid you?" Irene prompted gently.

I was surprised by that gentleness, but then Irene was the

compleat confidante. She could take whatever tack another required, despite her own feelings. Or, rather, she could mask her own feelings to serve another purpose. I felt a stab of pity for Queen Clotilde, shown by her bearing to be royalty in name only, and so obviously ill equipped to deal with crisis or even a minor social matter. She would be mincemeat in the courts of any land, especially Bohemia, with her obstreperous in-laws, the family von Ormstein.

Irene could have handled them, and had. Oh, how unfair life was! What a queen Irene would have made, to quote the King of Bohemia in one of his rare, perceptive moments. She would have played the role to perfection, and would never have lost herself, or her humanity, to it. Instead, King Willie had made this mail-order princess his bride. Now the unhappy creature was coming to Irene for aid. Aid for what? What did a pampered queen have to fret about?

She was about to tell us, but first she must wet her fish-belly-pale lips. They had cracked from such frequent gestures, adding to her lackluster air despite the rich garb and the soft, ever-present flutter of gray ostrich feathers that framed her person like dust-ridden gilt.

Such a complete and total loss! A shaking little white rabbit with nervous pink eyes. That the King must recognize each day of his life when he thought of the vital woman he had betrayed, whose blood was unblued by royal birth but whose every other attribute was of a royal nature.

"I am not sure that anyone can aid me," the Queen confessed, her brows knitting, I assume, since I could see only furrowed skin and a dusting of down. "I find it most embarrassing to name my ill. Perhaps I should begin with my personal history."

Irene expertly managed to conceal a yawn without lifting a rude but veiling hand to her face. I felt inclined to groan myself. The Queen of Bohemia looked to be a thorough sort of young person, seriously dull beyond her years.

"I am my father's second-born daughter," she began.

Irene's and my glance intersected. We had read all we wished to know of her in the newspaper.

"It was always intended that I wed the future King of Bohemia."

"Oh, really?" Irene beat the sarcasm from her voice but a particle remained. King Willie had never admitted as much.

The Queen smiled nostalgically. "I first met him as Crown Prince when I was fourteen. Wilhelm is such a tall, massive man, much like Czar Alexander of Russia, both six-and-a-half feet tall. They must be related, as many members of various royal houses are. The King is a man of uncommon height, with great blond sideburns and a mustache. Very handsome, I thought, a Viking prince. I was not averse to the marriage, though I would have to leave Sweden and learn German—very large matters to a young girl."

"And Bohemian," Irene put in.

"What?"

"You would have to learn Bohemian."

"Why on earth would I?"

"It is the language of Bohemia."

"But the von Ormsteins speak German. Bohemia is part of the Austrian Empire, and the court at Vienna speaks German. As a child, I learned English, French, Italian and German so I should be able to marry into whatever acceptable royal house, but from the first I was promised to Bohemia."

"Hence why bother to speak Bohemian?" Irene muttered to herself.

The Queen didn't notice; her mind had moved again to her unpleasant present lot, and her face reflected its poverty. "We married last spring, a splendid ceremony in Prague," she said, rallying a bit. "The city is pretty, but Prague castle is vast and gloomy. Little has been done to add modern comforts. Yet I was wed to one of the most handsome and eligible Kings of Europe. I . . . intended to do my duty."

"Which was?" Irene prompted.

Queen Clotilde looked first amazed, then mortified. She eyed her entwined and gloved hands. "My first duty is to extend the royal line."

Impatience flashed across Irene's face. "And you have made no progress in this required enterprise yet? Consult a physician, then. I can recommend Doctors Sturm and Drang," she added wryly.

Only I understood the danger the Queen ran in consulting Irene about her domestic disappointments. Sturm and Drang were the mock names Irene had given the Bohemian royal physicians during our disastrous stay in Prague two springs before. I bit my lip in a mirroring gesture as I watched the Queen's hypersensitive face threaten to collapse.

"I would, Madame Norton. Save that there is no physical fault. I cannot . . . breed if I am not . . . approached."

I could not decipher such delicate phrasing, and, for a moment, neither could Irene. She sank back against the down-filled cushions, her flame silk gown setting like a sullen sun against the twilight of the black upholstery.

"You mean that—?" For once, even Irene was lost for words.

"I mean that my husband, the King of Bohemia, has not consummated the marriage."

Or perhaps Irene had wanted to hear that admission from her rival's lips, without having to put soothing words into her mouth. But Irene was not usually cruel.

"Consummated the marriage," I repeated in the lengthening silence. I believed that I knew what that meant, in a general sense.

"Miss Huxleigh is right," Irene said, clearing her throat. "We must be absolutely clear on your meaning. You say that the King has not . . . visited your bedchamber."

"Oh, he has visited. As far as anyone would suspect the marriage is sealed. But . . . nothing has happened."

"Are you sure?" Irene asked sharply.

That pale face flushed as the dawn does when the light is thin and all color is only a hint. "I believe I would know. I have been told little, only that I must obey my husband and do my duty. Surely my duty does not require me to sleep alone, always. Nothing has passed between us but public courtesies. I cannot say that I was eager to solve these mysteries that are kept from maidens, but I expected to have them solved for me, certainly by now. I remain as ignorant as ever, and most puzzled."

"Perhaps," I said stiffly, "you have been granted the better part."

"Not if I fail to produce an heir!" Emotion animated those frail, pallid features for the first time. "That is my calling. My obligation. And then, the King is not . . . unpleasant in countenance or demeanor. Perhaps he finds me so. Perhaps he resents my being forced upon him by my royal blood. I feel despised in what should be my own palace. As if the servants—the very walls!—knew and were laughing at me."

Irene sat in abstraction. She idly stroked the small channel above her lip, that was not too short, nor too long, but just right . . . for a queen.

"You say, Your Majesty, that Wilhelm von Ormstein has not consummated the marriage."

At this bald repetition, Queen Clotilde nodded and swallowed simultaneously.

"Wilhelm von Ormstein?" Irene repeated in disbelief that was far more personal than the Queen would credit. Then she shook her head as if to clear it. "Could he be ill?"

"He appears to be in the finest of health."

"Could he be sparing you? Waiting for you to settle into the duties of queenship?"

"It is possible, but before we wed he led me to believe that he anticipated our union in more than ceremony. I cannot say that he was overattentive, and he did often seem brusque and involved in his own affairs. Yet every so often he would turn to me as if remembering that I was there and offer some gallant phrase or gesture. He said that his father's death had reminded him of his own mortality, that he had delayed too long in waiting until he was past thirty to marry, that he desired children.''

Irene sighed so slowly that her escaping breath seemed to be thought incarnate. "He sounds a man ready to meet his obligations and go forth and multiply according to divine providence and the bloodlines of Europe.''

"So I thought! I admit that I was nervous, and oddly excited, about my first encounters with these duties, but now I find myself far more nervous about their lack. What have I done wrong?''

"The King of Bohemia weds, but goes no further," Irene mused. "That does not sound like the King I know." I saw a pleased gleam grow in her eyes, and could guess in which direction her speculations wandered.

"You know the King?" the Queen was asking incredulously.

"What? Oh, only by reputation. The newspapers overflow with the exploits of royalty, which breeds a sense of false familiarity among the reading public. I would agree with you: by all repute, the King is a handsome, healthy, virile man. One would expect him to do his duty, and even find pleasure in it.''

Queen Clotilde blushed in awkward blotches. "Then it is I. I am so . . . ugly, so stupid, so ignorant that he cannot bear to be with me!''

Sweet words to one who had been asked to make way for this very woman by becoming the King's secret mistress. Irene let them wash over her for a long moment, then she sat taller, as a flash of anger lit her dark eyes like bright summer lightning.

"You are nothing of the sort," she said in the tone often used to goad me to some enterprise beyond my habits or inclination. "Obviously, there is nothing wrong with you, so there must be something wrong with the King."

"But what, Madame? Can you find it out? Can you fix it?"

The Queen's heartsick pleas, laden with imminent sobs, gave even Irene Adler Norton pause.

"I don't know. I should have to think about it. How long do you remain in Paris? May I reach you somewhere?"

The Queen seemed grateful for the opportunity to lower her face while she probed the gray Persian wool muff at her side.

"My card, Madame. I leave in two weeks. The King insisted I come to Paris for a new wardrobe. Most women would be ecstatic. I felt myself . . . banished. Gotten rid of." She bit her mangled lip again. "You are a woman of courage, Madame, and an American. No doubt you have never contemplated such silly problems as I face. You know nothing of the obligations of royal houses; perhaps they seem cold-blooded to you. I envy your certainty and your freedom, but I know only the life I was bred to live. If I am wife in name only to the King of Bohemia, I am an utter failure. I dare not tell anyone of any significance of my dilemma. It would cause a scandal of the highest order, that would shake the thrones of several nations—not because I am important, but because international familial and territorial pride is at stake. Bohemia is no great nation, only a modest bauble stitched to the hem of the Austro-Hungarian Empire. Only maintaining its royal line will keep Bohemia sovereign, and from becoming a prize contested for by larger, encroaching countries whose names I dare not breathe. If I bear no children—no son and heir—I will be sent home disgraced. My name will go down in history as Clotilde the Unloved, Clotilde the Unlovely, and who knows what the fate of Bohemia and all Europe will be! If you can help in any way—and I throw myself on your mercy—I beg you, do so!"

She rose and fumbled for the veiling on her bonnet,

pulling until its dark folds fell past her face like the blade of a guillotine. The result made her seem headless, faceless, a well-dressed animated dressmaker's dummy bereft of a soul.

Irene rose with her. "I cannot promise anything."

"Promise nothing," the muffled voice begged, "but try something, anything, if you can. I will pay whatever you wish."

We watched her go, both of us wrapped in invisible veils of silence neither was eager to lift.

Irene gathered her reticule and glanced my way at last.

"Notes were not necessary," she observed, "yet I rather imagine that your diary will have some rigorous use to-night."

Our coachman grumbled copiously to himself when he assisted us into the carriage at the door of Maison Worth. Apparently he judged that we had taken overmuch time within.

Irene, usually ever-ready to cajole the grumpy into good humor, ignored André's ill temper.

Even before he cracked his whip over the horses' cognac-colored backs, she was huddled in the carriage corner, excavating the depths of her reticule for the familiar mother-of-pearl case. A tiny lucifer struck and then sparked in the dim interior, and Irene had soon wreathed herself in a defensive moat of smoke.

I sat back and said nothing, not even about the annoying smoke, aware of the great shocks she had sustained this day.

"Well. Wednesday," she said at last. "What wonders will Monsieur Worth show us then?" she ruminated. "A showman born. And the Queen. What is your diagnosis, Nell?"

"That her problem is no difficulty at all. I cannot see that the *absence* of a man from her bed would trouble most women, especially those in an arranged marriage."

I deduced Irene's smile rather than saw it through the smoke.

"No, of course you would not see that, Nell, but Clotilde Lothman von Saxe-Meningen von Ormstein is not most women. She may be a symbol, but she is human still, and she has been treated most shamefully."

"You almost sound her defender."

"Do I?"

"Has it occurred to you, Irene, that the King may not be undertaking his husbandly role—whatever that is, exactly; I am sure it is uncomfortable, rather unpleasant and possibly undignified—because he has not yet recovered from the loss of yourself?"

"Hmmm," Irene purred in the self-indulgent way of black Lucifer when partaking of a bowl of fresh cream. She wriggled deeper into the tufted leather upholstery, as if settling into a velvet cradle.

"I confess that was the *first* thing that occurred to me. It does salve the savage soul: Willie bereft beyond duty. Willie unable to approach even his blue-blooded young wife, haunted by my memory, by my loss, by tardy repentance. Of course I would like to think it was true, but often the most satisfying explanation for such things is also the most self-deluding."

"Much as I abhor stressing it, Irene, for your self-regard is already too strong, the King was a broken man when he left the Serpentine Mews after finding the photograph gone and you eloped with Godfrey."

Irene shook herself out of her foggy reverie, and leaned forward to crush her dying cigarette's ember under her boot heel on the carriage's wooden floor.

"Broken men mend, especially when they are pampered royal personages with a high opinion of themselves," she said. "And I did not elope with Godfrey. We married in haste and left England in even greater haste. Speaking of Godfrey, you must mention nothing of this to him."

"I cannot lie!"

"He is not likely to ask anything that requires a lie. Simply don't blurt out any mention of this."

"I never 'blurt.' That sounds quite vulgar."

"What I will do to you should you tell Godfrey anything of our interview with the Queen will be more vulgar still," Irene promised.

"That sounds like a threat."

"Only a warning, dear Nell. Men are too high-strung to deal with certain matters."

"Such as their wives' former suitors?"

"Such as their wives' former suitors—especially if they are kings, and certainly if they are showing an inexplicable reluctance to consort with their own wives."

"She is not beautiful," I said then.

"Nor is she that hopelessly unattractive. She merely lacks polish. Besides, the Willie I knew did not show such nicety in these matters that any reasonably presentable woman would fail to interest him."

"He had not been spoiled by knowing you then."

"You are too partisan, Nell. I possess certain assets, but none that can surmount blue blood and a fat dowry, as I learned to my sorrow in Bohemia. The women in the salon are right, no matter how I berate them. I do not play fair with the world on its own unfair terms, and I have been—and will continue to be—punished for that. But Clotilde Lothman did play fair, so far as she was given leave to know, and I do not like to hear that Willie has treated her so badly. I do not like it at all."

"Does that mean that you will assist the Queen? Irene, how can you?"

"I don't know what I will do, but whatever it is, it will be interesting."

I repressed a chill of presentiment. What Irene and I considered "interesting" differed dramatically.

Chapter Five

SPLENDOR IN THE GLASS

I awoke that night in our Neuilly cottage to the faint sounds of Antonín Dvořák's lovely folk songs.

In fact, I did not awake at all, having lain for some time in an abstracted yet restless state. Like any keeper of someone else's secret, I found that hidden knowledge narrowed and darkened my view of the world around me.

Irene's normal dinnertime gaiety—she always rose to an audience, no matter how small or how familiar—took on a forced air in my eyes.

Godfrey's ordinary yet courtly attentions to us both made me feel the worst sort of hypocrite. In the parlor after dinner, while Irene demonstrated to vivid comic effect our introduction to the great Worth, Godfrey frequently turned to ask my opinion.

"What do you think this man-milliner of Paris will put on Irene, if peacock feathers are not grand enough?" he inquired in his way of teasing her by consulting me.

"Something daring beyond belief, no doubt," I answered in the same spirit. Godfrey always bestirred me to mild rebellion. "Perhaps sackcloth," I went on despite her gasp, "trimmed with diamante."

"A Cinderella in diamonds." He laughed at my word

picture. "How I wish I had seen and heard Irene sing that role at La Scala while wearing Tiffany's diamond corsage."

Irene threw herself into an easy chair, her theatrics over for the moment. "You have seen the newspaper sketch of me in that role and wearing those jewels."

"A sketch is not sufficient," Godfrey said. "You are always far more affecting in person. In the flesh," he added rather wickedly.

"So are diamonds. In the flash," she retorted. "Ah, me. I wonder where that magnificent Tiffany corsage is now?" she speculated wistfully. "You never saw it either, did you, Nell?"

"Of course not. You sang at La Scala alone. It must have been heavy, wearing that showy swag of diamonds from shoulder to hip."

"Not in the least. Like wearing meringue or angel hair. How cleverly it was designed, like a lacy sash of rank, to enhance any gown. They told me it shimmered like a comet on stage."

"Nonsense!" Godfrey lit a long cigar and stretched his slipper-clad feet to the fire, for the nights had grown chill. "*You* shimmered like a comet; the diamonds merely reflected your glory."

"There, you see," Irene urged me, laughing. "My most devoted audience. He is won over by the very thought of my performance."

Godfrey did not answer, nor did I. We were suddenly both too aware that Irene's future musical performances would be haphazard and private. She had retired from the stage only because the King of Bohemia had high-handedly cut her career short in Prague and then her risky encounter with Sherlock Holmes had forced her into premature anonymity.

I thought about Irene's great talent so suddenly and circumstantially silenced as I lay awake that night. She never spoke of it, and I dared not mention the subject. Yet it must secretly chafe her spirit, though she would never let that show. So I was unsurprised to hear the piano's faint tinkle in the sleepless wee hours, knowing as I did that the day's events must bring Irene's thoughts back to Bohemia, back to a past in which she had envisioned a glorious future that included neither Godfrey—then unmet—nor myself, save in a now-and-then way.

But Irene did not reign as queen of stage and palace in Prague; she was an English barrister's wife in Paris. Another woman no doubt treasured the Tiffany corsage that Irene had introduced to the fashionable world in Milan. Another woman wore the crown jewels of Bohemia that King Willie had himself arranged upon Irene for the incriminating photograph. Godfrey had never seen that, either. Irene told him that the sight of the King and herself together was history that would only pain him. Now I began to wonder if she feared that the sight of the jewels she had forsaken would pain him more.

Still the distant Dvořák melody unwound like a music box. I sat up, thrust my feet into slippers before they touched the cold wooden floor, then rose and donned a shawl.

Moments later I was feeling my way downstairs in the dark, too timid to light a candle and risk awakening Godfrey. Halfway down the steps my own shadow began to softly accompany me: Irene's parlor light seeped into the passage to bathe me in a vague glow.

A few steps more, and my darker self hunched in huge and twisted relief on the whitewashed passage wall. I pattered over the hall's slate tiles onto the softness of faded French rugs.

The leashed moon of a paraffin lamp glowed above the grand piano and reflected in its burnished rosewood, so two soft eyes beamed at me in the semidark.

Matching green embers smouldered near the fireplace. Apparently Lucifer had an ear for music as well as an ever-open eye for mischief.

At the piano, I saw only the rich gleam of Irene's hair

meandering down her back before vanishing into the satin folds of her peignoir. Her hands, white in the artificial moonlight, moved out and in along the ivory keys, as if invoking a spell or weaving on a loom.

Notes came forth, sometimes a separate trickle that gathered into watery falls, sometimes hunched together in throat-tightening chords. She played quietly: some notes were imagined moments strained for. She had meant not to wake us, but the effect was to haunt our dreams with an undercurrent of melody. Dvořák's music could be melancholy, and so this playing struck me.

I sat on a leather hassock, unsurprised when something black arched into my lap. Lucifer balanced on his clawpoints, neatly puncturing my knees, before settling down to pummel my abused flesh.

"I'm sorry I woke you." Irene spoke without turning or stopping, her words overlaying the music like a recitative. I refused to be unnerved by her recognition of my presence.

"You did not wake me. I never slept."

She played a while longer, then her fingers pressed a pair of chords into the keys, holding them down until the last almost inaudible vibration stilled.

There was a calm fatality in the way she throttled the instrument silent. I caught my breath as she turned to me at last, her face cameo-creamy in the lamplight.

"You mustn't worry, Nell. The Queen's confession is a mystery in a minor chord. I am puzzled, I admit, but hardly intrigued enough to act on it."

"You would like to," I accused.

"True. I am perishing of curiosity, but I am hardly in any position to lift so much as my little finger on the Queen's behalf. My hands are tied. I cannot go to Prague—"

"Of course you cannot! If you think Godfrey was perturbed when you ventured back to London and the vicinity of Sherlock Holmes last summer, can you imagine what he would say to your dallying near the King and Prague?"

"I was speaking for myself," she said. "And Godfrey *did* endorse my London trip once I had convinced him that I would be unrecognizable. I could visit Prague incognito as well."

"What you can do is not the question, only what you should do."

"Agreed, and what is it that I should do, Nell?"

"Nothing! Nothing that rekindles the old wounds that you received—and inflicted—in Prague."

"You mix metaphors with great dash, my dear girl. One usually rekindles memories or passion, not hatred and wounds."

"You know what I mean to say! You yourself admitted that the King is not one to forget a slight. By fleeing his offer—his assumption—that you would be his mistress, by evading his agents across half of Europe, by outwitting his chosen delegate in London, Sherlock Holmes, you have earned his eternal enmity. This distressed young queen may merely be a tool he uses to lure you back to Bohemia and into his clutches—"

"A pathetic tool! And how could Willie believe that I would go running off to Bohemia at the first whisper that he has not consummated his marriage?"

"Curiosity," I answered. "Your fatal flaw."

"I am curious, but I am not mad. I will not be going to Bohemia. I will not be delving into the intriguing intimate confessions of the Queen of Bohemia, poor creature. But I can remain safe at home and speculate to my heart's content, and that right I claim."

"You are married."

"What has that to do with it?"

"You should not think of other men under any circumstances."

"Ah!" Her hands lifted as if to strike thundering chords on the piano, then dropped with a sharp slap to her lap. "I am not to think, then, because I am married. I fear that not even Godfrey would agree with you on this."

"Yet you don't want him to know of the Queen's proposal."

"Nor do I want him to know of the women's gossip. Both are . . . rumors, idle speculation. They can only do harm."

"So can your dwelling upon any conundrums that involve the King of Bohemia."

Irene smiled slightly. "I do not dwell. I muse. And I amuse myself." She turned away to lower the key cover without a sound. "But fear not. Wild West horses could not drag me back to Bohemia. And now, back to bed."

Irene rose, collected the lamp and laced a companionable arm through mine as she led me to the stairs. She even shook my arm admonishingly as we parted in the upper hall.

"Don't worry, Nell! Today's events were tiny, unimportant incidents in the vast, daily flow of present into future. What I really dwell upon is what Monsieur Worth has in mind for my new gown."

"Now there," I agreed, "is a matter worth worrying about!"

Wednesday came all too soon for my taste; also for André's. Our coachman glowered from the moment he drew up before our country cottage until he deposited us before Maison Worth in the heart of the city.

Already idle drivers and their carriages lined the streets, their equipages far smarter than ours. Perhaps that is why André stewed; the French do not like to appear less fashionable than anyone, not even a fellow servant.

The page boy and master of the salon greeted us like old friends. Irene swept boldly into the antechamber, only to find it empty. Her chastened critics of Monday were disappointingly absent, from her point of view.

I began to breathe again, but found that pleasant condition interrupted when we were once again shown into an ornate dressing room. Against the far wall's pale paneling hung a sinister dark cloud of taffeta and tulle.

Even Irene was taken aback by this sober apparition, and turned toward our *vendeuse* in silent surprise. This young lady, a slender girl in light lilac surrah, rustled toward the diabolic-looking gown.

"This will take some care in donning, Madame. If I may assist—?"

Irene's theatrical background had made her the mistress of her own image. She scorned personal maids and hairdressers, preferring her own expert attentions. No matter how rich she became, I suspected, she would never sit easily while another arranged her. But now the intimidatingly mysterious gown that hung like condemned goods on the wall forced her to acquiesce.

I aided her undressing, relieved to see that today Irene wore the full complement of necessary underthings: pale yellow chemise, silk combinations, frilled drawers, rose-colored shot-silk petticoats and crimson brocade corset, silk vest and white bust bodice, all covered by a lace-edged camisole.

Soon all this sensible attire vanished under a rustling ebony cataract of fabric. A murder of crows had descended en masse upon my unfortunate friend; I was quite relieved to see her auburn head finally rise above the smothering gown.

The *vendeuse* pulled and prodded while I watched from the sidelines, then fell back when Irene was at last installed within her new carapace. Carapace is the proper word for it; the gown was a dark, iridescent, glittering shell reminiscent of some mystic scarab.

"Well!" Irene eyed herself in the mirror. Well she might. The gown's low-cut bodice was entirely fashioned of cock feathers—a glossy black tracery that shone with highlights in a borrowed share of the peacock's emerald, turquoise and burgundy hues.

Airy masses of black tulle, tufted here and there with tiny jet feathers and dotted with exotic embers of black opal, formed the huge, puffed sleeves and swaggered across the iridescent black taffeta skirt.

The *vendeuse* produced a pair of long, emerald velvet gloves scattered with jet beading. I was reminded of the Divine Sarah's twin green bracelets: living serpents.

"Sublime," Irene pronounced, turning in a crackle of brunette glitter when she had donned the gloves.

"Monsieur Worth will wish to see." The *vendeuse* bustled to the door. "But first he has ordered that you view the gown in its proper setting—gaslight."

This time we veered left through the main salon, into a series of chambers draped, as in Mr. Poe's Masque of the Red Death, in sumptuous fabrics of various colors. Cunning light bathed costly folds. My few days at Whiteley's could only help me guess at the rareness of these tempting lengths.

The fifth and final chamber held the same drama as Mr. Poe's penultimate room: an environment of eternal night lit by gaslit sconces and an overhead gasolier. Under this artificial illumination, Irene's gown glimmered like the discarded skin of a jeweled serpent, perhaps even of the one that had cost mankind paradise.

"Marvelous!" she exclaimed, turning before the wall of mirrors to watch the gown ring through its black rainbow changes. "Superior to common peacock feathers, more subtle."

"Monsieur Worth has outdone himself," the *vendeuse* said. "Now he must see the results."

Once again we paraded to the upstairs salon, Irene's train dragging like a funereal peacock's half-folded tail.

Only the man-milliner himself was present on this occasion, wearing a puce dressing gown over his shirt and loose necktie. The spaniel deserted its well-dented sofa cushion to waddle over and sniff Irene's hem.

"*En promenade*," Monsieur Worth ordered in dictatorial French. The language lends itself to dispensing orders. No wonder the nation spawned a Napoleon.

Irene complied with the uncustomary meekness to which I was becoming used. Perhaps she felt as if she had inherited the earth. Certainly she looked it in the extravagant gown.

She paused to let her green-gloved hands fan expressively. "What accessories should I carry, Monsieur? And jewels? Perhaps a simple diamond necklace?"

"Nothing that is not by Worth," he responded haughtily, nodding to the *vendeuse*. "Not so much as a stickpin."

The young woman bent to a large flat box spouting tissue and soon came bearing an encrusted undulating fringe like a living thing across her hands. This she put around Irene's neck. The upstanding collar of iridescent jet exploded into a dusky firework of design over Irene's décolletage, ending in a swaying rainfall fringe of supple beads. Diamonds did indeed seem redundant in the face of such extravagant artifice.

Irene fingered the necklace through the cushioning gloves, a moment later reaching for an item the *vendeuse* also presented reverently on open hands, a similarly beaded reticule.

"Monsieur Worth, what can I say?" Irene asked in bemusement, going on nevertheless. "The gown, the entire ensemble, is magnificent beyond words."

"Wear it and say nothing," he advised. "A woman in such a gown should be seen and not heard."

"In that I fear you ask too much of me," Irene replied. "I must at the least sing your praises when I appear in public in such a toilette."

He tilted his head, a very French moue of false modesty upon his weary face. Before he could answer, a door slammed in a distant area of the building.

The man-milliner frowned, obviously unused to domestic disharmony, and clapped a hand to his forehead.

"Please," he murmured to no one in particular. "My migraine—"

A person rushed into the room, the only one upon whom his wrath could not fall. His wife, Madame Marie.

"Charles!" she cried, giving the word its soft "Shh" French twist, instead of the forthright English "Chuh."

"What is it, my dear?" he responded in concerned French.

Luckily, I could follow short and sweet exchanges in this sour language, no matter how rapid, and there are no people like the French for chattering faster than a telegraph operator.

"A terrible thing." Madame Worth groped for the sofa and sat heavily, only then spying Irene, and perhaps myself. "*Magnifique*, Madame Norton," she paused to murmur. Then she addressed her husband again. "I am devastated to intrude but . . . one of the bead-girls has died." She eyed Irene distractedly. "The very girl, in fact, who made Madame Norton's rainfall neckpiece only yesterday. Such an agile hand."

"Sad news, my dear," he answered, "but hardly a matter of such import that it could not wait."

"Perhaps not. But—" Madame Worth's plump, capable hands sketched a helpless gesture. "Not merely dead, my dear husband, but . . . killed."

"Killed?" he repeated dumbly.

"Murdered?" Irene asked in a rising tone of interest.

The Worths regarded her, *père* and *mère*, their eyes dawning with the same notion at the same moment.

Madame Marie clasped her hands in overwrought beseechment. "Oh, Madame Norton. You know about such matters. Could you not see to this one?"

Monsieur Worth nodded until his mustache ends fluttered. "We will have to call upon the gendarmes, of course, if this proves to be a case of deliberate death. If not, perhaps Madame Norton could put our minds at rest."

"I should be delighted to assist you." Irene managed to subdue the relish in her voice to a hushed tone of concern.

Yet even I, God help me, felt a welcoming thrill at this possibly macabre diversion. There would be no more talk of Bohemia and King Willie's lack of marital effort if a murder victim was in the vicinity.

Monsieur Worth collapsed to the sofa, groping for either the spaniel or an abandoned compress. Madame Marie absently thrust a vial of smelling salts into his hand and stood.

"Follow me, Madame." She nodded briskly at me as well. "Mademoiselle."

Thus we found ourselves hastily winding down the rear, far less grand stairs of Maison Worth on the heels of the establishment's dignified mistress.

Despite the fashion house's grand but discreet exposure along the rue de la Paix, it contained much unsuspected space. We found ourselves weaving through workrooms crowded with French sparrows—those thin, doe-eyed, working-girl waifs, some apprenticed as young as twelve or thirteen, one often sees rushing home in the Paris twilight from twelve hours of labor in the shops and factories.

Ordinarily these industrious creatures chatter with that peculiar French effervescence, but now their large eyes were serious as they watched us pass. Irene's unearthly gown went uncommented upon, if not unnoted.

At last the endless rooms of worktables and rows of white-fingered girls opened into an empty room, one vacant only because of the ghost-faced mademoiselles clustered outside it.

One girl only remained in the room, lying apparently asleep upon the empty table glittering with a comet's tail of jet, beads and diamante stones. A small, richly dressed figure stood on the table before her, an idol worshiped by a mute supplicant.

"The supervisor did not at first suspect." Madame

Worth's deep voice hushed in the presence of sudden death. "So many of them fall asleep at their work."

Irene approached the motionless figure while our guide held back. I followed her, patting my skirt pocket for the small mother-of-pearl-covered notebook and pencil Irene had bought me since our arrival in Paris. I had remarked that such grandeur was inappropriate for the minor or macabre matters I might jot down on an outing.

"*Au contraire,*" she had enunciated in her perfect French. "Macabre matters require more formality than most. Consider the funeral."

I did indeed consider such macabre ceremonies as I stood gazing over Irene's fountain-of-tulle shoulder at the slumped figure of the bead-girl. I noticed little: the cheap woolen bodice and skirt; fingertips still reddened from the pressure and punctures of the thin beading needle; a knot of tobacco-brown hair; a pallid slice of face.

All the shopgirls were wan, even the youngest, and the French naturally tend to sallow complexions, but no doubt I am jaundiced, so to speak, against them.

"Perhaps she has merely fainted," I suggested.

For answer, Irene stepped aside, the movement acting as the drawing of a bejeweled black curtain on a living tableau. *Tableau vivant,* the French put it in that Frenchy way of theirs, only this scene was a depiction of death.

Now I saw it—the means! A sewing shears was embedded to its large, looped handles in the maroon wool of the girl's bodice back, a darker ring of red soaking into the surrounding fabric.

"An eternal faint," Irene commented, leaning over to eye the pearls and crystal beads that scattered from the dead girl's extended hand like semiprecious birdseed. The figure toward which the tiny treasures were flung stared open-eyed at the human sacrifice before it.

Irene nodded to the figure's lavishly beaded skirt. "The

bead-girl was working on this fashion doll when she was murdered."

"Fashion doll?" I stared at the small form, which had previously struck me as some wicked, well-dressed fairy presiding over the death scene.

"Fashion doll," Irene repeated a bit impatiently. "The finest French dressmakers send samples of their latest styles to the great ladies of many lands, to the courts of St. Petersburg, St. James, to Vienna, Madrid, Rome."

I studied a pale bisque face with rounded cheeks and chin both tinted dawn-pink, with round blue-glass eyes and painted lashes and brows. This fat, waxy doll seemed cruelly complacent keeping guard over the spare form of the dead girl. Her yellowish lean hand stretched toward a feeble trail of tawdry glitter, toward the heavy blue satin hem that clothed the doll, the raw, needle-pierced fingertips still ruddy despite the clutch of pale death's chill hand.

The doll's toy fingers were the color of ivory, each tiny nail sculpted into place. One finger wore a miniature ring of gold and topaz.

"No rings," Irene said, taking inventory of the corpse as if it were a different kind of doll. "She was not engaged, but that doesn't rule out a rival among her sister sewers. Stab wounds usually indicate a crime of passion—and opportunity. The fatal weapon was near at hand."

She looked up at Madame Marie. "Surely there were witnesses."

The Frenchwoman shrugged. "Their work is taxing and leaves little time to take their eyes from it. According to what the other girls said when I was called, they heard only a deep intake of breath, a gasp, and looked up to find Berthe slumped among them. They, also, suspected sleep at first. One even shook Berthe's shoulder before she saw the shears."

"I would speak to that one," Irene said.

Madame Marie looked to the open door crowded with

worried faces. "We have twelve hundred such girls working here. I do not know their names—"

"Twelve hundred?" Irene recovered from her surprise.
"Ask the one who first noticed to step forward."

At first Madame Worth's request was met by dropped
eyes and shuffling feet. Then a harsh wave of whisper agitated the girls, who stood askance with the haunted eyes of
a Greek chorus.

Finally one of them limped forward, her body twisted
into a hunchback. I could see why she sat at a table all day
and strung beads; what other work could such a one seek?
She approached reluctantly, and gave her name even more
reluctantly to Madame Worth.

"Genevieve Pascal," Madame Worth repeated, turning
to Irene, who had already heard the name forced from
those bloodless lips.

"Mademoiselle Pascal," Irene began with great politeness. "Tell me, please, who she is."

Genevieve's lusterless hazel eyes lifted to Irene, first traveling over the intricacies of her gown. Such humble seamstresses seldom saw the full results of their labor, I realized,
or the women who wore them.

"Berthe Brascasat," Genevieve whispered.

"What of her family? Who must be notified?"

The girl shrugged one already high shoulder. "Who
knows? She came each dawn to sew, and left each sunset
with the rest of us."

Irene ran a hand over the glittering Braille of her necklace. "I understand that she made this wonderful piece."

"Part of it, the center. Others did the fringe."

"And this doll, she was working on the skirt?"

"Berthe was given the most challenging work. Her eye-
sight was perfect and no one was so delicate with a needle.
She could anchor a bead with a single thread."

Madame Marie nodded heavily. "Our best bead-girl. I
saw that she received the most demanding work."

Irene glanced toward the doll. "This porcelain face is oddly familiar."

Madame Marie smiled ruefully. "The gown is destined for Maria Feodorovna, Empress of all the Russias."

"The *doll* is a double!" I blurted out, despite my swearing only twenty-four hours before that I did not blurt under any circumstances. "A doll double."

"Exactly, Miss Hussey," Madame Marie agreed. "We have many such."

"Did Berthe work on other dolls?" Irene asked.

"But of course. She was superlative at her work. She beaded many a miniature skirt as well as the yards and yards of a full-size one, such as yours."

"Mine," Irene repeated with some irony, her gloved fingers tightening on her skirt's elaborate encrustation. "More hers." She nodded at the slight form lying so still amid the fallen glitter. Irene, I think, had not until now considered the blinding, blood-pinching labor that went into such luxury as she admired. "A great pity."

"Yes, her death is a terrible loss for the house," Madame Worth said.

Irene, I knew, had not been speaking of the bead-girl's death, but of her drudgery-ridden life. She seemed almost about to say more to Madame Marie, then lowered her eyes and set her lips.

"The gendarmes must be called," she said instead. "You must consult the records of the other workers to find her family, so they may be notified. And I—I must change clothing," she announced abruptly, turning and rustling toward the young women still blocking the door.

They parted for her as the Red Sea for Moses, and, like the trusting Israelites, I followed meekly in the path Irene had created.

She said nothing after we returned to the dressing room, allowing the *vendeuse* to ungown her as if she had become as senseless as a fashion doll. She did not speak until we were again in our carriage, the boxed gown occupying the opposite seat, rattling back to the peace of the country.

"Twelve hundred, Nell," she repeated with a shake of her head. "Twelve hundred young women toiling away until their fingers bleed and their eyes refuse to focus. It is hopeless. Murder could walk those crowded rows clad in scarlet streamers and they would hardly notice."

"Perhaps jealousy," I suggested.

"You mean because poor Berthe was the best bead-girl?"

"Among so many it does not take much to instill envy."

Irene nodded, looking tired, then leaned her head back against the tufted black leather. Her bonnet feathers jostled to the bound of metal wheels over city cobblestones and later country pebbles.

"Twelve hundred. I wonder what they are paid? Not much," she answered herself. "Still—" She shook herself upright again. "Murder is not always so nice as to choose a select circle of suspects. And one must take what presents itself."

"You will look into this girl's murder?"

"That is apparently all I am free to do at the moment. Certainly I owe it to the poor child who only hours ago was laboring on my new gown." She eyed the oversized parcel opposite us almost bitterly.

"Will Monsieur Worth bill you, do you think?"

"We shall see," she answered with an air of distraction. "I must occupy myself as I can," she added fiercely, with no great relevance.

Murder at Maison Worth and the confidences of the Queen of Bohemia had not inspired Irene with a harmonious mood, I feared. Both incidents had reminded her of the ugly face the World is always ready to turn to the unprepared, and of how helpless most of us are in the face of fate or fact, incident or coincidence.

My friend Irene Adler Norton did not at all relish feeling helpless.

Chapter Six

BANKING ON IT

❧

We returned home at dusk to find the parrot Casanova's cage discreetly covered, the cat Lucifer cavorting unsupervised in the side garden with Messalina the mongoose, and Sophie gone to church. (These Romans are most devoted to evening services, the better to burn a queen bee's ransom in beeswax candles, I sometimes think.)

Godfrey was sitting in the wing chair by the fire, a brandy snifter in his hand and an expression of brown study upon his brooding face. Had he not been so handsome, I would have been reminded of Miss Jane Eyre's Mr. Rochester.

"One day," I expressed myself with some feeling on the threshold, "I am absent and the entire establishment collapses? What shall we do for supper?"

"Sophie left a cold quiche," Godfrey replied.

"Quiche is awful enough, but cold?" Words could not express my amazement and outrage. "Even the French would find that quaint comfort." I bustled toward Casanova's cage. Much as I abhorred the bird's all too understandable rantings, he was unused to enforced silence before ten o'clock.

Godfrey raised a languid hand. "Let the bird be. His ravings do not permit me to think."

I paused, appalled. Godfrey had covered the cage? I reserved the right to gag Casanova to myself, and jealously guarded it.

"Lucifer is boxing outside with Messy," I reported briskly. "They must be separated before they do each other harm." Ordinarily I could count upon Godfrey to attend to domestic adjustments out of doors. In fact, he would always shoot up like a jack-in-the-box to mend such matters in the past.

He did not move. "The cat was intent upon sitting on my lap. I thought it better to set him upon more lively prey."

I gaped at Irene, who was removing her bonnet and approaching Godfrey on cautious cat feet. Behind us, I heard André depositing the large dress box in the hall. For the moment, fashion was forgotten, no matter its costs.

Irene had sunk beside Godfrey's chair, her gloved hand on its rolled arm. "What is it, my dear?"

He glanced at her upturned face, his own features losing some of their distraction.

"I have just had a most immodest proposal today, and I'm damned if I know what to do about it."

"Oh?" she asked. "Does this involve a can-can girl from Le Moulin Rouge, by any chance?"

"If only it did!" he replied feelingly. Before Irene could bristle at this defection, Godfrey looked up to find me fading on the threshold. "No. Stay, Nell. This involves you as well."

"I? I am sure I have nothing to do with it!"

As usual, my response amused him despite his distraction.

"You are always so sure," he replied, "and most often when you know little about the matter at hand. Why are you so certain when you know absolutely nothing about this matter?"

"Because . . . it is so clearly out of the way. You are not behaving as yourself. Even Irene is stupefied, and I certainly do not want to be drawn into any . . . matter so convoluted and assuredly personal to yourself. Yourselves.''

He laughed then, sounding like himself again. " 'Stupefied.' Irene is stupefied? Stand by the fire," he urged her, "that I may study this unheard-of state."

She did so, enjoying his attention, and even turned coquettishly as if to better display this quality.

I very nearly stamped my foot in frustration. "Oh, you both know what I mean! Something has happened, and I fear it is none of my business."

"But it is." He stood as well, gesturing me to a seat before turning again to Irene. "Did you have an interesting day at the dressmaker's?"

She laughed, relieved. "Imagine Monsieur Worth's face, Nell, if he could hear Godfrey reducing him to a dressmaker. No, darling, I did not have a nice day at the dressmaker's. First, I was presented with a divine gown, for which I may not have to pay—we shall see; then I was presented with a murdered seamstress, one of twelve hundred such girls so employed at Maison Worth."

Now Godfrey looked stupefied. "Surely you jest."

Irene sadly shook her head. "I wish I did, for the latter problem has severely curtailed my pleasure in the first matter. And what adventures have put you in such a quandary, pray?"

"Quandary. How do you know that I am in a quandary?"

"Godfrey, you are the most even-tempered of men. When you put out the cat, smother the parrot, let the maid waltz off with nothing in the larder but cold pie and resort to a solitary brandy, you are obviously in grave difficulty. I deduced a blackmailing hussy, but then I am your wife and I cannot be expected to be objective in these matters."

Her words, lightly offered, sobered his face nevertheless. "I have been remiss," he admitted.

I straightened in a chair, expecting to have the domestic upheavals attended to shortly. Instead, he repaired to the Irish cut-glass brandy decanter. "A brandy," he said to

Irene, suiting gesture to words. "New gowns and murder are most fatiguing, each in their own way. Nell?"

"Nothing. I am right in supposing that this is the Napoleonic brandy you bought with the proceeds of Queen Marie Antoinette's Zone of Diamonds?"

He nodded.

"Too French," I sniffed.

Godfrey resumed his chair and his contemplative air even as he admired the liquor's topaz color in his glass. Irene perched on the wing chair's arm and stroked a charmingly errant dark lock back from his brow.

I was more than ever minded to retreat, for certain domestic scenes should remain private. Godfrey stopped me by speaking, facing into the fire as if recalling a distant day.

"I have had an offer. A most strange offer."

"In your work?" I prompted.

His glance was sharp. "For my work, yes." He sighed. "As you know, I have taken what legal assignments I can, specializing in cases that cross borders and involve knowledge of English and English law. This is modestly remunerative, and damnably dull."

Irene nodded sympathetically. Much as I deplored Godfrey's use of expletives this evening, I had to admit that our stop-and-start lives since leaving England left much to be desired. We were either idle, or engaged on some dubious venture involving crime and its consequences. And the funds from the Zone of Diamonds had to be dwindling.

Ever since, as a girl, I had come to make myself useful to my late parson father about the manse and the parish, I had taken content in a purely domestic role, but Godfrey and Irene were more worldly than I in more than the customary sense. They had thrived on invention and on contention, in court or on stage.

Now fate had denied both their proper arena. In some ways, they were as much exiled from their natural environments here in Paris as Quentin Stanhope had been in Afghanistan. Thinking of Quentin, who might be alive—must be alive!—made me clasp my hands in anxiety. Godfrey saw the gesture and misread it. How could he not?

"Pray, do not worry, Nell. One might say that I have a golden opportunity; good fortune in such stunning and sudden degree that I do not know quite how to take it."

"Then the news is good?" Irene cried. "Godfrey, you always take things so seriously, I thought—"

He raised a barrister's cautionary hands. "The matter looks promising. Too promising. There are other considerations. And conditions."

Irene's hands lifted and fell in rapid turn. "Oh, for heaven's sake, Godfrey! Do not keep us teetering on our chair edges." (She spoke for herself; her appealing perch required teetering. I was firmly anchored on the commodious bergère and in no danger of toppling.) "What is it?" she urged.

Of course he sipped the brandy before replying. I sometimes think such eternal dithering is the sole function of men's clubs.

"You have heard of Ferrières?" he asked.

How like a lawyer to answer a question with another question! By now I was ready to install Casanova's cage cover over Godfrey's attractive but aggravatingly noncommittal face.

"Ferrières?" Irene repeated. She prided herself on knowing of anyone of consequence in Paris. "I have heard of no such person," she admitted, crestfallen.

"Ferrières is not a person, darling oracle, but a place."

"Oh," I interjected. "Is it a . . . prison?"

"Hardly." Now Godfrey was showing frustration. "It is the country home of the Rothschilds, and there I—we—have been invited."

Irene almost fell off her chair arm, save that Godfrey threw an arm around her waist to steady her. "The Rothschilds? We—you—are invited to the Rothschild estate?" Her amazement turned to suspicion. "The autumn season in Paris has started. No one of any cachet would be caught dead anywhere else, and the hunt season does not begin until November. Why are the Rothschilds receiving guests in the country at this time of year?"

"Because these guests are also potential business associates; they wish the association to be discreet."

"Business?" She frowned, this mistress of insight and deduction, then leaped up, clapping her hands. "The Rothschilds wish you to handle some affairs for them! Wonderful. They are the most prominent bankers in Europe. The fate of royal houses and entire governments have lain in their hands in the past and will likely do so in the future. They have branches in London, in Vienna, in Madrid . . . my dear, they are a nation unto themselves and as rich as Croesus. They should be extremely lucrative to work for, and assuredly it will not be in the least dull."

Godfrey's mood visibly lifted as Irene's optimism sprang into full flower. He smiled and nodded throughout her speech, and at one point I thought that he would actually applaud.

"Then what on earth is the matter?" she finished up rhetorically.

He sighed and sipped, sipped and sighed. Men are so deliberate at times!

"Baron Alphonse's emissary was most definite on a certain point."

We leaned forward as one, Irene and I, recognizing the crux of the matter as hounds scent prey. "Yes?" we chorused.

"You must also attend this meeting."

I sat back, satisfied. "Of course it is only proper that your wife be present at such a vital juncture. The Baron shows much nicety for including Irene."

Godfrey regarded me complacently. "The Baron exhibited enough nicety to insist that you also attend."

"I? Surely not! Why would Baron Alphonse de Rothschild even know of my existence?"

"You sound insulted, Nell," Irene said with amusement.

"I imagine that the Baron is aware of you because his family operates the most efficient spy network in Europe."

"Spies!"

"Information gatherers and dispensers," she amended. "Every successful business depends upon such servitors, and bankers more than most."

"I do not like the notion of some 'spy' knowing about my existence," I said.

"At least we can rest assured that the Rothschild spies are thorough." Irene turned to Godfrey again. "Are Casanova, Lucifer and Messalina included in this rather blanket social invitation?"

"No . . . but they were mentioned."

Even Irene was impressed. "What are your reservations?"

"You have named them. The Rothschilds are rich and powerful. Such people draw envy and enemies. They are also of the Jewish faith. Such folk draw controversy, particularly in these times. Working for them might be dangerous."

"A wonderful recommendation!" Irene cried, carried away again. "You yourself said Paris law was dull."

"I am also troubled by their inclusion of you and Nell in the meeting, and its secrecy. I cannot be sure what they have in mind."

"Of course you cannot," Irene said. "That is what makes life exciting. Don't be such a . . . barrister, Godfrey. Obviously the Rothschilds have become aware of your sterling qualities. If they take notice of we humble females attached to your star, so be it. We can only be courteous and go and find out what they want."

"Curiosity," I warned, in a voice of doom.

"What?" Irene asked.

"You can only be curious," I responded, "and think what trouble that has caused you in the past."

"Yes," she agreed happily, rising to dance over to Casanova's cage and whisk away the chintz cover.

"Arrhhk!" The bird protested past indignities as his blindfold lifted. He sidled along the perch, cocked his gaudy head and, for the first time in his long and blasphemous life, supported me to the hilt.

"Curious!" he barked at Irene, thrusting out his neck until his feathers ruffled. "Curiosity killed the canary."

"You've got it wrong," Irene told him, nose to beak.

The large yellow beak opened, but she darted back before he could close it on her nose.

"Has he?" I wondered.

Godfrey caught my eye, his expression as he watched Irene half doting and half apprehensive.

I feared that our little domestic trio was to the family Rothschild and their minion birds of like ilk as canaries are to hawks, but I said nothing.

Chapter Seven

STAG PARTY

Why is it that large French country estates resemble nothing so much as the overblown public buildings of London? Perhaps, even in retreat, the French cannot help showing off.

Certainly Napoleon is a prime example of that, even if his antecedents were Cretan offshoots of an obscure but prolific Italian family. I have no reason to be fond of the island of Crete or any of its products, however infamous, given its sinister role in another of Irene's adventures the previous year.

The Rothschild chateau of Ferrières reminded me of the Royal Courts of Justice building recently erected on Fleet Street opposite the Temple where Godfrey and I had toiled together: acres of shining white stone interrupted by an excessive number of spire-topped towers.

We had much time to gaze upon the massive edifice as our coach, pulled by two ponderous, feathery-hocked horses, ground up the circular drive. Following a train journey from Paris to tiny Ozoir-la-Ferrière and a subsequent jolting in the Rothschild conveyance, I was not surprised to find that the great house cast a double image in my tired eyes.

At last, however, we all three stood on solid paving stones gazing up at what, to me, resembled an inverted chest of drawers belonging to a giant. I said so.

Godfrey looked askance, for a gentleman of dignified bearing was descending the stairs toward us even as I spoke. Irene's eyes again swept the grandiose facade as if she were viewing it for the first time, then she attempted, successfully, to stifle a snicker.

We were all in reasonable order as the dignified gentleman offered a welcome and led us indoors. If Ferrière's exterior was imposing, its interior positively intimidated. The Great Hall was ornamented in Napoleon III style. Unfortunately, the Buonaparte influence had not only changed the face of Europe on the battlefield but had altered the facade of many a house and garden on the fashion front for some decades after his well-deserved defeat.

My humble English pen balks at listing the quantity of preciosities strewn about, save that they included several plump towering pillars, a king's ransom in ormolu and gilt, paintings as ubiquitous as postage stamps and an outright infestation of fringed and tasseled furniture, much of it velvet in vivid shades of rose and moss-green.

The centerpiece of this domestic exhibition was a tall marble column surrounded by a circular couch. Atop this column sat a clock with a figure that I supposed to be Atlas bearing the world on his weary shoulders. On the other hand, it could have represented the architect of Ferrières facing the task of constructing such a bloated edifice.

The distinguished gentleman turned us over to the guidance of a soberly dressed woman, who conducted us up a massive staircase. I resisted the urge to turn back and gaze on the impressive room below, for fear I should fall, or at least turn into a pillar of salt. My attention was fixed, at any rate, by a succession of heroic-sized paintings depicting ancient gods and goddesses in the pursuit of game both animal and human, and all of it virtually undressed.

"Shocking," I muttered.

"Rubens," came Irene's reverential whisper. "Snyders. "Desportes."

Being wise, Godfrey took in all and said nothing.

We were shown in turn to separate suites along an endless passage of such accommodation.

Although my bedchamber was spacious, it featured a canopied bed, which I dislike due to dust and other invasions of an insect nature. And the walls were covered in a colorful fabric with a design of . . . perching parrots. Was there no escape?

The moment the conductress had opportunity to disappear in the manner of good servants, our doors popped open on the common passage, and we began a round of visiting, inspecting and judging each other's chambers.

"A veritable fairy-tale palace!" Irene exclaimed at the entrance hall of her suite, as she led Godfrey and myself through bedroom and toilet chamber into a private bathroom with fireplace. "Everything appears as if from invisible hands. Look! The fires are lit, the proper bags are delivered before we arrive."

"Monsieur le Baron was most cordial in greeting us," I put in, determined to make the best of our summons to this palatial pile.

Irene gawked at me most rudely. "That was not the Baron, silly Nell; that was the butler. The Baron will greet us at dinner, which the housekeeper told us was at nine."

"Short rations for a long time," Godfrey commented as he sat on the wood-enclosed bathtub and began fiddling with the spigots. "And we may not even see the Baron himself. I was visited by emissaries."

"Surely we have not been brought all this way—before the Season—to see only an understudy!" Irene objected.

"Most ingenious," Godfrey adjudged the plumbing, "especially considering this chateau was constructed thirty-odd years ago."

"Yes," I agreed, "the sanitary facilities are almost English in their efficiency. At least I shall have a good bath."

This last was an oblique comment on the tiny room that so poorly served this function at Neuilly. Irene, deaf to complaints about her cherished cottage once she was ensconced in a palace again, chattered on.

"Fruit baskets bedeck every room," she told Godfrey, "which ought to staunch your appetite. Our Nell has attained the proper Englishwoman-abroad's dream: hot water and lots of it. And I will have a Rothschild in the flesh for dinner tonight, or I will raise a ruckus that will shake the Rubens from their walls."

"You sound quite a cannibal," I protested as a timid knock rapped on the entrance-hall door.

Irene strode to answer it and discovered a white-capped maid in midcurtsy. It seemed we were all simultaneously subjected to such visitations, and were needed in our suites to direct our attendants in unpacking.

I also heard mention of assistance at our baths and dressing for dinner, but hoped that I had misunderstood the extremely misunderstandable language of France. At least a manservant stood waiting beside Godfrey's suite door.

Of the further ordeals of being a guest at Ferrières I will not say much more. The maid found my disinclination to disrobe in front of her most incomprehensible, but did insist on drawing my bath.

I confess that I found sinking into the warm fragrant water of a zinc-lined tub while firelight fluttered on the gilded fittings rather amenable. Despite the acres of time that stretched to the dinner hour, finding the clothes the maid had tucked away and then dressing—by myself, of course—used up sufficient time that I barely had a moment to eat an apple before a knock on the door called me to the feast below.

Godfrey wore white tie and tails, which always made him look taller and more handsome, neither of which quality required amplification. Irene had restrained herself from bringing her new Worth gown, instead donning midnight blue velvet softened with pearls and silver cord. I wore a "surprise" dress—not my staple costume of black and old rose with the reversible revers, but the second Liberty gown, a luminous ivory satin over pale pink taffeta that blushed through like a tinted seashell lighted from within.

"Nell positively glows," Godfrey said, gallantly offering me his free arm.

"She is one of the fortunate few who can wear pink without looking fatuous," Irene commented. "I, on the other hand, look like Little Bo-Peep in pink."

"In midnight blue you look as if you would lead a great many sheep astray, rather than merely lose them," Godfrey told her, eyeing her gown's formidable décolletage.

"I hope I am appropriately gowned to meet a Rothschild, as I will not be fobbed off with a mere flunky of two," she responded quite sternly.

"Irene, you are tediously curious," I warned her again.

"Better than being curiously tedious," she retorted. "Onward, to dinner at Château Questionmark."

We three tripped down the long, broad royal staircase like the Three Musketeers off to mutual duels with D'Artagnan.

From the main hall, the head butler conducted us to a drawing room appointed all in white. Irene flounced into that pale background like a royal widow, but I was afraid to sit anywhere, lest I leave some disarray behind, some unseen soil, even an indented cushion that would create a gray shadow.

The butler poured us each a sherry in glasses as delicate as a crystal bird's egg, then withdrew.

Irene settled onto a white brocade bergère, a blue-black rook nestled on a snowbank, cosseting her burnished liquor. "We seem to be our own best company so far this night."

"Interesting," said Godfrey, flipping up his tails one-handed and sitting on a hard chair.

I hovered by the closed doors, hoping for footsteps.

"This is carrying invisibility too far," Irene said at last, rising. She floated soundlessly over the pale Aubusson carpet to another door and jerked it open.

Two pale-faced men in evening dress stood there.

Godfrey leaped up. "Durfort. Marbeau."

"The gentlemen who called upon you?" Irene inquired in a deceptively limpid tone.

He nodded slowly.

"Now they eavesdrop upon us," she went on, her voice gaining timbre. "You appear to have been visited by a delegation of sneaks, Godfrey."

One man stepped into the room. "You mistake us, Madame. We were about to announce the arrival of Baron Alphonse from Paris."

Irene's tilted head and lifted eyebrows made her face a mask of polite incredulity. "The Baron arrives by the back way?"

"The Baron arrives discreetly," the other man returned.

"In his own house?"

"Sometimes, Madame, even that is required."

The click of shoes over shining marble echoed, then silenced. Irene drew away from the door, standing beside Godfrey and myself. The Three Musketeers, indeed; and now were we about to meet our manipulative Cardinal Richelieu?

The man in evening dress who entered was not tall, but he was elegant and commanded the attention. His features—as I would see later when I had studied the château portraiture—bore the stamp of his late father, Baron James, a Rothschild stamp that at least the French branch of the family had passed on and perfected: pointed chin, pointed nose, shrewd eyes and remarkably humorous, well-arched eyebrows. Wrinkles above the good-natured brows imitated their inquisitive vault. Wrinkles ran from the corners of his eyes in merry little rivulets. His prominent girth promised a love of plenteous food and wine. Baron Alphonse was at once a man supremely sure of himself and equally willing to spend time making sure of the others around him.

"You will pardon," he began, "the secrecy. I fear I have a rather melodramatic matter to discuss with you three tonight."

Three! My heart quickened despite my resolve to remain cool in the face of such titled wealth.

"Perhaps we should begin with business and dine after," he suggested, leading us from the white drawing room. The two men followed our party. Or did they contain and watch us?

Imagine my astonishment when our urbane host led us down a grand hall to a far less grand passage, and then to a narrow stairway . . . to the basements!

The Baron paused at the top of this unimpressive staircase. "Apologies to the ladies. Much of the basements are unlovely, although some quite respectable suites lie down here, but it is essential that we meet in some security."

With that he descended, Godfrey following, Irene and I trailing after. Behind us came the two—what? Associates? Spies? Guards?

The Rothschild basements were the utter reverse of the showy palace above, as if that were a whited sepulchre reflected in an oily pool and only now showing its true colors: we traversed a vast network of dark corridors interlarded with pipes. Anonymous closed doors led off in every direction. I envisioned storage rooms, servants' quarters, kitchens, pantries, root cellars, wine cellars and the like, also possibly crypts, dungeons and torture chambers.

We shortly lost our sense of direction, although the occasional gaslight sconce kept us from total darkness. The Baron led on without slowing his steps, finally pausing before a dark oaken door.

"Ladies are forbidden this room, which is used exclusively after the hunt, but tonight I require it for our business. I apologize in advance for the odor of old tobacco."

"You need not apologize, Baron," Irene replied in an amused tone, "if you are willing to allow us to add the scent of new tobacco to your older vintage."

"Us? You smoke yourself, Madame?"

"On occasion I even hunt, Baron."

After a moment's stalemate, the Baron nodded to his men. They stepped past us to flourish open the double doors.

We entered a huge chamber furnished with fur-draped divans. The gaslights, already lit, winked like Roman vigil lights around the room, reflecting from the brown glass eyes of mounted heads—shaggy bear, sleek stags, and wicked boar.

Unlike Sarah Bernhardt's exotic salon with its eccentric mix of animals living and dead, this room was hung heavy with generations of death, of slaughtered deer and boar by the hundreds, the thousands, falling hard to earth and being reborn again in macabre wall decorations.

I did not like the place, nor did Irene or Godfrey, for they were silent.

"Ferrières is a paradise for hunters," the baron said, mistaking our silence for stunned admiration. "We hunt only on Sundays, but such shoots we have—hundreds of partridge and pheasant and hares in a single afternoon."

"Sunday was the day the Lord rested," I choked out. "Could not His creatures also rest on that day?"

The Baron looked at me for the first time. "You are Christian, I understand, Miss Huxleigh, a formidable Christian. My faith does not keep Sunday."

"The Creation was recorded in the Old Testament," I retorted breathlessly.

The Baron's humorous features relaxed. "You are right, and it was also recorded that mankind was given dominion over all the beasts of the earth."

"Dominion, but not death in such numbers."

"Men die in numbers as great in forgotten corners of the earth, some of them very near to us."

"Women as well," Irene said. "And children."

The Baron nodded. "You touch upon the matter that has brought you to me."

"Death?" Godfrey asked quickly.

"Possible death. Potential death. Please, be seated."

We eyed the bestiary of surfaces to choose from. Godfrey shrugged and sat in a red velvet-upholstered chair formed from a thorny crown of antlers, against which his dark and light coloring and black and white garb appeared to great distinction. Irene sank upon a long-haired throw of creamy Mongolian goathair that perfectly set off her blue-black gown. I found a stool of some unidentifiable hide and sat before I had long to study it.

The Baron moved to a massive desk formed of an exotic gnarled wood and sat behind it.

"I am accustomed," he began, eyeing Godfrey principally, "to transacting business with men."

"So are most men," Irene put in a trifle tartly. "That is why they own most businesses."

The Baron raised a soothing hand. I almost expected to see a frill of lace at the wrist, so graceful was his gesture.

"I am well aware of Madame's distaste for custom," he went on. "In this case, I welcome it. But the American-born perhaps do not understand our Old World order. The house of Rothschild is founded upon one man and his five sons, and I am proud to claim Mayer Amschel as my grandfather."

"Did he and his wife have no daughters?" Irene inquired.

The Baron nodded. "Five."

"An equal number of sons and daughters? What became of Mayer Amschel's five daughters when his five sons began forging the links of the Rothschild financial empire?"

"They married and had children."

"That is all?"

"They worked hard to maintain their families and lived to see their sons move into financial enterprises in England and France, far beyond the Frankfurt ghetto where Rothschilds began, and to see their daughters marry sons of Rothschilds."

"But that," said I without thinking, "is too close a relationship for marriage!"

"First cousins to first cousins," the Baron admitted, "but by the third generation some foreign blood had strengthened the stock. Certainly all of us have proven to have a decent head for business."

With this I could not argue; the Rothschilds were the uncrowned kings of European finance, and only tales of the American financiers like Jay Gould could rival their princely ways.

"You have not invited us here, Baron," Godfrey put in, "to debate the Rothschild pedigree."

The Baron's face turned into a merry mask for several moments before audible laughter poured from his mouth and eyes as well. "We are considered an international and rather intimidating family, but I confess that I find myself confounded by the united front you three present, with Madame Norton's American verve, Miss Huxleigh's British rectitude and your own incisive Anglo-Saxon sangfroid, Monsieur."

"I am a barrister, not a banker. I cannot afford to be anything other than cold-blooded," Godfrey replied.

"Perhaps we can change that sad state of affairs," the Baron suggested with a twinkle, nodding to the door.

The distinguished gentleman I had taken for more than a butler advanced with a trio of boxes on a silver tray. He presented each in turn; first to Godfrey, then Irene.

Godfrey settled against his upright chairback with a decidedly Lucifer-like expression of satisfaction and a long, thin cigar between his fingers. The butler bent to light it, then moved on to Irene. From the smallest box, an exquisite thing of ruby enamel and sterling silver, she selected a small dark cigarette, which she installed in her own mother-of-pearl holder, extracted from her reticule.

While the skeptical Rothschild eyebrows remained

quirked toward heaven, she accepted the butler's lucifer and shortly exhaled an expert, stiletto-thin stream of smoke.

The servant disappeared and I forgot him utterly—until he was bowing before me with the silver tray . . . and a crystal bowl filled with wrapped hard candy.

My more innocent enjoyments had never before been catered to with such social thoughtfulness. I accepted one in a gold and crimson paper, making much of unwrapping it and popping it into my mouth. Only then did it occur to me that I had effectively silenced myself for some time. Unlike the disgusting cigarette, a sweet cannot be plucked from one's mouth and held casually in the hand while speaking, then be reinstated later.

Still, the sweet was flavored with strawberry and honey, and was very good.

The Baron had settled deeper into his chair with a cigar that matched Godfrey's for length and was twice its circumference. Again the butler made the rounds, this time with four flutes of blond, bubbling champagne. My flute, I discovered when I hoisted it, was filled with sparkling mineral water.

The Baron's uncannily apt hospitality made me regard him as a devil in disguise, and indeed, smoke seemed to swirl from his ears and mouth as he puffed away happily on his outsize cigar.

"You have made your point, Baron," Irene said, removing her cigarette holder from her mouth and contemplating the bejeweled gold snake that twined the stem, while smoke curled up from the cigarette like a ghostly extension of the serpent's tail. "You know a good deal about us, even to our personal habits."

"Why not? We Rothschilds have the most efficient spy network in Europe."

"Efficient, yes," Godfrey agreed, "but with more demanding work to do than turn its efforts to such discoveries as that Miss Huxleigh neither smokes nor drinks."

The Baron rose and strolled around his ornate desk, sitting on one corner and crossing his legs. Had Oscar Wilde tried such a posture he would have looked like an overbalanced Humpty Dumpty. Baron Alphonse looked at ease.

"At first I determined to speak only to you, Mr. Norton, until various reports indicated that Mrs. Norton would not respond well to overlooking." He bowed in Irene's direction. "Indeed, she suited us far better than you. Then I became convinced that Miss Huxleigh's participation was also necessary. You may not be a family, but you certainly amount to a force of three. I concluded that no one of you would be as effective as all three."

"Effective at what?" I finally asked, having sucked the sweet to a small enough pellet to swallow. "Spying?" I said tartly.

The Baron raised an instructive forefinger. "Exactly, Miss Huxleigh. Only the English are so forthright. That no doubt accounts for the fact that my uncle Nathanial in London has done better than any of us. You see, by scattering to the winds, each branch of the family Rothschild has developed its own character. Mine, as the French flavor in the recipe, is diplomatic and subtle, but you have boldly broached the heart of the matter.

"It would suit the Rothschild fortunes and family to have the three of you act as our eyes and ears. You travel on the fringe of certain circles and are admirably suited to learn things others less felicitously placed could not. With Mr. Norton's entrée to matters legal and international, with Mrs. Norton's ability to charm aristocrat and artiste alike, with your own invaluable gift for going unnoticed, you form a formidable syndicate, as it were, for gathering information crucial to not only Rothschild interests, but those of all civilized Europe."

"Which are no doubt one and the same thing!" I responded indignantly, feeling a sweet, hard lump melting none too swiftly down my esophagus. I hiccoughed and was forced to sip water and be silent.

"What drew your attention to us?" Irene asked sharply.

The Baron smiled and also withdrew his cigar to contemplate it. I wished I had done as much with my sweet, as I choked into my flute of sparkling water. I cannot imagine what possesses those afflicted with the smoking habit to make so many self-indulgent gestures with the objects of their obsession.

"Your intervention in the affairs of Alice Heine, the Duchess of Richelieu, soon to be the Princess of Monaco, thanks to your busy work."

"Ah." Irene had sat back to exhale the word in smoky satisfaction. Her silver gown trim glittered like smoke rings against the midnight-blue velvet darkness she wore. "Alice is related to rivals of yours, the banking family of Heine."

"Founded by Salomon Heine of Hamburg," Godfrey added.

"You see? How quick you are, and with no warning. From sixteen groschen Salomon Heine became one of the wealthiest bankers in Germany. Mayer Amschel started with less, but there were more of us."

"Why should we spy for you?" I demanded when I could breathe well enough to speak. I had framed the question from the high moral ground of demanding why he would think we could be persuaded to spy for *anyone*.

"Perhaps because we have asked you first? Not sufficient reason for Miss Huxleigh, I see. Then I would argue that our 'spying' has often kept the topsy-turvy towers of European capitals upright. The Rothschild coffers have more than once opened to save a crown or a parliament. Money breeds best in peace, yet Europe has tottered on the brink of disastrous realignment and dissolution since the Corsican ran roughshod over most of it."

"The sad state of European politics has persisted for decades," Godfrey said suspiciously. "That did not spur you to consider recruiting us now."

"No. But a specific country troubles, and a certain crown lies uneasy, and an even more . . . individual matter has arisen, one that I could not dare speak of to most people. Perhaps it will be too much for you, as well."

"What?" Irene demanded eagerly, drawn to the Baron's bait as a snapping turtle is to a dragonfly.

The Baron spread his supple hands, the cigar leaving a train of smoke like a steam engine. "You know where we came from: the ghetto of Hamburg. Twelve feet wide that home and haven and prison was, yet roomy enough to beget in, and die in, and be killed in. You have heard of the blood price?"

We were silent.

"The pogrom?"

Godfrey and Irene nodded.

"I have not," I spoke up.

The Baron addressed me so exclusively that I became restive after a while. His words were short and clipped and the picture they painted was as harsh.

"The pogrom is only on the large scale what all Jews have faced on a small scale. We are periodically reviled, herded, forced to leave where we have lived. In the ghettos even we are not safe: on high Christian holy days mobs attack and demand a blood price of many deaths for the single, ritual death they blame upon us. Then we die: men, women, children, and the thirst is satisfied until the next time."

"That," I said, realizing it for the first time, "is what you left behind."

"That is what we came from; to become barons of France and lords of England, we first had to become wealthy and powerful beyond all others of our kind. Thirty pieces of silver may buy betrayal; thirty million will buy—ultimately, grudgingly—respect; titles; prominence."

"Why, you are like Mr. Worth!" I said, amazed.

The Baron regarded me in puzzlement.

"You are respected by dint of talent, but only tolerated by dint of birth," I explained.

He smiled. "I believe that we Rothschilds are more than tolerated now, at least in France and England. Austria is another story. Even when we kept a major bank in Vienna, a Rothschild was not allowed to become a citizen or buy a house because he was a Jew."

Irene stirred, as if roused from some melancholy reverie. "The tale you tell is ever the same. If the Rothschilds cannot protect the Jews of the ghetto, how can we?"

"We are our brothers' keeper," he said a bit bitterly, "yet in these latter days we grow careless in our religion and smug in our safety. Only my brother Édouard pours money into the wild and doomed dream of establishing a Jewish homeland in Palestine. As well commandeer an ice floe and call it Israel! No, most of us Rothschilds do not seek to reshape the world, only to keep it from disintegrating further. We cannot stem the Russian pogroms, but we can aid those who flee them. We cannot level the ghettos, but we can leave them and make it possible for others to live beyond them, as we do. Other matters we cannot affect, only wonder at; one such example is much on my mind of late. Have you ever heard of the Golem?"

The Golem. The Golem. "I have—!" I stared wonderingly at Irene. "A kind of . . . monster, was it not?"

She shrugged. "One person's monster is another's messiah, and that is precisely the role the Golem played." Her tone dropped into the soft, hypnotizing range of storytelling. "The Golem was a man of clay. A medieval rabbi used the words of the Cabbala—the secret, oral tradition of Judaism handed down from Moses to the rabbis of the Mishnah and the Talmud—to breathe life into its huge frame. Supposedly mute, but powerful, the Golem defended the ordinary ghetto dweller from rampaging mobs. Yet this clay man could love—the rabbi's daughter—and so he was unmade. Some believe that the tale of the Golem inspired Mary Shelley to write *Frankenstein*. Yet the historic Golem is more than monster, it is myth. Its story explores the nature of creation and responsibility, that draws the fine line on which balance hatred and humanity. It would make a splendid tragic opera, as I told my dear friend, Antonín Dvořák, but who would play the title role?"

"Surely," I said, "no one today believes in such a creature?"

The Baron was silent, then pushed off the desk edge. He had long since allowed his cigar to burn to a last inch of ash in a crystal tray beside him.

I grew aware that the chamber was still, and smokeless.

"Reports—serious reports from unimpeachable witnesses," the Baron said, "indicate that the Golem has been seen—twice within the past three months—stalking the ghetto byways," the Baron said. "Taller than the ground floor of a house, with a face that is not a face, nearly blind and able to choke out only raw, ungoverned sounds . . . but alive, moving, back from the undead."

"Where? Where has such a thing been seen?" I demanded, still a doubting Thomas.

Then I remembered when and where I had heard mention of the Golem on Irene's lips and jerked my head. I met her eyes already staring into mine with an expression of mingled mystification and triumph.

"Prague," the Baron answered my question. "In Prague, of course. That city historically has been the richest source of the Golem legends. Something is rotten in the state of Bohemia, in its politics, and in its people. Now the Golem walks again for the first time in four hundred years. I want you three to go to Prague immediately and discover what is wrong."

"Prague," I whispered, stunned and dismayed.

Irene's lips silently mirrored the motion of my own, her face transformed by an expression of unholy satisfaction.

Chapter Eight

AN EMBARRASSMENT OF ROTHSCHILDS

"**I am** not persuaded," Godfrey said into the lengthening silence. "My wife has reason to fear for her personal safety in that city. Vague rumors of social and political unrest and the even vaguer reports of this mythical creature hardly justify the risk."

Godfrey had spoken with perfect politeness, and utter indifference. When he finished, he contemplated the thick ash on his cigar end as if the issue of when it would fall was of much more import than the Baron's astonishing proposal.

The Baron's dark eyes sparkled almost as brightly as Irene's did at the hint of a mystery.

"Monsieur is prepared to negotiate, I see, but time is of the essence, and I must be blunt. No doubt you refer to the current King of Bohemia's frustrated ambitions in your wife's direction?"

Godfrey did not blink—nor did he stop eyeing his irritating ash—but I could not avoid exclaiming, "You know of that?"

"Of course, Miss Huxleigh. When the King of Bohemia directs five of his top secret agents' attention to pursuing a pair of misses absconding from Prague, the action is noticed, please believe me. That is why you may rely upon our information that maneuvers of great moment are taking place in Prague; such plots may undermine the delicate national harmony of Europe itself."

"European nations," Irene pointed out, "have had no harmony since Buonaparte."

"All the more reason to watch every trembling of the earth and its inhabitants, whether in France or Bohemia. The various nations and their governments are all intertwined. We Rothschilds know that better than most, having sunk our roots into various quarters of the Continent. We listen when the feather of a pigeon drops unwarranted in Warsaw; feel the tremors when the royal coffers overflow in Bremen. When the Golem apparently walks again in Prague, we see it not only as a manifestation of spiritual unease, but of political unrest."

"If you know of the King's enmity toward my wife," Godfrey said, "you realize how senseless it would be to send her there. Without her presence, Miss Huxleigh and I are mere babes in the Bohemian woods."

"You must not devalue yourself and your able assistant," the Baron chided. "Happily, I do not accept your diagnosis." He turned to Irene with a smile. "Nor do I expect that Madame Norton will fail to find an apt way of reintroducing herself to the city, be it in disguise or in the manner of some brilliant, bare-faced approach. Am I not right?" He bowed to Irene.

"Perfectly correct, Baron," she agreed, "but my husband is also correct. I cannot be sure how the King would react to my presence in Prague, and that possibility must be considered. He may wish to kill me—or kidnap me; neither course would suit myself and my companions."

"Yes, yes, I admit the risk to you, Madame. Yet such risk did not keep you recently from the home turf of a far more formidable opponent than Wilhelm von Ormstein."

Irene donned her most skeptical expression, but I could
see her fingers tightening on her dainty cigarette holder.
"You refer, Baron—?"

"To your expedition to London, a city far more perilous
to you than Prague. In addition, this Colonel Moran with
whom you involved yourself is the most dangerous man we
have encountered on three continents. I predict that he is
not done with you."

"Then he is still alive?" Irene demanded.

The Baron smiled. "I may not say more."

"And Quentin Stanhope?" I broke in breathlessly, unable to restrain myself, unable even to check the hopeful
quaver in my voice.

The Baron's smile grew more mysterious. "I may not
speak on that issue, either, Miss Huxleigh, but I believe that
you are wise to have forgone wearing mourning just yet."

"If you know so much about us," Godfrey put in a bit
sternly, "you obviously have . . . spies of far greater experience than us at your command. Why recruit us?"

"Because spies are merely that, functionaries. This mission to Bohemia requires more finesse. I may have the
confidences of the servants to the great, but rarely witnesses among those with whom the great rub elbows."

"You do indeed resemble Monsieur Worth!" Irene exclaimed admiringly, flashing me a glance of acknowledgment. "Except that you require not a *mannequin de ville*,
but *agents du monde*."

The Baron did not scorn her comparison to Monsieur
Worth, as I feared he might, but he did look puzzled.

"Monsieur Worth," she explained, "wishes me to wear
his most exquisite gowns out and about as an inducement
to wealthier clients to buy them."

The Baron clapped his hands once, in understanding and
pleasure.

"So you are already placed, Madame, as one who may go
anywhere in great style for purposes of Fashion? Excellent.
You have a gift for attracting the support of merchant

princes like Worth and Tiffany, if not the honor of actual princes like Wilhelm von Ormstein. This new arrangement will suit my plans admirably."

Once again Godfrey intervened, and with a well-taken objection.

"You are not dealing with your usual sort of agent, Baron," he said. "Spies act at your command, as I said; I doubt that we will be so malleable."

"True," Irene added mischievously. "We will do as you wish only so long as we are convinced that it abets the greater good."

"And what is the greater good, Madame?"

"Why, what we believe it is."

"I see. You warn me that you may be contrary."

"We warn you," Godfrey said, "that we serve our own integrity before any other's cause, no matter how high-sounding."

The Baron upheld a forefinger. "But not your own interests?"

"Interests," Godfrey repeated, consulting Irene and me in turn with his eyes. "No. We are all capable of sacrificing our own interests if the need be dire enough."

"Excellent. I can ask for no more than agents accompanied by consciences. Our family goals are as I said: to insure the peace of Europe's many, often-contentious nations. Wars kill people, destroy lands and property, and ruin economies. The House of Rothschild has never thrived on devastation; we came from it too recently."

"Still," Irene put in, "you have not done badly for yourselves."

"And for those who serve us," the Baron added with a bow. "On that note, I would like to present you with some tokens of our confidence in this association. Of course you will be paid, and well, if your mission proves successful, but until then—"

He turned to the two men by the door who had stood to attention as stonily as well-trained dogs while we talked.

"You may bring in the items from the vault."

The word *vault* caused Irene's eyebrows to elevate in pleased anticipation. Godfrey merely looked wary, while I had visions of damp stone and large, red-eyed rats. We were, after all, in a basement, no matter how imposing the edifice above it. While the French like to fancy themselves too grand for vermin, they have a long history of consorting with them, just as all peoples do.

The first object was presented to Irene. The silent bearer stood before her, an inlaid ebony case supported on the crook of one arm—a case large enough to hold the family silver.

Irene's spine straightened even beyond the call of her superb posture, though she kept her bare shoulders admirably down, and her neck lengthened in a swanlike gesture, as if she were a child trying to stretch herself tall enough to see into a tempting dish atop a stove. Her expression was a study of innocently serene, utterly controlled and frightfully fierce anticipation.

I pitied the poor Baron if the contents of his chest failed to meet her expectations.

He nodded at the man, who plucked open the lid like a clamshell, revealing an interior of blackest velvet magnanimously lit by a Milky Way of blinding light.

Irene had risen with the lid to stare down at the case's contents, her features almost illuminated by that eerie, cool, profligate azurine-albino glow. Godfrey, too, stood and stared. And I.

"I must add," the Baron said, "that your old acquaintance Mr. Tiffany would be grateful for any news of royal jewels coming onto the market that you encounter on your journey. It was he who suggested that this bauble might serve well as an 'introduction' to those we wish you to consort with. He will, of course, be delighted to accept any commission its presence might stimulate."

Irene was still speechless, something neither Godfrey nor I was used to. But, then, we too were struck dumb.

At last she clapped her hands softly together at her bosom, a gesture I recognized from her operatic repertoire as one that preceded the delivery of an especially affecting and gorgeous aria.

"The diamond corsage that I wore at La Scala in Milan, when I debuted as Cinderella! How . . . thoughtful of Mr. Tiffany and yourself," she said in gargantuan understatement. "I am to understand that this . . . bauble is mine if I—we—accept your mission to Prague?"

His nod was half bow. "And other assignments as they might turn up."

"Oh. Very clever. This gift elevates me to the aristocracy of the fabulous. It will make me welcome—and envied—anywhere."

"It will make me nervous," Godfrey put in. "Think of the jewel thieves."

"Yes, you are quite right!" Irene's eyes sparkled like black-gold diamonds. "It will be quite amusing to find ways of outwitting them as well." She eyed the Baron. "May I—? They have never seen . . ."

"My dear Madame, they are yours if you say so."

Her gloved fingers plucked the fierce fire from the black velvet, but she seemed to me to be juggling white-hot embers with her bare hands. I couldn't help fearing that the diamonds would burn her somehow.

She held their length against her torso, anchoring one magnificent glittering rosette at her shoulder, the other at the opposite hip. The middle rosette reposed in the cleft of her breasts and all three were linked by a limpid lace frill of diamond brightness.

"You see, and it can be worn as a conventional necklace as well, although a bit overpowering. Even Monsieur Worth would approve: it is asymmetrical, after all. Brilliant," she purred to herself in utter indulgence. "Simply brilliant."

Whether she referred to Mr. Tiffany's inspired and lavish design in diamonds, to Mr. Worth's asymmetrical dressmaking, to the Baron's seductive gift, or to her own nature was questionable, as many things often were with Irene.

"Quite overwhelming," Godfrey commented in dry lawyerly tones.

The Baron heard the reservation in his voice and nodded to the waiting second man, who vanished.

Irene sighed and let the diamonds sink softly to their velvet bed. "They must be carefully donned to show their full effect."

"And carefully worn," I added.

She quirked a smile in my direction, but before she could say anything more the second man returned, bearing another box.

"My," Irene said as he paused before Godfrey, who looked none too pleased by the honor. "We are like Portia confronted by her three suitor's chests. What can the Prince of Morocco have to offer Godfrey?"

She sank back into her seat to watch Godfrey's presentation as she would a scene in a play.

The box that confronted him was nearly as large as Irene's, and of finely wrought Morocco leather, as she had noted, with inlaid silver designs. What, I wondered, would the persuasive Baron use to win over a skeptical barrister? Or did he make the mistake of underestimating Godfrey?

Once again the case lid elevated at the Baron's gesture. Once again a rich velvet—crimson as blood this time— lined the interior.

Godfrey stared blankly at the contents, which gave a gleam of polished wood and metal. And then he lifted something long and elegant and lethal.

"Dueling pistols!" he said in a tone that mixed cynicism, rue and wonder. Then he laughed. "How apropos, Baron Alphonse. I shall certainly require these after the gift you have given to my wife."

"They are French, of course, made at midcentury. I am told that they shoot absolutely true."

"How fortunate," Godfrey said, sighting down one long gleaming barrel, "for I will no doubt shoot false." He eyed the Baron. "I was not reared as a gentleman."

"Godfrey means," Irene put in swiftly, "that he was not introduced to the methods of dueling. As a gentleman, he has no equal."

"My dear Norton," the Baron said softly, "you cannot have had forebears who were reared less rudely or gently than mine." He stepped forward to pick up the other dueling pistol. "These have been in the family for forty years. I would be honored if you would accept them, and would consider the acceptance to include an invitation to meet with my own personal tutor in these lethal yet gentlemanly arts, the foremost duelist in Paris."

"Who?" Irene demanded.

"Coquard," he told her in surprise, unruffled by her curt query.

"A master of both sword and pistol," Irene said in satisfaction. "Good. Then Godfrey and I can practice fencing together. I fear I grow appallingly rusty."

"I can see," Godfrey said, "that it will behoove me to master such things. I recall now some mention of a duel in Monte Carlo." His fine gray eyes narrowed as if sighting on a target—Irene. "A man must have some way of settling an argument with his wife."

"But we never argue," she said blithely.

"To every rule there is a lamentable exception."

Godfrey carefully, almost reverently, laid the pistol he held back in its self-shaped velvet cradle. I saw that it was as dangerously attractive to him as diamonds and detection were to Irene; he saw possibilities for himself in it that he had never glimpsed elsewhere. So much for the barrister conquered. I should like to see what the clever Baron had decided to bestow upon me!

I was soon to get my wish, for the first man laid the case containing the diamond corsage on the Baron's desk and went out of the ghastly room—in which smoke and brandy and treasures were surrounded by glassy animal eyes in severed heads—to collect my trinket.

I sat again, as erect as Irene at her most imperial. I should not be seduced by diamonds and death. Although something fine but tasteful—perhaps sapphires, so dark, deep and reserved. Perhaps a lapel watch for formal occasions. Or . . . a gilded scissors, being both practical and lethally suited to a future spy.

The Baron was watching me with barely contained excitement, rather like a small boy in my charge who was giving the governess what he conceived to be the perfect gift—a toad, no doubt, to make me shriek, or a toy boat that would not float in a bathtub, or something equally unsuitable. I almost felt sorry for the man. I would so hate to be the first to disappoint him, to ruin his lucky streak with my easily impressed associates. . . . Oh, I, too, was the recipient of a large box. Mahogany, with scrolled brass corner pieces and great hinges at the rear.

I found myself stretching like Irene and reined in the impulse. Once again a lid popped open, revealing an old gold velvet interior, so aged that it was mottled darker and lighter here and there. And . . . a book. A great, thick book with an upholstered cut-velvet cover and golden spine, corners and gilt-edged pages. A . . . Bible.

I rose, speechless.

"Sixteenth century," the Baron said. "I have taken the liberty of inserting a parchment with your forebears listed to the date of the Bible."

"My forebears? Back to the sixteenth century?"

"Indeed. You come of solid English stock, Miss Huxleigh." He turned the heavy front cover and I saw a hand-lettered document that listed my parson father's first name, and my late mother's and then many others, each with years of birth and death written in spidery script.

"I thought it discreet," the Baron added softly, for my ears only, "to omit the pig thief hung at Tyburn, but the pedigree is otherwise complete. Of course, this is an early Protestant Bible."

"Of course," I murmured weakly. "Tyburn."

"Tyburn?" Irene asked alertly.

"Apparently . . . a, a maiden name in my family," I answered quickly, catching the Baron's twinkling eye as he shut the elaborate cover on my otherwise blessedly undistinguished family tree.

Chapter Nine

DOMESTIC CONTRETEMPER

We had dined like Renaissance princes at Ferrières, then returned to our chambers to redon our traveling clothes. Like Cinderella, we were returned to our ordinary rags and ashes at the stroke of twelve, when we were whisked in the ducal carriage to the tiny railway station, and thence to Paris. There our coachman waited with our more humble conveyance, though it was no pumpkin.

Two o'clock tolled in the cottage clocks' chorus of soprano and bass voices before we were settled once more safe and cozy in our Neuilly parlor.

There we sat, like heedless children on Christmas morning, ignoring the gargles of a yet-uncovered Casanova, our trophy cases—or bribes—before us.

"So clever," said Irene, happily exploring the complexities of her treasure chest. It masqueraded as a traveling vanity case, with the diamond corsage hidden in the top lid. The rose moiré lining fitted with ivory nail implements, crystal and silver cosmetic and perfume bottles and other fripperies struck me as ample enough a bribe without the added extravagance of the diamonds.

"Do you suppose that Mr. Tiffany never found anyone rich enough to buy the corsage?" Irene asked suddenly. "I despise looking a gift horse in the mouth, but he might as well get some good out of it, then."

Godfrey sat with the pistol case open on his knees, studying each elegant weapon. "Here is the maker's mark, on the barrel," he said in sudden triumph. "I wonder if he still lives."

"You are more likely to meet the Maker of us all," I noted, "should you resort to using those pretty but deadly toys."

"Nell will certainly meet her makers in that book," Irene put in. "How thoughtful of the Baron to have your antecedents researched. A most personal touch."

"Most personal," I said dryly. "A pity that he did not also investigate yours."

"Ah, but we cannot know that he did not," Irene said. "And Godfrey's family tree would have been most intriguing. A pity that Baron Alphonse did not elect to give either of us Bibles and backgrounds."

Her note of self-mockery was not lost on me. "My family tree is excessively dull, and Godfrey has no interest in his, since he disowned his wicked father at an early age. You are the only one of us left with mysterious origins."

"Origins are a most unoriginal obsession," she said. "One's own history is enough burden to drag behind one like a damask train: I do not require the particulars of a number of people I never knew, and who will never know me."

My "tsk, tsk" was ably aped by the parrot, who followed it with a lewd whistle.

"Can that vile bird not retire?" I asked in no good temper. "I have been forced to dine upon a surfeit of French cookery, and then to jolt home for two hours besides."

Godfrey had already set the pistols on a side table and risen to drape good English chintz over the parrot cage. Grumbles within slowly subsided, to the familiar tune of "Cut the cackle."

Godfrey did not resume his seat, or his examination of the pistols, but strolled slowly around the chamber.

"I was quite serious, Irene," he said. "Those diamonds are more a liability than a boon."

"What is the use of rare, beautiful things existing, if it is too dangerous to own them? And see! I could keep a tiny mother-of-pearl pistol in this indentation, where the cologne bottle is to go."

"A tiny pistol will not foil a reckless thief, Irene," he said, "and the Baron's dueling pistols are for more formal occasions."

I stifled one of my usual shudders. "I hope that you never find occasion to use them, Godfrey."

"Oh, I am willing to learn, Nell," he answered with a smile. "They are a less dangerous possession than the diamond corsage."

"But think how magnificent the diamonds will look!" Irene said. "I am so glad that one of Mr. Tiffany's stout American matrons or snippish, skinny heiresses did not buy them. They suited me perfectly from the first; even Mr. Tiffany allowed that they could have been made for me."

She had unfastened the lid's hidden spring while she spoke, so that the revealed corsage struck our eyes like a clash of fire and ice, lightning incarnate.

"A liability," Godfrey repeated. "As bad as returning to Prague."

"I have returned to London with no ill effects," Irene said. "Apparently the Baron's spy network is not so superior that it managed to uncover the role of Mr. Sherlock Holmes in the Colonel Moran affair. Or perhaps Mr. Holmes is simply too good at hiding his candle under a bushel." She glanced at me. "I believe that there is some exhortation against that tendency in your Holy Book, Nell, and that you also practice it a bit too literally."

"You refer to a New Testament passage. Matthew," I

said. "And there is no habit—either bad or good—that I can possibly share with Mr. Sherlock Holmes."

"Do not be so sure," she said in that irritatingly sure manner she used on occasion.

Godfrey stopped in front of Irene, drawing her attention from the diamonds glittering in the open case in her lap to a new and steely gleam in his eyes.

"Irene, you are not listening to me. Your plans to return to Prague are not agreeable to me."

"Not agreeable?!"

Irene was truly amazed when one of her intimates proved less than eager to dash off on an escapade. I wondered if Godfrey had ever objected before; certainly not in my presence.

"This is a splendid commission for us all," she went on. "It will open new vistas of . . . travel, fresh acquaintances, knowledge, monetary reward—"

"And it will unfold new visions of dangers from old foes. Do you think the Baron sends us to Bohemia as a kind of lark solely for your entertainment and enrichment? If he says the political situation there teeters, it is worse than before, when a king was killed, as you should well remember: you solved the murder of the present King's father, after all. Do you also forget how two lone women fled Prague Castle by night, yourself disguised as a man, and evaded pursuing agents in the train stations of Dresden, Nuremberg, Frankfurt, Cologne and Brussels? Even St. John's Wood in London was not safe from the incursions of King Wilhelm's agents. Why do you think you can dare the streets of Prague now, only two-odd years after you fled them?"

"I know the city. I know how to avoid attracting attention there, unless I desire it. I know the political climate; how restive Bohemia's native population is under the Austrian thumb." She paused, resuming in persuasive haste.

"And I . . . know the King. I will better be able to put my finger on what unrest is afoot."

"And he will better be able to put his hands upon you, as he has always wanted!"

"Godfrey, are you—jealous?"

"No—only worried, and mystified that you are not. But . . . should I be, Irene? This blithe determination to return to Bohemia is most unlike you."

She set the heavy box on the sofa seat beside her and stood.

"It makes perfect sense, Godfrey, if only you would listen to your barrister's logic instead of your foggy, old-fogey Londontown misgivings. We are all of us out of place and profession here in France. While our money from the Zone of Diamonds lasts, we are in no danger of starving, but we also have no challenging work! You say I dare not venture west to London because of Sherlock Holmes. Now you say that I dare not dance east to Prague because of the King of Bohemia. I cannot sing, I cannot go here or there. Where then may I go, pray? How may I earn my keep, and you and Nell yours, if we are to be chained to Paris, which is pretty and urbane, but hardly a center of much excitement?"

"I would think that you had enough excitement on our last venture to London, with Stanhope gone."

She blanched, even as I winced at Godfrey's reference to Quentin's apparently dire fate. Yet only tonight the Baron had hinted . . . and the strange box containing Quentin's medal had arrived for me last summer.

Irene's fists clenched against her midnight-blue velvet skirts. "You do not seem to see the same opportunity that I do in the Baron's offer," she said in low, deep tones.

"Oh, I see it, and I welcome more lucrative and challenging work as much as you. But why Prague, Irene?"

"Because it is there! Because that is where the Baron asks us to go. How many would even know the legend of the Golem, as I do? I actually suggested it as an operatic subject to Mr. Dvořák. And . . . I have unfinished business there."

"As I feared," Godfrey said grimly.

Her head came up, eyes burning bronze-hot with emotion. "Not with the King! In other areas. It is my city, that I knew and grew fond of, as I did its people."

"You once thought to be its queen," Godfrey said. "Do you feel a noblesse oblige, then, to rescue it, Your Royal Highness?"

His angry taunt revived the humiliation of Irene's last days in Prague. The pride she had been forced to hide from the King broke free in a rush of long-repressed fury, though now only Godfrey stood before her, not Wilhelm von Ormstein.

"No," she said flatly and unconvincingly, her cheeks coloring at last. "But when I fled Prague, I believed that I escaped a man who would curtail my freedom." Her face flamed, even as she choked on her last, bitter words. "I never dreamed that I would so soon find another man who would do the same!"

She wheeled, sweeping from the room like a blue-black velvet stormcloud, Godfrey fast behind her hissing, swaying hems.

"Irene, freedom has nothing to do with it!" he shouted up the stairs at the swift pound of diminishing footsteps. A slamming upstairs door punctuated his sentence.

Godfrey's steps bounded halfway up the stairs, two at a time, then stopped. After a long and utter silence, they clattered down again, then grated against the hall slate. I glimpsed his dark form passing like thunder in the softly lit hall, then heard the front door open and bang shut.

I sat as quiet as Casanova under his demure chintz cozy, and devoutly wished that I could be as invisible. My fingers gripped the Bible's plush covers, seeking to hold on to something, seeking warmth and solidity in a home that suddenly was bereft of both. The cottage clocks tolled the half hour, and still I sat.

* * *

When the front door opened softly a bit later, I jumped guiltily. (And I had done nothing!) I looked up to see Godfrey, hands in his trouser pockets and bare head lowered, looking at me.

"I fear that we have scandalized you, Nell," he said.

I was not sure whether I was relieved or upset that he had remembered my presence at last.

"I have seen Irene's explosions before."

"But you have not seen mine." He came slowly into the room. "She has been this . . . excitable before?"

"On occasion. Perhaps not so intemperate, but nearly so. It is the operatic inclination to overact. I am sure that she doesn't really mean it."

He walked back to the passage to stare up the stairs. The subdued light formed a halo for the fineness of his profile, but shone enough to illuminate the fresh, sharp strokes of strain on his familiar features.

Abruptly, he started up the stairs, his steps sounding like the house's heartbeat made audible. My own heart leaped into a Highland fling of anxiety. When Godfrey's steps stopped suddenly, I was left marooned in the private blood-storm in my head.

Don't be such a mouse, I told myself. It is only a quarrel. Yet I had never seen Irene and Godfrey quarrel in any serious sense, and the sight both embarrassed and terrified me.

I crept out into the hall, unable to resist that ominous silence.

Godfrey sat on the uncarpeted wooden stairs, his elbows braced upon his spread knees. The lantern at the newel post painted his comely features with a medieval devil's shadows and gloom. I came to the foot of the stairs, and he looked up.

"Why are you sitting here? It cannot be comfortable and the bare wood is icy at night."

"If I go up," he said, "I will find out whether the door is locked or not."

"Oh. And if it is?"

His mouth tightened. "It is better that I do not know. So I will stay here for a while." His expression softened despite the harsh light. "Go on to bed, Nell. It's late and our follies are no concern of yours."

"But they are! I suppose that they oughtn't to be, that it is none of my business, but—"

"I cannot for the life of me understand why Irene is so set on returning to a place where she was so wounded, where she was ejected from a singing role in midrehearsal, and forced by a onetime suitor to flee."

I eased up one step. "Sometimes Irene is like a child denied Christmas; her heart becomes set on something impossible, and even dangerous to her, because it is forbidden."

My explanation stopped. How could I tell Godfrey of the Queen's revelation at Maison Worth? How could I explain that her insatiable curiosity had been roused about the one man who had caused her to overleap herself, to miscalculate, to send her pride plummeting in flight and a humiliating banishment?

"Bohemia," I added, "happened before she truly knew you," I said in what I meant to be consolation.

"Exactly!" He pounced upon my humble defense like a barrister before the bar. "What happened in Bohemia that I may not know about? And with whom?"

"Nothing," I whispered, coming another step closer.

"Can you be certain?" he asked in a low, fierce whisper that made my own fade.

"Irene could never dishonor you without dishonoring herself."

"You mean that there is nothing she will not tell me?"

I paused. Already she had "spared" Godfrey and myself news of some minuscule matters in the course of our adventures. Like all clever people with a gift for stage-managing others in plays of their own making, Irene relished the element of surprise. And certainly she had not mentioned the plea of Queen Clotilde; in fact, she had expressly forbidden me to breathe a hint of it to Godfrey. What was a God-fearing woman to do? My misery must have shown on my face, for Godfrey patted the bare tread beside him.

"Sit down, Nell, before you swoon. It is not so bad as it looks. I am as likely to be out-of-temper as the next man, and Irene, as you say, must be allowed her artistic eruptions. I won't bite, I promise. Sit down and keep me company before I become bitter. I'm told my late father had a black temper; I have no wish to emulate him at this late date."

I did as he suggested, drawing my skirts close to my knees. We sat there like two naughty children banished to some dark quarter: silent, troubled, yet taking quiet comfort in having a partner in exile.

"We are a flamboyant pair for you, Nell. We shall worry you into an early grave if you take our contretemps so seriously," he cajoled.

I recognized that his concern for me was distracting him from his puzzlement and anger toward Irene. I may not be a particularly imaginative or dramatic person, but at times I can be useful.

"The devil of it is, Irene is right," he went on. "Work for the Rothschilds would enhance our situation. I myself would be the most public beneficiary, for doing their legal and diplomatic groundwork would raise my stock considerably. Irene does require a challenging pastime; I cannot argue with that. And you, Nell, especially, thrive on industry. No doubt we have lounged on the windfall of the Queen's diamonds long enough." His palms slapped his knees. "But why Bohemia? I could countenance anywhere on earth except Bohemia!"

"Except also perhaps London and the vicinity of Baker Street," I suggested.

He nodded. "I could do with less of London—and of Baker Street, as well."

"And of Monte Carlo, where that odious marquis fenced with Irene?"

"I was not enamored of her escapade with the villain, no."

"And think of Paris, where that vicious Colonel Moran first met us under a pseudonym a child could have seen through, had we only known of his real persona."

"Ah, Nell, you are too devious for a simple barrister, especially one whose mind is muddled by emotion." He smiled and took my hand. "Your litany only serves to point out that Bohemias lurk everywhere for the faint of heart and frail of faith. I trust Irene. I admire her. I love her. But sometimes, I could—" He sighed and released my hand.

"It frightens me to see you quarrel so violently," I confessed of a sudden.

He quieted at once. "I know. It frightens me. This has never happened before. Yet I cannot agree with Irene merely because her force of conviction is so strong. She would lose all respect for me."

"Then you mean that quarreling is beneficial?"

"Perhaps, in its contrary way, dear Nell, it clears the air."

I sighed in my turn. "The relations between men and women are most confusing."

"No, only complex."

"Godfrey, you are a man—"

"I should hope so."

"I mean to say, you would be expected to know what another man might think, or feel."

"It depends upon the identity of the man."

"Quentin Stanhope, for instance."

"Oh."

"You said that just like Irene when she thinks she knows better than everyone."

"I simply said 'Oh.' You mustn't read anything into that.

It is a lawyerly time-passing device while I endeavor to think without appearing dull."

"Oh."

"You see, you do the same thing, and mean nothing by it."

"I suppose so."

"What of Quentin?"

"Is it possible that a man . . . a gentleman of such fine upbringing and yet unimaginable misfortune in foreign lands, could he possibly . . . take a liking to someone as beneath him as myself? And why?"

"First of all, you are beneath no one, and Quentin Stanhope knows that better than most."

"If I am beneath no one, it is because I am no one."

He snorted in my defense. "I am no one. Sherlock Holmes is no one. The Rothschilds were no one until recently, and so with Charles Tiffany and Frederick Worth and Alice Heine and Sarah Bernhardt. Even Irene is no one, and would be the first to admit it."

"We don't know, do we, of her antecedents, though. She might be someone. Wouldn't it be ironic if she were royalty and didn't know it, and the King rejected her wrongly?"

"Don't recall my immediate irritations, Nell; your job is to distract me, remember?"

I smiled slightly at this mock-stern reminder. "You are wrong about Irene; she would never admit to being no one. She would say we were all Someones."

"The same thing, from a more self-certain angle! As for Stanhope, Nell, you must understand that he rejected the society life in which you first met him. He has lived as an exile in wild climes and among strange peoples. He has experienced things you and I cannot imagine—"

"Women," I said. "Exotic women. I heard reference to these. Why would such a man pretend to a liking to someone as homebound as myself? Does he mean to mock me?"

"No, no . . . he means you no harm, Nell. He would be

appalled if charged with such intentions." Godfrey's expression grew abstracted. "That doesn't mean that he may not do you harm, unintentionally."

"But why would he even care, even involve himself to the point where he might unintentionally harm me? I do not understand that, as deeply as you do not understand Irene's need to duel the past. Quentin Stanhope cannot truly like me!"

"He does, Nell, as we do. Do you doubt us?"

"Not you and Irene. But, if I were to allow myself to think that Quentin's liking went so far as . . . fondness. If it was of the sort a man might feel for a woman—why? It cannot be."

He smiled again. "It is unlikely perhaps. You do not invite men to bear a tender regard for you, but you cannot stop one if he insists upon it."

"And you think that Quentin . . . does?"

"I don't know, Nell. We saw so little of him, and you only know what passed between you. But to answer your first and most pertinent question: yes, Nell, a man of Stanhope's strange and unconventional life experiences could very well admire a woman who represented the restricted and secure background denied to him."

"You mean an ignorant and silly woman of no importance past her prime. But why, Godfrey, why?"

His forefinger tilted up my chin until I was looking directly into his amused gray eyes. "Because she represents a challenge that he knows that he can find nowhere else on earth."

Before I could ask another question, and I had several after this bewildering response, an upstairs door creaked.

We both turned, startled.

Irene's figure gleamed ghostlike in one dark doorway. She was clad in creamy satin and lace, and her dark hair snaked over her shoulders.

"There you are," she said as if nothing had happened. "I need help brushing my hair."

Despite her nonchalant air, hesitation touched her voice and its characteristic clarity was slightly clogged.

Godfrey and I exchanged a look that said: shall it be you or I?

He stood, leaning against the wall. "I could think of more appropriate use for that brush than grooming hair."

"Yes," she said a trifle sulkily, "but you will like brushing my hair better."

Still he hesitated, and she waited. I did not move, but crouched on the stair like a scullery maid.

"It is cold on the stair," Irene noted, the silver-backed brush flashing through the long tendrils curling over her shoulder. "Come to bed."

Suddenly he was striding upstairs. I expected that to be that, but just before the door closed I heard Irene's voice again: "Come up, too, Nell, or you shall catch your death."

I rose stiffly, sighed, then fetched the lamp from the newel post and made my way to my own chamber, where a heated brick set there by Sophie hours before awaited my chronic cold feet.

Chapter Ten

TRIFLING CONDITIONS

The late and trying night so upset my equilibrium that I woke unforgivably late the next morning, my feet as icy cold as the brick within my bed.

I dressed and hurried downstairs, impeded only by Sophie dusting the passage. Irene was in the breakfast room, slathering goose-liver pâté on thick slabs of crusty French bread with such gusto that she seemed to be conducting an invisible orchestra.

I admired the flourish of her lace-flounced sleeves, then eyed her face. Other than an infinitesimal puffing around the eyes, I could detect no sign of the previous evening's histrionics.

I decided to beard the lioness in her den directly.

"Where is Godfrey?" I enquired, sitting and snapping the folds from my linen napkin.

"Where he always is this late in the morning," Irene said, yawning. "Out."

"Out?"

"In town, of course."

"Of course."

"He has business to attend to."

"Naturally," said I. "What sort of business?"

"Business . . . business."

A platter of French breads and rolls shared the center of the homely wooden table with a crock of butter and an array of jams. I helped myself.

Irene yawned again. As an opera singer, she could accomplish quite awesome yawns.

"Baron Rothschild," I said, "is inconsiderate of guests who dwell near town."

"Had Ferrières been open for the Season, we would have stayed the night," Irene said. "Still, we were rather generously rewarded for keeping such late hours." Thoughts of the Tiffany corsage glittered in her topaz eyes, like diamonds viewed through a bronze mirror.

"How unfortunate that we shall have to return the lot." I poured intertwining streams of milk and tea into my country-size cup.

"We shall do nothing of the sort!"

"How can we keep these gifts—bribes, I almost said—if we do not go to Bohemia?"

Irene's hands cupped her delicate mug of black coffee, and she inhaled the steaming aroma as if indulging in a drug. She smiled.

"Because we *are* going to Bohemia, Nell. There is nothing to return—except our own selves to that lovely land."

"Going? To Bohemia?" I set down my sturdy cup so hard that a dirty tan wave slopped onto the bare tabletop. "How can we? Godfrey will not permit it."

"Well, you may heed such impediments, but I do not. I am not a former employee used to taking orders."

"I will be no part of any scheme that violates your husband's wishes and authority."

"Wishes only, Nell. Authority does not come into it except with dispensers of moral rectitude, of whom there are none on earth that I recognize, or with civil rulers, none of whom I call sovereign."

"Apparently your own husband has little to say on the matter."

"Oh, he had a great deal to say. So did I."

"And?"

Irene smirked—there is no other way to put it—over the brim of her cup. "We are going to Bohemia."

"We? All three?"

She glanced carelessly away. "There are a few . . . conditions."

"Aha!"

"Minor, trifling conditions."

"So it always seems at first, with a lawyer."

"We shall see how it seems at last," she answered with a satisfied smile. "Godfrey is in Paris now making preparations."

"So quickly you have converted him."

"Conversion does not quite describe my influence over Godfrey, Nell; but you are not in a position to understand the fine points of such negotiations. Let us say that I . . . persuaded him that the benefits of this mission outweigh the drawbacks."

"I do not think you argued openly and honestly."

"But I did! Godfrey himself admitted the boons of an association with the Rothschilds in your presence."

"Still, I think that you pressed some unfair advantage. I imagine that you did not tell him of Queen Clotilde's unhappiness and plea to you."

"And you claim you lack imagination, Nell," she mock-chided me. "We were both sworn to keep the matter of the Queen's discomfort private. Would you violate the poor woman's confidence?"

"A husband—"

"Need not know everything. Wait until you have one and then judge."

I felt myself reddening. "I have not the time," I snapped. "And if you recognize no sovereign, why do you honor a queen's rights over your own husband's?"

"Nell! I swear that awful muddle of milk and tea you drink clouds your brains as much as it clouds your cup!

You will understand these things better when you know more of the world, and that conflicting loyalties must each keep their proper place. The persons and events you and I knew in Bohemia are our own business. I had only briefly encountered Godfrey when I knew the king-to-be, and I never expected to see him again, much less marry him. Yes, I am determined to fully decipher the mysteries of Bohemia, be they royal dereliction of marital duty or seven-foot-high clay men stalking the streets. If Godfrey knew my full reasons, he would understand."

"Then tell him!"

"I said he would understand. I did not say that he would like them."

"You have put me in the middle," I charged.

She regarded me calmly. "No, you have put yourself there. It cannot be comfortable, but no doubt moral confusion builds character. I am sure I have read some religious adage on the matter."

"And I have promised not to tell Godfrey of the Queen's request," I complained, "so my hands are tied."

"Yes, you have," Irene mused, sighing. "There will be nothing to regret, dear Nell, except missing this opportunity to better our finances and return to Bohemia to solve greater mysteries than we left behind."

"Much to regret," I predicted, sipping my now lukewarm tea, "What conditions has poor, deluded innocent Godfrey set?"

" 'Poor deluded innocent Godfrey' has decided," Irene said dryly, "that I must pass in Bohemia under a pseudonym and in disguise."

I sat up. "Most wise. You are notorious there, after all."

"Apparently I am notorious everywhere. In fact, Godfrey has declared that he will be the excuse for the mission, and its prime implementer. He is visiting the Baron's Paris office today to set the machinery in motion. He will go openly as legal representative of unspecified Rothschild

interests in the neighborhood. I will come along later in my
. . . new persona.''

I smothered a smile. "So Godfrey takes the lead and you
must follow. Highly sensible. He has not lost all his senses.
I commend his strategy.''

Irene yawned again. "How fortunate that you do, for you
will accompany this vanguard expedition as his loyal secretary.'' Her eyes glittered with lazy wickedness. "Ah, how I
envy you, Nell, in your humble but underestimated role!
You will see the new Bohemia first. You will pry—with
Godfrey, of course—into the manipulations of court and
city. You will gaze again upon His Royal Highness, King
Wilhelm von Ormstein, first. You will no doubt have an
opportunity to consult with the Queen on her delicate
problem. I am sure that she will recognize you at once and
accept you as a delegate of mine, and consider you her
discreet confidante. Ah, how I envy you!'' Her voice grew
more stern than gently mocking. "And you will seal your
lips on the subject of our previous meeting with Her Royal
Highness, even if Godfrey should become suspicious and
ask.''

"Yes,'' I said dully, realizing that Godfrey's and my jaunt
to Bohemia would not relieve my moral dilemma, but in
fact intensify it. "I will do my best.''

Irene smiled and shook out the Paris paper. She eyed me
not unsympathetically over its serrated rim. "That has always sufficed in the past, and I am sure it will do quite
nicely now.''

Where Irene would have dashed off to Bohemia at the drop
of a royal enigma, Godfrey proceeded to prepare for the
mission with all deliberate slowness and groundwork.

I do not think he could have better infected Irene with a
seething impatience she dared not express.

He was in Paris all the day now, every day, consulting
with the Baron or his minions—which was not clear. A new

energy drove his step, even as a new reticence dogged his evening conversations. Had I not known better, I would have said Godfrey was being deliberately mysterious about his whereabouts and actions. He claimed that he was being discreet, that it was necessary to familiarize himself with the political and legal ground he would encounter in Prague.

Irene took her revenge by flitting off almost daily to the House of Worth for more fittings with the "maestro."

Even here I was carefully excluded. I was sent to the library to read crabbed texts concerning the Golem of Prague, and asked to report nightly on this preposterous fairy tale.

Perhaps fairy tale is not the proper description, unless it was one told literally by some set of Brothers Grimm children were not allowed to read.

I admit that I am not fond of the French, nor sympathetic to the Irish, nor at ease with the Oriental, either in individual or cultural form.

As for the Jews, I had been reared to think of them as a race of benighted people too foolish to recognize their own vaunted Savior when He came. So I learned at my father's knee, and so I had not thought further until I combed the heavy, gilt-edged volumes of the Paris Bibliothèque.

I had taken the liberty of also investigating the history of the Rothschild family in its many national branches. If any form of aristocracy is by nature untrustworthy, that acquired solely by the criteria of great wealth must be the most suspect.

I left my sessions at the library with my eyes bleary and the bridge of my nose tweaked scarlet from my pince-nez. I also left them so disturbed that I rode home in the carriage in numb disbelief, recalling Irene's and my one expedition into Prague's Josef Quarter (to find a fortune-teller, much against my inclinations) with a shudder of hindsight.

What my readings told me—that I dare not tell anyone else lest I be considered half-mad—was that good precedent

existed for such a being as a Golem, and that if there was
a God and He was Just—this I firmly believed—then the
Golem might walk the byways of Prague as a sign that
injustice had prevailed too long in Bohemia and, indeed,
upon the earth. For the first time, I began to regard the
demon in Prague as other than King Wilhelm von Ormstein, onetime admirer of Irene Adler, and something very
different and not at all human.

"Nell, do you think that Godfrey is not telling me something?" Irene asked me one evening when we sat in the
parlor, she at her piano, I at my stitchery.

Her rare, plaintive tone caught my instant attention.
Even the odious parrot sidled along his perch to press his
tilted head against the bars as if to listen better. His hearing,
in my observation, was only too excellent.

Godfrey was absent, as he had been on occasion, dining
in Paris with our new "employers." So he had said.

"Why should Godfrey not tell you something?" I inquired reasonably.

"Because he is so satisfied with himself of late!"

Her hands, deceptively strong despite their grace, drove
a crashing chord into the hapless keys.

Casanova squawked and uttered meaningless parrot for
once, lofting above his perch with beating wings.

"That is exactly how you behave when you are involved
with an unpleasantness," I pointed out.

"Precisely why I am worried," she retorted, striking a
less truculent chord. Her fingers relaxed into a liquid arpeggio that trickled up and down the keyboard. "It is not like
Godfrey to be mysterious," she added wistfully.

"The shoe," I said.

She eyed me quizzically.

"It pinches."

Another exasperated chord. Casanova cackled fluent
parrot.

"On the other foot," I finished, tying off a knot.

"If you are going to prate clichés," she said, "you could at least rattle them off in one go."

Irene spun around on the velvet-covered stool, hopelessly twisting her skirts. Candlelight invariably flattered her, but now it illuminated a faint pleat of worry in her forehead.

"They also serve who stand and wait," I complied dutifully.

She gritted her teeth, and being an actress and opera singer, managed to speak with perfect diction despite it, or perhaps because of it. "Sit, Nell. We sit. We sit here night after night and know nothing. Surely the Rothschilds did not mean us to . . . dawdle our days and nights away in Paris while all Bohemia burns!"

"I am certain that Godfrey is putting matters into fine order in good time. He was always most efficient in court. A paragon of organization."

"International politics do not wait for the finesse of impeccable paperwork," she spat. "Nor do monsters like the Golem."

Lucifer, sleeping by the ember-bright hearth, stirred and yawned to show his rose-red maw equipped with formidable white thorns of teeth. He growled slightly.

Irene's hands fisted on her lap, then crashed again on the piano keys. "I am not patient, it is true. Yet I am bound to abide by Godfrey's timetable. He is in communication with the Rothschilds, and I am not."

"Spying is men's work," I noted placidly.

"You have not read your Bible," she returned, pointing to the plump volume that occupied the whole top of my side table. "The example of Judith in the camp of Holofernes contradicts you."

I found my nose wrinkling. "That was butchery in the name of spying. Not all Biblical tales are suitable for emulation. One sometimes forgets how brutal the old ways were."

"They are still brutal." Irene turned back to the piano and uncoiled her skirts. "And I am brutally bored. We shall have to do something about it until Godfrey's brilliant and dilatory organization—whatever it is—is completed."

"We?"

"You, as usual, will bear the brunt of the task."

I looked up over my pince-nez, hoping I embodied my most forbidding governess resolution. "What will I be required to do this time?"

"Only what you do exquisitely every day." Irene's fingers were wandering the keys amiably again, and her voice had lightened to a careless, cajoling mezzo-soprano trill.

"What is that?"

"Sew," she said, glancing coyly over her shoulder as I plunged my needle firmly into my forefinger.

Chapter Eleven

SEW WHAT?

❧

So it was that, past my thirtieth year, I was rechristened "Agatha"—I do not think that Irene could have concocted a more abominable pseudonym—and introduced to the crowded workrooms of Maison Worth as the replacement for the late and apparently unlamented Berthe.

To excuse my less than fluid French, I was made out to be a remote English "cousin" of the Worth family. Playing a "poor relation" was nothing new to me, although pretending to be an accomplished "beader" was.

"I doubt there is any danger in this assignment, Nell," Irene had speculated the evening before my first day with a certain sangfroid that I found unbecoming in a dear friend. "But certainly we will learn nothing of the true circumstances of that poor girl's death without some notion of her life and work."

"I thought that you are a regular at Maison Worth these days."

"The workrooms form their own world. Neither of the Worths, nor I, will see what truly goes on there. This masquerade will only last for a few days."

"No doubt Godfrey will have completed his arduous preparations for Bohemia by then," I said fervently.

"Let us hope so." Irene echoed me with even greater
fervency. "He has been tiresomely . . . distracted of late. All
work and no play make Jack a dull boy and Jill most irritable."

I could not argue with Irene's current irritability, but I
could never find Godfrey dull; no matter how distracted he
might be, I always found him rather charmingly distracting.
But I was used to working with him, and Irene had an
entirely different relationship, so perhaps I did not understand her complaint.

What can I say of the fashion-house workrooms? Imagine a convention of female Casanovas chattering away in
high-pitched rapid-fire French in a dozen different provin-
cial accents. The Tower of Babel would have been a relief.

While carriages idled at the establishment's entrance on
the rue de la Paix and great ladies lounged in the front
salons, we sewing girls in back lined long, plain tables,
separated from the stitcher opposite only by our lengths of
fabric and a clutter of trims.

Our days began at dawn and ended at twilight, with too
few necessities breaks and an unsatisfactory lunch "hour"
that lasted less than half its supposed time. Luckily, this
was no shock given my early clerking work at Whiteley's
Emporium in London. It was indeed a shock, however, to
find how poorly I tolerated such hours and such labor in
these latter, lax days.

Strong cheeses perfumed the faces and garments around
me. Garlic and onions scented their conjoined breaths.
Given the forcefulness required to speak a language as awkward as French, this vegetable stew of odor hung foglike
over the workers.

Several sang or hummed as they stitched, an effect that
would have anguished Irene's sensitive ear. Indeed, my first
day was spent contemplating how ill-suited Irene would be
to survive such an ordeal, although perhaps I do her an
injustice. The only song in my ear was the rhythmic syllables of Mr. Hood's poignant "Song of the Shirt."

Another (and unwanted) thing I was given: poor Berthe's very seat. (I would never forget first seeing her slumped gray figure embedded with the shining steel shears and the small, dark red rose of blood blossoming around that silver thorn.) I was even given her work: dressing the fashion mannequins.

Never had I seen dolls so beautiful. At first I was afraid to touch these elegant female figures only two feet tall. When I expressed my awe, I was told by the haughty dame in charge of the sewing room that these were "Juneau Bébés" because of their finely done bisque heads.

What can I say of those pale, exquisitely round little faces, with their startling lifelike blue- and gray-glass eyes, their tiny pierced porcelain ears dangling semiprecious stones, their strongly drawn brows and delicately traced painted eyelashes? Those unearthly eyes were made of "paperweight glass," I was told. Even their hands were finely molded, and because their bodies were made of kid gusseted for movement, they could assume postures eerily similar to those Irene struck when modeling her Worth gowns.

Yet, despite their blond and brunette mohair wigs (some had real hair, though it was duller and certainly more macabre than the mohair) and elegant wardrobes, I found them slightly sinister. Perhaps I was put off by those hard, babyish faces with limpid glass eyes and timid rosebud lips, some hoarding two tiny rows of sharp teeth gleaming in the darkness within . . . or the uncanny way their articulated necks and wrists moved ever so daintily.

I was shocked on my first day—while embroidering a lacy set of white muslin underthings (I felt it best to start with items that would not show and work outward as I became more confident)—to discover a naked wooden form beneath the modest pantaloons and corset cover, jointed everywhere as in life. Such blatant mimicry struck me as nearly blasphemous, as did the bare, lifelike puppet beneath the elaborate garb.

Perhaps my recent readings in the medieval legendry of the Golem had reminded me of sorcerers' simulacra and homunculi, of forbidden experiments and fallen idols; even of primitive magic. Perhaps Berthe had been slain because of the idolatrous nature of her work, was stuck with a pin like the object of a savage curse.

The workrooms were not the place or time for fancies, not even macabre ones, laboring twelve hours a day with neck bent and fingers flying until needle pierced flesh as often as fabric.

> Stitch! stitch! stitch!
> In poverty, hunger and dirt,
> And still with a voice of dolorous pitch
> She sang the "Song of the Shirt"!

Yet the object of my labors was not coarse linen; far from it. Callused hands could not have managed the silks, satins and velvets that slid through my fingers without snagging the stuff more precious than a mere seamstress's flesh.

No, my sewing song was far more cheerful than that of the piecework drudge celebrated in Mr. Hood's poem. No matter how my neck and back ached, the workrooms were clean and decently aired. More than a straight seam was required of me.

Madame Gallatin, the supervisor I had mentioned, brought the tiny clothes the other women had cut and half-finished, rustling toward me with tissue-paper designs that I was to translate into beadwork on the miniature skirts and bodices.

I pushed my pince-nez more firmly onto my nose to study these intricate patterns.

"You must first baste the tissues over the proper part of the gowns, Mademoiselle Uxleigh," she instructed, sounding unfortunately like the Divine Sarah in dropping the

initial "H" in my surname. She mistook my cringe at the
memory for fear of the work.

"It is not so difficult," she went on more sternly. "Surely
a relation of Monsieur Worth will have a modicum of skill
in her fingers, not to mention the head." Here she tapped
hers, her sharp features screwed tighter by hair drawn back
mercilessly into a coal-black topknot that sat the crown of
her head like an angry question mark.

She set a series of glass jars down before me. "You will
use these beads as indicated in the sketch. Do not deviate
from the pattern on the sketch and you will do nicely."

I nodded to spare her my atrocious French and set to
work.

The partially attired doll who would wear my stitchery
stood before me, her pale, placid face cocked, her plump,
painted cheeks and tiny features wearing an expression that
blended pert expectancy with a waxen deathlike calm.

Her tiny, curled hands, so like a sophisticated baby's,
could grasp anything—tiny fan, mirror, opera glasses,
gloves, parasol, reticule. I could not picture that fragile
bisque extremity grasping anything so heavy or dangerous
as Irene's wicked little pistol.

This doll was to wear a spotted grosgrain silk in palest
ivory with fan-shaped beadwork designs worked on skirt
and corsage in a heavenly array of beads ranging from
faintest aqua to deepest midnight blue.

I basted on the first tissue, threaded with medium-blue
silk a needle almost as fine as an eyebrow hair and plunged
it up through the skirt's heavy ivory silk and tissue overlay.
An instant later my first bead was fixed in place. An unpleasant flutter of half-fear, half-pleasure trilled in my
chest.

"That fashion doll is destined for the Empress of all the
Russias," Madame Gallatin's guttural voice admonished
from above my bent head. "Be careful," she added in an
almost sinister undertone.

Startled, I looked into the only face gazing my way—the

doll's frozen features. The deep brown eyes held a weary, vacuous stare, but now I recognized the brunette coiffure, the petite figure: the very likeness of Maria Feodorovna herself, whom I had seen in Paris not months before!

Had she come to Sarah Bernhardt's salon fresh from a call on Maison Worth that resulted in the commissioning of the doll before me? Could I ever have dreamed then that many weeks later I would be sewing beads onto a miniature gown destined for her eyes and hands thousands of miles away in St. Petersburg? Could I have guessed that a murdered girl would link us, when before the only person we knew (if one could call it that) in common was the murderous Colonel Moran, then masquerading as Captain Morgan?

Life was indeed exceeding strange.

> Work! work! work!
> While the cock is crowing aloof!
> And work—work—work,
> 'Til the stars shine through the roof!
>
> It's oh! to be a slave
> Along with the barbarous Turk,
> Where a woman has never a soul to save,
> If this is Christian work!

When Irene asked me after a late dinner that evening how my day had gone, I responded with that stirring verse of Hood. She was not much impressed.

"I doubt that you would prefer employment with the barbarous Turk, Nell. Melodramatics and fancywork aside, what did you *learn?*" she demanded.

"How to sew on decorative beading."

"Well." She thought. "That may ultimately prove useful for my wardrobe, but what did you learn of the dead girl? Her friends, foes, passions, problems?"

"There was no time for talk."

"Make time," she ordered as imperiously as Madame Gallatin. "A spy must never sacrifice her secret purpose to the mere outward demands of her guise."

"If I am let go, I will be of no aid whatsoever."

Godfrey lowered the London *Times*, which he read assiduously after dinner every evening. "If Nell is let go, it will not much matter. We leave for Bohemia in two days."

"What of my inquiry into the Maison Worth murder?" Irene asked indignantly, although I could not much see that it was "her" inquiry when my fingertips were pierced purple.

"Irene, you adorable ingrate," he answered calmly, "you who have caused me to move heaven and earth to accommodate your desire to meddle once more with the affairs of Bohemia. Now that I have accomplished the necessary groundwork, you can at least let the murder of a fashion-house bead-girl simmer for a while, and allow Nell to trade her trying needle for her more customary pen and pencil."

"Then it is true!" Irene tossed aside the novel she had been reading—Balzac's *Eugénie Grandet*; imagine Irene eating up a tale about a miser!—and stormed to the side of Godfrey's chair. "We are to go to Bohemia at last!"

"Nell and I are to depart Thursday noon. Arrangements have been made for you to follow—under your assumed name—in four days." He glanced at me. "Can you bear to leave your sewing, Nell, that soon?"

I eyed the crocheted doily in my lap. "I will take along my own fancywork, but will leave the routine of a bead-girl behind as gladly as I left the life of a typewriter-girl. This will be quite official? We shall work together as before?"

He nodded. "To all appearances, but with greater causes at stake than most court cases—or so my wife and Baron Rothschild tell me."

"Oh, good," I replied, cheered by the notion of accompanying Godfrey on legal business, no matter how distant or dangerous. Perhaps I had missed my role as secretary and clerk.

While we conferred, Irene had sunk onto a stool beside Godfrey's chair, from which she teased Lucifer with the last strands of my unraveled ball of crochet twine. Between them, they had snarled the string beyond any damage either one could have accomplished singly.

"When do *I* leave?" she asked.

Godfrey smiled and removed a cigarette from the malachite box on the sidetable. "As soon as your chaperon arrives."

Irene popped as upright as a jack in a box. "Chaperon! I require no chaperon!"

"The Baron and I beg to differ. Your role as a woman traveling alone will be more believable if you are properly accompanied." He lit his cigarette with a flourish.

Irene's hands pounded the upholstered arms of his chair as if they were flesh. "Godfrey Norton, you have taken to very secretive and high-handed ways of late, and I do not like it one bit! I said nothing about your silence and your endless absences in Paris—one would think you had a secret mistress!—because I understood, and was foolish enough to respect, your deep personal reservations about an enterprise in Bohemia. But now you simply . . . schedule me like a departing train, and book unwanted passengers for me as well! I have been meek, I have been mild and I have been silent, but enough is enough. I require no chaperon."

By now she had risen to her knees on the stool, and her face was on a level with his.

He turned away to blow a polite stream of smoke in the direction of Casanova's cage.

"It is ludicrous!" Irene stormed on. "I am perfectly able to take care of myself, and as for scandal, when has the threat of that ever stopped me?"

"Not often enough," he said, turning back to her.

"I will go armed. What chaperon could you produce that would be worth as much to me as myself? Alone!"

"I had considered Sarah Bernhardt."

"You had?" Irene's flexible voice moderated, took on an intrigued quality. She sat back on her heels and held out her hand for a cigarette, which he provided, as well as a lit lucifer.

She tilted her face toward the lucifer, looking much like a cat that expects a petting, until her cigarette was lit, then conceded. "Sarah might not do too badly. I could say that she was my maid." Her voice had deepened into a pleased purr.

I rolled my eyes at the notion of anyone taking Sarah Bernhardt for a lady's maid, *anyone's* lady's maid. I rolled my eyes in the other direction at anyone having the temerity to consider her in such a secondary role.

"But Sarah is an actress, and must honor a playing schedule," Godfrey purred right back.

Irene bristled, then huffed out a furious stream of smoke, without politely turning away her head. "Then who?" she puffed like an angry locomotive imitating an outraged owl.

Godfrey smiled. "I happened on just the solution."

"What!?"

"You will see how perfect it is when Allegra arrives."

"Allegra? What is this? I am to travel with a musical direction?" Her hands were pounding the chair arm as if it were ebony and ivory and not mute stuffing.

I, however, sat up with a pleased chirp. "Allegra, Godfrey? Not really?"

Irene snapped her head in my direction. "This word means something to you, Nell? Am I to be utterly excluded from the schemings of my so-called friends?"

I gave her the look that she gave me when I was being uncommonly dense. "Allegra, Irene. Dear, charming Allegra. Quentin's niece. She has been longing to visit me in France. An ideal solution, Godfrey."

"Thank you." He turned to Irene with a smile, which was akin to facing the Medusa with a pocket mirror. "She is a delightful girl."

"Girl? You saddle me with a green girl when I am on a

woman's business? I have never met this Allegra person."

"That is true," said I. "You never did. Allegra Stanhope is most astute, Irene, and quite charming."

"She will fit perfectly into your plans," Godfrey said. "You can say she is your maid, or your niece."

"I am not old enough to have a niece," Irene noted dangerously.

I came to Godfrey's rescue, as I wholeheartedly approved of his scheme. "Of course you are, Irene, had you an older sister. Do you have an older sister?"

"No, nor do I have any friends," she added pointedly, glaring at me. "Apparently, neither does this poor Allegra Stanhope, or they would not allow her to venture into darkest Bohemia."

"But," said Godfrey with a lawyer's pounce, as Lucifer leaped to take full control of the abandoned twine, "she will be chaperoned by the most dangerous woman in Europe. Poor, dear Allegra could not be safer, save in her own bed in Belgrave Square."

Irene considered. "That is true." After a last draw on her cigarette, she handed it to Godfrey to extinguish. "I could say that she is my sister, my protégée. It will be inconvenient"—she glared most effectively at Godfrey—"but I will manage."

He laughed. "I am sure that you will. Frankly, Allegra has turned up on her own, impetuous impulse. I received her letter yesterday, and she herself arrives Wednesday. Nell will write to her family and assure them of her safety. I saw little else to do than take her with us."

Irene, mollified, nodded. "I do not relish traveling across Europe for five days with a stranger. At least I will have someone to talk to while I wonder what you and Nell are up to in Bohemia."

"And," I added, winding my thread until I hit the snag of fourteen pounds of fierce black fur, "while you contemplate what else is up in Bohemia, besides the arisen Golem."

"Yes," Irene and Godfrey agreed in concert, she now sitting on the arm of his chair, while his own arm encircled her waist.

They were the very picture of utter domestic harmony. I thought of another picture—a photograph much desired by the King of Bohemia, which Irene kept in a bank safe in Paris.

A pity such scenes could never last.

Chapter Twelve

DEATH BEFORE DISMISSAL

I fear my heart was not in my work at Maison Worth the following day. Although Irene had promised, rather wolfishly, to attend to my packing while I was pursuing duty to the penultimate moment, my mind was not at ease.

Small stabs of memory darted in and out of my mind as my needle pricked in and out of the rare fabrics it adorned: Allegra, my long-ago charge, albeit briefly. Belgrave Square. Her uncle Quentin. My distant vision of the blithe young uncle. My very recent reacquaintance with the jaded man of adventure returned from darkest Afghanistan.

Allegra, a delightful child, met again as a young woman as intemperate and charming as Irene herself. Dear Godfrey. A Solomon in modern dress. A Daniel come to judgment. Harnessing Irene's wildest, unconfessed impulses with a new responsibility, Allegra. Protecting Irene from herself and her past, protecting Allegra and her future even as he endangered them both. For if Bohemia was all that Baron Rothschild implied it was, there was no safety there for anyone, especially a vagrant lamb like Allegra Stanhope.

Beads flew through my throbbing fingers. I imagined myself to be a Sleeping Beauty who had been pricked by a multiplicity of evil fairy godmothers. Irene traveling with Allegra, who reminded me of . . . Quentin. I abroad with Godfrey, tracking the ghosts of Irene's disastrous almost-romance with the King of Bohemia. Clotilde. Queen Clotilde, where did that unfortunate woman come into our dramatis personae? And where—heaven forbid!—did the Golem?

"Mademoiselle Uxleigh!"

The voice thundered from above, like the Lord's, although I doubt that He would deign to speak French.

"Yes?"

"You have altered the pattern. Have you no brain above the wrists? Look at this!"

I looked at the miniature skirt I was embellishing. "It seemed more pleasing to continue the loop to the left."

A crumpled sketch was shaken under my shaking nose.

"This! This you follow. The pattern. Do not deviate from the pattern. This is no place for daydreaming. Here! Perhaps you can follow a new pattern better."

The mannequin of Maria Feodorovna was whisked from before my quaking gaze. Another small, stiff, elegant figure was pounded into her place like a nail.

I took in a corona of dark hair with red-gold highlights, gold-brown glass eyes as melting as licorice-butterscotch candy, an impeccable, imperious posture. . . .

I stood, breathing hard.

I looked at Irene. A doll of Irene.

"Monsieur Worth's latest model," Madame Gallatin announced. "Perhaps she will inspire you to do your best."

No.

"No!" I said. "I cannot!"

I cannot sew for an Irene in miniature while sitting on the hard wooden seat last warmed by a dead girl. I cannot—

"You cannot? Or you will not? Relation or no, I cannot tolerate an arbitrary worker. Miss Uxleigh, where do you go? You cannot leave—!"

But I did leave, for good, and breathed better for it.

* * *

Irene expressed surprise to see me home at midday. Perhaps she was merely surprised to see me.

"My dear Nell! Why are you at home—? You are so pale. And perspiring. Here, sit down. Have you an ague? A fever?"

"No, not at all. I am not perspiring," I added indignantly. "I am . . . dismissed. Again." As from Whiteley's, when Irene first found me on the streets of London years before.

"Oh. Oh! Do not fret. That silly business at Maison Worth is not worth fretting about."

"It is not? You insisted that I must go there and learn things."

"Yes, but that was before Godfrey's preparations for Bohemia had matured. Now we have bigger fillets to grill. You seem most upset, but there is nothing to fret about, I promise you. I will even tolerate this Allegra Stanhope who has been foisted upon me. What has happened at Worth's to unnerve you? I will have words with them if they have behaved badly."

I sat in Godfrey's chair while she fussed over me, and must admit to a moment's satisfaction. "You do not wish to endanger your standing with Monsieur Worth."

"Defending my friend will endanger no standing I value. What has gone wrong?"

"It is that awful Madame Gallatin who supervises the seamstresses. She allows for no invention in her workers. I merely changed the design a scintilla, not even thinking about it, but I have some aesthetic sense, you know, and do fancywork of my own, and she was most overwrought by my innovation."

"Overwrought by your innovation!" Irene puffed up like an angry peacock. "What enterprise does this woman imagine she directs? A bakery? Every loaf, every slice, must be of regulation size? Are *you* not to embroider a more pleasing design? Am *I* not to sing a more inventive aria? My dear Nell, I cannot think what I was doing, sending you into that den of . . . conformity. Monsieur Worth will know of this."

"No!" I caught her hand before she could rush off to write a letter, or dash into town, or seize a horsewhip like her idol Sarah Bernhardt. "I am not suited for such workrooms. And . . . I was distracted."

"By what?"

My hesitation quieted her of a sudden, made her sink beside my chair, as she had at Godfrey's the previous evening.

"I was thinking of"—my voice quavered despite myself—"dear Allegra."

Irene nodded sagely, looking regretful. "Of dear Allegra, and of her absent uncle. And also of my headstrong trek to Bohemia, and of the King, the Queen, and Godfrey. Oh, Nell, you worry too much about us, who are not worthy of your devotion—"

"And, and . . . they brought me a new mannequin. Irene, it was you!"

"I?"

I nodded.

"I. Then . . . Monsieur Worth has decided upon me as a *mannequin de ville*! I am to set the standard. This is wonderful news!"

"No! No, it is not. I sat there, not believing my eyes. You—reduced to bisque and paint and kid leather. You a puppet of other people's purposes. Then I thought of the Rothschilds and the Golem, a creature animated by no desire of its own, made to walk, made to sleep eternally as it suits someone else—no wonder it is restless, and mute, and angry!"

"Nell, darling Nell. That is legend. We face far more lethal dangers, in others, in ourselves. Only you know why I must return to Bohemia. Or guess it. You must not take all this so seriously." She shook my hand, my icy fingers clasped in her warm ones. "I know that you feel the contradictions, as Godfrey can'not. Dearest Godfrey, he thinks that I do not know how much this enterprise troubles him. It goes against his very core, yet he will do it, because I must, even if I will not—cannot—tell him precisely why. Forget the latest foolishness at Maison Worth. Godfrey will take fine care of you in Bohemia, and you must take care of him."

"I? Take care of Godfrey."

"Of course, you darling ninny!" She shook my hands. "I rely upon you. Godfrey is a babe in Toyland there; you have seen the lay of the land at least. You must advise and protect him, as I must the inopportune Allegra. Surely you and I could handle this better ourselves. Did we not together defeat the King's every stratagem on our last encounter in Bohemia—and beyond? Are we not up to another skirmish? I think so."

"You do?

"Certainly." She loosed my hands to clap hers together with resolution. "Well. We must do our best, as you say."

"If you are Monsieur Worth's new *mannequin de ville*, as you say, will it not harm your standing to desert Paris?"

"Nonsense! Even so, I do not truly care. Besides, absence makes the heart grow fonder in other than romantic matters. But you must promise me, Nell, to keep a weather eye out in Prague, so that Godfrey does not go astray. I bank on you."

"I will watch him as if my life depended upon it!" I swore.

"Excellent!" Irene sat back on her heels with a satisfied expression that much reminded me of Lucifer's.

Godfrey returned from Paris that evening so altered that we both almost did not recognize him, and indeed forgot any unpleasantness at Maison Worth, be it death or dismissal.

Irene was in the music room trilling her scales at Casanova, who showed much interest and repeated the exercise in a crude falsetto that nevertheless managed to be irritatingly on key. I, naturally, am tone deaf.

I was occupied with my sewing. When a shadow crossed the threshold, I expected Godfrey, so I did not eye him with much attention. Yet even my distracted glance detected a change. I turned immediately to Irene, expecting her to act as my weather vane and point to the source of the new wind in his sails.

She, too, glanced carelessly over her shoulder, smiling and *eeee-eeee-eeee-EEEE-eeee-eeee*-ing her endless vocal scales uninterrupted. Then she stopped, her mouth still impressively open and her motionless, curled hands hovering above the chords.

Godfrey always cut a quite respectable figure in my view, but now it was as if I saw him through a freshly washed window. Everything about him was sharp, new, and shiny in some subtle way.

Irene's hands descended into a discordant chord that made Casanova squawk in disgust.

"Godfrey! What have you done to yourself?" she demanded.

"Nothing that I am aware of, except work excessively hard these past two weeks," he said innocently.

Irene glanced at me for rare support. "Is he not more splendid than usual, Nell?"

Before I could answer, a frightful racket exploded in the passage. Lucifer hurtled into the music room like a furry croquet ball that yowled. Something thumped the hall slate with the dead weight of a corpse. A French curse drifted into our civilized scene, to be quickly emulated by the vile parrot.

Another dreadful thump brought Irene and myself to our feet.

"Nothing to worry about." Godfrey returned to the threshold to call out a *"Merci"* and dismiss our man-of-all-work, André. Godfrey glanced back to us with a sunny smile. "Merely some necessities for the journey to Prague."

"Ah." Irene beamed as she rustled over to the doorway.

"Trunks, I deduce, and a good many, from the sound. What have you brought me?"

"Nothing," he said. "They are for me."

"For . . . you?"

"I cannot go to Prague as emissary for the Rothschild banking concerns attired like a court clerk."

"I see." Irene looked him up and down, then caught his lapel in her fingers and gave her impeccable diagnosis. "A morning coat of finest twilled cashmere in charcoal gray. Silk-lined and—oh, my dear, stayed in the seams so the tight cut at the waist will not buckle. A satin brocade waistcoat with, think of it, Nell, mother-of-pearl buttons!" She ran her forefinger along the buttons in question as if presenting evidence before the Bench. "Black and gray finestriped worsted trousers and pointy-toed boots. My, you are quite the dandy; one might even say, the Masher."

"Godfrey is not a Masher!" I said hotly in his defense. These young men about town were not dandies in the Oscar Wilde manner, but known accosters of young ladies. "He looks," I said haughtily, "like a diplomat."

Irene was not to be gainsaid. "Like a most fashionable diplomat and more attractive than any of that calling that I have ever seen."

Godfrey remained unruffled by her prowling around his person, examining and petting his every article of clothing.

"Really, Irene," I added, "I cannot see much different at all in Godfrey's clothing. I have myself noted in my diaries than men's garments are for the most part like as peas in pods, and most undistinguished. Though, Godfrey, of course, has always appeared distinguished to me."

"Nell," Irene said, sighing, "you have the discrimination for fine points of men's clothing that Messalina the mongoose has for parasols. Take my word upon it: our man Godfrey has made a most astounding change in the cut, style and, I would say, the cost of his clothing."

Godfrey laughed. "Cost I grant you, but it was underwritten."

"By whom?" Irene demanded.

"By Baron Rothschild."

"And by whom is your splendid new clothing created? By Baron Rothschild's tailor?"

Godfrey shrugged, which did nothing to disarrange the fine fit of his morning coat. "I confess it."

"Really, Irene," I added, "if you will bask in the good favor of the Worths and Tiffanys of the world, I see no reason why Godfrey should not have the use of a Baron's tailor."

"Exactly, Nell!" he said, vanishing into the hall and leaving a fascinating sentence behind him. "I have also brought a token for you."

"For Nell?" Irene asked the empty threshold.

Godfrey filled it again, handsomely, brandishing a middling box wrapped in shiny paper.

"For Nell," he said firmly, moving to present it to me.

I retreated to my chair, where my sewing scissors abided, to open it. Godfrey came to stand before me, anxious as St. Nick on Christmas Eve.

"Truly, I require no presents," I muttered, cutting the lovely gilt ribbons and savaging the pretty crimson paper.

"Nonsense," said Irene. "You do not get them often enough."

I opened the box and unfolded the interior tissue. Sterling silver winked as me, as solid and shiny as only the real thing is.

"A . . . ring of keys," I began, reminded of our find in Godfrey's father's chest so many months before.

"No!" Irene crowded near to see. "A . . . chatelaine."

"A chatelaine? It must have cost half of Hyde Park," I said in dismay.

Godfrey had gone down on one pin-striped gray knee to better point out the article's advantages.

"A very special chatelaine, Nell. Every item is designed for your especial use. See, here is a tiny scissors, so you may always cut knots, be they of crochet string or puzzling conundrums we encounter in our adventures. This is a tiny automatic pencil. The lead descends with a twist of the wrist. And here is a true key—to Irene's traveling vanity chest and the Tiffany corsage. I deemed it wise to have a second key and you are the best keeper of that."

"And this—?"

"A magnifying glass, for unraveling threads or ciphers."

"And this is . . . a thimble case! Oh, is it too clever for words. And a needle case. Smelling salts. A tiny perfume flask. Oh, most handy for surviving ill-scented foreign climes, Godfrey, and foreign climes always have the oddest smells! And this . . . little knife? Surely this tiny thing is not meant to serve a similar role as Irene's pistol?"

"It is a penknife, Nell, for sharpening regular pencils so you can take accurate notes, a great quantity of them that will require much pencil-sharpening."

"Oh, it is lovely. Thank you, Godfrey. But what is this fine silver chain?"

"So," Irene explained, "you may wear it around your waist or your neck if you do not happen to be wearing a convenient belt. It *is* a clever conglomeration," she added a bit wistfully.

Irene never saw anything rare and beautiful, but she yearned for it, as a child does for a bright bubble, with an innocent greed that makes virtue out of vice.

Godfrey smiled at her. "If you are good in Bohemia, I shall find you a chatelaine of your own on our return."

"I am always 'good,' " she said indignantly, "and do not require bribes."

"But you have been known to accept them," he pointed out, lifting the key to her vanity case from my chatelaine.

"Only from strangers," she murmured.

He laughed and rose, assisting Irene to her feet, so they stood at last entangled, almost embracing.

She spoke in the same, soft teasing voice she had used

earlier. "I will have to investigate the rest of your booty, to insure that you have not smuggled any other exotic articles into our simple home."

"Investigate what you will. You will only find that clothes do not make the man," he promised.

"Ah, but sometimes they make the man too interesting for his own good."

I found the issue of Godfrey's new clothing rather tiresomely trivial. No one worried how *my* wardrobe should impress the Bohemian court or the connivers we were en route to Bohemia to confound.

There are certain advantages to being sane and sensible, I concluded, as I listened to Irene and Godfrey wend their slow, murmuring way upstairs arm in arm. I doubted that they would be down for dinner for some time, but then Sophie was most slack about putting out her aunt's contortions with the menu, and besides, the French can actually eat an unbelievable number of foods stark, raving cold.

I sighed and sacrificed the notion of a decent dinner for yet another night. Yet before I took up my crochet hook and string, I fastened the gleaming silver chain around my waist, with its jingling accoutrements of cryptic silver objects. I tested the tiny silver folding knife. Quite satisfactorily sharp.

Chapter Thirteen

BOHEMIA BOUND

❧

Our train steamed out of the Gard de Nord station. Our first-class compartment housed an unlikely pair of adventurers, I wearing my somewhat lethal chatelaine beneath my traveling cape, Godfrey carrying his handsome new malacca cane with the clouded-amber head of a dragon.

Beside me sat the rich and oiled contours of Irene's vanity case from Baron Rothschild. Godfrey insisted that the diamonds travel with us rather than with Irene and Allegra. Irene had rolled her eyes at this decree, but said nothing. I suspected that she trusted more to her revolver than to the security of any male escort, even if the escort were her own husband. I also suspect that she respected Godfrey's common sense. Though neither spoke it, I did not look the sort of woman who would be concealing diamonds in her luggage; indeed, I did not look the sort of woman to be carrying a vanity case, though even a country mouse such as I might be allowed my plain toilet water and my discreet face powder.

Beyond the compartment window, Irene waved a kid-gloved farewell, her smiling features blurring behind frothy furbelows of steam and managing to look mysterious.

Beyond her loomed André's dour face: long, unattractive and indubitably French. At least Irene would travel home, safe in male company, until beginning her own long journey eastward to Bohemia.

"How this reminds me of our recent trip to England," I told my seat partner, who kept his nose pasted to the window for a last glimpse of his wife even as she seemed to glide away into the stream with our train's motion. However stylish Godfrey's new clothes, I felt with him the soft-slipper comfort I might have shared with the brother I had never had. Godfrey and I had worked together too long in the crowded Temple quarters for any exterior alteration to off-balance our easy affinity.

"I trust that this mission will end less dramatically," he said, referring to Quentin Stanhope's final London contest with Colonel Sebastian Moran, of which I had been the only witness.

I bit my lip, reminded of that awful night's headlong hansom race. It had ended on a bridge where two men fought to the death despite my presence, despite my pleas. We three had reason to believe that at least one man had survived that joint plunge into the swift, icy Thames. I hoped that the survivor was the one who wore my heart as a keepsake.

"And we will not have to cross water," Godfrey reassured me. "At least no more than a river."

"Oh, you are thinking of the Channel. I refuse to call it 'the English Channel.' Nothing English could be so stomach-churning."

"I am told that this will be a staid but tedious journey."

"To say the least. I have made it twice, coming and going." I smiled. "On this occasion I have gallant company and no worries of imminent pursuit."

"Even if you did harbor such concerns, worry not." He twisted the cane's amber head to reveal a flash of polished steel.

"Your walking stick is a . . . sword?"

"Of sorts."

"Pardon me, but what do you know of swords, God-frey?"

"More than I knew a fortnight ago."

I considered that declaration as the train chugged ponderously through the suburbs of Paris under skies as gray as Godfrey's candid yet twinkling eyes.

"You have availed yourself of more than Baron Rothschild's tailor!" I guessed suddenly.

"How astute you are, Nell, when you wish to be. In a word, *oui*."

"Oh, stop using that vile language! Between us, at least, we need not resort to slippery syllables that tie the tongue in knots my chatelaine scissors could not slice. I assure you, we shall hear a vastly more complex and incomprehensible set of syllables when we reach Bohemia."

The dashing cane-top spun between Godfrey's black-leather-gloved hands until the dragon's ruddy head seemed to breathe smoke. "I welcome seeing that quaint little kingdom at last, Nell. After all, it has played a major role in Irene's life. I first feared going to Bohemia because of the ghosts that haunt it—and her—but now I am eager to meet them. Do you find that strange?"

"No, Godfrey. You are quite right. A man must know his wife's past as well as her pastimes, and in Bohemia is buried Irene's operatic career as well as whatever foolish hopes of queenship she cherished. He did worship her, you know, that self-indulgent, aggravating, spoiled bully-boy of a king."

"I know." Godfrey gave his lethal cane a savage twist. "And he saw her perform leading roles in opera, as I never have. She must have made a splendid diva, and would have made an even more splendid queen in real life."

"She is far happier now," I confided. "Irene never relished for long being subject to anyone's whims, be he a conductor or a crown prince and his court, though she may not admit that."

"You think so, Nell? I have fancied these last weeks that

Irene felt peculiarly compelled to return to Bohemia; that she would have found a way to accomplish this object no matter the turn of events, even without the convenient excuse of the Rothschild commission. I don't know why, though I can speculate until I sicken myself with conjecture."

"You fear the King of Bohemia more than Sherlock Holmes!" I said with sudden realization.

Godfrey smiled ruefully. "Sherlock Holmes is an eccentric; an original. He would have to be to become the world's first consulting detective. Yet he cannot be too unlike me in his upbringing, or his bourgeois roots. And however brilliant, however his mind catches Irene's imagination, his personal aspect is not especially impressive, from your description, Nell, which I take as Gospel. But the King . . . even you prattle in awe of his great height, his golden crown and hairs, his damned imposing, Germanic royal presence! I picture him as the hero of a Wagnerian opera, insufferable, but winning the maiden fair." He looked down at the wooden floor of our compartment, which the elegant brass ferrule of his cane pierced like a stickpin. "I feel I am a David confronting a Goliath."

"Then you cannot understand the depth of Irene's disappointment, Godfrey, when the King revealed his true colors. I myself have never seen her so . . . shocked into utter paralysis. Only anger roused her from that frightening state. Anger saw us both safely out of Bohemia."

"The other side of anger is passion."

"I would not know," I said slowly.

"Passion is often a two-faced emotion that does not endure," he mused, "although it is most pleasing at the time. Yet there is nothing worse than unsatisfied passion, whether it call itself love, or loathing."

"I would not know," I repeated, although I felt a dim stir of resentment at having to confess this fact.

Godfrey glanced out of the window again, distracted by his thoughts of Bohemia. I eyed his composed but troubled

profile, for a moment reflecting that a barrister confronting
Bohemia's ancient, aristocratic and autocratic ruling class
with a cane-sword was indeed a David dueling a broad-
sword-armed Goliath with a stickpin.

Of the many scenic delights found in journeying by rail
through Belgium and Austria I have written before. The
avid travel reader can consult a guidebook, if needed, of
which great numbers abound.

Although I enjoyed pointing out sights to Godfrey—
particularly the commendably upright telegraph poles
alongside the railway (in France, the same poles lurch like
drunken toothpicks)—neither he nor I were easy enough in
mind to sit back and enjoy our lengthy excursion.

When our route required an overnight stopover at some
railway hotel, I most appreciated Godfrey's escort to and
from the train, and his fluid French, which accomplished
our purpose where English did not.

I had been too greatly distressed on my rescue mission to
Irene and the return flight by rail to much remark on the
accommodation along the route. This time I noticed. I
found the mattresses piled so high on the ancient bedsteads
that one required a ladder to get into bed; despite such lofty
ambition, and although I had no pretensions to princess-
hood, the mattresses seemed pea-infected. Perhaps I mean
"flea." Certainly I was thankful for the sensible nightdress
that covered me from chin to knuckles to toes, and a night-
cap as well.

The common bathing areas were the subject of much
embarrassed negotiation between persons of the opposite
sex, or even those of the same persuasion who were unknown to each other.

By the second night, I wondered why on earth Godfrey
and I should hurl ourselves like battered dice in a rattling
wooden box to such an outpost as Prague on no more cause
than a banker's insecurity and Irene's insatiable curiosity.

And the food at the hotel dining rooms left much to be

desired, unless one is fond of lumpy soups with anonymous inhabitants, tough veal drenched in grease-laden
bread crumbs, and the inevitable vanilla ice accoutered
with a wafer that has much in common with cardboard.
Apparently the French nation's greatest rivals in abysmal
cookery are the Germans.

It was over another uninspired dinner that I spied the
odd gentleman. I believe the city was Cologne, or perhaps
Frankfurt or even Nuremberg. From a train one city is
much like another.

"Godfrey, that gentleman at the window table has been
regarding us all evening."

He managed to drop his napkin in a nonchalant manner
that Irene would have applauded (and I would never have
managed), then turn to look where I indicated.

"Ordinary enough chap," Godfrey pronounced on
drawing his chair back to the table and attacking his Wie-
ner schnitzel with the gusto all men seem able to apply to
even the most mediocre food.

"What of the blue-tinted glasses?"

"Eye trouble," he suggested tersely before excavating a
pile of sliced potatoes attired in a loathsome yellowish
sauce.

I used my fork tines to push my potato mound to the rim
of my plate. "I have seen him in the train stations as well."

"He may be traveling to the same destination that we
are."

"Is that not suspicious?"

Godfrey stopped eating, reluctantly, to give my questions the full attention they deserved. "We are not the only
persons with business in Prague, Nell. As for the gentleman's regarding us, he probably has as little to occupy his
mind on this trip as do you, which is why you noticed him
in the first place."

"He has a great amount of facial hair."

Godfrey managed another discreet survey of the man

under discussion. "So do German professors, Nell. That is precisely the species I think you have uncovered. Look at the thickness of the book that he has set beside his plate."

"Then why is he not reading it, instead of looking at us?"

"I do not doubt that we are more interesting than it is." A tone of exasperation had entered his voice, which I recognized from my own governess days when dealing with an unquenchable child. "Perhaps he is a Masher," Godfrey added with sudden inspiration. "The only way to discourage his regard is to pay him no mind whatsoever."

I sighed. If I was not to be suspicious of strangers, I would have nothing better to do than to attack the unattractive dinner. I bent my gaze and my fork back to my plate. Beets, I noted mournfully, a great quantity of beets leaking carmine liquid and—my fork withdrew from my mouth too late for me to do anything but chew and swallow despite myself—cold! Cold beets for dinner, can it be imagined? Prague, I reflected, had been a great mistake the first time as well.

Although Godfrey pooh-poohed my apprehensions all through that despicable dinner, when we rose to leave he turned to inspect the now-deserted dining room.

"The object of your speculation has left his book," he noted, leading me past the table we had noted.

Godfrey paused to pick up the tome and riffle the gilt-edged pages. "A commonplace treatise on the city of Prague. I will return it to the gentleman in the morning." The moment I opened my mouth to protest, he forestalled me. "We may learn something of the gentleman from his book."

So he saw me to my door and retreated with the mislaid volume under one arm. I itched to peruse it, but dared not say so; lost property was not common goods.

The next morning, Godfrey arrived at my door to collect me at the prearranged time, cane in one hand, book in the other.

"Well?" I demanded.

"An ordinary travel guide. I will leave it with the concierge."

But that reliable depository of lost articles and general information was of no help at all. She insisted that no gentleman answering to our description had recently resided at the hotel, even overnight.

We left burdened by the stranger's book. Godfrey shrugged off the incident.

"If we spy the man again, he may have his book back."

"If we spy the man again, he may *be* a spy!"

"For whom?"

"The forces in Prague that the Rothschilds fear, or even—"

"Yes, Nell?"

I lowered my voice. "The King."

"He does employ spies, like any modern monarch," Godfrey admitted, "but I doubt he would waste them on us. We have been troubled by no sign of the King's interest since Irene and I left London eighteen months ago."

"True . . . except—" I was thinking of Irene's and my accidental encounter with Queen Clotilde. Had it been mere happenstance, as it seemed? Could the unknowing Queen have been sent to the House of Worth to encounter Irene and lure her back to Prague and the King? Even Irene had not envisioned such a plot. I was sorry to have thought of it so tardily, and sorrier still to see Godfrey frowning at me worrisomely.

"Except what, Nell? Has the King shown some awareness of our new address in Neuilly that I am unaware of?"

Now I would have to produce a plausible excuse for my unguarded turn of phrase! I hated to mislead Godfrey, especially in the middle of a public hotel lobby.

"Except—oh, I don't know what I was thinking, Godfrey! Of course the King has not found us." Inspiration struck so suddenly that I did not even consider the ethics of such a wild story. "Except, as you pointed out when the mysterious box with Quentin's medal arrived at our Neuilly cottage, it could have been sent by that murderous heavy game-hunter, Colonel Moran, rather than Quentin himself. And that monster spied for the Russians. If he sent the medal, he knows where we live. He could be employed by the King of Bohemia now—or by his enemies." By now my fairy tale seemed all too alarmingly possible, even to me!

"Nell, Nell, Nell!" Godfrey chidingly shook my gloved hand. "You have been infected by an overdose of Irene's imagination. It is far more sensible to suppose that Quentin himself sent the medal, that he survived his apparent death. And you know that there is no harm at all in Quentin Stanhope's knowing where we live. For one thing, he has already been a guest there. For another, he wishes us no harm; quite the contrary. You mustn't see ghosts and spies behind every pillar and pair of tinted glasses. I began to fear that this return to Prague is likely to be as harmful to you as it may be to Irene."

Now I had worried Godfrey in my attempt to weave a tangled web from odd pieces of truth and pure conjecture! I nodded in guilty shame, which he took for meek agreement. He squeezed my hand for courage and led me into the bustling street, which smelled of old cabbage and fresh bootblack. Shortly after our luggage was brought down, we were ensconced in a carriage for the short ride to the station and the final leg of our trek to Prague.

Perhaps Godfrey was right that I saw danger in disguise behind every eyeglass and saw a mask in every mutton-chop. Yet the odd gentleman vanished after that night as if cued by Godfrey's and my discussion of him, and I had learned from Irene the uses and techniques of deception. I peered around the crowded terminal in Prague, but spied not a single pair of tinted glasses. And we remained in undisputed possession of the travel guide to Prague.

Chapter Fourteen

FEET OF CLAY

The city of Prague straddles a sharp bend in the river Vltava, whose nine bridges fan like spokes between the Old and New Towns on the east bank, and the Hradčany fortress and Lesser Quarter, or Malá Strana, on the west.

Prague is a pleasant city, situated neither high nor low, and famed for its "hundred towers," though they no doubt number more by now. The city is often likened to Venice (for its cluster of water-threaded islands near the National Theater) or Vienna (for its lavish Baroque architecture with its heaped-on plasterwork and gilt that amounts to nothing more than architectural marzipan).

Had my associations with the capital not been so unhappy, I might even have experienced some nostalgia at a return.

Godfrey had reserved rooms for us at the Europa Hotel in the New Town, a splendid modern hostelry that nevertheless hinted at the city's Baroque past. From the balconies outside our rooms (bed and bath suites that were needlessly luxurious), one could see the late-afternoon sun winking off the glassy river and dyeing the red tile roofs of the Malá Strana an oxblood color. Godfrey and I stood on our separate but adjoining balconies, eyeing the spectacle of Prague spread before us like a picnic on a gentle green blanket.

Godfrey was squinting at the appropriated travel guide in the dimming light. "Where would this Golem-creature show itself?"

I pointed to the northeast behind us. "One cannot see the Josef Quarter from this direction, but it is nearby."

"A veritable tangle of rooftops and towers," he noted of the town below us. "Some of those distant byways look hardly wide enough to accommodate Jack Sprat, much less a massive, seven-foot-tall man-monster."

"The Josef Quarter is most congested," I agreed, remembering an ill-conceived outing there with Irene, "and full of dark passages and queer signs in strange languages. I would not wish to go there."

He nodded absently, paging through the thick guidebook in the waning light, then lifted his eyes to the horizon. "And that. What is that? Surely more than a church."

He pointed to a long, high ridge to the west, behind which the sun shrank like a guttering candle. I had forgotten how this massive architectural cliff face dominated Prague's unambitious profile, or how the light glanced from its long lines of windows so it looked like a treasure chest studded with cut steel.

"The spires belong to St. Vitus's Cathedral, a Catholic church," I added unnecessarily while avoiding the true issue.

"Ah, here it is—'St. Vitus's Cathedral at the heart of the Hradčany fortress . . .' "

I tautened at the sight of the church's three serrated Gothic towers looming like spearheads over the long low bulk of the building that surrounded it.

"Hradčany," Godfrey repeated uncertainly. "Is not that the site of Prague Castle? Nell?"

"Yes, Godfrey?"

"Is that where you and Irene stayed with the King?"

"Yes, Godfrey."

"Why did you not mention it sooner?"

"I . . . forgot it. Truly I did. I was used to seeing the city from its windows, not to viewing it from a distance. It is most imposing."

"Indeed," he said indignantly, "but for all its vast mass, rather unimaginative."

I could not help but think that he was comparing the structure with its master. "The outer walls are eighteenth century," I explained. "Inside are bits and pieces of older architecture dating to the ninth century, so I was told. Parts of the interior are Romanesque and Gothic, and quite interesting, particularly the row of tiny medieval houses within the castle, which is called Golden Lane and once housed guards and, later, it is said, alchemists. Do you suppose the alchemists had anything to do with the Golem?"

"I have a perfectly adequate guidebook, Nell. You need not regale me with the odd detail." Godfrey sounded a bit out of temper. "How far back does this Golem date?"

"Medieval times."

"And the King's direct ancestors; how far do they extend into the mists of history, I wonder?"

"There you have me. Earlier rulers of Bohemia include Charles the Fourth, who was also Holy Roman Emperor, and Rudolph the Second. I am not so sure that the current King Wilhelm is descended from either of those distinguished gentlemen. Prague and Bohemia passed back and forth between waxing and waning empires for some time. No doubt the King's family tree bears several transplants and truncations."

"No doubt. Certainly I am not fond of my own family tree, and my disillusion goes back only to my father. Imagine what a train of scalawags a king with a proper pedigree might find hanging upon his ancestral branches."

"I need not imagine faults for Wilhelm von Ormstein, Godfrey."

"No. It has grown dark, and I cannot read this useful

little volume any longer. I suggest that we repair to dinner and plan our next moves. Thirty minutes, then?"

His voice came from the descending dark—a good voice: crisp, quietly carrying and thoroughly English.

"Yes," I said, hearing his shoe-pivot on the balcony stone answer me.

I remained in the almost-dark, hanging over the city with which I had such brief but gloomy acquaintance. Bells began tolling from the hundred-some towers as they had for centuries, each in its own distinctive voice. Irene, with her instant musical recall, could name each bell-note, I knew. I heard them with tone-deaf ears, yet their vibrations touched the harp strings of my memory, and I was sorry to be here again.

Did Queen Clotilde high on Hradčany hill lift her head to listen? Did the King pause in his regal pursuits to remember the bells? When he sat in the National Theater to attend an opera, did he hear Irene's unforgettable dark, rich voice echoing? Did the resurrected Golem in his cramped and hidden byways halt at the sound so blessed to me, yet cursed to him—Christian bells tolling an assault upon the Jews of Prague; alarum bells of warning to Jews; avenging bells of holy war to Christians?

Who in this city of sublime music and ancient hatreds, of beauty and beastliness multiplied to the seventh power, heeded the bells?

Who would heed us, or Irene, now that we were coming back?

The very civilized hotel dining room eased my primitive fancies and fears. Peach-colored linen dressed round tables set amid the warm gleam of wood paneling. Candlelight polished leaded glass insets and burnished the gilt figurines holding fresh flowers that decorated the chamber.

If only the food had matched the decor! My national pantheon of atrocious cooking became an unholy trinity: roast pork indifferently done; a slick lumpy offering the size of a croquet ball, and about as tasty, called a dumpling; bleached shoestrings of cabbage served hot in vinegar. Not only was the meal tasteless, but colorless as well. In terms of untouchable cuisine, from now on it was Rule, Bohemia!

Godfrey eyed the undemolished condition of my plate. "This does not suit you, Nell? What did you eat at the palace?"

"Very little. I was most worried about Irene and had no appetite. Then, when she detected poison as the method of the old king's death . . . I had even less appetite."

"And did Irene's theories affect her own digestion?"

"Hardly! Irene is as deaf to good food as I am to true notes. She will happily eat anything, and a good deal of it. I cannot understand why her figure remains so slender."

"Injustice, Nell," he said with relish, attacking the dumpling with knife and fork so it should not escape his plate. "Irene is the embodiment of cruel injustice, the model by which the rest of us fall short."

"Is that why you have saddled her return to Prague with the company of young Allegra?"

He smiled angelically. "Even Irene must have a cross or two to bear, not that Allegra is other than a delightful girl. Still, it will temper Irene's adventurous instincts to have an innocent in her care. Besides, the young woman was bound and determined to visit us, and she shall get her wish, and then some."

"She cannot have easily obtained her family's permission," I added.

"Oh." Godfrey grinned, and there was nothing angelic about it. "I doubt that she has bothered to ask them."

"And you have compounded the situation by inviting Allegra to Prague!?"

"Where else can we keep an eye on her? What else could we have done but shipped her back to her family in disgrace?"

"Allegra is a well-brought-up girl," I continued, most distraught. "How could she have done anything so ill considered as to undertake a trip abroad under false pretenses?"

"I said from the first that she reminded me of Irene." He smiled and set aside his napkin with a satisfied air. "I wonder how Irene will like having a younger, more impetuous version of herself on her hands."

"This scheme of yours may recoil upon you, Godfrey."

"Why?"

"Schemes generally do—even Irene's."

He lifted the pale wine provided for our dinner. "In this case, let us hope the schemes of the schemers we are here to hunt prove more vulnerable than our own."

"Amen," said I, toasting before drinking from my glass of the only Bohemian consumable I found palatable—water.

After a dessert of heavy torte I only picked at, we repaired to Godfrey's sitting room. (As a delegate of the Rothschild interests he would be expected to have grand accommodations, he explained.)

As soon as he was seated, Godfrey handed me the travel guide we had acquired.

"You have studied the Golem legends and have visited Prague before, Nell. Tell me if this book contains anything of interest I should know."

I donned my pince-nez and paged through, lingering at the tissue-covered plates featuring local landmarks. The volume, I discovered with approval, had been published in London, and was dedicated to a "Professor Moriarty, Corresponding Member of the Royal Scientific Society of Bohemia, who has so largely contributed to making Bohemia known to England."

Frankly, the professor's quest is still largely unfulfilled, for Prague remains one of the more obscure cities of Europe, and nowhere more so than in England. Indeed, although the term *Bohemian* has been appropriated from this land to describe individuals of an impoverished, irresponsible and artistic bent (a commonplace, even clichéd,

trinity of attributes), it has taken on a French association
that puts Bohemia in shadow even when it names a modern
phenomenon. From my observation, there are few things at
which the French excel, but in Bohemian attributes they are
unparalleled, thus outflanking the Bohemians, who are obscure to begin with, at being Bohemian.

I studied the usual small etchings: the chapel in St.
Vitus's Cathedral, the East Gate to Prague Castle; the Pow-
der Tower at the entrance to the Josef Quarter; Strahov
Monastery, whose magnificence is a model of the Roman
Church's thirst for ostentatious display.

"The index does not mention the Golem, Godfrey," I
finally pronounced, "but I do find an intriguing entry about
Rabbi Lowi Bezalel, who would seem to be the Rabbi Loew
of legend."

He bent over me to study the page, but the type was so
small and close that he begged me to read the selection
aloud. There is nothing I like better than giving an edifying
reading, even if it is merely informational rather than inspi-
rational. I complied, reporting that the Jewish colony in
Prague was said to date from before Christian times, from
before the Crucifixion even, thus supposedly protecting
Prague's Jews from Christian anger at presumed participation in the Crucifixion.

"This cannot be completely true." I interrupted my
reading to eye Godfrey sternly over the gold rims of my
pince-nez. "The book also reports a great persecution
of Jews here in thirteen-eighty-nine. Although Rabbi
Lowi Bezalel enjoyed the favor of Rudolph the Second,
ruler of Hungary and Bohemia, he was treasured for his
cabbalism because Rudolph sponsored many an alche-
mist, including John Dee. So the rabbi would hardly raise
up a Golem to defend the Jewish colony if there were no
danger."

"Impeccably argued, Nell," Godfrey said with a smile.
"You have put your finger on a grave inconsistency; but,
then, this is reported history, which thrives on inconsis-

tency. In my pagings through this book I am struck by the inconsistencies of Prague itself. It harbors three divergent races and religions: Catholic Bohemians, Protestant Germans, and Jews. At one time, Catholicism was forced upon the population; at another, Protestantism. Such a political-religious stew could indeed invoke as fabulous a creature as the Golem, and each faction could easily believe in the others' demons, if not their God.''

"You are saying that someone other than the Jews might have raised the Golem—if indeed there were such a creature and it was capable of raising?''

"I am saying that another faction might *use* the Golem legend to upset the populace for its own political ends." He considered his next opinion distastefully. "A barrister is not fond of the supernatural, but it is possible that some other faction could even have found the defunct Golem and reanimated it.''

"How . . . without the power of the ancient Cabbala? That occult agency I credit far more than our current form of spiritualism. At least it stems from the Bible, where wonders indeed were performed, and not from any latter-day drawing-room hocus-pocus.''

Godfrey frowned. "All these eastern European lands are caught in a crossfire of religion, race and a brutal taste for conquering their neighbors, coupled, of course, with a fierce thirst for their own freedom even as they decimate their enemies. Here East met West in ways Kipling never dreamed of, and long before Mother England touched toe to India. Huns and Turks swept westward and left their mark on these lands even after Catholicism and then Protestantism conquered them.''

"You mean to say that the old religions still survive here?''

His shrug was the supreme gesture of a rational, modern man, but his mind remained on the mystical.

"Shrines to Christian saints still decorate roads throughout Poland, Transylvania, Moravia and Bohemia, but yet the people placate pagan gods, demons and superstitions. Though centuries of religious and racial contention have leached them of their life, liberty and peace, they still see vampires on the doorjamb and werewolves among the trees. The Russian Orthodox Church clings to its eastern mysticism, and shamans—holy men—rule the neglected peasants of Siberia. Yes, I think the region's hapless history hints that these strange, contentious people are quite capable of stirring up each other's demons."

"Some faction other than Jewish, other than Bohemian even, would use the Golem and Prague as the fulcrum of its own purposes? How appalling!"

"Speculation, Nell. Mere moonshine." Godfrey smiled and shook his head as if to dislodge a sinister veil of thought. "Even English barristers can fall prey to the seductions of these ancient lands. Ordinary political machinations are danger enough without imagining supernatural plots as well."

"I cannot imagine the Germans subscribing to such nonsense," I added, "and it is they who have the greatest stake in Bohemia."

"You are right, as usual. Certainly the German ascendancy has dominated the nation for some centuries. Consider the King's string of Germanic names—Wilhelm Gottsreich Sigismond von Ormstein. Sigismond, after all, was a fifteenth-century king of Hungary, not Bohemia, according to this book, proof that the Bohemian bloodline runs as thin as watered milk in his veins.

"Irene did well," he added, "to avoid an alliance with such a watered-down king. But do you notice anything odd about the book itself?"

"Only—" I paged through. "—that some of the pages are dog-eared. One would expect that in a reference book."

"Yes. But what of the one page that is double dog-eared?"

"Which?"

He took the small book from me and quickly turned the pages to the one in question.

"Yes, the corner has been bent down," I said, "then bent again in a reverse direction. Most destructive, but people are so careless."

"Or their carelessness could *only seem so*, as perhaps the act of leaving a travel guide in the hotel dining room at Cologne was not careless or accidental."

"The man in the tinted spectacles! I told you then—"

"I only guess, Nell, for the Rothschild agents in Bohemia must find some discreet way of contacting us. But what this particular page tells us puts me at a loss."

I studied the small type. "It reveals only the bibulous nature of the Bohemians. This section is a discourse on beer making and drinking, apparently the lone area where Bohemians excel! Humph. Springs beneath the basement taverns, and breweries on the very premises. It discusses a Prague tavern that was old in the eighteenth century and is still in the same family as then, U Fleků. 'U' means 'at the,' followed by the tavernmaster's name. Apparently a benighted couple named Flek purchased the place in 1499. The text claims that the place spawned political plots, revolutions and more than one ill-considered marriage. Godfrey, this U Fleků sounds a most disreputable establishment—a low, dark cellar whose long tables will seat nine hundred. Can there be that many debauched souls in Prague who would wish to sit in such a place and drink beer?"

"Decidedly! And if U Fleků still exists and is vital enough to appear on the double dog-eared page, I believe that we should go there and find out."

"We? Godfrey, this is a common tavern."

"We are here on uncommon business. You mustn't fear, Nell; I am armed to protect you." Godfrey picked up and flourished his cane.

I was unimpressed. "You do not understand, Godfrey. I

am not *afraid* of going to U Fleků; I am embarrassed by it."

"Oh." He stood stock still for a moment, looking disappointed. "I did not come equipped to banish mere embarrassment, Nell. You will simply have to suffer in silence."

I rose to find my cape, bonnet and gloves. "That is nothing new."

Later, I carried the travel guide on our outing to the tavern. Godfrey insisted that a scholarly look would add to my respectability. I suspect that he wished to have his hands free to employ his unusual cane, if needed. Indeed, I suspect that he secretly hoped for such an eventuality. Boys with a new toy are predictable at any age.

Prague's cobblestoned streets thronged with gay crowds. Every other doorway we passed—sturdy double wooden doors reminiscent of church portals—exploded open, spitting out revelers and sucking in replacements. An odor of raw beer and stale food coughed into the street for a moment before the heavy doors swung shut, entrapping their victims.

Every other sign shouted U SOMETHING, announcing a tavern.

Our route took us over one of the fabled bridges. Beneath us, the Vltava's black water burned here and there as it reflected torchlight. Carriages passed on the bridge, moving almost as slowly as the pedestrians.

How I appreciated Godfrey's strong, defending presence! Though the sword-stick was a dubious and unproved weapon to my mind, merely having a male escort made a respectable woman seem buttressed by the best that society has to offer her. I clung to the arm Godfrey had offered me when we left the hotel, clasped the inconvenient book under my outer elbow and minced over the uneven cobblestones as we left the broad way of the bridge for a narrow, tilting side street.

Under an archaic clock in which the notorious letters U FLEKŮ formed the dial, doors massive enough to have come from the Wittenberg Cathedral, to which Martin Luther had nailed his earthshaking theses, shook to my right, then creaked open. A blast of overheated, intoxicated air perfumed my face like a drunkard's breath.

"Here," said Godfrey, stopping to look aloft at the quaintly medieval wooden sign swaying, not in wind, but in sympathetic inebriation, it seemed. U FLEKŮ, read the wretched sign.

We stepped into the dark, mysterious warmth, then tripped down several broad stone steps into greater darkness and unholy noise.

This descent into hell indeed held a medieval fascination. A great, barrel-vaulted, smoke-stained ceiling spread above us like some reverse Sistine Chapel in Hades. Dimly seen figures cavorted in the vast chamber, dancing and lifting beer steins and singing and juggling empty bottles and generally behaving like profligate demons.

I hardly noticed when Godfrey steered me to a seat on a bench before a long, much-scarred wooden table. At least the room bore the name of St. Wenceslas. I hardly felt seated, so madly did the crowded, noisy room whirl around me with its forced merriment.

Gradually, I noticed light from rosy lamps scattered through the chaos. Waiters skated among the tables, trays lofted high. Steins thumped to the ancient wood, seasoning it further with a dribble of liquid hops and barley.

Godfrey leaned near to shout in my ear. "Put the book on the table, Nell!"

It sounded like a sentence from a French language book: *Put the pen of my aunt on the settee*. I did as told, grateful that no aunt of mine (had I possessed one) lived to see this moment.

A waiter swooped low to accost us. I shrank away, but Godfrey shouted something and he vanished. Thank goodness. My relief proved premature. Two minutes later we were again assaulted by waiter and tray, and a stein came to rest before Godfrey—and then myself!

"You must appear to be an ordinary customer," Godfrey advised at the top of his lungs.

No one would hear; I barely did. I moved the small book away from any overflow from the massive stein and watched with interest as Godfrey cocked the lid and sipped from the thick pottery rim.

I was rewarded by watching him choke on the contents, and pounded him helpfully on the back with rather more vigor than was strictly called for.

"Black lager!" he sputtered when he could again speak— or, rather, shout. "Thick, heavy and black as India ink."

"You may have my stein as well," I offered in a discreet screech.

"You say you feel unwell?" he shouted back, looking concerned.

I shook my head. Communication was hopeless in this bedlam. A clandestine meeting with an unknown spy seemed even less likely, but I was in no mood to attempt to tell Godfrey so. One of us, at least, should retain the power of speech if we actually encountered an agent of Baron Rothschild.

In our mutual silence, I gazed around the vast, dim environment. Come to think of it, this subterranean dungeon resembled the Baron's basement smoking room. Here, at least, I observed some decently bonneted women among the clientele, and what appeared to be entire families of aunts and uncles and grandparents. Evidently such debauchery was a family affair in Bohemia, although I doubted that we would spy a von Ormstein among the devoted beer drinkers gathered here.

A woman wearing the unattractive Bohemian national dress swayed our way. I do not comment on her sobriety, but rather her many-petticoated and layered short skirts, which stopped well above the ankle. This swaying bell of fabric tolled ponderously toward us. I thrust my untouched stein at her, hoping that she would take the hint and claim it. Instead, she smiled mindlessly, swept her skirts back and sat beside me on the bench. I was reminded of Little Miss Muffet and a rather overdressed spider.

My seatmate's chubby hand prodded the slim book before me. "Most provocative reading," she said in perfect English.

I studied her ruddy cheeks, her braided brown hair pulled back tight from her temples, her husky arms in the coyly puffed-sleeved peasant blouse. She smiled and slid my stein in front of her, quaffing an audacious swallow.

Godfrey watched her with respect. The black beer of U Fleků did not cause this Bohemian maiden the slightest difficulty.

She smiled, wiped her mouth with the back of one plump hand and tapped the book again. "I have lost one just like it lately."

"You!" I sputtered. "You were not on the train from Cologne."

"No." She had sobered suddenly, nodding. "But my 'brother' was." Her thumbs and forefingers made approximate "O"'s and lifted to her bland blue eyes. "Man with tinted glasses."

I nodded numbly while Godfrey leaned across me quite rudely to demand at the top of his lungs, "Where is your brother?"

"Outside," she mouthed. "Follow me."

Never have I been so delighted to leave an establishment in my life, and the girl's swollen skirts were better than bread crumbs to follow in this Stygian darkness.

I leapt up like a deer in her wake; only the custodial cling of Godfrey's hand to my arm informed me that we two had not been separated.

Oh, the cool, silent dark of night! I stood in the empty street and inhaled the nocturnal air, so often said to be a source of ill-health and pollution. Those who claimed such could never have spent a choking half-hour within the bowels of a Bohemian beer garden. All I had seen was beer, and no garden, although such a bucolic place no doubt lurked somewhere behind those forbidding double doors.

The woman beside me inhaled until her ample frontage threatened to puff up like a pigeon's jabot of feathers. "Ah. On such a night one could almost see the Golem walking."

"You have seen such a phenomenon?" Godfrey asked sharply.

"No, but I have heard of those who have. Come. My brother awaits."

"Is he really?" I asked as I trotted in her sturdy footsteps.

"My brother? Do not be foolish."

"Easier said than done," I muttered.

We ducked down a narrow, dark lane, then into one even slenderer and dimmer. We crossed a passage between two tall, cramped houses. Godfrey hit his hatted head on a low-hanging sign and cursed in what I hoped was a gentlemanly remonstrance mode.

Our guide giggled and waltzed on, her skirts flirting before us like a gingham-check flag of sanity.

At last we found ourselves in a tiny, deserted courtyard. Our guide retreated before we could bid her adieu. A figure detached itself from the dark wrapping of an inset doorway: the man from our hotel, still wearing the tinted glasses, though it was night!

Godfrey stepped manfully in front of me to confront this person, inadvertently treading on my toe. I swallowed a ladylike exclamation.

Here our voices were hushed, like the night. Distant revelry tinkled beyond this solemn courtyard.

"You have the book?" the man asked.

Godfrey nodded at me—I could barely discern the gesture in the dark—and I handed it to our . . . secret friend. He glanced at it, running his fingers over a few pages as if they were Braille and he was blind.

"This is the book. Then you are who you claim to be. See Werner at the Bank of Bohemia tomorrow. He will introduce you into the proper circles. As for improper circles—" Here the husky, slightly accented English voice developed a sardonic tone. "—I am to lead you to the areas of the Old Town where the Golem has been seen."

"Oh," I couldn't help wailing. Er, saying.

The man turned on me with the swiftness of a serpent. "You believe in supernatural beings, miss?"

"Only . . . angels."

"The Golem is no angel, but a creature of solid clay and cruel justice and spilt blood."

"You have seen . . . it?"

"No, but some in the Josef Quarter who are not known for lies or superstition claim to have seen him. Follow me, I will show you where, and then I will show you the way back to your hotel on the river."

I glanced at Godfrey, seeing only a top-hatted silhouette bearing a cane. He took my arm, and we once again trod slippery cobblestones through the circuitous town, seeking a site where a legend had walked only lately.

Although the distance was not great, the district was ancient and its streets unwound in a corkscrew of high narrow streets. We were lost nine times over that night, and only the sound of our own footsteps kept us company.

I remembered visiting a gypsy fortune-teller in this quarter with Irene, and light glowing through a skull-shaped lamp. I recalled palms glittering with gold and cryptic lines, and a fortune frighteningly apt given subsequent events: Irene would wed a man with the initial "G." She, her eloquent eyes still starred with visions of queenship and the King of Bohemia, thought of his middle name, Gottsreich. I knew Godfrey then, but could I have ever imagined that he would be the "G" of Irene's fortune? So although I was not superstitious, still I knew that this quarter contained an uncanny portion of occult knowledge. Might not the remnants of a Greater Age of Faith, a medieval mannequin formed from clay and the Cabbala still stalk these mean byways?

"Cheer up, Nell," Godfrey said behind me. "It is too much to expect that on our first night in Prague we shall be granted a glimpse of its resident demon."

Of course he was right. Dear Godfrey, so sensible. No wonder he made the perfect partner for Irene, who was oft so insensible, or do I mean the ungrammatical "unsensible"? I will leave it to future readers of these diaries to decipher my meaning; as for me, Godfrey's comment greatly reassured me. I was able to gaze around sagely when our guide stopped to point out the intersecting street where the Golem had first been spied in recent times.

"A cramped and narrow way," Godfrey noted. "Even a man of ordinary height would seem taller there."

He stepped into the byway as if to demonstrate. I caught my breath and stifled my warning cry. Perhaps it was blasphemy to mimic the Golem's path.

But Godfrey was correct. He stood a solid six feet high, perhaps a shade more. In the confines of that cramped street, in the dark, he looked larger, taller, more threatening.

I sighed when he stepped from the shadow into the faint light of a distant lantern. Prague had no gaslights yet to dazzle the night shadows into daylight safety, and the narrow byways formed a stingy birth canal for the vastness of the night sky. Only a few stars at a time dared twinkle sparsely down on the old city's inhabitants, like sparks glimpsed in a mud puddle.

Our guide marched on, deeper and darker into the poor quarter. Meager light seeped out of closed doors and shaded windows. Even the robust smells of the tavern district were gone. Who lived here, what they ate here, were a mystery.

I thought I heard the distant chime of crystals cascading from a skull-lamp's lantern jaw, and coins clinking in a gypsy purse. I thought I heard footsteps hard behind me. Oh—Godfrey's. I thought I heard mumbled words in a foreign tongue, and saw a clay tongue accept a small roll of mystical paper as a Papist takes the Communion wafer. . . .

Oh, my imagination was wrought up! Why was I here, with Godfrey? Irene should be treading these dreadful cobblestones, with her hard head and her steel pistol to protect her, and Godfrey. And me!

She would laugh at my fancies. Godfrey would laugh. Our guide would laugh. I would laugh when I was safe at home with Lucifer curled at my feet and Messalina guarding the garden stoop and Casanova prowling his perch in the parlor and muttering Baudelaire. . . . Yet now I heard footsteps.

> Fee, fie, foe, fum!
> I smell the blood of an English mum.
> Be she brave or be she yellow,
> I'll eat her marrow; I'm a raw fellow.

Imagination. Fancy. Fright dreams. Nightmares.

Yet the footsteps came on, and our guide stopped, hushing us with a hand gesture.

We three halted against a house front. Godfrey's hand tightened on my arm, as if he would never let go. His cane lifted. I saw its faint, lean shadow on the dimly lit cobblestones.

And then the steps. Slow. Heavy. Black as Bohemian lager in their advance. One. Two. Three. Four. Five . . . On and on, louder and louder. A shadow fell dark as pitch on the charcoal-gray canvas of the street.

It thrust to the third story, that shadow, preceding the one who cast it. I heard the rattle of chains, though I knew I would see no ghost, no Marley come to take us on a Christmas odyssey. There was no Christmas for this phantom so physically advancing toward us. Six. Seven. Eight steps. Louder, and now moans. Horrible, anguished, frustrated moans of one pent up for too long, for weeks and months and ages and eons. Nine. Ten. The steps were the slowing beats of my heart, which could only throb in time to the oncoming strides. Much slower, and it would stop, my heart, my hearing, and I would know nothing of what came toward us, and would welcome that surcease.

Eleven. Twelve. As the Apostles. Thirteen. As is unlucky.

The maker of the shadow burst into the byway we occupied. I saw—no face. A blank face, worse than a doll's, lacking all features save a general outline that I longed to call a face. No expression, but the sound . . . the low, strangled, angry, hopeless moan! The huge feet, striding like an automaton's. Fourteen. Fifteen. Sixteen. Toward us, over us. Washing us like cold waves of imagination made incarnate. The Golem. I had seen It. Heard It. Feared It. Believed in It. At that moment, faith quavered before fear. I heard a metallic rasp. Godfrey's sword. I saw a thin pin of darker shadow fall across that great, moving, mechanical Shadow.

The sword hesitated, and the Shadow shuddered on. Past. Into memory. Into disbelief. Into rationalization. Into shivers and sobs.

"It's all right, Nell," Godfrey was saying, over and over, as if to convince himself. "It's all right."

Chapter Fifteen

HIS FRENCH CONNECTION

London: *September 1889*

''**Bah!**'' **said** my friend Sherlock Holmes as he pitched the *Daily Telegraph* Agony Column into a sagging tent on the footstool. "Crime has taken a holiday. No evildoers of any imagination whatsoever remain in London. I edge more perilously close to boredom every hour."

"What of the continuing atrocities in Whitechapel?" I asked in a mild tone. Now that I was married and residing in my own establishment, I took Holmes's dramatic outbursts of despair in stride. I could afford to, since I could easily leave them behind for the more tranquil company of my dear wife Mary in peaceful Paddington.

Holmes cast himself across the chamber in one great bound to stare gloomily out of the bow window, reminding me of a housebound boy in need of suitable occupation.

"You know my opinion of that sad string of events, Watson. The Whitechapel Ripper is likely no more than a disenchanted ticket-taker seeking a bit of attention."

"He has certainly achieved it." I eyed the latest sensational illustrations in *The Illustrated Police News* with a physician's scorn for the crude anatomical renderings. "Surely the contradictory information about the method of slaughter intrigues even you. Call it mere 'butchery' if you will—God knows I saw enough of battlefield butchery in Afghanistan. Yet this Ripper fellow apparently possesses basic surgical skills. I find myself speculating on his likely history. A surgical apprentice perhaps, or a barber—"

"Soon you will be resurrecting Sweeney Todd, Watson!" Holmes twitted me from the window. Yet I saw that my fumbling theories had lit embers of analytical fire behind the banked ash-gray of his eyes. He sighed and let the curtain fall back into place, a sign that he had seen no promising, agitated figure bustling along Baker Street to beg for his help.

"I do have one paltry request to consider a puzzle at present," he added, still lost in the fog-bound view that acted as a mirror of his mood. "A communication of such insignificance that I would use it to light my pipe were I not eager for any distraction."

"Excellent," I said, lighting mine and puffing away as regularly as the daily mail train, which habit I knew drove Holmes's more quicksilver temperament to abrupt and involuntary revelations. He could never tolerate life at a rhythmically steady pace, but thrived on the unannounced disruption. His thoughts must ever be drops of water sizzling on a hot griddle, ever exploding into new and daring notions.

"This case would require a trip abroad," Holmes said a bit too casually.

"Oh?" I had never ventured abroad with him, though crises took him there now and again, and he had never asked me to do so. Now that I was married, and newly married at that, such a likelihood was even smaller.

A measuring glance darted from those lowered, lazily speculative eyes. "The matter is minor, but halfway puz-

zling. You have been reading the newspapers, Watson; anything strike your fancy that hints of oddities abroad?"

"Well—" I shook the papers in question and puffed a
few more times to teach Holmes's more mercurial temperament patience. "I find the revelation of this ring of Cuban
counterfeiters rather intriguing."

At the window, Holmes's long, lean hand waved dis-
paragingly. He did not trouble to turn. "Closer to home,
Watson."

I shook the papers until they rustled like Mary's best
taffeta petticoat, meanwhile raking the news columns in
search of some outré event likely to have piqued Holmes's
always fickle interest. Matters of great political, or even
criminal, moment seldom fascinated him; no, only the odd,
telling fact or detail drew his formidable intelligence into its
keenest state. As the most minuscule physical clue could
solve a case for him, so the most trivial newspaper item
might set him off as swiftly as blaring hunt horns trigger a
pack of baying dogs.

I grasped at another peculiar item. "Here is a curious
report! A medieval monster prowls old Prague, a Jewish
demon called a Golem. Several eyewitnesses swear to seeing the creature on more than one occasion in the past few
months—most recently an English barrister only last week.
The report offers no name, but if an Englishman claims to
have seen the thing—"

Holmes made an impolite sound. "You know my opinion of what passes for the occult, Watson: fodder for the
foolish. There is more seen on heaven and earth than has
ever inhabited it. I would no more track this phantasm of
a Golem than I would try to calculate the number of archangels doing a mazurka on the head of a hatpin. Does
nothing in the multitudinous news from the globe over
reach out and catch you by the lapels, dear fellow? Has all
the earth become infected with the London malaise, so that
decent people may now walk in a stultifying paradise free

of crime and punishment? Perhaps I shall be forced to pursuing archangels and phantasms, after all."

"See here, Holmes, I can't imagine what blasted event might pertain to your request for aid!"

He turned to display the sliver of his smile. "When in search of the bizarre, one can never go wrong by looking to France."

I ran my eyes down the columns, hunting a French date-line—and found one, Paris. "Hmm. Murder. And then later a second murder. That might intrigue you more than the commonplace one-and-only murder, even if the Ripper's multiple slaughters repel you. Two young seamstresses at the House of Worth were struck down by a pair of shears amid a great number of their sister sewers. Is this it?"

For answer Holmes hied gleefully to the desk, lifted some pages of notepaper and tossed them into my lap on his return to the brooding post at the window.

I lifted the pale blue paper, surprised to find the writing in English. Holmes detested it when I skipped ahead of any logical progression—and no doubt lost vital clues—but I turned first to the last page to read the signature.

"Charles Frederick Worth! Holmes, this fellow is some-thing of a sensation himself. Is he not the man-milliner whose clothes all the women are mad about? Even Mary, modest mate that she is in her manner of dress and con-duct, has remarked on him."

Holmes clapped his hands together in sudden relief. "At last. A connoisseur."

"Hardly, Holmes. It's merely that a fellow can't be mar-ried these days without hearing a bit about this or that fashion."

"You are a veritable expert compared to my abysmal—and happy—state of ignorance on the subject of women's dress." He wheeled from the window. "The trail is appall-ingly ice-cold, Watson. The first woman was murdered two weeks ago; the second an entire five days before this. Quite an impossible commission, and yet . . . well, read the letter,

Watson. Perhaps you will see between the same lines that I did."

"I doubt it, Holmes. I am always the last to know anything."

He smiled again, that quick, stabbing yet charming smile that he reached for as rarely as another man might for a dagger. "But you are the first to tell it. How go your little stories?"

"Well enough." I disliked discussing my attempts to write up Holmes's cases as much as he loathed delving into areas that held no interest for him, such as women's fashions. I let my eyes concentrate on deciphering Mr. Worth's fussy yet sweeping hand, and looked up shortly.

"He mentions a relationship—"

"Yes, yes. The French branch of my family is related to his wife, Marie, who was born Vernet. A peculiar fix, Watson, for a man with as few relations as I have, to be called to the aid of a French shirttail. Odder still that she has a famous English husband on top of it—! Read on."

I did so, absorbing the distress that Mr. Worth and his wife obviously felt at the murders of two young seamstresses among the several hundred they employed. One could not help but wish to aid a pair who took responsibility for their workers to such heart. And then there was the gruesome nature of the deaths: both young women stabbed in the back by a pair of shears during the workday, yet no one had witnessed the bloody deeds.

I turned to the third page, and sat up to attention. I glanced again at Holmes, seeing the same slight, thin stiletto of a smile.

"Well, Watson. Have you reached the same conclusion that I have?"

"You refer to this 'American client, a woman known for having a way with delicate matters'? Apparently, the Worths called upon an amateur inquiry agent to investigate the first murder."

"At the suggestion of 'Alice Heine, Duchess of Richelieu,' a most prominently placed lady and a great patron of the opera. Does that not set any bells ringing in your cranium, Watson?"

"Naturally, I can think of only one woman bold enough to pass herself off as a problem solver of that sort—the woman you encountered in the matter of the King of Bohemia's photograph—but Irene Adler is dead, Holmes."

"Presumed dead. There is a vital difference between that and the evidence of one's own eyes. You know my position on that issue as well."

"Holmes, you cannot persist in seeing this woman behind every forward hussy who takes matters into her own hands!"

"No? What if I were to tell you that Irene Adler is not only alive, but that she meddles in mysterious matters with irritating frequency; that I have seen her face-to-face since the purported death of herself and her husband."

"You would say such things?"

"What if I were to say that she has stood in these very rooms in other guise, before your very eyes?"

"Holmes." I was momentary speechless before I noticed the challenging glitter in his eyes. "Then I should have many things to say, as a friend and a physician, among them that you were indulging overmuch in the seven-percent solution of cocaine you so rely upon. I should have to say that your use treads perilously close to addiction and delusion."

"Should you, Watson?" The glitter was gone, in its place a weary smile. "Fear not. I will not say such foolishness. You and I are far too rational for outright nonsense. As well say that the Golem performs the Empire waltz through the streets of Prague, or that Chinamen drink apple cider instead of tea. No, we will keep the planets in their courses and the stars fixed to their accustomed constellations. We will each see Irene Adler in our own way, I fear, and mine is to imagine that she is not dead. Is that delusion, Watson?"

"Only if you pursue her."

"The lady is married, whether dead or alive, and I pursue truth, not anything less. We will agree to disagree as to her state, just as we agree to disagree on the placement and nature of the wounds you received at Maiwand. Such differences salt an association, and ours is certainly well cured by now. And, finally, has Mr. Worth's letter sufficiently piqued your interest to bestir you for the first time from England's fresh-scrubbed stoop into murkier waters? Will you hop the puddle of the Channel and come with me to Paris?"

"Is that what this is about, Holmes? All this chatter of Irene Adler was a mere ruse to prod my curiosity and enlist my aid? You needn't go to such lengths. My practice can spare me for a week or so, and Mary will approve so long as I bring her back a trinket from this House of Worth, if anything to be found there is affordable."

"Oh, if we find who has killed these two young seamstresses, I imagine much will become affordable there. I thank you, Watson. There are few arenas in which I feel at a loss, but this French factory where women's clothing is concocted is one of them. I predict that I will sorely need the advice of an experienced voice in matters of women and fashion before we are done."

"Then I am your man," I said, "to the best of the ability that any mere male can have on that demanding subject . . . and providing that Mary will give me leave to go."

Holmes fluttered his eyelids in mute complaint, but forbore comment. He then headed for the drawer with the seven-percent solution. I, of course, could not object now.

Chapter Sixteen

AN ENGAGEMENT AT
THE PALACE

Why is it that expeditions to sterling civic institutions are never as fascinating as jaunts into the seamier side of whatever city one is visiting?

Whatever the reason for this phenomenon, it accounts for the fact that my diary entry on Godfrey's and my mission to the Bank of Bohemia is much shorter than my description of the previous evening's outing to the appalling and notorious drinking establishment, U Fleků. Even to write the name the next day is to evoke a thrill of exotic distaste. Perhaps I am simply overtired from describing at length the degradations of that cavernous place and its denizens, not to mention Godfrey's and my later encounter with the supposed Golem of Prague.

"Well, Nell," Godfrey began as we set out from our hotel the following morning, enunciating the words with the same relish as an actor rendering "How now, brown cow" for the edification of elocutionists everywhere. "Well, Nell," he repeated in the same rolling tone, "now that we are again safe and sound in the light of day, what do you think of our chance meeting with the Golem?"

"I think that if we are to resort to reason rather than rank superstition we would understand that the creature we saw was some drunken brute on a rampage, no doubt a regular client of U Fleků and its ilk."

He did not disagree. "Do you not find it odd that we should chance upon such an apparition, however ordinary our diagnosis, on our very first night in Prague?"

"Given the number of beer gardens I have observed now that I am staying in the city proper rather than at the palace, I should say that our chances of encountering a wild, careening drunkard are extremely high at any time in any quarter."

He nodded again, but said no more.

I had resolved to enjoy the day, fair as London days seldom are, and as Paris days are far too often to be appreciated. The vivid sunlight brought into knife-sharp relief architectural fancies that garnished the city's Baroque buildings like lacework formed by stone and shadow.

Godfrey had consulted the notorious travel guide for more than the unfortunate directions to U Fleků, and held forth on Prague's reputation as a mystical city of many faces, compared at various times by various poets and pundits to Athens, to Venice, Florence, Rome and other Italian cities, even to Jerusalem. His comparisons did not persuade me to a desire for visiting any of those locations.

Yet once we were inside the Bank of Bohemia's imposing stone exterior, we could have been within any civilized metropolis's most trusted institution. We glided across ice-smooth pale marble floors while green marble pillars and engraved brass grillwork slid by our wondering eyes. In short order, we were shown into the huge, cherrywood-paneled office of a high bank official named Mr. Werner and ensconced on tufted red leather chairs.

Godfrey was offered a cigar. I was barely offered a considering glance.

Our host was a stout, middle-aged man with a single lock of unconvincingly black hair drawn across an otherwise bare pate as polished as any marble pillar.

He told us, in impeccable English, that Baron Alphonse

had opened a significant line of credit for "your needs"—
he looked exclusively at Godfrey—with the Bank of Bohemia, and that we were invited to an important reception at
Prague Castle on Friday, which was only two days away.
Godfrey was to call upon Mr. Werner for any needs that
might arise.

Godfrey thanked him and suggested that our demands
would be modest. I thought him optimistic, for Irene had
not yet arrived, and her demands were never modest. I
began to worry about what I would wear to the palace
reception, even though I was a person of no importance
and nobody would care what I wore so long as it did not
disgrace the company. I wondered if a Liberty silk gown
would be considered disgraceful in Bohemia.

The banker rose, presented Godfrey with documents
allowing him to extract money from the Rothschild account and with a fat cream parchment envelope that gave
my heart and memory a nasty knock. I glimpsed the ornate
von Ormstein seal on the back, and realized anew on what
perilous ground I would again intrude, and this time more
was at stake than my friend's romantic future!

Godfrey sensed my subdued mood on the stroll back to
our hotel.

"Well, Nell," he began, "are you surfeited with Bohemia
already?"

I tried not to set my teeth. It is indeed unfortunate when
one's nickname rhymes with a common introductory
word. At least no one can play the same trick with "Penelope," with the possible exception of Oscar Wilde, should
he set his mind and his Oxford classical education to it.

"Well, Godfrey," I replied, "I have already seen the
purported Golem and can report that a fraud. If we can
discover whatever nonsense is affecting royal politics as
quickly, we will be home before Casanova and the rest even
miss us."

Godfrey smiled. "I fear that politics are never as plain
and accessible as reputed monsters. Do not underestimate

the delicacy of our mission at the palace reception. There we shall begin to learn how the land lies, and there I will first lay eyes on the King of Bohemia. It should," he added, tightening his grip on his walking stick, "be a most provocative evening."

I instantly realized that I would likely also see the Queen of Bohemia, who might remember me from her interview with Irene at Maison Worth and blurt out some betraying comment!

"Amen," I said to Godfrey's last observation, so fervently that he eyed me oddly, although he said nothing.

We each had our own private mission in Prague, ones that had nothing to do with Rothschild interests, political maneuvering or monstrous stirrings of any nature other than ordinary human passions.

That Friday evening the slow-setting sun made Prague Castle's turreted silhouette into a harsh black border for the firmament of windows blazing brightly down on the town.

Our hired carriage climbed the long hill to the summit. Within it, Godfrey looked as splendid as a duke in a new evening suit courtesy of the Rothschild tailor. A man's evening dress in this unimaginative age is a rigorous uniform: white tie, shirt and vest; cutaway black coat and tails, black trousers. I am so ignorant of male tailoring that I cannot put my finger on the difference between an ordinary suit and one from a master tailor, save to say that this evening Godfrey looked at least the social peer of the King of Bohemia, if not of the Czar of All the Russias, or perhaps even of the Prince of Wales.

I had no choice but to wear the blue Liberty silk Irene had bought me on the sly. While Irene always went equipped for the most lavish of formal occasions as well as for rough-and-ready danger, I was always caught by surprise in both cases, and must make do with something halfway appropriate. At least I wore long white kid gloves of softest Parisian leather and tasteful ivory satin slippers that Irene had persuaded me to buy for "the small soirée."

There was nothing small about the train of carriages our conveyance joined as we crested the hill to face a blaze of exterior torches. Night had fallen as if cued to do so. We were aided from our carriage by footmen wearing powdered wigs and knee breeches, and joined a throng in being gently steered through the massive entry hall and down imposing passages to the reception chamber.

I had never entered the castle by the public way before; when Godfrey bent a mutely inquiring gaze on me, I could only shake my head. How useless I was already proving to be! Out of my element, experiencing the pangs of unhappy memory, I deeply regretted that we had allowed ourselves to be seduced by the Rothschild commission, that I had allowed Irene's obsession with the Queen of Bohemia's confession to overrule my native caution and sense.

Godfrey was navigating these candlelit halls as if to the manner born, but, then, barristers are born actors at heart, whereas a typewriter-girl is only a nervous supernumerary for life. Our progress had clogged into a crowd: we were stalled before a high double doorway, waiting our turn . . . to be announced!

Godfrey presented the heavy cream card to the footman at the door, who passed it in turn to a tall, stout man in puce satin and a powdered wig. This worthy struck a rococo staff upon the marble floor and bellowed our names so loudly that I hardly recognized them as they echoed in the upper vastness and bounced among the dazzling glass chandeliers alive with light and melting candlewax.

He announced our true names. My grip on Godfrey's forearm grew tigerish. "My name . . . should never have been used. The King and his family have met me."

Godfrey's reassuring hand covered my gloved fingers. "I believe that the official has pronounced it 'Foxleigh.' Don't worry, Nell; we will hardly cause a stir in all this crowd."

I hoped that he was right. As we strolled into the vast chamber, I recognized the decor from one of my ambles through the castle. Irene would know and remember every inch of the place. Despite our travels to Monaco and our brief time in the palaces of the wealthy and titled, for me to tell one palace from another was like distinguishing lavishly iced wedding cakes from each other. They were all huge and overwhelming, and it made one's mouth purse to see so much sweetness; to know each one was impossible.

Godfrey led me to a gilt-framed chair against the wall and went to fetch some refreshment. While I sat there, thankfully ignored and fanning my heated cheeks, I discovered that the steward's voice was clear and audible throughout the chamber, however garbled it seemed on the threshold.

I wondered at Godfrey's calm in letting his name suffer such a public bandying about. Surely Sherlock Holmes had confided to the King the identity of the man whom Irene had married in haste before escaping them both. Or did Godfrey *want* the King to know of his own existence and presence? Did I underestimate the unspoken motives he might have for this ill-fated faring to Bohemia? Was Godfrey as curious to meet Irene's onetime royal suitor as Irene was to find out why her former pursuer ignored the wife he had obtained at the sacrifice of Irene and his own deepest inclinations?

My head began to ache, no doubt an effect of the extremely silly arrangement of flowers and pearl beads I had affixed above my right temple because Irene had declared it went wonderfully with the Liberty gown. Inside the supple kid gloves, my palms were growing intemperately wet. At that moment, I would have rather dared another encounter with the muffled, lurching being of the byway than with either of the crowned heads present tonight.

"The freshest spring water!" Godfrey proclaimed, returning with two brimming flutes. His glass bubbled with the pale saffron effervescence of champagne, I noticed. "Shall we take a walk around the room?"

I stood reluctantly, studying strangers as if they were snakes that might turn and show me a familiar face, that might, in turn, find me all too familiar. But the crush permitted not even a mite to turn; after a few minutes of uninterrupted progress I began to calm. After all, who would pay any attention to an obscure British barrister abroad—or his secretary—at such a elegant affair?

"Mr. Norton! Miss . . . er . . . Mufflee." The banker, Werner, stood before us, recognizable only for the black serpent of hair bisecting his pate. "If you will remain here, the King and Queen will pass shortly. His Royal Highness is most anxious to meet you."

Godfrey started as my fingers clawed into the impeccable wool of his sleeve. He looked down, showing the same utter calm under pressure that Irene had made her signature.

"Do not worry, Nell," he assured me. "This is the moment we have been waiting for."

"But I have met the King before! I have sat at the same table with him, shared the same sitting room and library. He *must* recognize me."

"Nonsense. You have changed a great deal from your Bohemian days, don't you realize that? That long-ago Miss Huxleigh would never have worn a Liberty gown."

"Oh." I eyed my blue silk form downward. It did look alien.

"Nor that smashingly fetching hair ornament," Godfrey added with an encouraging smile.

"You really think so?" I asked, astonished.

I was so engaged in pondering why a gentleman should notice, much less compliment, such a ridiculous item that I hardly noticed when the banker popped back and presented us with great pomp to a couple that had paused before us.

Oh! While Godfrey managed a proper bow from the waist, I dithered between a bob and curtsy and produced an ungainly duck of my head.

Oh, indeed. There he stood. The King . . . he did look every inch a king, no denying that. Golden hair glinted like gilt on his head, eyebrows and mustache in the chandelier light. He stood so tall and regal that the nearest chandelier gleamed behind his leonine head like a crystal halo, although I was not so utterly undone that I could conceive of King Willie meriting a heavenly halo in any lifetime. His uniformed, royal-red chest glistened with royal-blue ribbons of rank and ornate gold medals and stars of office.

Beside him, Godfrey seemed . . . smaller, plain. Dwarfed.

And beside the King, at his side, stood the Queen, even more diminished—a sad, golden spaniel of a woman with silky hair and huge, humid eyes and a deferential chin. Daisy-yellow silk and silver netting—I saw at a glance now the unmistakable mark of a Worth creation—could produce no sparkling, sunny effect vivid enough to counter the sad confusion that Queen Clotilde carried like a crown of thorns, despite the diamond tiara glittering on her satin-blond head.

"Werner," the King commanded in English, and the banker jerked like a puppet. "I am confident that you will do all you can to assist Mr. Norton. We are most pleased that the House of Rothschild shows interest in underwriting the affairs of Bohemia, and will extend every courtesy to its emissary here."

"Certainly, Your Royal Highness." The man bowed low, the better to display *his* ridiculous ornamental hair.

Now that business greetings had been made, the King's attention then turned to such social pleasantries as he could muster from such a pinnacle of perfection. He looked down—and down—at me. My fan paused in midflutter, pasting itself to my bosom. The King eyed me with regal disinterest. "And this, Mr. Norton, is your lady wife?"

I gasped, wondering what Mr. Norton's true lady wife would make of such a misapprehension.

"Alas, no, Your Royal Highness," Godfrey answered with smooth, sincere regret. "This lady is my secretary only, but a paragon of efficiency. I quite depend upon her impeccable memory."

Mr. Werner, single carats of sweat beading his bald head, quickly consulted a card in his curved, gloved hand. Apparently he had decided that ignoring me yesterday had not been wise.

"Miss Huxleigh," he declared by way of introduction, pronouncing my name emphatically—and correctly.

The King regarded me. I cringed within but regarded him back, wishing that I were a cat looking at a Queen.

Next to me, I sensed Godfrey doing that very thing with lightning glances. The King did not notice him eagerly eyeing the Queen, which was very good for Godfrey.

Instead, the King stared directly at me, which was very bad for Penelope Huxleigh. The Queen stirred under Godfrey's scrutiny, then looked at me to avoid it. A vague flicker livened her sorrowful eyes.

"Most charmed, Miss Huxleigh," said the King, his eyes as blank of recognition as if I had been introduced as Miss Eel-Peeler of St. Elfing. He was already moving on and swept the Queen with him, but she twisted her head over her milk-white shoulder to give me a last quizzical, hopeful glance.

"She cannot hold a candle to Irene," Godfrey whispered fiercely in my ear. "The King was a madman to think that Irene would consent to be his mistress while he married *that!*"

"The Queen may be kindhearted. . . ."

Godfrey snorted indignantly. "Not much recommendation for the marriage bed. And, you see that the King did not recognize you or your name!"

"Perhaps I underestimate how overlookable I am. The King was never one to acknowledge servants. No doubt he took me for one. What did you think of him?"

Godfrey's vehemence died swiftly. He glanced down at his white-gloved hands as if wishing for a walking stick, then spread them in an empty gesture.

"He is indeed larger than life," Godfrey said dully in a tone of giving the Devil his due. "Robust. Barbarically splendid. Wealthy. Aristocratic. A Prince Charming out of an operetta. I had hoped for less."

I sighed so heavily that a passing gentleman paused to ogle my neckline, a new experience for me. Before I could contemplate my reaction to it, a voice thundered behind us, too imperious to ignore. The steward was announcing a new guest.

"Sarah Wilde of Kent, Lady Sherlock," came the clarion call.

Godfrey and I froze like a marzipan couple atop a wedding cake. We did not regard each other, nor did we turn to face the double doors behind us where another guest was making a fashionably late—and therefore unforgettable—entrance.

"I believe," said Godfrey between his teeth, with commendable aplomb, "that the King's memory is about to receive an even more formidable testing."

"So," I replied, between mine, "are we."

"And," boomed the steward, "her sister, the Honorable Allegra Stanhope."

"And," I added privately to Godfrey, "so is Irene."

Chapter Seventeen

SHERLOCKIAN SCANDALS

In moments, Godfrey and I were confronting a sea of faces. It became obvious that we were the only individuals in the ballroom not transfixed by the newcomer. With a mutually resigned glance, we braced ourselves and turned in unison.

We faced what could have been a scene from a play, or perhaps a grand opera.

Irene stood alone center stage, framed by the rococo double doors through which she had made her entrance. (With Irene, it is never any wonder that the noun "entrance" is spelled the same as the verb, if not accented on the same syllable.) Irene's entrances always managed to entrance. At least I assumed it was she! My eyes told me quite differently. Lady Sherlock (oh, odious pseudonym!) seemed taller than Irene, even thinner. Her hair was a glistening black arrangement in which diamond drops sparkled like dew on wet tar. I had never seen dyed hair of such a vibrant black hue before and began to doubt my identification . . . except that Milady Sherlock was attired in Irene's coq-feather Worth gown—and how it shone, like the iridescent ebony-tissue cloak-lining of Night itself, drawing all into its deep, secret, enveloping darkness! The

Tiffany diamond corsage slashed diagonally across that feathered bodice like a blinding-white sword-stroke of utter luxury set against a black taffeta background.

Only later did I notice the slight, brown-haired girl in ivory satin standing behind Irene, eyeing the gathered throng like a shy but crumb-hungry wren.

Silence held for a long minute as the guests wondered who Irene was and absorbed her extravagant appearance. When she had enjoyed enough adulation, speculation and envy, she unfurled her black ostrich feather fan with a snap of her wrist. The clack of the fan's unfolding tortoiseshell sticks echoed to the chamber's farthest corners.

So a conductor might have struck a downward blow with his baton, signaling a symphony to begin. Chattering voices resumed again as one, producing a roar like convivial cannon. Glasses tinkled like chandelier chimes. Air circulated again, and a thousand breaths eased out as one.

"A damnable pity that I have never seen her upon the stage," Godfrey murmured beside me.

He seemed unaware that he had used an unsuitable expression for the presence of a lady, but perhaps Godfrey had forgotten me as utterly as everyone else there had. Who could deny Irene's flair for the dramatic gesture? Not I, though I feared this trait would ensnare her, for there was no mistaking it, either, and the King of Bohemia *had* seen her upon the stage.

The next pressing question was whether the King of Bohemia would approach the mysterious guest or she would pay her courtesies to him first.

I watched his golden head bobbing above other, less lofty heads, even topping the ladies' wafting aigrettes. Its course, however circuitous, made for the Dark Lady who moved through that gay mélange of gowns as a black swan parts the pale water lilies with its stately, self-absorbed passage.

"We dare not go too near, lest we give away the game," I warned myself as much as Godfrey.

He agreed in a soft murmur, but guided me closer nevertheless. He may have missed Irene's operatic performances, but he was not about to miss her next encounter with the King of Bohemia!

Still, we kept to the fringes of the crowd, which gave way to Irene as it would to the Wicked Fairy Godmother at Sleeping Beauty's christening, with a nervous respect. She was, in fact, the uninvited one, but she had come despite it, on her own terms: back to Bohemia.

Allegra, who kept to Irene's rear like a dutiful daughter, or niece or sister or handmaiden, saw us suddenly. Her face brightened, then she doused her natural excitement with a bushel of false disinterest. We four must not speak until we were alone.

Yet seeing us had reassured Allegra, I noticed. New to Irene and her escapades, Allegra must have undergone a tremendous shock during this past week of travel and subterfuge.

I really cannot say who came round to whom at last. I only know that the rulers of Bohemia and my friend Irene Adler came face-to-face in a large circle of cleared marble floor, as might would-be dance partners or duelists. Allegra at Irene's rear could have played a shy second, and the royal couple were backed by a glittering host of guests and subjects.

Both the King and Queen had seen Irene as Irene, the Queen most recently. I admired my friend's theatrical talents—and she was a past mistress of disguise if not of kings—but could even she hoodwink those who knew her . . . ?

Irene swept into a lavish, low curtsy, fit for Windsor and its Widow, but unnecessary for foreign monarchs. She said nothing. Her face betrayed no emotion. Yet I saw a subtle mockery in that supposed subservience. Irene could never look properly subdued.

She was upright as swiftly as she had bowed, so the curtsy seemed an illusion. The King and Queen were left looking as if they had neglected to offer her a fit counter-courtesy.

"Lady Sherlock," the King said slowly, as if tasting the foreign syllables. Not so foreign! He had employed Sherlock Holmes, after all. Oh, Irene, must you always cut risk so thin? "I am not familiar—" he began.

"I should hope not, Your Majesty," Irene intoned in perfect uppercrust accents. She sounded more British than the Queen. "I have not been about much until recently. I am, you see—" Her expansive gesture, hands and fan spreading, indicated her gorgeous yet dramatic attire. "—a recent widow."

He nodded as slowly as he spoke, as a man in a dream or a nightmare, or one who dreamed that he might meet such a woman in a nightmare. "A widow, like your Queen Victoria. I am sorry."

"Thank you, Your Majesty." She smiled demurely as she turned to Queen Clothilde. "I am enchanted to meet Your Royal Highness, and to see your lovely city of Prague."

"Thank you," the Queen parroted, unaware. She too spoke in slow syllables, as if tangled in the heavy black cloak of Irene's presence. "Lady Sherlock, Prague welcomes you and your . . . sister?"

Allegra stepped forward like the good, well-spoken child I had briefly had a hand in rearing her to be. She curtsied most docilely. If Irene was the Red Queen gone black, Allegra made an adorable Alice in Wonderland.

"Yes, Your Royal Highness. I am Allegra Stanhope."

"How kind of you, child, to accompany your sister in her bereavement, and how fortunate she is to have a cheerful, young boon companion like yourself," the Queen said in a wistful but stately monotone.

Irene and Allegra exchanged the kind of glance that Godfrey and I had employed before their arrival.

"Yes, Your Royal Highness," Allegra said gravely.

Irene only inclined her head, as if signaling the royal couple to be on their way rather than accepting their taking leave of her.

King and Queen continued their royal progress around the room, while Irene made her own regal advance to the refreshments table, apparently at the behest of Allegra. Godfrey and I watched them go, bemused.

"You are English, is that not true?" an imperious accented voice suggested behind us.

We turned to find a tall, russet-haired woman attired in deep sapphire blue encrusted with gilt and silver thread. Ordinarily I would have found her elegance overwhelming, but Irene's entrance had put all other women in eclipse. A certain sour expression that marred this stranger's otherwise lovely face suggested that she, too, realized this.

"English indeed," Godfrey said with another elegant bow. There is nothing like arguing before the bar to imbue a man with a courtly manner. In this Godfrey matched every actor on the London stage, and this stood him in splendid stead in elevated company. "I am Godfrey Norton, a barrister who represents the Rothschild interests, and this is my secretary and colleague, Miss Penelope Huxleigh."

"Miss Huxleigh, Mr. Norton," the stranger murmured, although her eyes looked restlessly beyond us. "I am Tatyana," she declared haughtily, as if the one name should suffice. "Do you know this Wilde woman?"

For a moment we were both nonplussed into silence, not realizing that the woman was using Irene's false surname, rather than an adjective.

"Lady Sherlock," I supplied in the nick of time, to remind Godfrey of whom this Tatyana spoke.

"Yes," our interrogator said. "This Lady Sherlock appears to enjoy the limelight. What do you know of her?"

"Nothing," said I, too quickly.

"Very little," Godfrey added smoothly. "I have only heard that she is quite wealthy, now that she is a widow."

"Wealthy and a widow. A potent combination." Tatyana did not look pleased. "She has certainly made a great impression on the King."

"Perhaps," I put in, "he is in an impressionable position."

The woman looked blood-brown daggers at me. "All monarchs are in an impressionable position. It is to their interest that they know who seeks to impress them, that is all. Is she an adventuress, this Lady Sherlock?"

I was struck speechless at this bald attack on Irene's character, even under a pseudonym, but Godfrey replied quickly.

"All beautiful women are adventuresses, are they not, Madame Tatyana?"

For an instant those restless maroon eyes paused on Godfrey, but I do not think they truly saw him. They returned to the distant form of the King. Or the Queen. Or Irene. "Perhaps. I am Russian," she declared in a kind of non sequitur. "I am dangerous no matter what role I play. You will excuse me—"

She was gone in a flounce of flashing embroidery.

Godfrey smiled ruefully. "Irene has accomplished exactly what she intended. She has attracted all the wrong kind of attention. I would not be surprised if the Golem himself crashed through that window and asked her to waltz."

"Oh, Godfrey, what a notion! The day that Irene and the Golem of Prague go for a gallop around the room, I shall . . . I shall—" I could think of no eventuality dire enough.

"Please do not do anything foolish, dear Nell," Godfrey advised, taking my arm. "Irene has cornered that proclivity."

He led me to the refreshment table, where he plied me with anonymous abominations. Despite his distracting maneuver, I saw what he saw that night: a subtle social gavotte of heads pale and vivid—of the blond King and Queen weaving in and out of the crowds; of Irene's bold black in pursuit or evasion, and of the redheaded Russian woman's advance and retreat; of the entire assembly fading to bland beige and only those signal colors active on the chessboard of this occasion.

And Godfrey and I? Were we bland, faceless pawns? Or bishops in disguise awaiting our chance to hopscotch across the playing field and make our mark?

I can only describe that entire evening as odious. The sole shaft of hope was the wholesome figure of young Allegra reveling in the entire sordid scene as if it were a mad tea party and she were impromptu hostess.

Godfrey and I returned to the Europa in silence, both mulling the evening's disturbing implications.

He must of course weigh the worth of his wife's charade in the Rothschild quest. I mused upon the many risks of recognition Irene and I faced that night, and of how we had sallied through them all in good order. Had I truly changed as much as Godfrey said?

If so, I was an adventuress as well, because of my deceptive appearance. Had Irene truly deceived both King and Queen? Were the royal pair so unobservant? Perhaps they were, if they thought they viewed inferior beings. Do not all royalty possess myopia in that respect? That may be why they are the easiest of all to dupe.

At the hotel, Godfrey insisted that I join him in his sitting room after he had paused below to order a magnum of champagne.

"I do not imbibe, Godfrey," I reminded him when I arrived after freshening my toilette, and saw the massive, cloth-wrapped bottle reclining like a swaddled infant in its cradling stand.

"No," he said, grinning, "but Irene expects a postperformance celebration, and I believe that Allegra is not averse to a bit of bubbly now that she is free of the family mansion."

"You expect them to repair here?"

"I expect them to retreat here, boasting of their victories on the reception room floor. I arranged accommodation for them at the Europa, but not under Irene's proper—" He lifted a dark eyebrow. "—improper name. I corrected that omission just now. No doubt you will wish to satisfy yourself that Miss Allegra has sustained no damage during her long journey with an adventuress."

"Allegra, yes! Poor lamb . . . she looked quite bedazzled by the goings-on."

"Trust me, Nell. She will do more bedazzling than she will be bedazzled in not very long. Well! What did you think of the King and Queen?"

"What I always thought of them. I am no fickle sail to flirt with every wind. He is pompous, insufferably self-sure and will run to fat in middle age. She is . . . a sad creature, saddled with that arrogant man, but of course no rival to Irene in any real sense. Blue blood hardly can compete with—"

"Sheer gall. You are right, Nell. Irene has outfaced them all, and they none the wiser. Or are they? Has our Lady Sherlock deceived them as thoroughly as she thinks? Pride goeth before a fall, and Irene has much pride to tumble from."

"She has earned it," I said stoutly, or stiffly. "Still, I abhor seeing her back on this blasted ground. If the Rothschild commission were not so . . . generous—"

"And Irene not so curious—"

"Why do you say that?"

"It is obvious, Nell." He flipped up his coattails to sit upon a side chair. "Irene does not give a fig for the Rothschild commission. She's rather attached to the Tiffany corsage, but she could forgo even that in an instant. What she is insatiably curious about is the King and his new Queen. Even you could see that. A child could."

"Godfrey. I resent your comparing me to a child."

He smiled sadly. "Sometimes you are, you know. I loathe pricking your illusion, but it is likely—no, certain—

that Irene is here in Bohemia on a quest into her past, not on Rothschild business."

"Godfrey, you shock me!"

"I don't mean to, but I must be a realist. You know little of the world, Nell. It is your greatest charm. Why do you think I came here, to this forsaken corner of the world, in my borrowed evening dress, with my crippled cane, which is also a sword, all at the boon of the Rothschilds? I must either come and play the game, or be left behind. I much prefer an active role in my own doom."

"Godfrey! How can you say such things! Irene would never abandon you. Or me. She has her own peculiar morality, it is true, but I have never known her to hurt another soul who did not deserve it."

"Who deserves the hurt of an imperious integrity?" he asked rhetorically. "Her integrity will be the death of us, mark my word. I understand that she would do nothing to hurt us, but neither will anything stop her in her pursuit of the truth. And thus can she hurt us indirectly."

A discreet knock at the chamber door prevented me from replying.

I opened to admit a more fantastic figure than we had seen at the reception. Irene's black evening cloak was swirling folds of damask velvet foaming at hem and throat with midnight ostrich feathers. A black net scarf sprinkled with jet, diamante and tiny feathers covered her falsely raven hair, and became something of a redundancy. Behind her flickered the pale mothlike shadow of Allegra in a white mohair evening cape.

Irene swooped over the threshold, a hundred ostrich feathers trembling with every step.

"Brava!" Godfrey declaimed, greeting her with a brimming flute of champagne. "Even I barely recognized you."

"Really!" she exclaimed in delight. "That is indeed the true test of disguise."

I saw and heard no more, for impetuous Allegra had

launched herself at me in a fit of girlish greeting that was as surprising as it was uncalled for.

"Oh, dear Miss Huxleigh! It is so nice to acknowledge you at last! We have had such a jolly journey from Paris. Most exciting. Is that really a Liberty silk? You are becoming quite, quite advanced in your dress. I did so long to speak to you and—" She turned to include Godfrey in her enthusiasm, and I looked for him as well.

He and Irene had twined arms to sip from each other's champagne flutes and stood gazing into each other's eyes with an exclusivity that left both Allegra and I feeling like an unwanted audience.

She had the wit to lower her voice on her next outburst. "Mr. Norton looks divinely dashing as well! Of course, he always did, as did dear Uncle Quentin, only distance and time do seem to make men more . . . interesting. Why is that so, Miss Huxleigh?"

"I believe that the change is in the observer, not the observed."

"Not always! Look at Uncle Quentin. A foreign spy, fancy that. Or rather, a spy on foreign soil. There. But we are spies, too. Irene has made that plain. What a fascinating creature she is." Allegra flicked a wistful glance to my oblivious friends, lost in champagne and other self-indulgences that it was better not to regard too long. "I had expected to be jealous, but there is no point, is there?"

"No," I agreed heartily, having never dared to cherish ambitions in that direction.

"At least," Allegra went on in resignation, "I can learn a great deal from her."

"I would not model myself upon her too much, Miss Allegra."

"Whyever not? She is a paragon of wit and daring and fashion. I pine to grow old enough to wear black and drip with jewels as she does and have gentlemen—even kings!— mooning over me. Did you see those diamonds—!?"

"You look more charming in white and pale colors, my dear. And mooning men swiftly become either maudlin or boring. And I not only have seen those diamonds, but I carried them to Prague."

I led her to a pair of chairs, as Irene and Godfrey seemed likely to stand and sip and stare indefinitely.

"You did! *You* were the guardian of the diamonds?"

"Certainly. Of course, Godfrey was there should some unpleasantry arise. By the way, how did Irene retrieve them for tonight's affair?"

"You and Godfrey had already left for the castle when we arrived at the hotel, so Irene whisked into your chamber and fetched them."

"How could she whisk into my chamber? The door was locked."

"Not after she picked it."

"Picked it? That is a new trick. With what?"

"A hatpin," Allegra said ecstatically as she sat. "Irene says that a good, strong hatpin is a woman's greatest glory and useful for ever so many things, including stabbing Mashers in crowds."

"Gracious! She is telling you a great deal that she should not. A properly brought up young woman would never be in a position to repel Mashers because she would never be anywhere, alone, where she might encounter such an individual. And you must not call her 'Irene.'"

"Why not? She told me to."

"Still, you must not. She is your elder and a married lady. You owe her the respect of a proper title."

Chastened, Allegra's tender brown head bowed. Then she looked up with a gleam in her bright eyes. "Then, since you are unmarried, I may call you 'Nell'?"

"Marital status has nothing to do with respect between generations! You may call me 'Miss Huxleigh.'"

"I am twenty!" Allegra burst out irrelevantly. She forced her clasped gloved hands to her lap, a much-advocated posture for proper young ladies that I was pleased to see her remember. "And I am so tired of crossing my feet at the ankles and twiddling my thumbs in the drawing room. It was only because Mama feared I had gone into a decline after the adventure of the summer that she permitted me to travel to Paris. I was escorted by my second-cousin Broderick." She pronounced the name with a pucker, then brightened. "But he brought me to . . . Mrs. Norton's doorstep. It was quite all right after that."

"I am sure that it was quite not all right. You must understand, Miss Allegra, that your arrival at Neuilly was not properly announced and rather awkward. Your presence here is against everybody's better sense, but we did not wish to send you home in disgrace. So you will refrain from being seen and heard in Prague, and keep yourself out of dangerous intrigues."

"Of course, Miss Huxleigh," she said quietly. "But you must remember that we are no longer in the schoolroom, and I am not your charge and you are not my governess. Therefore, you will call me 'Miss Stanhope.'"

I drew back, feeling insulted. "What have I been calling you, pray?"

"'Miss Allegra,' as if I were thirteen years old and still wore my hair down."

"Oh. I was not aware. It is just that I am so used—"

"Well, Miss Huxleigh, I am used to being addressed as 'Miss Stanhope,' unless I allow you to call me 'Allegra,' in which case I should call you 'Nell.'"

Confused, I threw up my hands. Had I journeyed all the way to Bohemia to debate the fine points of address with a former charge? I think not.

"Since we are both unmarried," I said pointedly, "we will be 'Misses' to each other."

She glanced at my friends. "I should like to be married, if I could be sure of such a handsome and attentive husband as Mrs. Norton has."

"You will be married," I assured her, "in good time and to a man who will appear as handsome to you as Mr. Norton does now."

"You think so?" she asked with a touching trace of uncertainty. What a child she was, under her excessive airs and impatience!

"I know so! But you will never be 'Mrs.' Anybody if you poke that inquisitive Stanhope nose into the wrong business."

"Oh!" She covered the offending feature. "Do I really have the Stanhope nose?"

"Yes. It is a splendid nose, only highly curious. Quentin has it too."

"You mean Mr. Stanhope."

"I mean your uncle Quentin," I said severely. "Since we are adults, and old acquaintances, we have decided to use our first names."

"And don't you mean 'had'?"

"I beg your pardon?"

"I mean—" Allegra's honest brown gaze (so like another Stanhope's of my acquaintance) fell. "You speak in the present tense. My uncle, my dear Uncle Quentin, is . . . dead. Pleasant as it is to speak of him to another who knew him, we must not forget that."

I could have strangled myself. No one but I, Irene and Godfrey knew that evidence existed which might indicate Quentin's survival of the deadly trap Colonel Sebastian Moran had set for him. I had nursed that hope in my secret soul, and seeing this engaging child again, forgot what a slender hope it was, and that I must not encourage it in Quentin's relations without greater proof.

"No," I agreed in a throttled voice, "we must not forget that he is dead."

Silence fell upon us both: mine because of my possible deception of this dear child who deserved to share the hope I cherished; hers because she feared, with a youngster's wisdom, that her elder had failed to reckon with reality.

Into this awkward pause came Irene and Godfrey, among the conscious again, bearing champagne glasses.

I eyed the flute my friend presented to Allegra.

"Miss Stanhope is too young," I objected, seeing in her still the schoolroom miss.

"Then is Miss Huxleigh too old?" Irene demanded so mockingly that I accepted the glass Godfrey offered in patient silence.

Indeed, I needed a distraction. Meeting Allegra again had been unsettling. She set me vibrating between two separate poles: my long-ago role as governess to her and as no one of significance to her uncle, and my new role as friend to her long-lost uncle and herself. A gulf of years and social position separated us, yet was rapidly shrinking in both cases. If only I could give Allegra a hopeful word of her uncle's survival!

Irene, as usual, apparently read my intemperate thoughts. I found her admonishing eye upon me—a particularly dark eye. She had again been using the preparation that enlarged her pupils for a disguise.

"We traveled long today," Irene noted, myopically watching Allegra sip her champagne with flushed cheeks. "One glass, my dear girl, and then to bed."

"Shall you retire also?" Allegra asked ingenuously.

"I am retired," Irene said into the awkward silence. "From the stage, from the opera house. One glass, then Godfrey will see you to your room."

"He will?" Allegra brightened immediately and downed her champagne with the same speed as if it had been as repulsive as cod liver oil.

Chapter Eighteen

THE MAKING OF
MONSTERS

Irene sighed, then unfastened her cloak and let it collapse over a vacant chair. The Tiffany diamond corsage burned upon her bosom like incendiary ice.

"Can you come help me loosen this diamond anchor, dear Nell? I am quite weary from traveling all day."

I rose promptly to adjourn with her to the bedchamber, suspecting that more than a need for a maid was behind Irene's request.

She turned to shut the door as soon as I entered, then smiled wryly. "And spending five days and nights with Allegra's chatter, dear child that she is, is also enormously taxing. I pray that with Godfrey seeing her to her rest later she will sink into blissful peace, quiet and long, long sleep when we share our suite tonight."

"She is somewhat taken with him," I said carefully.

"She is utterly mad about him! Can I blame her? Girls of tender age often fix upon an older male acquaintance, even a cousin or an . . . uncle, as a romantic target." She eyed me inquiringly.

"I am glad that *I* am not young any longer, and prone to embarrassing misattachments."

She smiled. "I am glad that *I* am not young any longer,

and prone to embarrassing misattachments! Did you see
the King? What did you think of him?"

"Yes. He looked . . . splendid."

"Oh! All starch and pomposity. How I ever—! No matter. Clotilde appears even more distraught than when she
approached us in Paris. I must arrange a rendezvous with
her."

"You are here on Rothschild business!" I said sternly, at
last unfastening the awkward yet fragile diamonds.

"Rothschild business will benefit from my worming my
way close to the throne. Would you rather I closet myself
with the King?"

"No!"

"Then Queen Clotilde it is. Did you and Godfrey learn
anything interesting?"

I sat on the adjoining chair, the Tiffany diamonds a glamorous doily across my lap, watching Irene fan herself until
her fringe of black curls lifted from her face. Inactivity was
death to her; physical fidgeting only indicated the constant
working of her mind.

"We have made the acquaintance of two Rothschild
agents."

"Two whole days in Prague, and that is all you have
accomplished?"

I bridled. "And . . . we have made an expedition to a beer
garden."

"Indeed! Most daring." Irene wafted the corsage from
my lap into its harbor in the lid of her traveling case. "I am
impressed. For what purpose?"

She drew me up from the chair as she passed and herded
me back to the sitting room, where Allegra and Godfrey
waited. I immediately saw that Allegra's champagne glass
was brim full again; even superior men may overindulge
pretty young girls. The minx herself sat demure and silent,
content with her hero's recent sign of favor and not eager
to attract Irene's attention to her forbidden second glass of
champagne.

"What purpose?" Irene repeated as she sat and lifted her empty glass in both toast and request to her husband.

"To meet with the first Rothschild agent," I said. "What transpired afterward was more . . . unexpected."

"Nell, when one is spying, one must expect the unexpected. What was this untoward event?"

"We saw the Golem," Godfrey put in, ruining my careful introduction to the subject.

"At the beer garden?" Irene demanded incredulously.

He approached Irene's chair to collect her glass. "Outside the beer garden."

"Even a Golem must crave to have its thirst slaked," she observed while Godfrey poured her another full flute.

He delivered it with a flourish, glancing at my nearly untouched glass. "Perhaps that was why the fellow squawked so, Nell. He craved champagne instead of beer."

"He squawked?" Irene asked.

I endeavored to give a more rational report of the encounter. "He tried to speak, Irene, but was somehow prevented. The Golem is supposedly a mute creature, but this . . . figure struggled to speak, and failed. It was quite heart-wrenching, really, as if an animal should attempt speech."

Irene's eyes grew sober. "What would a pseudo-man who had been created only to serve men say? The Golem was not made to speak, but to serve. Yet our servants will always insist on speaking, eventually. It is most inconvenient of them."

"This was not the Golem!" I said impatiently. "Some fraud, some figment—"

Irene looked to her husband, who became the compleat barrister.

"Tall," he said as if testifying in a court of law. "Perhaps seven feet. I felt . . . diminished. Insufficient. A massive figure blindly reaching out—with his legs and arms, with his smothered, inarticulate voice. Such raw energy, contained power, pain . . . I have never before seen. Had it been a beast, I would have shot it to put it—and myself—out of its misery."

Irene had sat to attention during Godfrey's compelling—and unexpectedly vivid—description of our encounter with the Golem of Prague.

"This . . . figure was truly that large, that . . . awesome?" she asked.

He nodded, sipping champagne from the narrow apse of the glass. "I hope never to see such a wounded creature again. I—we—could only watch, stricken to silence more than fear. This was not a thing one tries to capture, or describe. One only experiences it—and lives to speak of it if one can bear to."

She turned to me. "Nell?"

Godfrey's description had shaken me. Hitherto, I had forced my mind to dismiss what I had seen as a delusion or a mistake.

Now I felt it, felt the blind flailing center of that manifestation, felt the inhuman, yet human, hurting heart of it. I knew that voiceless fear and rage, knew it for the thin, small voice of humanity arguing hopelessly in the face of universal dissolution and death.

I had been such a sightless, soundless, raging creature myself during moments I dare not remember on a bridge outside London not very long ago.

"Nell?" Irene was repeating. I realized that she wanted, that she required my opinion. I was not a mere witness, but someone whose views she depended upon for a certain consistency, even a certain clarity.

That Irene, with all her wit, many talents, greater worldliness and superior intuition relied upon me for balance was a realization I knew seldom. When I did experience this revelation, I felt less foolish, less useless, less idle. Now I must set aside my deepest prejudices and speak to what I had seen, as truly as possible, so that Irene could see through me to the greater mystery that was hers to solve.

I spoke softly, slowly, aware of Allegra's enormous, and impressionable, eyes and ears upon me.

"You know me, Irene. I believe in the spiritual too deeply to fall easy victim to the merely supernatural. Yet this Golem is the product of a spiritual process, however base its common clay, as we all are. What did I see?" I sighed, striving to be utterly accurate. "I saw a being. Male. Large. Huge, in fact. Something chained about it, something confined. Something vacant, masked, unfinished in the face. I saw a powerful . . . blundering, witnessed a Hercules unchained. It did not see us, not in any common sense. It could have just broken free of a long-ago past, for the street itself was older than many cities. It was not a normal thing that we saw, that I saw. Larger than life. Perhaps larger than death. Was it the Golem? I cannot say. But it was not . . . ordinary. It was not . . . right."

Irene stroked the bridge of her nose, as I do when my pince-nez pinches, but she wore no spectacles. Her eyes closed as if consulting an inner vision. Then she nodded.

"There is no doubt. You and Godfrey have seen something extraordinary. I had not reckoned on that, upon there being substance to these rumors of the Golem walking again. Most troubling."

"What is this 'Golem'?" Allegra asked eagerly, no longer able to contain herself. "Is it something like a Guy Fawkes effigy?"

And a little child shall lead them. I smiled at Allegra, that most innocent of us innocents abroad. "The Golem, my dear, is like a giant from a fairy tale, only more profound. It is both living and dead; wise and stupid; victim and avenger. It is protector, and sacrificial lamb."

Only I had studied the old tales. Only I knew the Golem's proper place in ancient Prague. Only I might predict its reality in the present-day city. Of all my duties as a governess, I loved best telling tales, especially if they were morally instructive. Or if I could make them so.

"Have you heard of the Rothschilds, child?"

Allegra nodded, eyes wide. "The wealthiest and most powerful bankers in Europe."

"The fiscal frog princes of Europe, my dear girl, who sprang from a small, dismal pond no one else wanted: the Jewish Quarter of Frankfurt, but twelve feet wide, and that twelve feet extending forever into poverty and despair. You know that most humans failed Our Lord when he finally came to Earth. Only a few knew the promised Savior, and pledged allegiance even at the foot of the Cross. You know how Christianity, persecuted and reviled, came to convert half the world—the most civilized half, of course. You know how Greeks became Christians, and Romans and half-wild Huns. But not Jews. And, in time, Christians reviled the Jews for their ignorance of the Lord's arrival. The Jews were forced to wander the earth, and to them Christians assigned the distasteful task of handling money, as Judas had handled the thirty pieces of silver. Only they could lend and borrow, could thrive on the interest of such transactions."

"Like Shylock!" the dear girl prompted.

Irene started from her reverie. "Oh. I thought you had mentioned my current pseudonym."

"Like Shylock," I reiterated pointedly. "At first we despised them because they did not believe as we did. Then we despised them because they did what we considered ourselves too noble to do. Despite their money handling, most Jews remained poor, and even the rich among them dwelled in the same crowded, filthy alleyways, the Jewish quarter, in the great cities of Europe.

"Then we began to suspect them of occult wrongdoing, of ritual murder of our children. Did not Herod order the Slaughter of the Innocents? So on great Church Holy Days, particularly at Easter, when Our Lord was crucified and resurrected, Christian anger boiled over. Then they would storm the gates of the ghetto, then riots ensued, and then Jews would pay the blood price for the Blood of the Lamb they had shed, and may still be shedding."

"But did they do it?" Allegra demanded. "Murder children, like the evil butcher who pickled them in the St. Nicholas legend? That was so long ago, Miss Huxleigh! And the ancient Jews didn't know, did they, who the Christ was? If they had known, would it not have made the prophecies of their disavowal wrong? Weren't the people of Israel needed to reject the Savior, so that he could save us all? And is it fair to blame the descendants for their forebears' stupidity?"

I smiled at her impassioned, naive wisdom. "Perhaps. That is not for the likes of you and I to decide. Even Christians all suffer for the foolishness of Adam and Eve, our own forebears."

"Ah," Irene interrupted, "is that why life is sometimes so vexatious? I shall have to have a sharp word with Adam and Eve in the Afterlife."

Allegra opened her mouth as if to say something more, then shut it. I resumed my tale, which had all the drama of grand opera, not appreciating the interruption. Irene had been right; the Golem legend provided the perfect text for such a work, could only a baritone big enough be found to sing the part of the Golem.

"To know the legend of the Golem, one must know the meaning of the Hebrew word. It means 'germ,' also 'formless' and 'mindless.' "

"A blank slate," Godfrey put in, sitting back and folding his hands. "A perfect tool."

"There are many variations of the Golem story, and who may say where the truth most lies?" I went on, quelling Godfrey with a governess's glare.

"Certain elements remain: the High Rabbi, one Loew, used the Cabbala, the mystic Jewish occult powers, to bring to life a huge man-figure of clay. He put a paper, on which was written the vivifying words, including the shem, the secret Name of God, into the Golem's mouth to raise it. But the Golem must not defile the Sabbath with its unnatural life, so each Friday evening the rabbi must remove the paper bearing the sacred shem. On one such midnight, the rabbi forgot."

"Just as Cinderella forgot!" Allegra burst out, much annoying me.

"The Golem is no Cinderella," I said sternly. "For one thing, it would require a large rather than a tiny shoe."

"Clementine," Irene added absently, and mysteriously. "Number nine."

"There was no number written on the paper, simply the occult formula for the Golem's creation. What do you suppose happened when the Golem was not set to rest for the Sabbath?"

Allegra blinked, looking weary. Perhaps the hour was late for old folktales that seemed to have no point. "He turned into a pumpkin?"

"No. He turned into a madman. He went berserk, uprooting trees and running wild through the streets of Prague."

"Like the figure you saw!" Allegra exclaimed.

"Exactly. Like the figure Godfrey and I saw. Legend has it that the appalled rabbi realized that the Sabbath had not yet been consecrated at the Old-New Synagogue. He pursued the Golem and drew the sacred scroll from its mouth. The clay form fell to the ground and shattered. Even today the pieces are said to lie in the attic of the Old-New Synagogue."

"A stirring tale," Godfrey put in over the smoke of a cigarette that he now passed back and forth to Irene, a most unsanitary habit, but then I imagine that married persons indulge in even more unhygienic pursuits.

"That is one version," I added, sitting back, pleased to watch my attentive audience pucker a common brow.

"There is not a single legend?" Irene asked. "How . . . very annoying."

"Perhaps not. The second version is much more political."

"Political?" Godfrey abandoned his careless slouch to sit to attention.

"Indeed," I answered, and went on before I had to endure any more interruptions. "Some say that the Golem was destroyed only after the rabbi was called to a midnight audience with Emperor Rudolph the Second. This mystical ruler, some say a madman, made Prague his seat, then invited the day's alchemists and crackpot astronomers to the city.

"The year was fifteen-ninety-two, and Rabbi Loew was conducted in secret to the Emperor's chamber. What came of that conference, we cannot know. Some say that in exchange for putting the Golem to a final rest, the rabbi had the Emperor's assurance that the attacks on the ghetto would cease.

"Some say that Rabbi Loew returned from Prague Castle to tell Joseph Golem (that was the Golem's first name) that he must sleep henceforth in the attic of the Old-New Synagogue, where he had been created. On the thirty-third day after Passover, the rabbi and two assistants entered the attic and walked seven times around the sleeping figure, intoning magic formulas. By the seventh circle, all life had left the Golem. It has not been seen since, but many believe it has lain in the attic of the synagogue. Waiting."

I turned to Allegra. "As for your Cinderella dreams, I must add that in some versions of the legend Joseph the clay man falls in love with the rabbi's lovely daughter, and has slept ever since, dreaming of her after her father took the words of life from his mouth forever."

"How sad! No wonder the poor creature blunders through the streets," she responded from her sympathetic young girl's heart.

Irene merely smiled and said, "Herr Frankenstein's monster, I presume."

Godfrey frowned, then added, "Does not Hugo's novel, *Notre Dame de Paris*, portray yet another 'unnatural' man— the hideous hunchback Quasimodo, in some versions created by the magician Frollo—who covets a maiden fair in Esmeralda, the beautiful gypsy girl?"

Irene nodded. "Scratch the day's new works of art and uncover an old legend. A pity neither you nor Nell thought to scratch the surface of the Golem you saw. I wonder what—or whom—you would have found?"

Allegra shivered. "I would not wish to know! I am so grateful that I was on the train with Mrs. Norton instead of in the streets of Prague with Mr. Norton, Miss Huxleigh and . . . that thing."

"You are young, Allegra," Irene said, more severely than she was wont to speak, "and think in extremes. Better to pity the creature than to fear it. Scratch a legendary monster," she added, "and often you will find a martyr."

Chapter Nineteen

QUEEN'S GAMBIT

The next morning, Godfrey was commanded to the Bank of Bohemia to report on his progress. I was not mentioned in Mr. Werner's message.

This left me somewhat miffed, and at the mercy of my enterprising friend, Irene, who was always more dangerous when left to her own devices.

"Let the men go talk their men talk!" she said when I reported my snubbing in the rooms she shared with Allegra. "We have better things to do."

"Such as—?"

She glanced at the dear girl by the window, then leaned close. "We must arrange an audience with Her Royal Highness, the Queen of Bohemia."

"We?"

"You were present when the Queen sought my aid. You will reassure her when she meets us again and finds me . . . changed."

"Yes, I am always useful for reassurance. What of Allegra?"

I give Irene some credit for sense. She understood immediately that I was concerned about our charge's disposition.

"Allegra will accompany us. What better excuse for an

insignificant social visit than a triumvirate of women, one of them a mere girl?"

"She is indeed only a girl. How can you involve her in such a scandalous intrigue?"

Irene shrugged. "A knowledge of such intrigue is the best defense one can give a girl in this dangerous age."

"It has not done the Queen of Bohemia much good."

"Ah. But she knows nothing of intrigue, or she would not have been driven to seek our aid." Before I could challenge Irene's convenient, and inaccurate, "us," she cannily changed the subject. "What did you think of the King last night?"

"What I have always thought: a most impressive figure face-to-face, but impervious to the gentler considerations involved in being a gentleman."

"You thought him a pompous prig!"

"Irene, you put words in my mouth, as usual! I cannot deny that Wilhelm von Ormstein is most overbearing in person. That feature has not changed. But now I know the man beneath the monarch, and he has not only treated you despicably—"

"Yes?" Irene purred.

"He has additionally been most insensitive to the poor Queen, who, being an unimaginative creature, cannot understand his dereliction of duty—"

"Yes, Nell—!" she encouraged me.

"But me he has always treated as an exceptionally invisible piece of furniture, and so he did last night. Nothing has changed with him."

"Ah, you think so?"

"You say differently?"

"No. Only he did not recognize me."

"Irene! Why on earth should he? You have marshaled all of your considerable theatrical arts to insure that he should not do so. Why are you disappointed that you have succeeded?"

"Not disappointed, Nell. Interested. No matter what disguise I had donned, Wilhelm von Ormstein should have seen through them, had one red corpuscle remained among the many blue in his blood."

"My dear Irene! I question neither your arts of disguise nor your affect upon the King of Bohemia, indeed, on the whole of the opposite sex. I have seen the success of both too often. But. Why should the King remember you after an interim of more than two years when he is now wed and you are got up like a Spanish dancer?"

"Spanish dancer?! Nell, you wound me."

"I am sorry, Irene, but there is nothing subtle about raven hair, and you are on occasion less than subtle."

She mock-pouted for a moment before adopting a preening gesture that ended in her petting the glossy locks in question. "At least Godfrey does not agree with you."

I sighed. "Godfrey may be a paragon among men, but I imagine that he is typical enough of his gender that the sight of his wife in a radical new light may give him the safe illusion of variety without risk."

"That is a rather profound observation, Nell, and quite worldly. A good thing that I whisked you away from wicked Paris and off to stodgy old Prague."

"Old, but not stodgy enough for my taste."

Another voice answered me.

"Are you talking about the King?" Allegra inquired, joining us on the settee. "He seemed utterly, too, too stodgy to me, though he is the first king I have met. Of course, he is old, as you observe, Miss Huxleigh, and perhaps I expect too much of royalty."

We both stared at Allegra's eager, innocent face. Old? At one-and-thirty? The King was exactly Irene's age. Irene herself had keenly noticed the implication, as was shown by her next remark.

"My dear 'little sister,' you will soon find that age is relative, and especially relative as one ages oneself. The King of Bohemia is in the prime of life."

"Perhaps, but he struck me as a stuffy old sofa."

"What was your impression of the Queen?" I asked.

Allegra made a face. "Quite, quite ordinary! So disappointing. A milksop, although she seemed pleasant enough. Irene . . . I mean, Mrs. Norton . . . was the only regal person present. And Mr. Norton would make a most distinguished king, with all those medals glittering on his frock coat. It is too awfully bad that the right people never are born to the right parents."

"Adorable child!" Irene kissed Allegra's cheeks in turn in the French fashion I found so affected. "What impeccable taste you have." Her impending hilarity broke out so flagrantly that we ended by laughing with her until tears filled our eyes.

"You must understand," Irene continued, taking Allegra's hands and becoming serious, "that the Queen may seem so colorless and stiff only because she is deeply troubled. In fact, that is a secret reason for our presence here in Bohemia. You must not judge where you do not know the entire case. Do not forget, we are the Queen's women here, and we owe her at least the benefit of the doubt."

"Oh, I am sorry," Allegra said, contrite. Real tears sprang as quickly to her eyes as those caused by laughter. "How easy it is to mock those apparently more fortunate than we. I never dreamed that the Queen could harbor a Secret Sorrow. Does . . . Mr. Norton know?"

Irene shook her head and put her finger to her lips. "Some things even the best of men cannot be privy to. The Queen's trouble is our sole knowledge. She risked much to tell even us."

"Oh, it is tragic!" Allegra wrung her hands. "I had no idea that such unhappiness could exist under a diamond tiara, in the face of such ceremony and bright light. I will say nothing to anyone, not even to Mr. Norton, I swear!"

Irene nodded, satisfied that Allegra knew as much as necessary, and no more, and that the girl was sufficiently impressed by Irene's melodrama to quell any youthful tendency to . . . blurt out . . . untimely revelations. Poor

Godfrey! Now he had three women determined to keep him in utter ignorance, all for his own good.

As usual, Irene had invented a fiendishly clever and simple method to gain us entrée to the Queen. She had written a note the first thing that morning and asked for an audience.

"The Queen has no reason to know us from Eve," I pointed out when she confided this fact.

"No," Irene admitted, "but I write a most persuasive note. You do recall my masterful epistle on the occasion of leaving the King and Mr. Holmes an empty safe in St. John's Wood?"

"Every word," I said fervently, hearing again *the* man's somewhat high and grating, yet impeccably expressive voice, reading Irene's ironically corrosive syllables as if he were casting literary acid at the King. I do believe that he disliked the man as much as I did. The real mystery was why—and how—Irene, the most discriminating of women, had become even momentarily enamored of the Bohemian monarch.

"I do not know why you expect the Queen to be so accessible to intrusive strangers."

"I know Prague Castle, Nell," Irene said with a rueful smile. "It is vast and ancient; the Queen is isolated and lonely. In her state, she will welcome any kind of attention."

"Poor thing," I commented tartly.

The answer came after lunch on the heavy paper I found to be favored by royalty. We were all invited for tea at Prague Castle the next afternoon.

"Why?" I demanded, taken aback. "Surely we must seem an unlikely triumvirate."

"Nothing more natural," Irene said in blithe triumph, waltzing around the room with the proof of her victory. She ended by fanning herself with the imperial paper. "You are English. I am English—at least in this persona—and

Allegra is English. No one is more clannish on foreign soil than the English."

"But you are Lady Sherlock and the Honorable Allegra. I am a mere secretary!"

"Secretary to an emissary of the Rothschilds. That alone is worth . . . oh, seven thousand pounds, say. Half the royal houses of Europe owe their continued existence to the enterprise and support of the Rothschilds, even and especially, I suspect, the Saxe-Meningens."

"Do you mean to say, Irene, that in this spurious and inferior role I am now Somebody?"

"I fear so," she said contritely.

"Oh."

"Dearest Miss Huxleigh." Allegra approached me most docilely. "You are always Somebody in any role, as I remember clearly from your time as our governess."

Her use of the word "dearest" reminded me most disastrously of her uncle, Quentin Stanhope, now presumed dead. I dared remonstrate no more against Irene's imperious plan with my usual objections, for I quite hung on the brink of a lamentable emotional collapse.

We dined that night with Godfrey, who instructed us on the political ramifications of the situation. We heard a great deal of Russian ambitions, which were not restricted to the lust for the English possession in India, but wished to stretch outward to Europe's eastern edge.

"Poland. Bohemia. Transylvania," Godfrey explained enthusiastically over the sweets. "Even Austria itself. You see how simple, and diabolical, the progression is. Napoleon has inspired imitators." He rubbed his hands together in a gesture quite foreign to him. "You see how matters of great moment brew in this bucolic corner of the world? I fear our island England blindfolds itself. Since I have lived abroad, since I have glimpsed the hidden maneuvering of crowned heads and bankers, I have come to see that our globe, our world, our lives are all caught up in an international game of catch-as-catch-can. The Great Game extends to playing fields Great Britain has never imagined. We are the advance guard, like Maclaine's guns at Maiwand, only it is not Tiger who confronts us, but the great, greedy Russian Bear.''

We could say nothing, we women who knew nothing of such great matters. Only I saw a similarity in Godfrey to Quentin that both saddened and satisfied me. I wondered what the Rothschilds had drawn us into, and where it would end.

I felt a sudden sympathy for the Golem, poor thing made and manipulated at its master's command, then unmade as easily. What blind force was marching across Europe, and where would it stop, if it ever did?

Tea with the Queen of Bohemia began to seem the better part of valor.

Chapter Twenty

SCENE OF THE CRIME

I cannot speak for Irene, but our return to Prague Castle was the most difficult pilgrimage of my life.

We entered by the public gates, an instant reminder of our former intimacy with the castle and its residents.

Bless Allegra! The girl's innocent wonder in the vast and ancient stone edifice distracted both Irene and myself from painful memories.

Had it only been two-odd years before that Irene had been a bedazzled innocent expecting to become Queen of Bohemia by the grace of a besotted King? Had it been merely thirty-some months before that I had journeyed here alone to witness Irene's illusion collapse like a house of cards, with the Jack the most fickle of the face cards?

She had not known Godfrey then. I felt a twinge of traitorous guilt to know that he was now kept ignorant, if not of our destination, at least of its true significance.

"Keep alert for any tidbit of gossip that might shed light on the political situation," he had advised as we left the Europa Hotel that day. "You may even unearth some rumor of the Golem, though I doubt such superstitions penetrate the castle stones."

Indeed, such raw concerns seemed remote within those

aloof, impenetrable walls. Irene was the usual mistress of
her emotions, engaged in playing the part of the fictional
Lady Sherlock. Her choice of name was hardly lost upon
me. Irene knew that Sherlock Holmes had despised the
King and his treatment of her. So she came here again,
attired in a remnant of the man's scalding persona: investigating, observing, judging, as she had failed to do before
until too late. Now, she was impervious rationality, when
she should have been raw nostalgia.

We were shown to the Queen's private rooms, formerly
those of her sister-in-law, the Duchess Hortense, as she
explained endlessly when we arrived.

"The moment we wed, the King resolved that in-laws
should not inhibit our married life. His brothers—even his
dear mother—were banished to distant castles. They were
not overjoyed to leave the capital, but Wilhelm was King,
and they could not contest his will. I cannot understand
that such an authoritative bridegroom would prove so
. . . hesitant."

"Kings are ever arbitrary beings," Irene said, with good
reason to know. "So the royal relatives have been sent
packing. Interesting. The King has a genius for exiling inconvenient persons."

"Perhaps I am another," the Queen said.

Clotilde was as pale and impossibly shy as I remembered.
She was pathetically eager to see us, leading us to a pair of
eighteenth-century sofas. Why did I resent in a queen the
characteristics that resided so much in my own soul?

"Tea is vital to the English, I hear," she added in a rush
that implied a fear of silence. "I have arranged for some
Viennese trifles, but I fear I lack the proper—" She eyed me
as if I were some social arbiter. "What are they called, Miss
Huxleigh? Sandwiches of cucumber?"

"Cucumber sandwiches are unnecessary," Irene said,
"and vastly overrated. I myself adore Viennese pastry."

"How kind of you to say so, Lady Sherlock." The Queen
sounded as if even she did not believe her own words. "I

am new to Prague and its customs. Foreign visitors set me
at ease; perhaps it is because they are as at sea as I am."

I cringed during her self-abasing chatter. She was, if anything, even more pathetic than in Paris. How could Irene
tolerate sitting in this palace where she had hoped to rule,
watching this inept creature stutter through the most every-
day motions?

Allegra, following the precept that the young should be
seen and not heard, remained admirably silent. Yet I saw
her open, honest face showing wonder at this woman who
was so little mistress of herself.

Irene was deliberately unreadable. Cool, contained, in
utter control, she was the exact opposite of the queen. Even
her false raven coloring seeming more genuine than the
Queen's pallid, natural blond hair. And the more the
Queen dithered, the more icily regal Irene became. How
could she not lash out with her anger and contempt, as she
had with the silly women at Worth's?

"I do not entertain many guests," Queen Clotilde chattered on. "I am most fascinated by Englishwomen. So eccentric, yet not at all offensive, as are American women. I
must say, Lady Sherlock, how much I admired your Worth
gown at the reception. Only an Englishwoman would have
had the grace to carry off such an extravagant toilette."

American-born Irene smiled her tightest smile and
sipped from her overpainted teacup. "Your Royal Highness is most gracious. If you recognized the source of my
gown, you must be a client of Monsieur Worth."

"Indeed I am," the Queen confessed, avid for anything
in common with her guests. "The King insists that I be
fashionably attired. It was he who urged me to Paris and
Maison Worth, although I loathe to travel, and I speak
French so poorly . . ."

"You speak it exquisitely," Irene declared, "as you do
English. But surely you cannot be immune to the wonder-
working of Worth?"

"Our Danish court was more conservative, and I was

among . . . my family." A sudden wrench distorted the
Queen's voice. "Here, I am expected to set a standard. I am
. . . new in my role. I much prefer, in fact, to commission
my gowns by way of fashion dolls. In fact, a shipment from
Worth has just arrived."

"Fresh from Maison Worth!" Irene's Lady Sherlock
grew of a sudden rapturous. "Oh, but we must see, Your
Royal Highness, if we may?"

"If you wish." Queen Clotilde seemed taken aback; then
her cheeks turned faintly pink. "Perhaps, if you don't
mind, you could help me choose. You seem to have a sure
fashion sense," she added wistfully. "The King wishes me
to be handsomely gowned, although he does seldom notice
what I wear. Perhaps he feels that a queen should advertise
her husband's rank." She laughed nervously. "We were
careless about such matters in Denmark; the dogs were
always leaping up on our skirts anyway."

"Dogs," said Irene brightly. "Charming. Did you hear,
Nell? What kind of dogs? Miss Huxleigh tells us that she is
most partial to cats and parrots, and even keeps a mongoose, but she has never had a dog."

"A mongoose, Miss Huxleigh?" Queen Clotilde regarded me as if I had climbed Mount Everest in her estimation. "I knew the English were eccentric!" She frowned,
then stuttered, "F-forgive me for being forward, but . . .
have we not met somewhere before?"

Clotilde was rising in my estimation by kilometers. She
was proving more perceptive after a half-hour's previous
meeting than her esteemed spouse was after hours spent in
my company.

"No doubt!" Irene rose and took the queen's arm to
usher her from the room. "Miss Huxleigh has one of those
ever-familiar faces. I tell her that is the legacy of being a
parson's daughter and trying to fade into the woodwork
seven days a week. It never works. The Worth creations are
in here?"

"My bedchamber suite." The queen gestured to the grandly testered bed in an adjoining room before indicating a row of exquisitely attired dolls propped along the back of a Biedemeier sofa in the antechamber.

How bizarre to see an entire row of Worth fashion dolls, everyone in the pallid likeness of the Queen, yet all differently dressed! With their tiny arms lifted and their blank faces, they reminded me of an army of miniature Golems.

At any moment, I feared, they might come to life and march in insipid formation down to the carpet and up to our feet. So odious was this notion that I envision of myself kicking them away like so many oncoming, exquisitely dressed rats.

"Lovely." Irene waltzed over to one doll, plucked it up, then sat in its place. "Look at the lacework! Exquisite. One cannot blame the King for wishing his wife to have such treasures."

As she ran an appreciative finger over the skirt's intricate pearl beadwork, I had another disconcerting vision: that of Berthe bent over her table at the Maison Worth workrooms, a shears impaled in her back like a pin into a cushion and an abandoned mannequin toppled on the table before her.

Allegra, fascinated, ventured to the sofa, too. "May I touch one, your Royal Highess? I have never seen a doll so beautifully made, or so well dressed!"

Queen Clotilde's pale face waxed feverish at her guests' pleasure. "Of course, my dear child. The dolls are Juneau *Bébés*, but you cannot hurt them. They are rather dolls for grown-ups, aren't they? You must tell me which you like the best, and I shall order those gowns."

"Every one is so . . . lovely." Allegra turned the tiny figure over to examine the intricate back fastenings on the gown. "Why not order them all?"

"All? Oh, I could not?"

"Why not?" Irene asked.

"That would be . . . greedy."

"But the King wishes you to dress well," Irene pointed out.

"True," Clotilde murmured. "The only thing he requires of me, it seems—"

"Madame," Irene said, her voice suddenly her own. "Do you not recognize Miss Huxleigh and myself?"

The Queen looked up, stunned, with the same frozen porcelain expression as her mannequin. "Recognize you, Madame—? How could I? We have never met."

"Not in this place, and not under these pretenses, but not that long ago."

The Queen stared into Irene's smiling face, then blinked in amazement. "Madame . . . Norton?" She turned wildly to me. "You were the . . . maid." Her attention fixed on Irene again. "I don't understand. You wrote me in Paris that circumstances prevented your investigating my dilemma." She stared at Irene, trying to paste her likeness in Paris over the role she played here. Then she nervously eyed Allegra. "The child knows nothing of—"

"She knows that you need assistance," Irene said quietly, "and that is more the case than ever. Forgive the theatrics; I was indeed called away but have managed to come to Prague, and found an assumed identity convenient."

"You have not abandoned me!" The Queen sank onto the sofa in bewildered relief, seizing a fashion doll to take its place, then sitting the small, macabre figure on her lap. "Astounding. You have such . . . verve, Madame, to come here in disguise. Will you help me, then, if you can?"

"Certainly," Irene promised. "I will even help you choose your Worth gowns, for no recompense. I like nothing better than spending someone else's money, as Miss Huxleigh can well attest."

What an extraordinary afternoon it turned out to be! The queen's relief at the proof of our assistance was so palpable that we all became quite giddy from it.

First, a lively discussion ensued as to which of the many gowns the Queen should commission. Allegra, of course, had numerous opinions and displayed as much art as Irene in putting her finger on the most flattering styles and in convincing the Queen to accept them.

Clotilde herself became another person: animated, laughing more and blushing for imagined awkwardness less. I felt like a governess among a high-spirited set of charges playing with dolls, and Allegra's unaffected laughter echoed the Queen's more often than not.

"Then it is settled," Irene said in sober summation after some minutes of merriment. "You will take at least six of the gowns suggested."

"Heavens! That will bankrupt the kingdom's coffers."

"A few paltry French gowns will hardly undo the nation, or the von Ormstein credit line." When the queen's troubled silence continued, Irene took another tack. "You said yourself that the King wished you to dress in the first fashion. You can do no better than Worth."

"I know, Madame," Clotilde said, toying with a tiny frilled hem. "Monsieur Worth's selections are designed to flatter me as I have never been flattered before."

"He *is* a genius, you know," Irene said.

So was she, in her own insidious way. It struck me that Irene was already performing most admirably as a *mannequin de ville* by encouraging the Queen of Bohemia to patronize Maison Worth so lavishly, all the while making gleeful inroads on the King's purse to boot.

Yet I must admit that the Clotilde who had bid us goodbye was a vast improvement on the melancholy creature who had welcomed us. So eager was she to perpetuate our company that she escorted us back to the common areas like any Paddington housemistress. Since Allegra's light brown hair was the closest to the Queen's blond, the two chattered about the advantages of faded "rosebud" shades like mauve, coral, lavender and yellow.

This girlish dialogue was interrupted when Irene paused at the mouth of a long hall we were passing.

"Does the castle have a portrait hall?" she inquired mystifyingly, for she well knew that it did.

"How odd that you should ask," the Queen said. "This very passage leads to it. Would you like to see it?"

"Oh, yes," said Irene, veering in the direction she had always intended to go.

Allegra and I brought up the rear while the Queen pointed out notable paintings along our path.

"How horrid it must be to have such a long line of forebears cluttering up the walls and looking down painted noses at one," Allegra confided to me.

"I imagine that depends on the forebears."

"The Queen is quite charming and unaffected, when one knows her, is she not?"

"Perhaps; but I doubt that you 'know her.' "

I was feeling a bit distracted by the scenery, recalling Irene's and my similar stroll among the portraits. Too many canvas faces displayed the von Ormstein hauteur for my taste.

Whatever Irene's purpose in suggesting this detour, and I do not doubt that she had one that went by a better name than mere whimsy, we emerged into the common area of the castle's royal apartments.

By now Allegra was gawking about like a schoolgirl on an outing. She had glimpsed but a particle of the castle at the reception; now she was free to stargaze at a firmament of plastered ceilings and a veritable Milky Way of gilt-frosted architectural details.

My every step farther into the castle's more familiar areas sunk me into a quicksand of the past. The long walls became a tunnel lined by disapproving faces that had witnessed our first downfall in Bohemia. I recalled not only our shocked flight when Irene learned that the King intended to marry the very woman who was now our conductress (and therefore make Irene his mistress), but the grave events that preceded that revelation, including the murder of the King's father and Irene's solution of that crime.

None but the immediate family and we knew by what means Wilhelm von Ormstein had assumed his crown. Though the naive maid who poisoned the former King had been a mere tool of Bohemian patriots weary of Austrian rule, no one (including us) knew what had become of her once Irene had unmasked the culprit.

If Bohemia, and Prague, and Prague Castle could have hosted such deadly intrigues two-odd years ago, what more noxious stew might now be simmering here potently enough to attract the attention of the Rothschilds' international interests?

No doubt Irene and Godfrey would chide my overlively imagination, but I realized that a legendary monster loose in the city's oldest byways could do far less harm than the occupants of a royal palace who exercised supreme rule over an entire nation.

Even as I thought this, we passed a particularly dark and sober painting of an antique-garbed man with a sallow, sunken countenance and a raven mustache.

"Surely not an ancestor of the King?" I exclaimed, as startled as if I'd been accosted by a cutpurse in a dark byway.

The Queen stopped and retraced her steps to regard it.

"Quite a dour fellow indeed, but no direct relation to my husband. A portrait of a Transylvanian cousin, I believe. The King has cousins in every neighboring nation—Germany, Austria, Poland, Moravia—as far as Russia."

"There is virtually no family resemblance," Allegra noted, bending closer to study the odious visage.

The Queen blushed. "Not all of Wilhelm's cousins are . . . how can I say it delicately—?"

Irene, always in the forefront of delicacy except when it suited her not to be, stepped in quite literally. She strode to the painting as if to confront its subject eye to eye.

"An utterly different physical type," she pronounced,

"even for a 'cousin.' Ladies, the Queen is trying to spare us the ugly facts: not all royal relatives are legitimate." Irene studied the dissolute visage with satisfaction. "King Wilhelm's family tree includes some seeds that fell far from the trunk, hence the lack of resemblance, although most such unrecognized offshoots often bear the hallmarks of their royal lineage."

I am not a complete innocent. We were regarding no mere shirttail relation, Irene implied, but a *night*shirttail relation from the wrong side of the blanket! I took Allegra's arm firmly in custody and impelled her down the hall and away from such degenerate subject matter.

So determined was I to protect Allegra from the ruder realities of royal life that I did not slow my pace even for the Queen and Irene, but swept Allegra around the corner and away from the disreputable portraits.

A woman's rich, low laughter floated toward me, as if ridiculing my concern. I stopped, turning, amazed that Irene would mock my deepest sensibilities in public . . . and found her coming up behind me, quite unlaughing.

The laugh continued against a counterpoint of clinking crystal. Before our party could recover from our surprise, someone rounded an opposite corner of the foyer. Two someones, linked arm in arm, both tall, both bearing wineglasses, both looking away from each other to see us four at the same time.

No more alien species could have met at opposite shores of the same wilderness pond. We acknowledged each other's presence, then froze and said nothing.

The King, who had been leaning down to address his companion, straightened to his usual height and adopted his usual haughty look. His companion's head lifted as if delicately scenting prey. Her red-gold hair caught and held the light from the windows high above.

I looked back. Queen Clotilde's face was locked into a grimace of happiness curdled into distaste. Irene's eyes had narrowed at the sudden sight of her former suitor. How I wished I could have put a blindfold on Allegra! Even an innocent girl could guess that the King's recent tête-à-tête with the red-haired woman had been anything but innocent.

"You entertain guests, I see," the King said to his queen, almost accusingly.

Clotilde answered in a barely audible voice, as if *she* had been caught entertaining inappropriate company, not he. "English ladies. I hoped to practice my language skills."

"Why?" he demanded jovially. "You have none." His pale blue eyes rolled past us like vagrant marbles. Then his gaze fixed—on myself! A frown creased the lofty royal brow. "Ah. This is the English secretary of Mr. Norton, the Rothschild emissary, is it not?"

"Miss Huxleigh, yes," the Queen answered uneasily.

The King's demeanor softened. "I will have dinner with him tonight."

Irene and I exchanged a glance. Apparently Godfrey had been filling his social calendar as well.

The King was eyeing Irene now, with close appreciation. Now it would come: the recognition, the recriminations; the open scandal. A royal forefinger lifted as the King wagged it at Irene in belated understanding.

"Now I know you!"

We held our conjoined breaths.

"The English lady who wore such a magnificent gown at the reception. I am sorry," he said, although he hardly sounded it, "but I have forgotten your name."

"I am Lady Sherlock," Irene answered with matching imperiousness, "but I was born Sarah Wilde."

"Such strange names, these English syllables," the King commented.

Clotilde spoke abruptly, for she had not been listening. "And who is *your* guest?"

The woman answered for herself, with a dramatic toss of her head. "Tatyana."

The Queen waited politely, not her first mistake. Irene

could have told her that only the bold get answers, and so she leaped into the breach.

"A lovely name," she told the woman, "but I believe that her Royal Highness was inquiring as to your surname."

"I have none," Tatyana replied icily. "Nor title. I am . . . Nobody."

Nobody in the chamber believed that for a moment, least of all Tatyana herself. Irene's lips curved in a musing smile. She liked nothing better than a mystery, and Tatyana was providing her with a tempting one.

"Have I not met you at Ascot, perhaps?" Irene continued, "wearing a wonderful bonnet of black tulle and calla lilies?"

"I fear not. I have not been to Ascot. I have not been to London. And I would never wear such an obvious bonnet."

"I have seen you in Paris, then!"

"I have not been to Paris . . . recently."

"Neither have I," Irene blithely lied. Her swift skill at falsehood was most disturbing to one reared to speak only the truth. "I must be laboring under a delusion," she conceded. "And now my young sister and I must bid this lovely palace adieu. Thank you for your hospitality, your Royal Highness." She bowed to the Queen, then turned to the King and his strange guest. "Your Royal Highness. No doubt I shall dine out lavishly when I return to London, with my tale of meeting a King and a Nobody at Prague Castle. Au revoir, Madame Nobody."

With a last nod, she swept from the room, myself and Allegra at her heels. Something else was at her heels, or at her skirt hem, to be precise: an aggressive dustball of gray fur, yapping wildly for attention.

Irene froze like a housebreaker caught in the act, looking into the room we had left. The archway framed a vignette of King and Queen and mysterious interloper watching us leave.

Impulsively, Irene stooped to capture and elevate the

annoying animal. "What a little darling!" she exclaimed, holding the flailing bundle of yapping fur at arm's distance as if to admire it. "Such an unusual dog. Have you seen the like, dear Allegra?"

"No," Allegra answered slowly, looking even more surprised when Irene thrust the ill-behaved creature into her arms.

"My sister is fanatically attached to dogs of all sorts," she explained to the royal party. "They sense her instantly. I am sorry if her affinity has caused a commotion."

"Not at all," the King said, looking further bewildered.

"Perhaps Allegra can carry the darling thing until we leave the castle," Irene suggested.

"As you wish, Lady Sherlock," he said.

"Thank you. Your Royal Highness is most gracious. Come, Allegra. Oh . . . what an adorable creature—"

We proceeded on our way, Irene cooing over the struggling burden in Allegra's arms all the way down the hall. Luckily, Irene knew the castle like a guardsman. She whisked right and left in various sequences until we reached the main entrance, where a footman stood on duty to admit visitors.

Irene extracted the dog from Allegra's arms and thrust it at the unhappy footman. "Here. You must keep this darling dog from running out with us, although we would love to keep the sweet thing."

The dog's open maw displayed impressive teeth for its tidy size. With a last pat on the head, neatly avoiding a snap of those active jaws, Irene led us from the ancient huddle of Prague Castle into the daylight of an inner courtyard.

She breathed a sigh of utter relief as the footman, struggling to contain the dog, shut the heavy doors behind us. "At least the miserable dog recognized me, although I had rather he hadn't. You recall Spaetzl, don't you, Nell?"

"Not until now," I said grimly. "A dog as unmannerly as his master."

"You do not like the King?" Allegra inquired innocently.

Irene flashed me a cautioning glance, though she needn't have bothered.

"I am not much impressed by royalty," I told Allegra.

"That is what I love about you, Miss Huxleigh; you are not impressed by anyone. I admit that I am not so advanced. I am foolishly elated at having spent the afternoon with a queen, and at having met a king in private, even if he did not acknowledge my presence." She pranced ahead of us in high spirits.

"King Wilhelm is very good at not acknowledging presences of late," Irene said cryptically.

"Although you have done all you could to announce yours," I muttered. "Disguise, indeed."

"That makes his ineptitude all the more telling," she answered with a smile I could only describe as smug.

"It proves that royalty are deaf and blind when it comes to commoners," said I. "Even the Queen barely remembered us after mere weeks. Still, your luck with the King may not hold forever," I added softly as Allegra rejoined us.

We were walking through the various courtyards to the drive where our carriage awaited, Irene setting a brisk pace. I couldn't help thinking of the Three Musketeers again, though we made a poor substitute for those dashing swordsmen of Old France. Still, we compared impressions of our interesting afternoon, and thus shared an air of camaraderie seldom come by.

"You are quite right, Mrs. Norton," Allegra began. "The Queen is quite different in private. She was so gay when we discussed the fashions, and shy in a rather touching way. How fortunate that you convinced her to settle on the kinder colors and styles; she has the instinct of a chicken for fashion, poor thing."

"We cannot all of us be young, beautiful and supremely confident, my dear Allegra," Irene retorted mischievously.

"That is true," the silly girl responded. "It is comforting to know that a queen can be gauche." She tripped up the step leading to the carriage without waiting for the driver's assistance. Irene shrugged, and we "older ladies" installed ourselves within in a more orderly manner.

And so we returned to the Europa, Allegra still chattering about our tea party with the Queen, and Irene uncommonly quiet.

Not until we had arrived in the hotel hall near our separate rooms did Irene speak, and then only to tell Allegra to go to their rooms.

"I wish to speak to Miss Huxleigh about her impressions of this afternoon. Then I shall see if Godfrey has returned from his er, outing."

Allegra went on down the hall without a murmur while I unlocked the door to my chamber.

Irene rushed in on my heels and shut and locked the door behind us.

"Thank heavens!" she said, throwing herself into the room's sole upholstered chair and clawing through her reticule.

I sighed to see her extract the mother-of-pearl cigarette case, a cunningly made and lovely thing, but always a precursor of her favorite prop, the abhorred and reeking cigarette.

"Well, Nell," she began, innocently parroting Godfrey's unfortunate habit. Perhaps wedded people exchange each other's peccadilloes as well as vows. "Surely you were as conscious as I of the extremely provocative developments this afternoon at the palace."

"Ah . . . yes, of course, but I did not want to say anything in front of Allegra."

"Very wise. Offer your observations first."

I watched her fiddle with the case. A mechanism opened a small compartment that held a set of lucifers tiny enough for the Queen's fashion dolls.

"Well?" Irene demanded.

"How can I speak when your attention is on that revolting ritual? First you will remove a cigarette and then hunt for the holder. Next you will screw the cigarette into the holder and drop one or more of those ludicrously tiny lucifers. When you finally strike one on the rough spot on the case, you must light the cigarette end in haste so as not to scorch your fingertips. Then you will rush to extinguish the lucifer in a dish and huff out a noxious stream of smoke, which makes you look like a hibernating dragon. It is too distracting."

"Indeed," said Irene, going through just the gestures I had described, until she leaned back against the upholstery and sighed deeply. "You forgot the final aspiration, my dear Nell, but I admit that your description of my panto-mime is accurate enough. Now. You have my full attention. Lay all your suspicions and conclusions before me, and a tempting lot they should be."

She smiled magnanimously.

No route remained to me but Irene's favorite device: bluff.

"I find it quite amazing that no one recognized you, or me, for that matter."

"Whose dullness do you find most hard to counte-nance—the King's, the Queen's or that of the King's mis-tress?"

"Mistress!"

"Surely even you suspected."

"I *did* think their behavior rather improper for Allegra's observation."

"And consorting with her in the castle under the Queen's nose! Willie has grown quite brazen for one who wished me whisked to the wilds of the country not long ago. What do you suppose has given him such courage?"

"The Queen's utter fecklessness."

Irene flourished her cigarette holder with the entwining, jeweled gold snake as she expelled a matching spectral ser-pent of smoke. "And this was the woman he was so terri-fied of scandalizing! So terrified that he had me hounded across Europe, that he came to London himself to set Sher-

lock Holmes on my trail. All to reclaim a mere photograph
of the two of us together that he feared might compromise
him with his royal bride-to-be. I have heard that marriage
changes a man, but Willie has changed into something of a
monster. He openly caters to his own gratification at others' expense."

I pleated the folds of my skirt on my knee. "I told you
that a king is not like other men. You were too American
to understand at the time."

"When we return home, you must teach Casanova the
phrase 'I told you so.' Then you will not have to wear
yourself out reminding me."

"Irene, I seldom carp upon your past miscalculations."

"That is true. The present ones offer you enough material for correction. Well. I am not overestimating His Royal
Highness now. Again I ask you, *why* were we so unrecognized?"

I sighed and forced myself to think. "We had seen the
Queen most recently. Although you have altered your
name, your voice and your appearance, I am hardly so easy
to disguise. She should have remembered us, except that I
am often overlooked."

"And," Irene added, "the Queen was greatly distressed
when she interviewed us at Maison Worth. She could
barely look us in the eye as she described her most embarrassing difficulty; no wonder we did not make much of an
impression upon her! When she received my declining
note, I am sure all hope of help went out of her head. No
one is more unobservant than a person lost in the maze of
her own difficulties."

"She recognized us the moment you assumed your
proper persona."

Irene nodded. "She may not be completely hopeless, or
helpless. But what of the King? How could he have failed to
know me, no matter how much hair-black I use, or in what
kind of accent I clothe my voice? The man intended at one
time—when he was deluding himself, no doubt—to marry

me, after all! How could he forget no matter the guise? And I am told on good authority that this is not one of my more successful impersonations."

"If you were more willing to camouflage your beauty you might be more impenetrable."

"I am not returning to Bohemia looking like a frump!"

"Of course not. You wish to fool the King, but you wish him to yearn after you nevertheless, even if he does not know who you are. Vanity will be your downfall."

"Perhaps, but it will provide such a lovely exit." Irene airily brandished her elegant cigarette holder. "And you fail to mention the unlikelihood that some hair-dye and a different accent can conceal a woman from a man who once loved her, if he loved her. Godfrey would never be deceived by me in my present guise."

"Then why did you use such a fragile facade for the King? I will tell you. You *wanted* him to recognize you to salve your vast vanity, and this he has utterly failed to do. It has been almost three years since he last saw you, after all. He has grown so heartless in the interim that he neglects his Queen, his bride of less than a year. Now you tell me that he consorts with foreign women. I never did like King Willie, but he has descended to depths of depravity even I never imagined."

Irene nodded, an odd expression on her face. "Yes, Willie is quite unlike himself. However, if one must revisit an old suitor, I suppose it is best to find him descended to depths of depravity. And that brings me to the third person who failed to recognize us."

"Third person? There was no other . . . even the servants were strangers."

"Yes, they were. Most telling."

"What 'third person,' Irene? In a moment I expect you to inform me that the Maison Worth mannequins should have come to life and recognized us."

"What a notion! No, at least they are exactly as they

should be, something of a comfort in the Prague we find before us. I refer to the rather intimidating Tatyana. If she did not recognize us, and I am not so sure of that, surely you, Nell, recognized her."

"Of course I did! She briefly approached Godfrey and myself at the reception."

Irene jerked upright, wrenching her smoldering cigarette from its holder. "She did?! Neither you nor Godfrey mentioned this. When did this occur?"

"When you and Allegra made your grand entrance, or, rather, when you entered and Allegra followed. This Tatyana could not keep her eyes off of you, especially when you dallied for some words with the royal couple."

"And you mean to say that you never suspected her identity?"

"That she was the King's mistress? How could I? And, besides, you have only your instinct to attest to that."

"My instinct is apparently superior to yours. You truly cannot recollect where we have seen her before?"

" 'We'? You and I?"

Irene nodded. "And Godfrey."

I racked my brains, and then I applied thumbscrews, but could recall no occasion when we three had laid eyes upon the terrible Tatyana.

Irene tapped her fingers against her head while I watched, blinking. "Other women than I may dye their hair, Nell. Don't let that loathsome strawberry-blonde fool you. Think!"

" 'Strawberry blonde'?"

"An American expression for yellow-red hair. Imagine Tatyana without it."

I shook my head. Imagining Tatyana bald did me no good whatsoever, except to make me giggle to imagine the King with such a mistress. . . .

"Where?" I asked.

"Paris, as I suggested today, although she denied it."

"Anywhere in Paris in particular?"

"Twice; once publicly and once privately. You are only aware of seeing her on one occasion, and that formal."

I loathed it when Irene pretended to greater knowledge than I, and then refused to demonstrate it.

"A formal occasion," I pondered. "We have attended few formal occasions in Paris, unless one would consider that vile Bernhardt woman's salons such an event."

"Excellent, Nell," Irene encouraged, rooting in her reticule for another cigarette.

While she was thus distracted I subjected my poor brains to the equivalent of St. Lawrence's hot gridiron, but produced nothing.

Irene, ensconced again with a smoking cigarette, was looking smug. "Remember the tall blond woman present when I sang for the Empress of All the Russias?"

I frowned. "But, Irene, she was seen with the man passing himself off as the heavy-game hunter, Captain Sylvester Morgan, that night! You mean to say that this woman is associated with that murderous wretch, Colonel Sebastian Moran?! The man who, before my very eyes, plunged with Quentin Stanhope into the Thames not three months ago?! No—"

"You saw her *before* that night in Sarah Bernhardt's salon," Irene went on with the relentless air of a barrister, no doubt gained from her association with Godfrey. "I believe that she lingered on the cobblestones outside Notre Dame Cathedral when Quentin first approached us, when he fell at our feet subjected to a poisonous injection."

"No! Irene—"

"I further believe that this 'Tatyana' is the Russian spy Quentin had heard of in Afghanistan just before the Battle of Maiwand nine years ago, when he was known by the sobriquet of Cobra and Moran that of Tiger. You recall Quentin's cryptic reference to 'Sable'?"

"Irene! I recall none of this, and now you say this creature is the King's mistress? You will go to any length to preserve your pride and concoct any absurd scheme to justify that opinion. Impossible! I cannot believe that a woman associated with Colonel Moran nearly a decade ago would surface at one of Sarah Bernhardt's soirées; it is even more ludicrous that she would hie to Bohemia and become the King's mistress. Why? Simply to spite you? You have far too grand an opinion of your importance in the world, of your effect on kings and other foolish men—and of your memory and impressions."

"Perhaps," she conceded in a suspiciously meek manner. "I do depend a great deal upon your diaries for enlightenment. You are most precise about details, Nell, even if you do not fully comprehend them. I know you travel with these delicious little volumes. Please consult the proper book. We will shortly see how grievously I have erred on this occasion."

She directed a stream of smoke as thin as a stiletto in my direction.

Chapter Twenty-one

GUESS WHO'S GOING TO DINNER

Once again we had been forced to play false with our hotel rooms. Godfrey and I occupied separate rooms; Irene as "Lady Sherlock" and her "sister Allegra" maintained their own suite.

Irene managed to intercept Godfrey when he paused at the hotel after a day of consultation among the bankers and financiers of Prague, before he was off for the evening. He was indeed to dine with the King at Prague Castle that evening, upon His Royal Highness's especial invitation.

When Irene and Allegra collected me for another hotel dinner later that evening, she informed me of this arrangement.

"Apparently, no interlopers—that is, women—are allowed; not even the Queen will be tolerated." Her melodramatic sigh of disappointment did much for her décolletage. "I should *so* like to observe Godfrey and the King at dinner together!"

"No doubt," I responded, appalled. That was the last thing in the world that I would like to see, and the second-to-the-last thing would be the King and Irene together again in the same room.

"We shall simply have to plan our own adventures over

dinner," Irene added, linking arms with Allegra and myself on our way downstairs and leading us off at a brisk pace.

I had always harbored deep doubts about this Bohemian venture, but dinner was pleasant enough, thanks to the company, although largely inedible—until we retired upstairs again. Allegra once more was banished to their suite while Irene slipped into my room for a consultation. She intended to stop last at Godfrey's chamber, to which she had a spare key.

"I suppose that you will interrogate him mercilessly," I noted as I turned up the lamps.

"That depends on how forthcoming Godfrey is. I must say that he is taking an unusual relish in this masquerade. He seemed actually . . . enthusiastic about his tête-à-tête with the King."

"A man seldom has an opportunity to study his former rival. Besides, Godfrey takes his assignment for the Rothschilds most seriously. He will not let personal matters intervene."

"Do you think that I will?" Irene indignant was especially impressive.

"What scheme have you in mind for us tomorrow?" I asked narrowly.

"Nothing of much consequence. It seems that bankers, kings and barristers have so much in common that we poor ladies must fend for ourselves, and are condemned to minor matters. I propose an outing to the Old Town to hunt this convenient Golem of yours."

"Do you imply that Godfrey and I were diddled by the Rothschild agent? That it was arranged for us to see a false monster?"

She shrugged. "The Golem is a Gothic element that adds a picturesque quality to a common and sordid political intrigue. Certainly Baron Alphonse is well aware of my attraction to the exotic. So, no, I do not expect to find serious traces of the Golem, but I would like Allegra to see more of Prague than the autocrats on Hradčany hill. The streets teem with color and music, and I have missed them."

"The streets are as dangerous to us as any Golem! We will be three women alone."

"No, four."

"Four?"

"I managed a discreet word with the Queen during our visit yesterday. She has agreed to join us; in disguise, of course."

"The Queen! She is not suited for such expeditions."

"Neither are you, Nell, but you go."

"What are you up to, Irene?"

"Have you forgotten my first mission: to help Clotilde? I want to show her Bohemia, the real Bohemia, that she rules by a quirk."

"How will this revelation solve the problem of the King's indifference?"

"I don't know, but it will aid the problem of the King's and Queen's indifference to their subjects."

"You really think that Clotilde cares about such grand issues?"

"I think that Clotilde cares far more than even she guesses, and than this King could ever imagine."

"Irene, I confess myself at an utter loss. I have no idea what you think you are doing here, but such a scheme cannot be useful or even healthy."

"No," she admitted with that charming frankness I found it nigh impossible to resist, "but it may be effective."

A knock at my chamber door the next morning sounded like the pecking of a sparrow.

Puzzled—for neither Irene nor Godfrey were timid knockers, and the hour was far too early for the affected scratch of the chambermaid—I opened the door.

Allegra Stanhope stood before it, toying with her berib-boned sleeve cuff. In her cashmere green plaid Directoire redingote with its puffed sleeves, wide waist sash and lace collar, she looked as charming as a shepherdess.

"Are we ready for breakfast, then?" I inquired, more eager to learn the results of Godfrey's royal dinner than to breakfast like a Bohemian peasant.

Allegra looked away, clearing her throat. "I suspect that you and I will have to make a pair of it."

"Oh?" Her unusually diffident manner alarmed me, and I stepped back from the door so that she could enter the room and we could speak privately. "What of Irene and Godfrey?"

Allegra came out with it in a burst. "Mrs. Norton did not return to the suite we share last night."

"Irene is missing!? Heavens, child, why did you not say so immediately!?" I rushed to fetch my wrap, reticule, bonnet and gloves. Inquiries might be necessary, and that would require us to leave the hotel. My mind flailed for the last time I had been assured of Irene's whereabouts. "I saw her after dinner, of course. She planned to wait up for Godfrey in his room and discover what he had learned at the castle. We must ask Godfrey instantly when he came in, thus establishing when Irene might have . . . vanished. You *did* notify Godfrey first thing?"

I bustled Allegra out of the door, barely remembering my room key, and started down the passage. Allegra, rather than matching my haste, dragged her feet most annoyingly.

"Hurry, dear girl! Not a moment is to be lost. Irene may be off on some secret escapade, but then again she may have been kidnapped by the King's agents, or—Allegra, are you coming or not?"

The girl drew to a stop behind me, still fidgeting with the ribbons on her gown. I could have shaken her, and tried to do so verbally.

"Allegra!"

"I have not yet . . . disturbed Godfrey," she admitted.

"Then we must notify him immediately. Gracious! We

do not even know that Godfrey is in his room, or that he returned last night. Heavens! . . . Irene may have fallen asleep waiting for Godfrey, while he may have been captured by the King, who has known Irene's identity all along, and now Godfrey is being held prisoner in the dungeons of Prague Castle—"

"Miss Huxleigh," Allegra interrupted me, "I truly doubt that Godfrey is languishing in Prague Castle's dungeons, or that he is in the least discomforted at the moment. Neither do I think that you should actually . . . knock at Godfrey's door."

"Not knock? I have never been afraid to knock at a door in my life. I am not much noted for courage, but in that regard I am a lion. As long as one knocks politely, one can do no wrong."

"I considered doing it myself," she confessed, "but—"

"But? You have become a very schoolroomish miss. Courage! We may discover the worst, but we will at least know more than we do now."

I had pulled Allegra toward Godfrey's door despite her folly in hanging back. We must discover what had happened to our companions, no matter how mystifying or frightening the news.

"Either they are in here, or they are not," I told Allegra, poising a firm fist above the wood.

Allegra Stanhope stayed my hand, hanging from my arm like a distraught child.

"Please, Miss Huxleigh," she begged in an agonized whisper. "I do not think that you understand."

"Nonsense! It is you who are too timid to face facts."

"Miss Huxleigh, I am not afraid that Mr. and Mrs. Norton are *not* in the room; I am afraid that they *are!*"

The absurdity of her remark froze me in midgesture.

Allegra whispered in my ear. "Mrs. Norton has always returned to my room for the night until now. The reason for this abrupt change in habit may not be sinister, as you think, but merely . . . marital."

"Oh." My arm dropped back to my side.

I considered such matters as room arrangements in purely practical terms when we traveled. Once a person had accepted a room as hers or his, she or he stayed there, as one would in a home. I never thought of—but then it was none of my business.

I let Allegra lead me down the passage a little before I said, "What do you suggest?"

"Mr. Norton's and your rooms are single chambers, while Mrs. Norton's and mine is a suite. If we knock and are . . . precipitous, no other room cushions us from the . . . occupants. Perhaps we should breakfast on our own and investigate later. Mrs. Norton planned to await Mr. Norton in his room. If we assume that nothing untoward has happened . . . we must not intervene until a more suitable hour. If you are indeed right, and some perfidy has been afoot, then we shall berate ourselves bitterly for not acting. That is why I came to your door. I do not want full responsibility for whatever action we take."

I considered. Allegra was correct. How much better to assume we were witnessing the results of a domestic improvisation—however awkward and embarrassing—rather than a criminal attack.

"I will not be able to eat so much as a kipper until I know that all is well," I complained.

This time Allegra took my arm to lead me toward the stairs. "We must give time a chance, dear Miss Huxleigh, to prove that ordinary rather than extraordinary actions explain our dilemma."

"Irene's irregularities in habitation set a most improper example for you!"

Allegra's smile displayed her dimples. "On the contrary; I do not blame her in the least. As for propriety, they are married, after all."

"Yet to let you wonder and worry all night! She should have said something."

"What?" Allegra asked with eyes as candid as Evian water.

What, indeed?

We went down to the hotel's usual uninspired breakfast: strangely spiced sausage, eggs and potatoes, and the Bohemian national delicacy—leaden, lumpy dumplings.

We had survived the worst and were consoling ourselves with heaping bowls of fresh berries and cream when a motion in the dining-room archway caught our eyes.

Irene and Godfrey stood poised there, blissful as a couple on a wedding cake. When they saw us they waved blithely and came to the table.

I solved the mystery in one glance: Irene still wore the same gown with which she had honored the castle the previous day. I hoped that Allegra's anxiety would help her overlook the extremely improper example Irene was setting her. Obviously, she'd had no occasion yet to don fresh underclothes for the day!

This lack seemed not to have affected her mood, nor that of her spouse, who was in exceptionally good spirits.

"I could eat a horse!" Irene exclaimed as she sat.

"You may get your wish here, and never know it," I murmured in reply.

They ordered breakfast nevertheless, and I almost wished for Casanova's carping presence; certainly my air of dignified disapproval was having no effect. In fact, they did me the extreme discourtesy of failing to notice it.

Allegra, being young, had forgotten the uncertainty and embarrassment of the morning.

"Oh, Mr. Norton, we are writhing in agony to know what transpired at the castle! Do tell us, please."

"You are quite right to use the word 'transpired,' " he admitted with a conspiratorial smile, glancing round the dining room. Due to our late arrival, the chamber was deserted, so he dispensed a quick, if cryptic, diagnosis.

"Baron Rothschild was right. The King of Bohemia fancies himself quite a coming power in this quaint corner of the world. He seeks immediate funding to finance everything from spy networks to launching a possible military adventure."

"From Bohemia!" I demanded in disbelief.

"Hush," Godfrey cautioned me. "The notion is quite serious to him. Nor were we alone at dinner."

Here Irene leaned over the table to enter the conversation. "An unannounced guest of a surprising nature, or so Godfrey swears, joined the King and Godfrey for dinner." Her teasing tone was also a bit thorny.

Godfrey drew back. "The King's . . . associate. I understand that you three met her in the castle earlier, and Nell and I glimpsed her at the reception. She calls herself 'Tatyana.' "

I glanced indignantly at Irene, on her behalf, and was met by her understanding smile. "Odd, is it not? The Queen of Bohemia cannot be party to a dinner attended by the King and the Rothschild emissary, but this woman can. If I were Queen, such snubs should not happen."

"Interesting, Irene?" I answered. "It is shocking. Deplorable. Even I cannot believe that King Willie has sunk so low—"

Irene's expression warned me against further exercises of outrage, but Godfrey had already seized my comment as a fisherman might retrieve a baited hook.

"Well, Nell, you surprise me indeed when you find the King more reprehensible than your opinion. I confess that I found little admirable in him. He is supremely arrogant, rather slow-witted, and, though a robust-looking fellow, not half as handsome as I was led to believe."

Irene remained silent. Although her toe tapped beneath the table, only I heard or understood the sound. Her dilemma rivaled Allegra's and mine of earlier that morning. She was not averse to her husband finding a former suitor no serious threat, but neither did she wish him to dismiss such an erstwhile interest so sweepingly. The meeting between the two men had accomplished exactly what Irene would have wished, but at the cost of her vanity. This was never an ideal outcome for one of her theatrical temperament.

Godfrey shook out his napkin as if the topic of the King were a crumb to send flying. "Much overrated, His Majesty, Wilhelm von Ormstein, by the Rothschilds as well as by . . . others, including you, Nell. I am vastly disappointed. I had not thought you so impressionable at your age."

"My age?" I squeaked tardily.

Irene smoldered silently. I searched for the hidden cigarette, but found no sign of smoke.

Godfrey's eyes rested on Allegra with satisfaction. "One might expect an untried girl to fall victim to such royal bluff and bravado, but, believe me, Europe and the Rothschilds have little to fear from this quarter, if Wilhelm von Ormstein is behind it."

"What of her?" Irene asked in a dangerously low and modulated voice.

"What of whom?" Godfrey knew very well that he had been tweaking Irene's tail feathers unmercifully. I suspect he had grown so bold only because he had met the King on his own ground and come away unscathed.

"Her," Irene repeated. "The one woman allowed at your dinner of state, that even queens may not attend. Tatyana."

She articulated the word with foreign flair, yet musically, so it rang like Russian grand opera.

"The King's . . . toy," Godfrey dismissed her. "He has a colossal vanity."

"Kings generally do," Irene responded, "and sometimes so do barristers. I suggest that if you find the King a feeble opponent, you are not confronting the most powerful piece on the board."

He sat back. "The Queen."

"The Queen who is not the queen. If it is true that the King harbors ambitions that were alien to him two years ago, what has changed since then? His marriage? Tell me

that Queen Clotilde is a Lady Macbeth and we will all have
a good laugh. If you wish to be an effective emissary, Godfrey, you must cast the part of the power behind the throne
elsewhere. Tatyana."

"A woman is the puppetmaster behind the throne?" he
asked with just enough reluctance to set Irene's toe tapping
again. Like Mr. Poe's raven, Irene's irritable toe was an
ominous harbinger of no good.

"Humor me," she suggested in a voice of satin. "Arrange
to call upon this woman in private—and soon; today, if
possible—to test my theory. Measure her as you would any
opponent, rather than as a woman you view merely as a
king's amusement. And take Nell along as your secretary,
for a sensible assessment."

"Me?" I squeaked again. "I am to tour the Old Town
with you and Allegra and—" Irene's look was Medusa-
terrible, and it silenced me in time. "—and all the native
Praguers we can find who have witnessed the Golem's most
recent reincarnation."

"You two ladies hunt the monster of legend," Godfrey
said, "while Nell and I hunt hussies? A fair exchange, I
suppose. Certainly I will examine this lady more closely; if
I have overlooked her, you must credit a certain prejudice
on my part to other ladies more lovely."

He smiled around the table before letting his gaze rest on
Irene. The flattery was calculated, good-natured and
slightly jibing. Irene only smiled, but she seemed content.

"Why must I go with Godfrey?" I demanded when I had
managed to draw Irene away from the others after breakfast
by feigning a wardrobe difficulty in my room.

"You were dubious about our jaunt to the Old Town;
this will be less dangerous than chasing the Golem."

"But I shall worry about Allegra and the Queen. And
you."

"Worry rather about this Tatyana," she said a trifle
tensely.

"Irene, do you really . . . fear her?"

"Let us say that I fear Godfrey's optimism." She walked to the window to study the colorful tile rooftops of Prague. "He is like the tailor who has killed five flies with one blow, or like Jack the Giant-Slayer. To his surprise, the King has not proved to be the formidable rival he feared; hence, he is overoptimistic. He even derides my past attachment. Did his cockiness now not indicate the depth of his earlier anxiety, I might be inclined to take offense."

She turned to regard me. "I am not condemning you to accompany Godfrey, dear Nell; I am charging you to protect him. You will not take this woman for granted. You will not see her as what I was supposed to become for the King of Bohemia, a trivial ornament for a tyrant. You will watch her with unjaundiced eyes, and will keep Godfrey's vanity from blinding him."

"Vanity," I repeated, "is a fearful fault."

"Yet understandable," Irene said ruefully, "especially in ourselves. Watch well today, Nell. I have a suspicion that a wise witness will see much. Godfrey is a barrister, despite his current insensible state, and a clever one. I expect his call upon the mysterious Tatyana to be highly productive."

"And will your party make much progress in tracing the Golem, Irene?"

"The Queen," she said by way of evasion, "is the most powerful piece on the chessboard, if not in life. I think that in this case she will ultimately prove worthy of her reputation."

"Clotilde? Please, Irene, you ask too much of one."

She nodded, and this time there was no mistaking the grimness in her voice. "So do the Rothschilds."

Chapter Twenty-two

AN INTERVIEW WITH
A VAMP

At least the mysterious Tatyana kept rooms outside the castle, at the Hotel Belgrade. Somehow I saw this as more sinister than if she had been a guest in the massive royal compound on Castle Hill.

Would virtue need a respectable address?

I do not forget that two years earlier I had lectured Irene for residing at the castle, but the King had not been married then, or even betrothed.

I was surprised by this woman's alacrity in answering Godfrey's note of the morning. A messenger returned an answer after luncheon, shortly before Irene and Allegra were to leave for their foray into Old Town.

Godfrey fetched me as soon as the note arrived, and brought it to Irene and Allegra's suite. (We convened in Irene and Allegra's outer salon, where four could meet without crowding, or confronting a bed.)

Irene snatched the envelope, running her fingers eagerly over the texture of the paper and lifting the missive to her nose before opening it. Allegra watched this performance with saucer-shaped eyes.

"Irene masquerades as a hunting dog on occasion," I informed young Allegra.

Irene observed my comment, then held the unopened missive before her, as a palm reader might the top of a hand.

"Viennese deckle parchment notepaper, as thick as tough pastry. An odor of . . . iris and old roses," she declared portentously, fingering the heavy envelope. "Two sheets, because Madame Tatyana's handwriting is bold and greedy, consuming ink and paper in great, bounding loops. No seal; she has no surname of which to boast. Besides, she wastes no time on empty ritual, particularly if it could untidy her manicure. You will find some bizarre personal token enclosed within, as an insignia."

She presented the envelope to Godfrey over the support of her opposite wrist, as a man's second would offer him a dueling pistol.

"Most civil of you to allow me first reading rights," he noted to Irene. Godfrey slit the envelope with the fruit knife, then skimmed the contents.

"Was I correct?" she demanded.

With a smile, he turned the first page so we all could view it. Black ink stormed the page, almost gusting off the edges. There were indeed two pages, and between them something that slipped to the carpet.

Allegra bent quickly to retrieve it. "A pink tulle rose, as could have fallen from a corsage decoration! How pretty!"

"So pretty that you may have it," Irene declared, smiling to see her prediction proven. "The formidable Tatyana has another side: she is formidably sentimental. An interesting blend of characteristics. I am sure that Godfrey has no need or wish to retain another woman's tokens."

"Assuredly not," he said hastily. "Nor need I keep her communication to myself: a simple invitation to 'late tea at five.' What do you make of it, Irene? No doubt I am missing some nuance."

Irene eyed the pages in turn, shuffling them back and forth, studying the penmanship like a doctor his patient.

"A most . . . diabolical swoop to the crosses on her ts.

Quite lethal." She frowned. "As for the import, she obviously is previously engaged for tea, yet makes immediate room to see you later. I wonder what she will serve? An interesting quandary for any hostess, but I have no doubt that she will solve it by five. Does she suspect Nell's presence? No. Does she suspect anything? Possibly. The text is perfectly acceptable for a king's mistress who is welcoming one who could benefit her master, or perhaps herself. Go, my children, and find out more. Meanwhile, Allegra and I will potter around Prague and no doubt have a dull time of it."

"Perhaps you will return before Nell and I must leave," Godfrey suggested.

"I fear not," Irene said with regret.

I suspected that she would be responsible for the Queen's discreet exit and return to Prague Castle, no easy task even for a sleight-of-self artist like Irene.

"Watch the woman," she told Godfrey sternly in farewell, turning to me to silently impress the same command upon my conscience.

Then she gathered Allegra in her train and we all vacated the chamber, the two to sally forth; myself to my room to catch up on my diary; Godfrey to tiresome rounds of the banks, seeking information on the King's finances. With the Rothschild credentials, all doors—including those of many imposing vaults—were open to him. I could see that he liked that excessively well.

Frankly, I spent the afternoon moping over my diary. I missed Allegra's cheering company, and, furthermore, had decided that Irene had chosen the better part in leading Allegra and Clotilde into a "queen's holiday" in the Old Town.

Suppose they should encounter news of the Golem? I longed to know what Godfrey and I had seen, if it actually was some form of supernatural being, whether wrongfully called up or not. Few in this world are permitted to glimpse the supernatural, either in the form of good or evil. I am not so unimaginative that I do not wish to know whether I have done so or not.

Then, I found Godfrey's and my assignment to learn more of the cryptic Tatyana distasteful. I disapproved of the woman to begin with. What need had we to deal with such a tawdry individual? The King would see Godfrey; indeed, he courted him. And why was I needed to escort Godfrey to this lady's lair? Godfrey could take care of himself. How ludicrous to pretend that I could offer Godfrey any kind of protection whatsoever!

Still, Irene thrived on being mysterious as much as her ultimately successful rival for the King's affections, or at least his attentions. I resolved to dress for the encounter in my most prudent and plain ensemble. This elusive Tatyana should know that she was dealing with an Englishwoman!

Godfrey and I set off at four-thirty on foot, the Belgrade Hotel being nearby. We set a smart pace, Godfrey flourishing his swashbuckling walking stick, I eager to get the business over with so I could return to hear Irene and Allegra's true report privately, for of course Godfrey could not know about her adventures with the Queen, nor would he learn of her secret mission.

"I hope," he commented as we went, "that your attire does not indicate your expectations of the outcome of this meeting. It would do magnificently for a funeral."

"Men wear dull black all the time, and no one thinks them melancholy for it," I pointed out.

"Men are dull most of the time," he retorted. "No wonder they wear black."

"You really think so? I confess that the thought has often crossed my mind."

"Of course they are. They are encouraged to be so. Unless they are exceptions . . . like Quentin Stanhope. That native getup of his was not black."

"No." I blushed, confused. "I imagine that Sherlock Holmes is not dull, although he too wears citified black."

"I never worried about his dullness," said Godfrey, glowering. "Although, now that you mention the matter, I have decided what is wrong with the King of Bohemia, despite his gaudy uniforms."

"Yes?"

"He is unforgivably dull."

"Yes! Godfrey, you have put your finger upon it. I knew that there was a reason why he was so unsuited to Irene."

He paused. "We are unanimous, then: you, I and Sherlock Holmes. The King of Bohemia was—is—unworthy of her."

"Why, yes, of course. That is no new revelation, Godfrey."

"Ah," he said, taking my arm to resume walking, "but I never saw for myself before. Sherlock Holmes had the better of me even there."

"Now that you have, do you feel the better for it?"

"I do."

"Then it is worth this return trip to Bohemia, if you have resolved that one doubt."

"You were not in favor of the journey."

"No."

"You do not approve of the sponsor."

". . . No."

"You do not even wish to be walking with me to the Hotel Belgrade to interview La Belle Tatyana."

"Decidedly not! And she is not beautiful. Not really. It is all pose and gall."

"You are saying that she is not worthy to be Irene's rival?"

"Yes!"

"Yet, at times, you like to see Irene confronted with one, do you not?"

"She becomes . . . imperious."

"But she is so becoming when she is imperious." His devil-may-care grin quickly faded into a slight frown. "I have been a bit boisterous in throwing the King back in her face. I was worried, I fear; abashed by his rank and reputation. He is not what I thought."

"He is not what she thought, once—and I must say that he has declined even more since we left Bohemia. At least in those days he never intended to flaunt a mistress before his wife-to-be. Now that Clotilde is queen, he has no qualms in parading this Tatyana woman before her."

"Clotilde is helpless, and the deed is done now."

"What deed?"

"The marriage. He has Clotilde's dowry, an alliance with her influential family, a royal road to a properly regal heir. He will have his cake and eat crackers, too. That is a flaw that kings share with common men."

I kept silent. Everything Godfrey had said was absolute truth and made perfect sense. Only Irene and I—and poor, ignored, snubbed Clotilde—knew that the King was committing one incomprehensible error: he was not bothering to ensure a royal heir. Why?

Little time remained to ponder this puzzle. Godfrey and I had arrived at a Baroque facade in the Malá Strana that claimed to be the Hotel Belgrade.

Liveried men ushered us through gleaming leaded-glass doors. Godfrey's inquiry with the concierge further directed us up a grand staircase so thickly carpeted in a frantic floral pattern that it was possible to lose one's footing on the shallow stairs.

After two flights of gazing at this dizzying sight, especially with my pince-nez on, I had to be guided down the passage. The hall was not the narrow, functional tunnel of most hotels, but wide as a river and furnished with side chairs and paintings, like a palace.

At a carved, white-painted door on which a gilt number seven gleamed like a golden spike, Godfrey paused to knock. A maid in serviceable black topped with white organdy apron and cap admitted us. Beyond her lurked a sullen-looking individual in a crude, food-stained tunic, his

eyes a queer, intense blue that sliced through one like ice
daggers of lethal, clear Russian vodka. We passed into a
suite of rooms that could have been transported to Hradčany and no one the wiser. The maid took Godfrey's top
hat, gloves and cane, although he watched her set the cane
in an umbrella stand in the hall. Naturally, I kept all of my
accoutrements, though they were less deadly than his.

We were shown into a salon lit by crystal chandeliers and
paraffin lamps. Wine-red brocade covered the divan and
numerous large hassocks that flocked around the floor like
overupholstered sheep. What was not red in the room was
emerald green, or gilt.

Clutter crowded and towered around every table. Rare
artifacts winked from hither and yon, with enameled eggs
sitting on the glazed tiles before the hearth and gleaming
behind piles of gilt-edged books. Scarves of erratic design
lay like snakeskins over tables and chairbacks. Furs tumbled off chair seats. Vases erupted like Vesuvius with lilies:
tiger lilies, tulip lilies, calla lilies, sago lilies, even modest
little lilies-of-no-name staked a claim on every uncrowded
surface, giving off no scent, yet contributing to an effect of
hothouse enclosure.

Oil paintings burdened with wide gilt frames lined the
walls, many depicting the ballet; some were by the Frenchman Degas, whose messy little sketches I had seen in Paris.

Over a mantel bristling with gingerbread trinkets hung
the largest and most surprising painting, a colorful study of
some impossibly barbaric princess, half-dressed, and what
little she wore mostly beads and veils. Who this figure
represented I could not say. Salome? Messalina? Another
debauched temptress of legendary origin? Although her
hair glimmered dark beneath a decadent web of veils and
gold, I recognized the hard, haughty features for those of
the self-proclaimed Tatyana.

The original of the painting soon swept in from another
chamber, wafting a zephyr of cinnamon, roses and delicate
iris. We regarded her aghast.

Except for being pulled back at the temples by a beaded fillet, her hair hung ungoverned over her shoulders and back, in heavy, straight lengths. She wore a flowing, flame-colored brocade caftan edged everywhere in a narrow band of soft brown fur—foaming at the hem with each step, edging wide, drooping medieval sleeves and the impertinent neckline that skimmed her bare shoulders. A huge topaz the color of peach brandy dangled in an elaborate setting against the corpse-pale whiteness of her breast.

Compared to a Liberty silk, this gown was suited to boudoir, not sitting room, and certainly not to the presence of a member of the opposite sex. Some would argue with me, including Sarah Bernhardt and even Irene. Perhaps I should say that the toilette was not suited for the eyes of a *stranger* of the opposite sex.

Godfrey had practiced enough law to betray no shock at this unseemly sight. I maintained my professional expression of utter indifference, which some (such as Irene, and now Allegra) are so bold to describe as my "disapproving look."

Tatyana bloomed in her exotic environment like the most wild of her tiger lilies and smiled.

"So kind of you to come at such an unreasonable hour, Mr. Norton," she said in her fermented English accent. "Too late for a civil English tea; too early for a decadent Viennese supper. We will have Russian tea," she added, nodding to a huge brass samovar where the maid stood poised, looking much too proper for this tea party.

I looked upward, expecting to see the figured folds of a massive tent, but spied only a coffered ceiling.

"And this is your . . . secretary," she added, eyeing me as we threaded our way through the flocks of furniture to the round table heaped with piles of raw-looking food-stuffs. "I realize that many men of affairs travel with secretaries, but I have never known one to employ a woman. Such a thing is so improper in English circles, is it not?" She eyed me meticulously from bonnet top to boot tip.

"Yet who could suspect Miss . . . Rucksleigh, is it? . . . of being other than completely proper?"

I know an insult even when I agree with—in fact, applaud—its import.

"No one in this room," I answered, looking inquiringly at the bulbous samovar, which had the overblown, brassy presence of one of St. Petersburg's onion-domes. The Russians, on the whole, cherish an obvious, vulgar appeal that is not in the least subtle, but no doubt they would argue with my opinion.

Tatyana nodded to the maid, who drew steaming cups of something in pewter mugs.

"Russian tea," Tatyana taunted me . . . and Godfrey. "Prosit." She sipped, watching us over the crude brim, as if we were missionaries at a cannibal feast and she were imbibing blood. At least if she spilled any, it would not mar her incarnadine gown.

"Nine cheers to the Queen," Godfrey replied.

"Santé," I offered in sour French whose accent was no more to be trusted than the sincerity of my sentiments.

I sipped cautiously, along with Godfrey. The drink was heated! A kind of mulled wine, only without wine . . . spiced, yet sweet as well, and punctuated by something strong and searing that reminded me of rubbing alcohol. I contained a cough while Godfrey raised his eyebrows.

I set my mug upon the serving table and would drink no more.

Godfrey laughed. "You see why I break tradition. Miss Huxleigh is utterly dependable. I care not what others may think or say."

Tatyana eyed him with growing respect as he continued to quaff the mysterious beverage. "Yet you are wed."

When he looked surprised, she glanced at his left hand. "You wear a golden band." Her disdainful tone made it sound like the ring through a bull's nose.

Godfrey remained unstirred. "True, on both counts."

"Does not your wife, who is at home in—?"

"The French countryside."

"In . . . France. Does she not chafe at the notion of your traveling with a single woman as a secretary?"

Now that the odious Tatyana had summarized my position, I blushed for myself. Or perhaps the flush came from my one sip of the forbidden beverage.

"My wife is a confident woman," he replied, "and my work takes me often away. Perhaps she regards Miss Huxleigh as an ideal chaperon."

"No doubt." Tatyana prowled around the tea table, at last selecting a toast round heaped with a black mountain of tiny, shining beads.

I recognized thin slices of some rosy flesh, obviously cold, as were all the victuals, in contrast to the heated beverage. Other than a few pert sprigs of parsley, I could see nothing edible besides these unappetizing and slippery raw, iced foods of uncertain ancestry.

"You must forgive me if I do not understand the manners of the frigid West," Tatyana said. "Where I have lived for most of my life, women are either Everything, or Nothing. That is, to a man they are either the bounds of his whole existence, his whole mind and heart and soul, or they are mere functionaries. A woman who is neither the potential object of passion nor an indifferent object of use, is an exception."

"I have always considered Miss Huxleigh to be an exception of the first water," Godfrey replied promptly. "And I have always found women capable of more than two extremes, and far more interesting for that fact."

She glanced again at him, her gaze not the usual, rapid consultation of his expression, but rather a summing up of his whole person, from head to toe, from outer aspect to inmost essence. She seemed determined that not a pinstripe in his trousers should go unnumbered, that not a hair on his clean-shaven chin should be unanticipated.

This distressed me in a nameless way that was even more

worrisome. So hunters might eye prey from a distance before the chase was on.

"How have you become so exalted an emissary?" she asked then, crunching sharply on her bead-slathered toast. I was reminded of the fee-fie-foe-fum giant grinding the bones of an Englishman.

"There is little exalted about the Rothschilds, other than their recent rank and great fortune," Godfrey said in a tone of amusement that I would have found quite cutting. "Nor is there anything exalted about myself. I am an ordinary barrister who has some experience in international law. The facts about myself are that simple."

"I disagree, Englishman." Tatyana glowed before my eyes, visibly warming up to this verbal fencing match. "Great fortune and international affairs are the stuff of exalted drama, infinite wealth and much adventure, both remote and personal."

"Barristers know nothing of adventure," he said mildly, picking among the savage tidbits for something consumable.

She watched him eat as if she would taste him next. I had been forgotten, one of those nonessential functional women named "Nothing."

If I found this realization bitter, I found it satisfying also. Irene had bid me watch and wait, not an ignoble role. Now I could observe, unwatched myself. Now I had become a piece of furniture that would be ignored.

I did not extract my notebook and pencil. The matters I witnessed here required a more subtle record. I prayed that I would see—and remember—the germane parts. I slipped as silently as I could to a seat on a nearby hassock and joined myself to that which I was taken for. Furniture.

"What do barristers know of?" Tatyana asked, not moving as Godfrey roved around the table, thus forcing him close within her orbit. Even at my ignored distance I could inhale her heady perfume.

Godfrey smiled. "Horsehair wigs. Endless suits. Senile judges. The law's delay and the client's greater delay in payment. The injustice of justice. Some triumph, more defeat. The pleasure of waiting, and sometimes of winning. None of this adds up to adventure."

"Perhaps." She took his pewter mug, refilled it at the samovar, sipped from it, then replaced it in his hands, curling his fingers around the metal in a most familiar way, as if to warm them.

Godfrey's eyes narrowed, a sharp expression that only enhanced the striking clarity of his features.

"You are dark for an Englishman," she commented, "but your eyes are light as pewter."

"Common enough coloring for an English barrister," he said.

"Not in Russia, where we do not have many barristers, but an immense number of judges, soldiers and aristocrats."

"What are you there?" he asked suddenly.

She seemed taken aback.

"Are you Everything, or Nothing?"

"You know the answer," she said, her odd red-brown eyes as ruddy as the brew she served. "I was . . . a ballerina."

He glanced to the huge painting over the fireplace. "You danced that role?"

"Later I danced many roles. They were all . . . Everything."

"As dancing once was."

She nodded slowly, taking his cup between her hands to drink deep of her own lethal liquid.

"You no longer dance?" he asked. Despite his wariness, sympathy tinged his voice.

"Not the ballet," she admitted, thrusting the cup back at him and swirling away to regard the painting.

He set down the tainted cup. "An injury?"

"Yes. And no. An injury not fully physical."

"Is any injury physical only?"

"No." She turned. "Where did you learn that?"

"Not," he said, "before the English bar."

"How have you transgressed?" she demanded with sudden passion. "What have you done wrong? Why can you no longer practice law in London? Why do you live in France? Why does your wife not keep a shorter leash on you? What do you hope to gain for the Rothschilds? What are you doing here in Bohemia?"

"My dear woman," he remonstrated, "you must never rush your cross-examination."

She had drawn nearer to him on every question. Now she reared back like a still but striking snake.

" 'Rush?' " she asked.

"Hasten."

"I am . . . Russian," she answered, her smile askew, "therefore I rush. Yet I never invade where I am not wanted."

"I beg to differ. Russia has a habit of overrunning weaker nations. Consider the Afghanistan adventure."

"What do you know of that?"

"Only what I read in the newspapers. And what about the recent Naval Treaty England parlayed with Italy. Was not Russia eager to disrupt it?"

Now *her* eyes narrowed, not as attractive a sight as the expression was in Godfrey's face. "How does a simple barrister living abroad know of such things?"

"I read the *Daily Telegraph* and I work for the Rothschilds."

"What can they pay you for such employment?"

"You would be surprised."

"Nothing surprises me," she swore, drawing closer, then gripping the lapels of his frock coat.

I stifled a gasp, knowing better than to interrupt such an illuminating scene, though it racked my conscience.

Godfrey had grown very still, as a man might in the presence of a lethal serpent.

She leaned into him, against him. "I would surprise you, Mr. Barrister. I promise it. And I can offer you more than a Rothschild. I am Russian!"

"I believe it," he said fervently, but whether he referred to her boast to outdo the Rothschilds or to her claims of nationality, I am not certain to this day.

Certainly something odd was transpiring here. I itched to produce my notebook and jot down a few crucial notations. Irene would no doubt interrogate me as to every word employed when I reported on this encounter. I did not wish to miss a telling nuance. Yet I could not doubt that this Tatyana considered herself powerful enough in the current political struggle that she could tempt Godfrey with the promise of turning traitor to her own cause.

She might make a useful ally, but hardly one whom we could trust.

"Your sphere of influence is the King," Godfrey pointed out; indeed, he stressed her improper alliance.

"The King!" she spat contemptuously. "He is . . . Nothing."

"As am I," he reminded her.

"Not if I say otherwise." Her fingers twined in his lapels, wrapping themselves in the silk facing as if to bend him to her wishes, twining herself into his presence.

She lifted her face to his, swaying slightly, the fur ebbing over her bare shoulders, her eyes heavy and hooded. So I had seen Sarah Bernhardt enact a death scene . . . and some others.

He clasped her encroaching wrists. Odd. I saw his knuckles whiten, as if he exerted tremendously more force than was evident.

"I am here," he reminded her, "to inquire if you wish to aid the Rothschild interests."

Her voice grew low, and slowed. She spoke as thickly as the potent "Russian tea" poured from the spigot of the samovar. "I wish to aid where I desire. If you would serve the Rothschild interests and have Bohemia serve them, you must serve mine in turn."

"So little would turn you?"

"You mistake me. I do not dabble . . . in anything. I am an unforgettable ally, and a merciless enemy."

"Do you threaten me?"

"With that? Never. Never . . . you."

"Do you have as much influence with the King as you imply?"

"With more than the King! With the Czar."

"Then you admit that Russia is deeply interested in the doings of Bohemia and its king?"

"Yes!"

"Why?"

"It does not matter! You have guessed as much. You are not stupid. I prefer you to be not stupid."

"Is the King stupid?"

"Infinitely!"

"Yet you—"

"One is business; the other—"

"Yes?

She laughed then, lazily; at him, at herself; perhaps at anyone foolish enough to witness this bizarre cross-examination.

"The other is—" Her voice had sunk so low that he unthinkingly bowed toward her, as I leaned forward on my humble hassock to capture every word, every revelation. Was that not what we were here for?

She put her hands on his shoulders and thrust her face up suddenly to his, whispered fast and warmly into his ear, her face avid, triumphant.

Godfrey drew away as from an attack, but the weight of her entire body hung from his shoulders, all that ponderous brocade and fur weighing him down.

A moment later conventional space intervened between

them. I blinked, sensing the jaws of a steel trap released in some invisible fashion.

"I have told you all I can." She spoke in smooth, thick, sweet tones, then strode to the fireplace, leaning her forehead against the long, cool marble mantelpiece. Above her the savage painted empress glared out on the room and its occupants in surly defense.

The fur swagged so low over Tatyana's pale, naked back that it was clear she wore no corsets. Her shoulder blades seemed as sharp and severe as a shark's fins. I was shocked that a woman would reveal so much of herself to a strange man, even to a strange woman, but Godfrey seemed beyond shock.

He quickly came to me, took my elbow and piloted me to the door, where the pert maid curtsied as she let us out. Of the sinister and slovenly manservant I saw nothing.

By the time we arrived in silence at the street, we saw that dark had fallen and gazed around us, baffled by such a natural occurrence after the unnatural atmosphere created by Tatyana's rooms and presence.

"We should probably hunt a hansom," Godfrey said. Then he turned to me, agitated. "Can you bear to walk, Nell? I feel the need of . . . air."

"How close she kept that suite, everything overheated and cluttered! It was even worse than Sarah Bernhardt's salon."

He laughed, faintly. "How right you are! Worse than Sarah's by far. Would it shock you, Nell, if we paused at a beer garden on the way back? Some honest ale would be a boon."

"I cannot blame you for wishing to rinse your palate after that beverage you shared!" I agreed. "I will not object if you promise not to smoke and do not stay long."

"Not long," he said fervently, "and we must decide what to tell Irene."

"What is to decide? This Tatyana has admitted her illegitimate involvement with the King, and that her real interests lie with her native Russia. You masterfully extracted all the pertinent information, and we went on our way after being subjected to some bizarre and barbaric hospitality that I do not wish to describe or even recall, for my stomach's sake. I am sorry that I found it unnatural to take notes, Godfrey, but I can at least summarize what sense I extracted from the outing."

"Ah, Nell." He squeezed my shoulder as if I were young and foolish like Allegra. "Who needs fresh air when you are present and more bracing than a Channel breeze? Of course we will tell Irene all that, but first you must allow me one small detour to . . . recover from the contents of the samovar. What a man must subject himself to in order to accomplish a simple piece of spy business!"

"The food was as bad as the drink," I added. "I cannot think what the Russians hope to accomplish in the world if they can cook no better than the Bohemians, the Germans or the French."

"You are right, Nell; English cooking will conquer the globe. Now, I see the sign of U Kalicha banging in the wind. Only a beer parlor sign would bear the image of a chalice. Let us pause there."

"I can be no less happy than that awful Tatyana woman to serve my country," I said stoutly as he drew me in the torchlit direction of roistering voices, "even if the means are extremely unpleasant."

Chapter Twenty-three

A ROYAL FULL HOUSE

Godfrey's ingestion of Bohemian courage (and my renewed immersion into the smoky clatter of a beer garden) proved unnecessary. We returned after dark to the Europa to find Irene and Allegra safe in their suite, full of their own adventures of the afternoon.

"Look!" Allegra demanded, cavorting up to greet us. She flourished her wrist to display a bangle of deep-crimson garnets. "We bought it from a street peddler, can you imagine?"

"A pretty trinket," Godfrey said absently, eyeing Irene.

I examined it more closely. "No doubt glass, or an inferior type of garnet. One can buy nothing on the street worth having; remember that in the future, dear girl."

"And I had my fortune read by a real gypsy woman! Mrs. Norton knows such odd nooks and crannies. This particular place was absolutely . . . thrilling! Dark despite the daylight outside, lit only by a lamp shaped like a human skull, can you believe it, Miss Huxleigh?"

"Indeed I can, and did you manage to make an appointment with the Golem as well?"

"No." Allegra donned a face of grave disappointment. "But we saw the Jewish cemetery! Such a shiversome site!

All those piled tombstones tilting this way and that as if to loose their ancient occupants. Of course, no one has been buried there in more than two centuries, but the Golem's master, Rabbi Loew, has a prominent tomb—almost as large as a London monument. People still leave notes there begging his—and the Golem's—protection. Can you fathom it?"

While Allegra regaled me with tales of Prague street life, Godfrey divested himself of hat, cane and gloves and went to Irene, who sat (or lounged rather, after the habit of Sarah Bernhardt) on the sofa.

Allegra demanded a full audience, and capered up to him before he could sit. "What do you think the fortune-teller predicted for me, Mr. Norton? She said that I will marry three times! I will have fourteen children, and will travel to China. Do you think that possible?"

"Everything is possible. And what did she predict for Irene?" he asked, turning to his wife.

"Oh, nothing so interesting as my fortune," Allegra answered hastily for her. "She did say that Irene would have a tattoo."

"A tattoo?" I repeated faintly.

"Did she say where?" Godfrey asked, sitting beside Irene with an air of relief.

"In Tibet," Allegra said.

He smiled. "I meant, where on Irene, not where on the surface of the globe, would this be accomplished?"

Irene bestirred herself. She seemed unusually tired, or contemplative. "Some things even a fortune-teller cannot predict. We must leave something to the imagination."

"Tibet?" I repeated. "*I* shall never go there. It must be an even more ungodly place than Afghanistan."

Allegra again erupted in a fresh lava of words, catching hold of my hand in her enthusiasm. "Oh, and Miss Huxleigh, I asked if—when—I would ever see my uncle Quentin again, if he was alive, and she answered instantly. 'Within a fortnight, child,' she said in a quavery but most convincing voice. She was quite, quite strangely . . . believable."

I was not aware of paling; Allegra kept hold of my hand and seized my arm to guide me to a chair.

"My dear girl," I said when I had sat and caught my breath, "you must put no faith in these street entertainers. How irresponsible of that gypsy woman to have said that! Don't you see the opposite and more sinister implication?"

"Oh." Allegra sat on the arm of my chair, suddenly sober. "She could have meant that I will see Quentin soon because I, too, will ere long be dead."

"Nonsense!" Irene interrupted with her usual spirit. "Allegra is the apple of all our eyes and could not be safer. Gypsy fortune-tellers are amusing but not a source of honest information. Speaking of safety—" She eyed Godfrey and myself in turn. "How went your interview with the estimable Tatyana?"

"Vile woman!" I blurted out despite myself. "She makes Sarah Bernhardt seem the soul of sweetness and light. I sense a deep unhappiness in her, yet it is clear that her immoral relationship to the King is more a matter of politics than of personal satisfaction, and somehow I find that more detestable than honest passion. She spoke quite readily of betraying the King if the Rothschild coffers opened wide enough to persuade her."

Irene turned to her husband, who had become as withdrawn as she had been but moments before. "And what did you think of her, friend barrister?"

"A formidable woman and a wily opponent, as you suspected. She is surely the power behind the King, such as he is. One wonders if he requires a strong woman to lead him, either to good or ill."

Irene shaped her clever, pretty hands into a steeple, spreading her fingers and thumbs, and regarded this mirror image of opposing extremities.

"The King I knew," she said, "considered himself strong

enough to neither fear nor need an equally strong woman. Perhaps . . . vanity has since led him astray." Her glance at Godfrey was swift and piercing. "Perhaps I would have been a good influence." She smiled wickedly. "Then again, I am not thrifty. Perhaps I would have bankrupted the royal coffers and driven him into the hands of the bankers, the blackmailers and the political plotters sooner rather than later."

Godfrey spoke slowly. "He always was cold-blooded about his marriage, but at the beginning he at least wished to be discreet about his outside interests. I must wonder why he has capitulated to such an open alliance with this Tatyana when he would have hidden Irene in southern Bohemia?"

"If Tatyana is whom I believe her to be," Irene said, "she is not merely a mistress, but a fellow plotter, a cohort. She may not even be his mistress; that may be a mere subterfuge. Certainly, she has no true feeling for him. Nell? Did you watch and observe?"

"Religiously, Irene!"

Godfrey stirred in alarm. "What does Irene mean, Nell? Was more going on during the visit to the Belgrade Hotel than I realized?"

"I am sorry to disillusion you, Godfrey, but I had a hidden assignment. Irene is convinced—on very little evidence, I might add—that Tatyana is the Russian woman we glimpsed consorting with Colonel Moran at Sarah Bernhardt's salon."

"That woman's hair was a heavy, honey blond!" Godfrey objected instantly. "And she was not quite so tall."

Irene chortled triumphantly. "How specifically you noticed, husband dear! Yet men are so swayed by externals. It never crossed your mind, I would wager, that you have just spent nearly an hour in the same woman's company."

He frowned, trying to mesh his memories of the two women.

"Nell, however," Irene went on, "suffers from no such handicaps, although I admit she was as much a doubting Thomas as you. So, Nell, what is your verdict?"

"She could be the same impertinent creature," I admitted, "with her hair tinted red. And she could be wearing high heels. Yet, in that case, should she not have immediately recognized you and Godfrey, if not me as well?"

"Who is to say that she has not?" Irene suggested. "Certainly she will not oblige us by confessing that! If she is the spy that I suspect, she is far too subtle to give away a game until the last card is played."

"The fur is most suspicious," I added.

"Fur?" Irene inquired.

"Her gown tonight—other than being most shockingly . . . unanchored—was edged all over in some very soft brown fur, like Messalina's, only much lighter in texture and color."

Irene eyed her silent spouse, who was looking more appalled by the moment.

"No doubt Godfrey hardly noted such details of dress, even such interesting . . . unanchored . . . dress. Did you have an opportunity to consult your diaries, Nell, and did a blond woman loiter near Notre Dame when we encountered Quentin there?"

"Yes," I murmured unhappily.

Why it distressed me so much when Irene was right about some apparently trivial detail, I cannot say, except that I am the diarist and she rarely deigns to write down anything.

"In fact," I added, "on rereading my observations I must ask myself if she could not have easily administered the cobra poison injection that leveled poor Quentin to our feet on that unfortunate occasion. She brushed by him very closely, and she was wearing a gown edged in some brown fur, although the weather was warm for it."

"Ah!" Irene leaped up in a huntress's rapture. "I thought she might have been suspect in that, and this fur sounds the nature of a trademark. A woman like Tatyana is prone to a fatal vanity. Can you recognize sable when you see it, Nell?"

"I fear not, but if it is brown, fine, and looks costly, I suppose that is what she wears. My diaries also confirm the point you mentioned, that a Russian spy named Sable was in the neighborhood of Afghanistan when Quentin, as Cobra, went head-to-head with his traitorous fellow British spy Tiger, whom we now know as the hopefully deceased Colonel Sebastian Moran."

"Perfect!" Irene crowed, prancing around the room as gaily as Allegra. In fact, she caught the girl's hands in passing and they both galloped over the carpets as if at a May dance, until they collapsed together on a sofa, laughing. "We have named our mongoose and it is a Sable," Irene chortled.

"Oh, Mrs. Norton, you are such fun!" Allegra said, panting, "but I have not the slightest notion of what you are talking about most of the time."

"Welcome to the ranks of those who know Irene," Godfrey said a trifle grimly. "Why did you not tell me your suspicions?" he demanded of his wife in the next breath.

"I wanted an objective observer, and—pardon me, Godfrey—men are not always the most objective when it comes to femmes fatales. Now you may tell me what *you* think of Tatyana, her motives and ends, her scarlet-dyed hair and shifting furs."

"Nell exaggerates the furs," he said uneasily, "but I believe that you are right: she does not love the King. I doubt that she could love any man, she is so enamored of herself and her games of manipulation."

"It is possible to loathe men, and still use them; in fact, necessary. Yet if she is indeed a Russian spy of long standing, any alliance she makes will only serve her first loyalty—to her country and perhaps to a man who introduced her to spywork."

"Colonel Moran?" I suggested.

Irene whirled at my question. "I doubt that, although they may be associates of long standing."

Another matter puzzled me. "If we have deciphered her role and presence, why should she not know us?"

"She may, but she would no more reveal that than I would drop my pose of Lady Sherlock and go about as ordinary Irene Adler Norton."

"There is nothing ordinary about you, Mrs. Norton," Allegra intoned in the voice of pure heroine worship.

"Thank you," Irene said modestly, "but we dare not bask now that we have measured our opponent. Obviously, the King is the weakest link in this alliance, and there we should concentrate our attention. We know that rivals do not sit well with him. Perhaps we should try his soul. Perhaps Godfrey should pay some outward attention to the fair Tatyana."

He jumped as if scalded. "I think not, Irene. She is no one to trifle with."

"Oh, pooh! I am not suggesting any serious seduction; merely a few politenesses of which news may travel back to Prague Castle. You might send her flowers, for instance, in thanks for today's interview. You will always be chaperoned by Nell, of course." Irene glided to take hold of Godfrey's lapels in the same insinuating manner as the detestable Tatyana, although with a far more silken, mocking touch, as if she had anticipated Tatyana's wiles and their exact form. "I know I can trust you utterly, dear Godfrey, no matter what vixen with whom you are forced to associate."

"I have no difficulty associating with the trustworthy vixen; indeed, I am accustomed to it, but what of the untrustworthy vixen?" he murmured.

"A vixen is only as untrustworthy as her victim," Irene declared, "and I have implicit faith in you." She turned to us. "As well as in Nell and Allegra."

She regarded us with a blinding smile, but I noticed an

expression of deep unease on Allegra's face that rivaled a
similar expression on Godfrey's.

After dinner, employing wiles that I would hitherto have
attributed only to the despised Tatyana, I managed to separate Allegra from my friends by suggesting that I could use
her advice. I refused to say upon what subject—which
wildly intrigued Irene, but she could not harass me in public.

Thus Allegra came to my chamber for the alleged consultation, while Irene and Godfrey proceeded about their own
business of the evening.

"How so sweet and clever of you!" Allegra congratulated
me as soon as my chamber door closed upon us.

"Whatever are you speaking about?"

"Why . . . how you arranged for Godfrey and Irene—I
mean, the Nortons—to escape our tiresome presence so
they could be alone. Obviously, they were dying for some
privacy."

"What is obvious to you is far from so to me," I returned, affronted. "And my . . . request relates only to you
and I."

"Surely you realize that this rooming arrangement is
most trying for a married couple?"

"It is? I am afraid that has not occurred to me. Other
than the Incident of the Wandering Chambermate, I have
noticed no dissatisfaction with the present arrangement."

"You have been sleeping alone," Allegra pointed out.

"I should hope so. I am a spinster, after all, and I do not
see what is not my business."

"I am a spinster as well," Allegra pointed out with a
disavowing pout, "but I am not blind!"

"Nor am I," I retorted, getting to the matter at hand.
"There is a matter of which I must know more, that has
nothing to do with the rooming arrangements of my
friends, wed or unwed."

I sat on the upholstered chair, as I was the elder. Allegra, instead of taking the straight chair—as, say, Godfrey would do—plumped herself down upon my bed, wrinkling the coverlet.

"What, Miss Huxleigh, is your hidden purpose for this meeting?" she demanded mischievously. "And do you have nothing to eat? I am hungry already."

Since I had seen her consume great quantities of mediocre Bohemian food at dinner, I was surprised, to say the least.

"There is some fruit in a basket on the desk."

"Fruit! Oh, well."

She flounced over to capture some grapes and returned to my bed, which she proceeded to bounce upon. Indeed, I had forgotten the exuberance of the young, and blessed fate that my governess days were over.

"What are you worried about?" she asked, sitting up to peel a grape in a disgusting manner. "Cat's eyes!" she announced, swallowing the product of her depredation.

I tried to remember that even the young can be valuable witnesses if properly led during an examination.

"Allegra, dear; I am most fearful that I have not heard the full report of your and Irene's day about Prague. Certainly I have heard nothing of the Queen's role in all of this."

"Oh, the Queen. What a darling! So shy. So . . . well, shockingly unqueenly. Irene says that she has had a cruel trick of fate played upon her, and that whenever the World attempts to turn a Queen into a Pawn, it is up to We Women to Right the Balance."

"We women?" I stared at Allegra, who was lying prone upon my lofty feather comforter, popping peeled grapes into her mobile mouth.

Allegra sat up by pounding her fists into the overambitious feathers. "Yes! I think it quite remarkable of Irene to forgive her former rival and take her part. The King is unworthy of both of them put together, even though, between us, Irene would be six times the Queen poor Clotilde will ever be!"

"Irene told you of her former . . . expectations of the King? I did not know—"

"What do you think we talked of during four interminable days of rail travel across Europe? The King . . . men in general and particular. Fashion. Men in general and particular. My possible future. Irene's past. Men in general and particular—"

I had not expected to experience the spasm of jealousy that I did. Allegra now knew such things a decade before I even had considered them.

"What men . . . in general . . . did you speak of?"

"The King, of course. He is our main target on this mission. And Godfrey, a bit. Irene was most understanding of my admiration for him, but she says that it will pass. And . . . Quentin," she added, biting her lip.

Tears briefly polished her already bright eyes. "I remember him from the pinnacle of my youth, dear Miss Huxleigh—and you as well. He is the first person whom I have cared for who is supposed to be dead. I admit that I cherished a . . . fondness for him, although we were related, but Irene says that this, too, is quite natural. She said that I was fortunate to have such a worthy object of my admiration in my youth."

I had been young in those days, as well, as young as I ever was. I clasped my hands, then donned my pince-nez and took up a blank notebook.

"Allegra. I am most interested in your and Irene's visit to this fortune-teller. Did the Queen go as well?"

"Oh, yes. She went everywhere with us. She wore one of her maid's gowns and she loved being nobody. Really and truly! She is so much more pleasant away from the castle. Almost like an ordinary person. I cannot tell you what good our outing did her. She almost wept to return."

"What did the fortune-teller really say? I could see that you reported only part of it."

"Could you?" Allegra pounded the feather quilt like a child in a tantrum. "I did think I had been so . . . subtle."

"Allegra. I once was your governess. It is true that I was young myself then, but I was not blind," I said, paraphrasing the minx.

"Oh, Miss Huxleigh, you are not half so blind as you would have us all think! And I must tell you. My fortune spoke so glowingly of Uncle Quentin. I shall see him again, I know I shall! Only—" Her face sobered.

In an instant her high spirits fell. Childish fear touched her features.

"Oh, Miss Huxleigh, the woman said such . . . odd things. It was not the small thing here and there that struck me—that I shall marry many times and have many children. One expects to hear such nonsense from a gypsy fortune-teller. Or that Irene will have a tattoo and go to Tibet. How I wish that you had been there! Perhaps you could have made some sense of it. She spoke direly also— to all three of us. I confess that it haunts me."

I decided to begin with the fortunes that least touched me. "What did she say to the Queen?"

"Oh, that was odd! She said that Clotilde would rise higher in the world than she appeared to be at this moment."

"Indeed, Clotilde has already done that. Could the fortune-teller have recognized her?"

"In the Old Town? I doubt it, but it is possible. Then she said that she saw a chessboard—"

"Irene's metaphor!"

"Exactly. With three queens and two kings upon the squares."

"A chess set has two queens and two kings."

"I know. It is like a secret message from one of Uncle Quentin's anonymous spies! Clotilde was quite bewildered, but Irene leaned forward and listened as if she took this all quite seriously."

What could I say? That I had sat in the same rug-draped room with Irene two years before, and learned that the letter G named the man whose fate entwined Irene's? The King of Bohemia's middle name was Gottsreich, which Irene thought of at the time, not Godfrey whom I knew then as a kind employer who was hostile to her, not as my friend's spouse-to-be. So far as I knew from my one experience, the gypsy fortune-teller had an unnervingly accurate record, which Allegra could not know, and would not know until I had wormed every detail from her.

"What did this woman—she was old?"

"Aren't they always?"

"I fear so. What more did she say of Clotilde?"

"That true love had not found her, but would."

"A sop."

"Perhaps, but it cheered the Queen."

"Was a date given for this miracle?"

"No." Allegra blinked and bit her lip again. "Dear Miss Huxleigh—may I call you 'Nell'? I feel the fortune-teller has drawn us all together in common hope . . . and common disaster."

Who was I to insist on proper formalities when so much that was improper was unfolding around us?

"Call me what you will," I urged her, "but tell me what you know!"

"Dear Nell . . . I must say that although the woman promised me a reunion with Uncle Quentin she also promised much danger—soon. And for Irene—"

"What did she say about Irene?"

"She said that three queens reigned in Prague at present. One would triumph; one would escape; and one would . . . face mortal danger."

"Irene triumphs. Always."

"In . . . Prague? Always?"

"In Prague as well. True, we fled this city once, but that was triumph. It is all in how one looks at it, Allegra."

"Yet the old woman said that Irene was in mortal danger."

"She said so—specifically?"

"Yes. And . . . myself."

"You! Why should anyone wish to harm you?"

"I cannot imagine. Irene was disturbed, I could see, although she made light of all our predictions after we left the place. I sensed that she regretted taking us there."

"So she should! She has a fearful weakness for the lurid. Remember that most fortune-tellers should be on stage, and often have been."

"Yes, Nell." Said quite meekly, despite the personal presumption I had permitted in a weak moment. I had my own frailties.

"Did the old woman say anything more of . . . your uncle Quentin?"

"Oh, how careless of me! I have forgotten that you, too, knew him from years back, and that your reacquaintance is what returned him to our family, however briefly."

"Acquaintance," it seemed to me, would no longer quite describe Quentin's and my relationship, though I could not explain this to Allegra, no matter what she called me.

She grasped my hands as if wishing to warm her own, which were icy.

"The woman was most odd about Quentin. She spoke of one dead and not-dead. I wondered if she confused Quentin with the Golem! She spoke of one cast away and imprisoned, who would—pardon me, Nell, I know you take such talk seriously—'rise again.' She murmured of evil plots and 'plots' that sounded like grave sites. She was most cryptic."

"*Crypt* indeed is the word. All nonsense, as you would see had you not been infected with 'Prague fever.' This ancient town, with its medieval quarters and its Cabbalistic history and its current affairs shrouding reality in plot and counterplot, is not a wholesome influence. Now, I have

seen sights today that truly chill the blood, and I have not
had to leave the environs of the Belgrade Hotel to accomplish it.''

"How so?"

"You are young, and could not understand."

"Miss Huxleigh. Nell. I have told you all. You can but
reciprocate.''

"I am not sure that even I understand myself what transpired.''

"Then you must share the experience." Allegra patted
the feather quilt, which sank six inches at her attentions.

I eyed it askance. Sitting upon goose down always made
one sink like a stone, and look like a drowning goose.

"Do get comfortable," Allegra urged, "and we do not
wish anyone to overhear us.''

"Here? In my room?"

She leaned near. "The walls have ears."

"I doubt it." Yet I studied the wallpaper, which was
excessively busy in the Austrian style. Could not such
design mania conceal the subtle peephole?

"Hop up," Allegra urged.

I eyed the quilt. "I do not 'hop.' ''

"Then leap like a gazelle, dear Nell, and tell me your
deepest worries. Believe me, not a word of it shall pass
beyond these ears.''

I obliged, and found myself the proud possessor of a
peeled grape that I did not wish to touch, given her grisly
appellation for same.

"Tell me," the dear girl urged, and I confess that the
temptation was intense.

"Well," I began, "it seems that the archvillainess
Tatyana has conceived an ill-advised interest in Godfrey."

"Oh, there is nothing ill-advised in such an interest at
all," Allegra assured me. "I am surprised that you have not
realized that.''

"I was his typewriter-girl at the Temple," I said; "such an
interest would have been quite inappropriate."

"Yet it would have been such fun, Nell. Have you never suffered from an ill-advised interest in your entire life?"

"Once," said I, accepting another rather slimy grape and ingesting it.

"In whom?" she demanded rapturously.

I knew what she expected, the untrustworthy minx, and was prepared for her.

"A country curate," I replied, "of the name of Jaspar. With two *a*'s." Then I recited chapter and verse in all particulars about the unfortunate Curate Higgenbottom.

And so I soon had Allegra drowsy and begging to repair to her room—whether Irene was there yet or not. That left me free to speculate on the significant pieces of information I had cajoled out of her in two hours, with the aid of two given names and six grapes. Casanova would have been proud.

7

Chapter Twenty-four

MINUET IN G

My next interview was with Irene herself. I encouraged Allegra to send her to my room by allowing my reminiscences of the lamented Jaspar Higgenbottom to put me into an apparently distraught state.

By the time Irene arrived, I had recovered, but had decided to let her think my concern was due to Allegra's account of the gypsy's report on Quentin Stanhope. Irene's dramatic nature always responded best to extremes—be it romantic subplots or murderous main plots.

"Nell! What is it?" Irene demanded the moment she arrived. "Allegra said that you were most disturbed."

"I am. And I am . . . appalled that you would bring such innocents as Allegra and the Queen to that miserable gypsy fortune-teller we visited on our last time in Prague."

"Why should I not? I took *you* there, didn't I?"

"That is no excuse. And now I hear that this awful creature has predicted great danger for those I hold dear. How irresponsible of you to attempt such a thing without me present."

Irene smiled, gathered her lilac taffeta combing gown around her like the crackling tissue that wraps a Worth gown, and sat on my single upholstered chair.

If she extracted a cigarette, I expected to scream, but she fortunately had left her smoking apparatus in the suite.

"You want a complete report on the fortune concerning Quentin, I suppose," she offered.

"That would be nice." I sat on the straight chair.

"That would be more than nice. It would be most intriguing."

"Irene, you don't for a moment believe that woman with her crinkled hands and shriveled roots and lethal powders and jangling skull lamp speaks anything but drivel?"

"Well . . . she hit the mark last time regarding my romantic disposition. G. Who would have thought that meant Godfrey then? Not even you."

"That is true, but many men have given names beginning with the letter G."

"Name three."

"Ah . . . Geoffrey. Godwin."

"Godwin could be a surname as well."

"Geoffrey. Gregory . . . Gabriel!"

"The last is honestly angelic, but not common."

"Still—"

"Even fewer names begin with Q."

"Agreed," I said, my throat suddenly dry.

Whenever I tried to anticipate Irene, she usually jumped me from an oblique angle, as a knight outmaneuvers a rook.

"Can you think of three?" she asked roguishly.

"Only one," I admitted brazenly. "Quentin."

"There is Quinn."

"A surname," I snapped.

"And Quincy."

"Another surname."

"You are right, Nell, as usual. We always come back to Quentin."

"Did the fortune-teller introduce him by mentioning Q as a first initial?"

"Exactly. Of course Allegra immediately blurted out that

this must mean her uncle Quentin before I could stop her. I could have wished for more restraint. No one thought of 'Queen' Clotilde.''

"Of course! 'Queen' is her first name in a sense! What was said about this 'Q' person?''

"That such a person was possibly as good as dead and in great personal danger, but would shortly triumph, would in a sense be reborn. When Allegra pressed her about her uncle, the old woman assured her that she would see him again, and soon, but that Allegra herself was in danger.''

"I don't like that, Irene."

"Neither do I! The irritating crone suggested that we all were in mortal danger. That is no good way to insure return customers.''

"The Queen too?''

"The Queen above all, although the wretch was most cryptic about who really *was* the Queen. She could have meant Clotilde. Or myself. Or someone other.''

"Not I," I commented.

Irene smiled. "I fear not. How did your interview with the demanding Tatyana really go?''

"Such a strange woman, Irene. I believed that yours was a dramatic persona. Now that I have seen this Tatyana in closer quarters, I find her even more overwhelming than yourself.''

"How comforting to know that one's own excesses can be exceeded by another.''

I examined her face for traces of sarcasm but discerned none.

"You are certain that this woman is a seasoned spy," I asked, "and that she recognizes us all from our brief encounter at Sarah Bernhardt's salon?''

"I would stake my life upon it, and—now that I have heard the gypsy's prediction—fear that I do.''

"Can this Prague tangle truly be so serious, Irene? So far Godfrey's excursions among the bankers are routine. Aside from our spectacular vision of the Golem, Prague seems as sleepy as always, and the Queen's marital anxieties are not unique. Even men who do not wear crowns keep mistresses."

"Oh, how worldly and callous you are becoming, Nell! Does not her plight wring your heart? Poor Clotilde, a stranger in a strange land, isolated in Prague Castle, utterly rebuffed by the one Bohemian legally and morally obliged to care for her—!"

"Extremes," I reminded her, trying hard not to sniff in a superior manner. "I remember a day two years past when we sneered at Clotilde's portrait in the *Daily Telegraph*."

"Sneered? I do not sneer, no more so than you blurt." Irene on the brink of laughter was always a persuasive force.

I found myself smothering a snigger. "I must commend you for showing pity for a rival, and a successful one at that."

"I can afford to be magnanimous about Clotilde, dear Nell; I have found a far more formidable rival."

"You mean that Tatyana woman! I am so sick of her. She does nothing discernible save associate with the King and presumably do what mistresses do. To elevate her into some overwhelming force responsible for everything from Quentin's collapse at Notre Dame to the King's disinterest in his Queen is to make her more than any one woman could possibly be! Your fascination smacks of obsession, Irene; even of delusion."

"You think so?" she answered, unruffled as only Irene could be, even when confronted with the most outrageous challenge.

"I *say* so! The solution to the entire problem in Prague will be through Godfrey's efforts with the bankers and the officials, via the Rothschilds. The insanely silly rumor of the Golem and the matter of Clotilde's marriage bed will prove to be mere distractions to the central puzzle, which is the usual political pas de deux that I find most boring and annoying, however vital it may be to the Foreign Office."

"You are thinking of the matter of the Naval Treaty, which involved both Sherlock Holmes and Quentin Stanhope."

"Only because Colonel Sebastian Moran linked the two camps."

"He may live."

"So may Quentin, I am told on good authority, ranging from a Bohemian gypsy to my good friend Irene Alder."

"Touché," she said, sinking deeper into the upholstered chair. "We are balked until we can catch hold of some loose end of this puzzle."

"What puzzle?"

"Nell, you may not see any peculiarity in it, but I am most alarmed that a crowned head would not attempt activities of an engendering nature with another crowned head to whom he was specifically wed for that purpose! I am not encouraged that the most powerful banking family in Europe believes that political maneuvering in the tiny kingdom of Bohemia will shake the face of the Continent! I am not enamored of the fact that the two people whom I most trust in the entire world have apparently seen an apparition of the Golem of Medieval Prague, no matter the means or motive to which they attribute this vision!

"And I am most disturbed that a woman who a decade ago was a likely spy for an ambitious and devouring nation like Russia chooses to entwine her affairs with a minor king on the eastern edge of Europe, and may have been recently involved in a murderous plot involving those I know and hold dear, including our new friend Quentin.

"Lastly, I am compelled to wonder what our erstwhile rival Sherlock Holmes would make of such a tangle, and if he himself has begun to suspect the possible survival of both Quentin and Colonel Moran, as well as international intrigues that may shake the Continent in its boots!

"Now. Other than that, I am content."

I blinked. "What do you wish me to do?"

Irene sighed, not sadly or wearily, but as one who gathers herself for some immense task.

"First, I wish you to accompany me for the day tomorrow."

"What of Godfrey and Allegra?"

"Godfrey has his bureaucratic trail to follow. Also, I find it amusing to set him about making the King jealous, when the King was so envious of this man he had never met, whom I married."

"Irene—" I began, stirring uneasily. The pervasive Tatyana disturbed me, but I could not put my fear into words that she would understand.

"Allegra will be safely assigned to Prague Castle and the Queen," Irene went on quickly, as though to reassure me, "on a pretext of further wardrobe consultation. You may wonder that I delegate Allegra, a mere child, to this delicate task. A new shipment of Worth‑dolls is due, and the Queen's fashion sense is so appalling that any advice is worth its weight in gold. Besides, we shall know them both safe within the castle."

"Where will we be?"

"In the Old Town. My companions today were too distracting."

I could not resist a triumphal surge. "You hunt the Golem?"

"I hunt whatever is setting these events in motion. Something is very wrong, and some essential piece is missing. I sense the tremor of many filaments, of a malevolent web in construction of such vast size that it is all too easy to overlook. Ah, I am not a political person, Nell! And that is the basis of these events. I can only use what has served me in the past: my instincts, my own knowledge of this city and the personalities involved, my . . . dramatic extremes."

"Irene, did the initial G come up again during the gypsy's reading?"

She smiled cynically. "Of course. Do you think that old woman failed to recognize me, despite my disguise? She is no self-submersed King of Bohemia! Her livelihood depends on more wit than that. I may not believe her predictions, but I do not doubt her consistency. She saw danger shrouding someone whose name began with the letter G."

"Could . . . the G stand again for Godfrey?"

She nodded.

"And . . . Gottsreich? The King's middle name."

" 'God's right,' indeed. Yes, of course."

"Or could it possibly, quite insanely . . . stand for 'Golem'?"

Irene's face froze. "You mean that the danger may not envelop this unknown 'G,' but emanate from him. Or . . . It. I knew that there were reasons why I relied upon you, Nell. Thank you for reminding me."

Chapter Twenty-five

DOLLS TO DIE FOR

Holmes filled his pipe with the abominable shag he had brought from London.

Here we sat in a handsome hotel room in Paris, surrounded by the very perfection of everything that money and inclination can buy, and Holmes puffed away on twopenny tobacco.

"What did you think of our expedition to Maison Worth today, Watson?"

"I think that it is a grand establishment, and that Madame Worth was once an astoundingly handsome woman; indeed, she still is most impressive."

"No doubt you also wonder why such a family attribute took a turn for the worse when it crossed the Channel to England," he put in with a twinkle.

"Not in the slightest, Holmes, though I am surprised that you are related to such a family."

"The Vernets were ever artists, Watson. I find it interesting that Marie Vernet has married an artist in the sculptural art of dressing. What did you make of all those . . . draperies?"

"You mean the clothes, of course?"

"Of course, dear fellow. I am not interested in mere window hangings unless they contain or conceal a clue. In this case, I fear the clues are far from concrete, but involve the volatile world of ladies' fashions. There I must defer to your greater observations and interests."

"I am only married, Holmes, not an expert on women's dress."

"The two must be the same."

"As to what I thought—we saw some splendid specimens of womanhood today, Holmes."

"Did we?" he asked in all sincerity.

"Many great ladies of Paris were visiting the salons through which we passed, of that I am certain, although I am not Parisian enough to know their names. Oh, but their forms, their grace, their bearing . . . their *je ne sais quoi*—surely even you noticed that we were in the presence of great ladies!"

Holmes shrugged and puffed simultaneously. "I will take your word on it, Watson. I cannot say that I noticed. Mere mannequins, that is what I saw today strolling through that temple of gingerbread, of no more interest to me than the porcelain dolls that the dead girls worked upon; of rather less interest, in fact."

"Holmes, we have glimpsed the flower of French society—queens of the stage; noblewomen and women not-so-noble but far more beautiful, all wearing gowns of the most exquisite design and manufacture. I confess that I felt a pang for my wife Mary left behind in Paddington. She would have loved to glimpse such legendary luxury."

"There is only one queen of the stage in my estimation," he answered shortly, "and she is not here." His expression sharpened, then softened. "In spirit, perhaps, but not in person. Great ladies are not the object of our mission; what of poor Berthe Brascasat?"

"A tragic turn of events, Holmes. These blithe young things work a long and little-paid day. I admit that I will not admire a well-gowned lady as heartily now that I have seen the dozens of seamstresses who must labor to create such extravagances.''

"Yet you purchased a rather frivolous cape for your own Mary," he noted.

"I could hardly return home from Paris without some such frippery; if you were wed, Holmes, you would understand."

"I am not wed, yet I do perceive the married man's problem. You decry the exploitation of the bead-girls, but you wish your wife to benefit from their needlework."

"Wish has little to do with it, Holmes, as you would know if you were wed."

"But I am not, and not likely to be." He blew out a mighty gout of smoke. "Watson, ignorant as I am of such matters as fashion and women, and as cold as the trail is, I must confess that the murder of this young bead-girl, Berthe, and her sister sewer is as dastardly a deed as we have yet seen."

I sat forward. "The means—the scissors—were unconscionably brutal."

"Brutal . . . and so unnecessary."

"Are you saying that you have a clue to the murderer?"

"The murderer? No, but that is irrelevant. What matters is why these girls were slain."

"You are here to solve these deaths. How can the murderer be irrelevant?"

"I know murderers, Watson. There is no greater satisfaction than unveiling one who has allowed lust, greed or cruelty to guide his hand to the ultimate renunciation of common humanity. This is not such a case. Berthe and her compatriot were not killed for who they were, but for their position."

"Their position? Holmes, they were persons of no importance, mere bead-girls among hundreds."

"That is why their murders are so repellent. The hand that struck them down could have as easily killed their neighbors. This was a crime of mere happenstance, Watson, for a purpose I glimpse and find wanting."

"Yet, as you say, Berthe and young Nathalie were of no importance in the wider world; then their murders must be as meaningless."

"Your logic is as lacking as your conscience." He sighed. "No, Watson, their deaths were meaningless but the motive behind it is one of vast significance. Can you not see what is plain, what was plain before even Berthe's or Nathalie's eyes at the moment of death?"

"I see only a huge room lined with tables, over which dozens of young women bend to their stitchery. The products of their labor are ultimately valuable, but the pieces are mere morsels of lace and ribbon and glass beads . . . or jewels? Were there true jewels, Holmes, concealed among the glittering beadery? A scheme to steal and hide jewels, perhaps?"

"Jewels." He laughed. "You harbor the soul of a romancer, despite your scientific training. Yet who can blame you? To see these young women laboring over such elaborately attired dolls, these mannequins twinkling with tiny beads; some wearing earrings even. What small girl would not sell her innocent soul for such a toy? Is it any wonder that older individuals would sell even more than their souls for such things?"

"You confuse me, Holmes. First you say that the murders are not significant, then that the matter involves great brutality and the selling of something worth more than souls."

"It is crime we investigate, Watson! Crime roots itself in contradictions. Even I may commit a few in the pursuit of crime. Did you not notice a certain oddity about the fashion dolls?"

"Only that they were exquisitely made, and of course, dressed."

"You did not recognize any?"

"Recognize them? What an offensive idea, Holmes. They

are dolls, mannequins, made from molds. They are pretty and false at one and the same time. They may suit to satisfy small girls, and perhaps the larger girls who play with fashion as their younger selves played with dolls, but I should not look for any revelation among those frozen porcelain faces."

Holmes nodded. "No doubt your greater worldliness preserves me from a sad delusion, Watson. No doubt I was mistaken to detect a resemblance or two on that company of dolls."

"A resemblance? To whom?"

"One was to a face that is known the world over, one that even I have noticed: our good queen's daughter, now wed to the future czar of Russia."

"Princess Alexandria? No doubt she is a client, Holmes. How . . . enterprising of Monsieur Worth to order his mannequins to resemble his famous clients. Are all of them duplicates of some living person?"

Holmes shrugged. "I cannot speak for all; certainly another one that I recognized memorializes a person no longer living, or presumed so." The look he gave me was oblique. "Most of the dolls may be anonymous, except for a favored few. Did you notice the one that mimics our Queen in her younger days?"

"No! One would think Monsieur Worth would retire such a figure now that the Queen is a widow."

"Why should he? These cunning mannequins record the lineage and long custom of his most illustrious clients. He clothes every royal house in Europe as well as the uncrowned aristocracy of American wealth, my cousin Marie tells me proudly. I wonder if the ramifications of such a fact ever strike her."

"What ramifications, other than the fact that she has married a man who has become world-famous, wealthy and much honored?"

"He is also in a position to be used, my dear Watson, as are his wealthy clients."

"I can't quite see how, Holmes."

"No, that is why my cousin and her husband have come to me. I have business about Paris while I confirm certain theories. Then, I am afraid, we are in for a much longer rail journey than brought us to Paris."

"We must travel on? Where?"

"I fear the trail will lead us all the way to Prague, Watson."

"Bohemia? But why?"

"Because that land's Queen is involved in the matter that led to the murder of poor Berthe."

"The devil you say! Royal intrigue and murder? What a case. At least we are acquainted with the King."

Holmes puffed deeply on his pipe, assuming that dreamy expression I only glimpsed during his moments of deepest thought, or while caught in a cocaine trance.

"We are indeed acquainted with the King of Bohemia. It will be interesting to see him again."

"But you do not like the King."

"I did not say that it would be pleasant, Watson; only interesting."

He smiled, to himself, not me, and stared out over the Paris rooftops turning slightly golden in the twilight.

Chapter Twenty-six

CRYPTOGRAPHY

Irene and I strolled together up Karlova Street, she in the best of moods, I in the worst.

"Ah, what a splendid day!" she cried, stopping to fill her lungs with the lively Prague air. "I feel that we will make excellent progress. As much as an incognito venture into the Prague streets benefited the Queen yesterday, I could accomplish no real work with Clotilde and Allegra along.

"*We* two will make giant steps," she predicted, taking my arm and implementing her own metaphor until I was stumbling to keep up.

"Irene, slow your pace! People are staring."

"Of course they are; we are a notable pair."

She reluctantly released me to set a genteel pace more befitting our ladylike attire.

Irene had exaggerated when she declaimed our worthiness of interest: I wore an Empire green twilled wool, princesse-style redingote with dusky maroon trim on revers, cuffs and skirt and a green felt hat to match. No one would—or should—give me a second glance.

Irene wore a princesse-style polonaise, too, but her effect was far more queenly. Her gown was of silver faille in an all-over scallop design, with an upstanding collar and bodice of black lace. Swags of glittering jet overhung her bosom and hemmed the gown, so she faintly clicked as she walked.

She carried an ebony walking stick. Her brimmed black velvet hat was frosted with silver and dull red ostrich plumes, with a crimson velvet cluster of roses nestling under the wide brim near her left temple.

"I am so relieved, Nell. Since I left Paris, I have had Allegra to look after. Now, Allegra is consorting with the Queen at the Palace, and Godfrey is doing something dull with the bankers. I know all my chicks to be safe and am now free to track the Golem to his lair."

"Today?" I asked with some dismay. "With me?"

"Of course with you! Is it not wonderful to be tramping the Prague streets together again?"

"Perhaps," I said dubiously, "but you forget that you and I seldom went out unaccompanied by the King. Our small tramping expeditions were only to the royal doctors' infirmary and the gypsy woman you revisited yesterday."

"That may be true," Irene admitted, "but now we are free to tramp where we will, unimpeded by royal escorts and castle carriages. I have just the route."

She drew me to a stop beside a greengrocer's shop to rummage in her reticule for a much-crinkled piece of paper.

"What is that?"

"My scribbled notes, and a crude map I made. Yesterday's venture had more purpose than an en masse palmreading. I gathered testimony of the Golem's progress on the two other occasions on which he was seen."

"There are more?"

"Only the two, except for your and Godfrey's encounter."

"Three times. It does rather sound like something large and brutish is running loose in Prague."

Irene leaned near and dropped her voice into a stage whisper, which is to say that she attracted the attention of everyone within fifty feet. "Perhaps it is the Frankenstein monster. That would be a find, Nell, would it not?"

"Not," I begged to differ. "I hope this Golem proves to be as much fiction as the Frankenstein creature."

"I don't!" Irene avowed. "Such a turn of events would ruin my investigation. See this map; I have marked the sites of his appearances with an X."

"Most original."

"Here is U Flecků," she went on. "You notice the appearances cluster around the Old Town and the Josef Quarter."

"The likely area for a Josef Quarter creation to haunt."

"Please do not use such a negative word, Nell."

"Which one?"

"Haunt. I am convinced that the Golem is as solid as you and I."

"Then I am glad that we make your pilgrimage to find him in daylight; I wonder that you did not drag me out by the dark of the moon."

She eyed me askance, her amber earrings shaking indignantly. "Once we have verified the Golem's lair such an expedition may be necessary. Now, we need to see."

"How fortunate for me, although I really do not want to see any more of the Golem than I did."

"I am afraid that we must. He is the key to this entire business."

"He is a medieval legend, Irene, as Faust is. Sometimes, I fear, you take the unreal reality of the stage far too seriously."

"What do you think you saw?"

I pondered. "A large person, moving quickly yet clumsily. Were it not for the . . . unearthly . . . quality of the face, I would feel confident in saying that Godfrey and I encountered an exceptionally balky drunkard."

"What was unearthly about the face?"

I was loath to revisit my memories of that night, but Irene was a skilled interlocutor. I found the scene taking shape again in my mind.

"The face was . . . unformed, rudimentary. I sensed

where eyes, nose, mouth were, but did not see them fully formed. I saw a . . . melted . . . face, Irene."

She bit her lip and lifted her eyebrows, an expression that would have not flattered anyone else, but was enchantingly provocative in her.

"I am afraid that you describe with admirable exactitude the unfinished face a giant clay figure come to life would wear. Most disturbing, Nell, I don't mind telling you, for I trust your observations implicitly. I could not have described the Golem's face better myself, had I seen it."

"Then we do truly track the Golem?"

"It would seem so." She drew her reticule cords taut, then waved the crude map under my nose. "The Rothschilds will not be encouraged to hear that the rumors are true. Whatever the outcome, we will follow the trail to its logical conclusions."

So we walked on.

As charming as the streets of Prague's Old Town were, I could not help glancing worrisomely down every passing byway. Many of the streets could not tolerate more than six persons across. In such shaded, narrow and winding passages, marked by archways linking wall to wall, one could well envision an unearthly being on the prowl.

The citizens of Prague came and went in broad daylight. A baker's vendor brushed by, his tray half full of pastries dusted with poppy seed. The local population much treasured the tiny black poppy seed, but I could not see a seed-strewn roll without being reminded of mice droppings.

Buxom lace-capped Bohemian countrywomen passed us, their ample shawl-covered figures bursting from checked gowns and embroidered aprons.

We walked farther into the heart of Old Bohemia, until we crossed into the Josef Quarter. The area was named for the Emperor in Austria, Franz Josef, who had given the Jews in the ghetto their full civil rights some decades before.

Such largesse was unusual in Europe, and, perhaps for that reason, several Jewish synagogues thrived in this small area, the most significant of which was the Old-New Synagogue near the bend in the river Vltava.

In the crowded, narrow ways, Irene drew me into a nearby butcher's shop so she could further study her rough map by the light of the window.

I gazed at the foreign meat goods, at strings of fat sausages, some dark as blood, others pale and pink. Unknown spices seasoned the shop's warm air. Garlic rose from among them like a thread of French incense.

The entire scene was rather repulsive, but Irene was frowning at her map and would not be distracted.

"If there is a point around which all the manifestations center," she muttered, pointing a gloved forefinger at the much-abused paper, "it is here. I can find no other terminus."

"How far is 'here'?" I wondered.

"Only a couple of streets over."

"Then why don't we go and see what sits on that site?"

Irene turned unusually baffled eyes upon me. "Because I know what sits upon that site; lies, rather. That is the old Jewish cemetery."

A thrill crawled up my corset strings. "We saw such a place on a previous ramble in Prague. Graves, hundreds of graves, all piled one atop the other."

She nodded. "The Golem was said to have been both created and uncreated in the attic of the old synagogue, but when one thinks of him rising to walk again, the vicinity of such an ancient graveyard for his kind seems perfectly appropriate."

"Then we *do* speak of a ghost!"

Irene tucked her paper back in her reticule. "A most substantial one, I fear."

We walked on, with purpose now, with a single goal in sight.

The Jewish cemetery in Prague was renowned even years

before I first glimpsed it. I might say that it was perversely renowned, for to see it is to know that we do indeed pass as the grass which springs up and is cut down. Apparently, little land was allowed the ghetto for burying its dead. The result over decades and centuries was that grave was set upon grave, up to twelve denizens deep, until the headstones came to thrust each other up like ingrown teeth. The effect given was of the dead bursting forth from their allotted six-by-two-foot spaces; of headstones pushed up and askew; of a whole City of the Dead elbowing one another for, er, breathing room; of man's inhumanity to man, alive or dead, reaching bizarre proportions.

Yet amongst such chaos, amongst such pathetic yet oddly dignified and touching memorials, one monument stood solid, level and unaffected by the raw jousting for space around it. That was the tomb of Rabbi ben Loew, the father of the Golem.

Irene had pointed out this impressive stone structure on our previous sortie into old Prague. Now we stood before it again, more awed than ever by the power of the Golem legend. At least, I was more awed; I can never say for certain what Irene is thinking, because she is an actress and hides that well when she wants to.

"When we were last here, Nell, I mentioned that to this day people place notes upon Rabbi Loew's tomb, seeking some boon or the other. Is that not suggestive to you?"

"Yes. Hope springs eternal."

"—beyond the need of humanity to see past its own mortality."

I thought. "The rabbi's tomb is a kind of post-office box between living and dead."

"Exactly! And why must we restrict the correspondence to between the living and dead? Why not between the living . . . and the living?"

I turned to stare at my friend's triumphant face. "A message center, you mean?"

She nodded slowly. "I suggest that we examine some of the slips of paper that have been left recently."

"Irene . . . it may be blasphemous to trifle so with the dead, and the living's hopes; certainly it is an ultimate invasion of privacy."

Her mouth settled into a grim line. "Sometimes one must invade privacy and even trifle with blasphemy to find the truth."

We advanced together on the tomb, a solid stone affair somewhat higher than our heads.

As we neared, the truth of the custom showed itself. Small white flakes of paper had been affixed to it by weighted stones.

"These petitioners believe that the rabbi himself will look upon their offerings," I objected. "We must not violate their expectations."

"And if a wrong is being committed in the dead rabbi's name?" she answered instantly. "Have we not an obligation to reveal it?"

"Yes! But you cannot know for sure until you violate the crypt."

"What did you say?"

"You heard me."

"Yes, but what word did you use—?"

"Violate—?"

"Most dramatic, Nell, and most in character, but, no, that other telling word, so wonderfully melodramatic."

I considered. "Crypt?"

"The very word! Crypt. Oh, it smacks of pyramids and mummified pharaohs; of speaking ravens, forgotten mists and the divinely decadent dreams of Mr. Edgar Allan Poe. Crypt. Yet this is not a crypt, Nell, but a tombstone. Why did you call it so?"

"I don't know! It looked . . . like a crypt."

"How does a crypt differ from a tombstone?"

"I don't know! I suppose . . . one can walk into a crypt, and one cannot enter a tombstone."

"Ah!" cried Irene, in rapture. "So simple. So obvious."

"I beg your pardon."

"Oh, you need not beg anyone's pardon, least of all Rabbi's Loew's, whose gravesite you have just saved from a dastardly desecration."

"I have?"

"Indeed. I was ready to rip every message from its surface, and read it. Now I think that such a course is uncalled for."

"I should hope so!"

"Now it is much simpler. We must return by the dark of the moon you mentioned earlier, Nell, and dig it up!"

Chapter Twenty-seven

FIT FOR A QUEEN

We returned to the Europa to find that Irene's scheme to desecrate the rabbi's tomb would have to wait: catastrophe had run rampant among our associates.

First, the majordomo intercepted us in the lobby with an urgent message: we were to repair immediately to Godfrey's room. Such news did not leave time for our usual sedate route of stairs.

"I cannot say that I am surprised by such a summons," Irene admitted complacently as we were whisked upward in the new and rather terrifying lift like trapped mice in a cage. "I am surprised that you are included in the invitation."

Before she could explain that cryptic uttering, the car came to an unsettling stop and the attendant drew open the gilded grille. We hastened down the long carpeted passage to the room in question.

Our knock was answered instantly. We were relieved to see Godfrey standing there, as hale, handsome and hearty as ever. He politely stepped back from the door, but did not invite us to enter. As we gazed into the chamber beyond we could see why.

The room was thronged with massive floral offerings on stands and in urns and vases, enough to soothe the self-regard of a Sarah Bernhardt. Huge stands held showy blooms of coral gladioli, blue hydrangeas, purple iris, copper- and saffron-colored asters . . . all displayed against blades of background greenery as aggressive as swords.

The heady scent of a hundred jousting blossoms suffused the air. Irene regarded Godfrey with a look that asked all. He answered it.

"I did as you suggested, much against my better judgment. I sent the estimable Tatyana a small bouquet in thanks for her hospitality of yesterday."

"A small bouquet," Irene repeated, "but apparently potent."

He shook his head and spread his hands in bewilderment. "A nosegay of no particular worth or significance."

"What was it?" I asked, for I am especially fond of flowers.

Godfrey turned his harried expression on me. "Only what I should send to any lady whom I wished to thank: tea roses, sweet william and Parma violets."

"Parma violets?" Irene was beginning to sound unsympathetic. "Those are my favorite flowers."

"That is why I thought of them," he said; "I am not accustomed to sending flowers."

"Apparently, she is." Irene ventured into the room, sniffing arrangements as she went, rather like a suspicious cat.

"That is not the worst of it," Godfrey added.

"There is more?" Irene turned against a background of lavish blooms.

He gestured to the desk, which was barely visible between two enormous fanned arrangements of iris.

Beside a tattered pile of ornamental wrapping paper stood an exquisite box formed from inlaid woods of such exotic color and pattern that they seemed to be painted on.

Godfrey went over and lifted the top of this treasure—to reveal a rarer prize within, something that gleamed silvery gray and sparkled with stars of inset diamonds.

Irene recognized it instantly. "A Fabergé egg. How profligate of her! I must interrogate Nell as to the specifics of your interview. What a peerless beauty! I mean the egg, of course, not the donor."

Irene elevated the bijou on its golden stand so that we could all appreciate its gleaming enameled surface.

"Certainly Tatyana is not hiding her Russian connection," she said. "Speaking of hiding, where is—"

Her fingers tested the egg's golden encasement until I heard a click, then the liquid notes of a lovely melody. The upper part of the egg snapped open to reveal a pair of animated bejeweled doves, made from baroque pearls, billing and cooing with mechanical industriousness.

Irene looked less than enchanted. "Tatyana's influence in St. Petersburg is sinisterly significant; this toy has arrived in less than twenty-four hours. Unless . . . she meant it for another and changed her mind." She throttled the mechanism to a stop by shutting the curved enamel doors. "Did either of you recognize the melody?"

Godfrey and I exchanged a blank glance. Music was not a strong point with either of us.

"The principal aria from *La Cenerentola*. You do remember, Nell, that I sang the role of Cinderella in my La Scala debut."

"Yes, but I never heard the music."

"I would let you hear the entire selection now, but I am not quite in the mood."

Irene delicately replaced the jeweled egg on Godfrey's desk, as if it were something that might bite.

"I cannot explain—" he began.

"Oh, I can explain it," she answered swiftly. "I simply do not care to. Did any message accompany this unparalleled generosity?"

"Only a card suggesting that she looked forward to seeing me at the castle reception and ball on the morrow."

"And so she shall," Irene decided.

"You recommend that I attend? After this?" Godfrey sounded dubious.

"Of course. We have all been invited by the Queen, not the King. Now the King's mistress underlines the invitation. You have proven successful beyond dreams in your assignment. Why would I suggest that you abandon the playing field now?"

Again Godfrey's and my glances crossed in silence. Irene was being far too magnanimous for one of her temperament.

Godfrey cleared his throat. "Perhaps because the . . . extravagant Tatyana seems to have contracted a . . . an interest in me."

"Why should she not? You are eminently interesting. Of course you will go to the castle tomorrow, and see her. But I do think—"

We waited—how else can I put it?—with bated breath. I am most displeased by my lack of original expression, but then this scene was very out of character for all of us.

"—I do think," Irene repeated airily, snapping a lush purple iris from its stem and thrusting the blossom into her hair, "that you should escort Lady Sherlock to this affair."

"But—" Godfrey began, dumbfounded. The entire charade had been constructed on the notion that Godfrey and I were total strangers to Irene and Allegra. "How shall I explain the connection?"

"You will not have to explain anything." Irene's voice was growing taut. "I will instruct Madame Tatyana on how things stand. With my usual subtlety, of course; or, rather, with Lady Sherlock's."

"Of course," he said, sounding not at all certain of that.

What more would have been said, I cannot speculate, for at that moment a knock on the door ended the discussion.

A maid brought us a note, a communication from the castle.

That was the second appalling development of the day,

a day whose events soon made me ache to return to the
Jewish cemetery and desecrate the rabbi's grave as a far
better occupation.

Irene opened the heavy cream stationery—the Queen's
personal stock—and read the brief message within, aloud
and with perfect diction:

*"Come at once! An event of ghastly import has transpired.
Clotilde is prostrate. You must insist on seeing only the Queen.
I remain with her to preserve what sanity I can. Try to maintain
a serene demeanor when you arrive. No one must suspect anything!*

"Allegra."

We decided that Godfrey should remain behind to make
arrangements for the flowers; actually, Irene decided, in the
autocratic manner that was becoming all too common to
her since we had returned to the picturesque and cursed
kingdom of Bohemia.

"The egg is worth half as much as my Tiffany diamonds," she told Godfrey. "You must find a safe place for
it. I suggest a bank, or the hotel safe if the banks are closed.
Then, you must find some suitable deployment for the
floral excesses. Whatever has happened at the castle, an
innocent visit from a pair of ladies will not aggravate the
uproar. I fear, Godfrey," she added a trifle severely, "that
whatever effect you have had upon Tatyana has somewhat
compromised your role in this intrigue."

"I did nothing," he protested, quite rightly, "save follow
your suggestions."

"Sometimes one must stand one's own ground, and follow one's own instincts for self-preservation!"

On this note she left, with myself in her train. I will never
forget Godfrey staring perplexed at his ring of floral trib-
utes, looking more alarmed than a civilized English gentleman should have to.

The sun was setting by the time Irene and I were en-

sconced in a carriage bound for Hradčany. Every spire in
Prague was tipped with liquid gold. Taverns and shops
beamed a rosy glow of twilight commerce as our conveyance passed and began climbing the winding route to the
pinnacle of the city.

Prague Castle, sprawling on the hill it commanded, threw
a dark and forbidding silhouette against the lowering crimson curtain of the sunset. Our horses' hooves clattered to
the private entrance far from the overwhelming public gate.

No one contested our request or right to see the Queen.
Even the servants betrayed an indifferent contempt for
what the Queen wished or did not wish. They deferred to
whatever another said of her wishes, rather than ascertain-
ing her will.

Irene, who had been grim during the entire journey, was
no less optimistic as we followed a knee-breeches-clad
lackey through those elaborate halls until we reached the
Queen's chambers.

One of the double doors was opened by a pale-faced
Allegra.

"Thank heavens!" she cried, sweeping the door wide for
Irene and myself.

"Where is she?" Irene demanded on entering.

"In her bedchamber, but she expects you. In fact, she has
been wailing for you for hours; I fear she has little confidence in one of my years."

"Yet you had the wit to write, and apparently quickly."

Irene paused in the bedroom's antechamber to remove
her gloves while she and I assisted each other out of our
short capes. No servants came to relieve us of our outer
things, so Irene tossed them cavalierly on a lounge chair.

"What is the mishap you write of?" Irene wanted to
know next.

"It may seem a trivial matter, but 'mishap' does not
describe its effects. Look around you. Do you see what is
missing?"

Irene's glance was as swift and sharp as a carrion crow's.

"The Worth mannequins are missing. Did Clotilde not like any of the gowns, after all?"

"Quite the contrary! We had a delightful afternoon examining the new arrivals and the old, and then—"

"Then? Allegra, surely you have not called us to the castle on some trifling matter involving the Worth mannequins? We have left Godfrey back at the hotel in a situation of grave danger."

Allegra was a charming, well-brought-up girl, but she possessed an imperious streak at least a quarter as wide as Irene's. She drew herself up and answered stiffly, "I cannot say what peril Godfrey faces, although I am sure that he will overcome it, but you must judge the Queen's case for yourself."

With this she knocked at the coffered doors leading to the Queen's bedchamber, a room we had never seen.

A smothered "Come" was not an encouraging invitation.

Allegra pulled down the rococo lever, and we entered a room of shining marble floors scattered with Aubusson carpets and a testered bed as soaring and stately as any altarpiece. It seemed odd to find a self-declared Virgin Queen ensconced in such luxury; perhaps the irony of her situation only goaded the Queen more.

She was prostrate, as advertised, but not upon the royal bed. She lay crumpled like an abandoned doll on the upholstered chaise longue near a pair of Louis XVI chairs by the tall windows.

When she looked up to see who had arrived, I was struck dumb. Clotilde even in full bloom was a pallid and spiritless blossom; Clotilde after hours of hysterical weeping was a sorry sight indeed.

Her large blue eyes (her best feature) were tear-swollen. While her eyelids were always pink around the lashes, like those of a white rabbit's, now her entire eye-whites were tinted unflattering scarlet.

Her pale skin was mottled with red blotches; even her

satin length of silky blond hair seemed dulled by the damp in which she had wallowed for so long.

Irene rustled over to her with the efficient concern of a crack nurse.

"Your Majesty has had an unsettling day!"

"Don't call me 'Your Majesty,'" Clotilde replied as testily as a sick and sleepy sobbing child. "I am queen of nothing but my own misery! Please, I wish I could go home and be just Clotilde. Call me Clotilde and I shall feel as if I am among my dear s-s-sisters again! I wish I had never heard of Bohemia or its King."

Irene's face took on an odd expression: half utter sympathy and half rueful agreement. She sat gingerly on the small corner of the chaise that Clotilde had not dampened with her weeping.

"Come, now; it cannot be as bad as you think. We are here to help."

"There is no help!" Clotilde wailed, putting her pale head on Irene's silken shoulder nevertheless.

I pay a keen tribute to Irene's self-control when I mention that she did not even wince as fresh tears baptized the rare changeable mauve silk of her gown.

"Tell her; tell them," Clotilde commanded Allegra, her tone pleading rather than imperious.

"It was dreadful," Allegra began, her voice taking on that indignant tone that Irene delivers so well at her most melodramatic moments. "We were in the antechamber, deciding among the gowns. And—oh, Irene, you should have seen the latest shipment. Superb! Monsieur Worth only gets better. I so long for my first Worth gown," she added meltingly.

"Time enough to think of that after you have finished your testimony," Irene said smartly, patting Clotilde's heaving shoulder and watching saltwater stains seep into the delicate silk's subtle pattern.

Allegra began to pace. "I cannot tell you what a shock it was; what a pleasant, innocent afternoon we were having.

I have never known a Queen so well," she added a bit self-importantly. "We were getting on perfectly. Then the King came in."

"The King?" Irene sounded puzzled.

"Indeed. He entered without knocking; simply burst into the room, this huge man bristling with mustaches and mutton chops. And then he took the dolls."

"The King came and took the Worth mannequins? Personally?"

"No, of course not. He had three lackeys cart them off, but first he strode about and stormed."

"What did he storm about?" I asked. The sudden and thunderous appearance of the tall King had reminded me unpleasantly of my glimpse of the giant Golem in the streets. Perhaps these two larger-than-life figures had a certain anger in common.

"The mannequins. He accused Clotilde of not knowing her mind, of not—" Allegra glanced to the Queen's bowed head and stopped.

"You must tell me whatever the King said," Irene encouraged her in a quiet tone, "exactly what the King said, no matter how painful."

"He accused the Queen of . . . of not even having a mind, and said that she had dallied with the dolls like a child, and would have them to toy with no longer. That is when he snapped his fingers and the lackeys appeared to cart them away. Even while the servants were present, he said that the Queen had no taste, no opinion, no sense. That . . . that Tatyana wished to choose some gowns for herself, and must be kept waiting no longer."

Allegra took a step toward us and lowered her voice, as if hoping that only Irene and I would hear. "That is when I noticed that vile woman waiting in the outer chamber; waiting for Clotilde's mannequins! Then the King swept away with Tatyana, the lackeys and all the mannequins. I have never witnessed anything so perfidious and cruel in my life. I cannot believe, dear Irene, that you ever saw anything in the King. He is a monster!"

Irene's face became a mask of alarm, for Allegra's outburst alluded to her prior acquaintance with the King, but the sobbing Queen was immersed in her own distress and did not hear, or understand, the allusion.

"A monster," Irene repeated in a hollow voice. "It would indeed seem so." She sighed, then tugged gently on one of Clotilde's lank curls.

"It is time to stop mourning what cannot be changed," she suggested, her voice a sweet yet seductive tool she employed with equal doses of sincerity and artistry, "and to decide what we will do about it."

Clotilde responded despite herself to that voice that had enchanted thousands. Her lifted face revealed even redder eyes, but one word in Irene's sentence had encouraged her. "We?"

Irene nodded. "I am sure that you and Allegra reached a splendid decision on the gowns. You no longer need those silly dolls; you have made your choices. Now you must order."

"But they are gone—" Clotilde threatened to drizzle again.

"Do you think that Monsieur Worth has not kept track of every design, every frill, on each model sent to you? He resembles the Great Creator in his own small way. Not a furbelow is dispatched to Prague or Vienna or London that his eye is not upon. You and Allegra must sit down now—while your thoughts are fresh—and list everything you wish to order. Worth will fulfill it."

"But . . . Madame Norton—" The Queen sat up and pushed flaxen damp strands of hair from her ravaged face. "You do not understand. The King entered my very bedchamber, as he has not done at any private time, and publicly ordered my . . . my mannequins into that woman's care and consideration! I do not wish to state the obvious

before such genteel women as your sister and Miss Huxleigh, but obviously this Tatyana is a personal interest of
the King's who outranks myself in his regard. She is his—"

"Mistress," Irene said plainly. "Of course. Kings have
ever had such things. They are as common as crowns,
among kings. Our own Prince of Wales . . . my dear, he has
had many mistresses."

"How does the Princess of Wales endure it?"

"With dignity, and, I should imagine, a certain distaste.
Yet that is her lot in life: to be a loyal and good wife to a
king too spoiled to rein in his every appetite. Even the
mistress has her role: to cater to the spoiled child inside
every king or wealthy man. Think what such a woman must
put up with; not only his fickle regard, but she, poor thing,
must receive him in her bedchamber. This is not always a
consummation devoutly to be wished, no matter what the
fairy stories say about kings and princes."

Clotilde nodded slowly. "You advise me to reconcile
myself to my lot. I confess that I do not now desire the
King's presence . . . personally, only I do wish to provide
the heirs I am obliged to. And I thought that children might
console me for the emptiness of my role."

"Perhaps they will," Irene said with a smile. "We will
have to wait and see."

"How can I have children, Madame, when the King
shows no inclination to visit me; when the very sight of him
repels me now that he has shown his true nature?"

Irene shrugged, an apparently callous gesture at such a
charged moment. Sometimes her grasp of the larger drama
was so great that she failed to ache for the heartbroken
minor character.

"Things may not be as bleak as you think they are.
Certainly they will seem better if you order enough Worth
gowns. I myself find such purchases most uplifting to the
morale. In fact, given His Majesty's high-handed appropria-
tion of your mannequins, you will be safest simply wiring
Monsieur Worth and telling him that you will take every-

thing he has sent, and if he believes a certain model to be particularly flattering to you, he must make it up in two or three of your best colors."

"But Madame Norton! That will cost a veritable fortune?"

Irene smiled angelically. "Yes, I rather imagine that it will. And imagine how the King will feel when he sees the bill!"

"He will be furious, even though he first urged me to visit Worth. He will stalk into my rooms again raging and towering."

"And—?" Irene inquired lightly. "What will he do about it? What *can* he do about it?"

Clotilde blinked, banishing a glaze of tears on her baby-blue eyes. "He can do nothing," she said in a hushed tone, "if I am not frightened of his blustering. He will have to pay."

"Yes." Irene's expression was seraphic. "He will have to pay, a good deal for a long time to come." She turned that smile on Clotilde, coaxing its pale imitation from the Queen. "And you will have a splendid wardrobe. You see what they mean by 'poetic justice'?"

"I do," the Queen said, nodding, "but it is a rather sad triumph."

"That is what most women have to settle for, particularly when they consort with kings . . . but, for you, my dear—" Here Irene's voice became an uncanny duplicate of the gypsy woman's we had first visited more than two years before as she took the Queen's hand to examine her palm.

"—for you I see a dazzling triumph of a moral sort, a humbled king, and many astounding revelations. You sit at the center of a complex web, and while your dilemma is tangential to the whole, it also forms the heart of the entire problem. Rest easy; be hopeful, the future will be better than you think—and, I predict, you will get a sublime Worth wardrobe out of it that will be the envy of an Empress."

By now even Clotilde was smiling.

"I am not as convinced as you evidently are, Madame Irene, of the power of a new set of clothes."

"Trust me," Irene said in her unabashedly portentous gypsy accent. "I know my kings, and I know my clothes."

Chapter Twenty-eight

TOMBSTONE TERRITORY

One would think that rescuing her cherished husband from an infusion of flowers and consoling the Queen of Bohemia would be enough accomplishments in a single day for any woman.

Alas, Irene was never so easily satisfied. We returned to the Europa to find that Godfrey had disposed of the bouquets by the inspired expedient of donating them to the National Theater and a local mortician.

The Fabergé egg he was less inclined to donate. Irene, after some jousting between feelings of jealousy and her natural acquisitiveness and practicality, had to agree. A rare objet d'art was an objet d'art, after all, and eternal; brazen hussies, even those who might be inclined to pursue her husband, come and go.

After a subdued dinner—Godfrey mused upon his unanticipated admirer . . . Allegra upon the Queen's dilemma . . . Irene upon Godfrey's unanticipated admirer . . . I upon all my friends' problems—Allegra was sent to her bedchamber for the night while we three consulted in the salon.

"I am not pleased by today's turn of events," Irene said.

"The puzzle turns vicious. We must attack it from another angle."

"Paris?" I suggested hopefully.

She eyed me with disdain. "You know very well what my next plans are, Nell. We must beard the rabbi's tomb."

"What tomb?" Godfrey wanted to know.

"That of the rabbi who raised the Golem. His tomb is a local landmark. I fear that it is also the key to much that troubles this city."

"Surely," I said, "you do not hope to unearth the Golem?"

"That is exactly what I wish to do, and at the precisely right moment, which is the intricate part."

"Can there be a 'right' moment for unearthing the dead, or for uncovering a monster?"

"My dear Nell, there is always a right moment for everything. I think that tonight is your *moment juste* for an after-dark adventure."

"What are you saying?" I glanced at Godfrey in alarm, but although he looked mystified, he was no help whatsoever, and moreover seemed somewhat distracted. I suppose that, having survived trial by Tatyana and her invasive flowers, he was willing to see me put to some new and unsettling travail in my own turn.

"I only propose," Irene said, "that Godfrey and I don discreet black tonight and investigate the rabbi's tomb. I also believe that you should accompany us."

"Indeed I should, if you toy with desecration of a grave-yard, no matter the creed."

Irene eyed me up and down in a most disparaging manner. "I am afraid that petticoats and petit point will not do tonight. I wear my best trouser-suit; you can do no less."

"I? Dress as a man? I think not."

Irene made a moue of resignation. I would have rested easier had not a twinkle of calculation also dawned in her eyes.

"I feared that you would object . . . so—" She rose from

the sofa and bent to withdraw a large cardboard box from beneath it. In a moment she was lofting the contents.

"You see here, Nell, a most respectable bicycling toilette for the active lady: black wool-and-silk bloomers; black sailor's-style blouse; black stockings and walking boots. Even black gloves. The most elegant lady could not object to such an ensemble."

"Bloomers! That is an American invention, and long since failed."

"Perhaps, but the melody lingers on." She held the foul articles up to my person. "They should fit perfectly. Do you wish to allow Godfrey and myself untrammeled access to an ancient tomb, or do you wish to dress for the part and accompany us?"

"It strikes me," I answered, "that you have been most forward today in advising other people on what they should wear."

"That is because I know better," she retorted with irritating certitude.

I glanced to the ever-sensible Godfrey. "What do you say?"

He gave a short laugh. "I believe that Irene is right; we will require spiritual guidance tonight if her suspicions regarding the Golem are correct."

"And she has told you what she suspects?" I demanded.

"No," he admitted, "but I recognize the symptoms."

"Very well, Godfrey. If you will assure me that you will not lose respect for me if I don this extraordinarily idiotic outfit, I will do so."

"My dear Nell, I could never lose respect for you, no matter what you wore," he promised me with a commendable sincerity that his wife would do well to imitate now and then.

I gathered up the repellent garb. "Were I not concerned for your spiritual well-being—"

"I know, I know, Nell!" Irene interrupted, leading me to her empty bedchamber, where we could change our clothes. "Think how poor Quentin had to don long, alien garb—the equivalent of women's robes in our quarter of the world!—in Afghanistan and India, when he did spy-work for Mother England! You do the same, after all."

"Not for Mother England," I reminded her, "and Quentin did not have to wear bloomers!"

"How, dear Nell," she asked in the same sly tones a speaking serpent might have employed in Eden, "do you know?"

Whilst I considered the interesting question of what Quentin had worn under his Arab robes, trying not to blush, Irene was swiftly drawing off her gown. In minutes she was garbed in the disconcerting men's clothes in which I had seen her before. I had donned the outfit provided and faced myself in the long mirror on a wardrobe door.

In my nautical black, selected for midnight camouflage, I looked like one of those American female cyclists contemplating entering a nunnery, both concepts utterly anathema to my British and Anglican upbringing.

"Charming," Irene declared, drawing an oversized black beret over my hair, ears, forehead and all. At least I was permitted to see. "Quentin would be impressed."

A city like Prague never sleeps, simply because the large number of taverns and beer gardens that populate its streets do not permit even the decently abed populace to slumber undisturbed.

We three—Godfrey now wearing the same dark seaman's garb he had employed on other such surreptitious expeditions in Monaco and Paris—made our sober and silent way through the convoluted streets. We were warmed by the flare of tavern lights, an ever-present distant whine of fiddle and harmonica and a faint chorus of merriment borne on a sour breath of beer.

Anonymous knots of pedestrians, loud and lurching with laughter or worse, passed, and occasionally jostled us.

Usually when we walked out together in our proper

clothes, Godfrey occupied the middle so Irene and I could take one of his arms should we require steadying while navigating the streets in our sometimes enmeshing garb. Now Godfrey and Irene bracketed me, a courtesy I much appreciated, for Godfrey carried the cane that only I knew contained a sword. I did not doubt that Irene's pistol weighted the pocket of her man's coat.

"Now I understand," Irene commented as our route took us into the twisted byways of the Old Town, "why the Golem's three rampages had witnesses. No street of this city, however narrow or deserted, is quiet all the night."

"Do you suggest that the Golem was deliberately paraded?" Godfrey asked.

"It is possible," she answered in that vague tone of intentional denseness that she uses to deflect too close questioning. "It is also possible that the Jewish Quarter has set guards in the cemetery. The recent sightings might encourage crowds or even vandalism at the tomb of he who first raised the Golem, Rabbi Loew. We must be cautious and quiet."

Fortunately, even midnight revelers seldom decamp to graveyards. When we came upon the black blot that was the ancient cemetery, the sounds and lights circled at bay in the distance. We saw no patrolling figures—not even a supernaturally large one, for which I was most grateful.

We plunged into this section of Prague as into a coal mine, for the city had not yet converted to gaslight. Only the occasional streetlight beamed feebly through dusty glass. I was terrified of stubbing a boot toe on one of the many aslant tombstones and tumbling into a picket fence of unknown markers.

Luckily, Irene carried the same black bag that had served so well in Paris. When she extracted and lit the hooded lantern she carried, a line of light wavered before us like the pale wand of a blind beggar's cane.

Most of the headstones were the modest, two-foot-high variety. What made the site so irregular, so remarkable and memorable, was how they sat one upon the other up to twelve deep.

Like the cabin on a ship, the rabbi's tomb loomed ahead of us, a monument of significant size in this landscape of upthrust but lowly slabs.

Irene ran the lantern's beam over the tomb's smoke-stained stone, illuminating a surface scabbed with notes. Some had shriveled from the admonition of the elements; others were as fresh-looking as the Hotel Europa stationery.

This time Irene endeavored to read some of these missives, handing Godfrey the black bag and myself the lantern.

"All written in Bohemian, Hebrew or German," she noted after perusing several.

"What did you expect?" I wondered.

"The lone anomaly. I can read most of these languages well enough, yet we do not have time to read the entire offering."

While she studied the messages, Godfrey had begun circling the edifice, patting it with his gloved hands. He made a full circuit back to us, then lofted the light from my hand to crouch down and cast it along the tomb's stone base.

"You are right," he told Irene, "a most curious structure. To all appearances it is simply a massive stone monument atop an ordinary grave; yet its size suggests the entrance to something grander, a church crypt, perhaps."

"That was Nell's observation, not mine," Irene pointed out with commendable accuracy. "No one has been buried here since the mid-seventeen-hundreds. The rabbi's grave—if not the monument surmounting it—dates back some two hundred more years. We stand on exceeding ancient—and sacred—ground."

"My point exactly!" I said in relief. "We should leave."

"Yes, but how?" Irene said, a smile in her voice even though the lamp lit only the impassive stone before us. "Godfrey, light my way around the monument."

"Wait!" I cried, as two shadows followed the light's beam around a stone corner. "Don't leave me."

"This will take but a moment, Nell." Irene's voice drifted back from the dark.

But a moment in an unpleasant place is an eternity. In fact, the moment they—and their lantern—vanished, I was plunged into Stygian dark. Perhaps my eyes had not immediately adjusted to the removal of light; perhaps I sensed the history of this venerable graveyard, collapsing under the weight of the outcast souls confined to its borders for so many centuries.

I groped after my friends, needing a glimpse of light, a sense of what was left and right, up and down, in the instant gloom. And I confess to a superstitious dread: of we three, only I implicitly believed in heavenly retribution, in the certainty of life after death for the saved; only I could conceive of such a thing as the Golem coming to life at the call of the ancient Hebrew text, the power of a rabbi who at the least was a remarkable and influential holy man for his time, if . . . not . . . more.

Why else had he commanded the imposing monument, the written supplications three-hundred-some years after his death, supposing that he was indeed dead?! If the Golem still walked—and Godfrey and I had seen something inhuman, outsize and impressive, there was no denying it—then why not its creator?

I felt an instant need to draw away from the monument, to gain some distance. I backed up into the empty arms of the dark, and the very thing I had been dreading happened.

I tripped—tripped on some not-to-be-imagined curb of stone—tombstone, curbstone, protruding bone turned stone; I know not what, nor do I ever want to know!

Shuddering, I retreated forward without thought.

Into the very monument that I feared!

My gloved hands came down hard on night-dewed stone, cold and dank as . . . well, I need not say more.

Worse, my mad scramble for escape upset my balance.

My hands scraped down the monument's slick sides, over groove and decorative scroll. I knew a moment of absolute conviction that I was about to fall forward on my face, directly into the adamant stone.

Qualms of serious physical injury as well as of spiritual danger for violating a sacrosanct and arcane place (for this was not a Christian cemetery, and the late rabbi had practiced the Cabbala) surged into utter horror. Choked by the prospect of facing my worst fear, I was even gagged from expressing my terror.

Mute like the Golem, my arms stretched out to cushion the blow both physical and spiritual. I stumbled forward, falling . . . falling . . . into solid stone, my hands clutching what small holds they could.

My anticipations were only too accurate. I felt my body fall forward until it seemed level. Yet . . . no impact with the monument met me.

For a moment I hung in vacant dark air, madly convinced that my scrabbling hands had *pushed* the monument away from me to avoid the inevitable collision. But that was impossible!

Then gravity and time asserted itself. I did indeed fall to earth—to loam scented with the rich aroma of growth and decay. My body jolted with the contact, my hands absorbing the worst stress and paying for that role. Now I made noise—an involuntary "ooof" of impact as I felt my bones shudder.

Dazed, I used my poor hands (thank God for the offices of the gloves, or they should have bled), to push myself to a sitting position.

Still the dark surrounded me without any boon of lamp or lantern light. How odd that my eyes were taking so long to adjust. . . . I struggled to my feet, on the theory that a woman on her feet is a match for almost anything, and reached out for orientation.

Ahead of me was only empty air. Yet, as I made a tight

circle, afraid to step from the solid ground beneath me for
fear of stumbling again, I found the monument's wall again.
Directly *behind* me!

This could not be! I had always faced the monument and
I had never changed my position until this rotation. Could
the rabbi's tomb move, as a mountain?

Something panted in the dark. I froze for long seconds,
before I realized that it was . . . I.

I crouched down and felt before me in my original direction. Oh! The naked, packed earth upon which I stood was
not level. As I feared, it dropped away before me.

So might a holy hermit of old on his high pillar feel,
unable to move left or right, forward or back, yet even
these holy men had not immersed themselves in utter,
unremitting dark.

Something whimpered in the blackness. I thrust a fist
into my mouth, and thought.

Where were Irene and Godfrey?! I heard nothing of
them, saw nothing of them. They could still pace only feet
away, circling the monument, looking for something only
they knew.

That was not I. They expected me to have remained
where I was.

With sight blindfolded, I was aware of being blanketed
in heady smells—earth, age, insects, decay—and of a certain motionless chill that wrapped my body like a shawl.

Shivering, I strained for any sight, sound or smell that
might call me, guide me. Nothing. I was surrounded by the
macabre silence of the tomb.

Prayers began mumbling through my mind as I moved in
a slow circle. Though my lips moved with the familiar
words, no sound came. I would not make any impression
on this blind captivity. I would not admit my presence to
the waiting dark. I would not hear my own despair.

Then, as if in answer, a fine wire of light, the merest hair,
hung taut and upright in the featureless dark before me. I

tore off a glove and clapped my bare palm to the phenomenon, feeling a barrier of cold, damp stone! Again, behind
me.

The light . . . moved. Up and down. Like a lantern in a
hand.

"Irene! Godfrey!"

My own voice berated me as if I and it were confined in
a closet and could only gibber at each other.

"Godfrey! Irene!" I heard nothing in reply.

The light winked out, leaving a cruel ghostly line on the
blank slate of my vision.

I swayed on my feet, disoriented again, like a drowning
person whose one lifeline has been yanked away.

Again the light seeped through, horizontal this time, at a
height I could just reach. My hands, both bare now,
reached to capture this slender thread, to warm my chill
fingers at its pale warmth. Ah, a red reflection on my flesh!
The light was real, the light was . . . moving again.

Down it went, vertical once more, sinking toward the
earth, and then winking out.

I pounded stone with fists. I shrieked and wailed. I
heard—and hurt—only myself.

After a few more moments of mania, I forced a fist into
my mouth to stop myself, to warm my icy fingers with my
own breath. My breathing huffed and puffed around my
invisible cell, but nothing blew down.

Yet even as my panting roughened into the first swell of
a sob, I heard something. A scrape. A chinking sound.

The line of light flared again at my left and paused at
waist height. There came the faintest of scrapes, like mice
feet on soapstone. Delicate creatures mice were, not truly
vermin, but rather endearing, after all. Even Messalina and
Lucifer had clever delicate claws that could insinuate themselves into almost-invisible chinks . . . even Casanova's
gross claws—if I had Casanova's claws now, strong and
curved, perhaps I could widen that narrow line of light,
perhaps I could push stone from stone, crack grout, break

the back of the granite, burst through the darkness and silence and . . . and musty smell . . . into wholesome clean night! But I did carry Casanova claws! I reached to the chatelaine at my waist and, amid a reassuring jingle, found and applied the small penknife on it to the stone.

Even as I echoed it, the tiny exterior scrape roared toward my long-denied ears, and suddenly became a grating, a freight-train howl. A coffin lid of darkness swung away from me, narrowing into an oblong of dazzling light peopled by a pair of vague silhouettes. And were not angels supposed to be light, not shadow? Why would Dark Angels come for me? I wondered; I had always been as good as I could.

Grasping arms, hands, protruded from the dark. Then I was plucked from my prison and dragged into the light amid a roar that resolved itself into confusing and commonplace chatter, like Casanova's, after the enforced silence of the tomb.

"Nell!" "Penelope!" "How on earth—? Come." "Oh, my dear—"

More than one voice picked at my muddled mind. Still light-blinded, I staggered forward, supportive hands upholding me.

Something crushed me to bone and blood.

"Oh, darling Nell! You have done it! I knew that there was some mystery to this monument! How dare you vanish like that and frighten us—"

Irene's voice; was she dead, too, then? And what did they mean, frighten *them*—?!

"Hush, Irene; she's terrified."

Someone large clasped me in an encompassing embrace, as I did not recall but suspect my father had done when I was quite young and frightened of something. A sense of security dropped over me like Casanova's cage cover. Oddly, I began trembling at that moment when I felt myself finally rescued.

Godfrey kept an arm around me, but I saw his hand

thrust the warm glow of the lantern toward the other dark figure. He lifted his cane-top into the light and then twisted it.

The gilt knob fell apart in his hands, but, undismayed, he tilted the cane toward it. A moment after something clinked on my teeth and a bolt of wet stinging fire washed into my mouth and down my throat.

Sputtering and swallowing, I struggled to speak.

"This is an abomination! Must I be drowned as well as incarcerated?"

A stinging warmth burned my chest like a poultice. Then I found that I could breathe without gasping, and speak without pausing.

"Irene! Godfrey! Where have you been? What are you doing?" Whether or not it was freedom or Godfrey's liquorous application, I was fully myself again, and fully indignant.

Godfrey laughed as he screwed on the cane-top again. "Brandy is for heroes, said Ben Jonson, and you have certainly merited your ration."

Irene's hands grabbed my shoulders as she crowed, "You are inspired, Nell! How on earth did you discover the mechanism to the secret entrance when Godfrey and I have been crawling around this cursed monument to no avail?"

"I would not call it 'cursed,'" I said first, coughing as genteelly as I could. Ben Jonson's heroes must have come equipped with iron esophagi if that had been brandy I had just imbibed.

"A mere expression," Irene interjected with customary impatience. "Godfrey was able to use his sword-tip—what a most accommodating cane he carries!—to find a break in the seam, but how does the door open without forcing? I am afraid that in the excitement Godfrey neglected to keep the portal from closing again."

I turned to look behind me, the lantern's dazzle lighting every stone cemented into the monument. I studied an apparently impervious wall, all of a piece. How annoying to have to admit that I had literally stumbled upon this wonder! Drawing my gloves on again in order to gain thinking time—and the night air was chill—I looked this particular surface up and down and still saw nothing.

Then I remembered my flailing hands, and ran my fingers over the decorative sills and down toward the monument's bottom, pressing hard. On the swell of an acanthus leaf, the stones separated with hardly a sound and swung inward upon a darkness so palpable that I recoiled. The cool, close air of a crypt hushed into my face. Thank God I stood outside of it now, and had other air to breathe!

Irene gazed raptly into this macabre space. "Did you have time to investigate it?" she asked eagerly.

"No," I answered. "Did you hear me . . . call to you from within?"

"No, dear Nell; the stones must be admirably muffling. Just think, this clever mechanism must have been constructed centuries ago, with still nary a squeak despite fire and flood and damp and decay."

"Just think," I repeated unenthusiastically.

Godfrey chuckled, a sound that went over both our heads.

Irene ducked hers into the dark, then thrust the lantern within and swept it from side to side.

I gasped. No wonder I had felt marooned on a mere slice of solid ground! An earthen stairway led deeper into the dark. Had I taken a single step forward, I would have tumbled farther into the gloomy throat of darkness.

"We must investigate!" Irene moved into the chamber, taking the little bit of light she carried with her.

I hesitated, but Godfrey's hand on my elbow both braced me and urged me forward.

"The worst is over, Nell," he bent to say in my ear. "You should have the honor of exploring your find."

I was hardly in any condition to decline honors, no matter how dubious. We three descended into the crypt, unaware of what awaited us below.

Chapter Twenty-nine

KING'S CASTLING

One of the most fascinating diversions during my life with the Nortons was to watch Irene attempt to conceal a yawn in company. Owing to her life as a diva, she could open her mouth to astounding dimensions. Irene yawned and sneezed as she sang, with head-thrown-back gusto.

Thus, when tempted to one of these vulgar necessities in public, she treated the onlooker to a battle royal between inclination, capacity and self-discipline.

On this occasion, Irene interred her yawn in the corner of her breakfast napkin and marked its passing with a celebratory sip of strong black coffee.

We broke fast on the cusp of elevenses, so late had we three risen after our arduous night in the graveyard. Allegra possessed that capacity so taken for granted by the young of being able to sleep late and heavily. She found nothing odd in our stirring so tardily, and joined us at the hotel table like a vagrant ray of sunshine.

"Did you have a jolly adventure last night?" she asked, drinking her tea and milk immediately after; no pitch-black liquids for her.

"Jolly does not do it justice," Godfrey observed, breaking apart a roll crammed with a tarry substance he had assured me was nothing more sinister than prune filling.

"Amen," said I, though the time for saying grace was long past. "And 'jolly' is not a proper form of expression for a young lady."

"Oh, fiddlesticks, Miss Huxleigh! I was merely asking."

"We had a right jolly adventure," Irene put in, "and will have an even jollier one tonight."

"At the palace!" Allegra reminded herself, and us. "Oh, I do wish to go and see poor Clotilde."

"She is 'Queen Clotilde,' and you shall go," Irene said smartly.

"I shall? To the reception? But I am not invited."

"Indeed you shall, but not to the reception. I have a greater assignment in mind for you."

"Really? At the palace? And I shall see Clotilde?"

"All of that," Irene answered smugly, biting with enthusiasm into a roll crawling with the vile seed of the poppy. "And—" She eyed me with mock meekness "—you will be home before six and safe in your suite, as Miss Huxleigh would consider only fitting and proper for an unescorted young girl in gay old Prague."

"Gay old Prague!" I added with what was not quite a snort. I may blurt on occasion, under stress, but I never snort.

"What is the plan for the evening?" Godfrey asked with a certain reluctance.

"We shall go together," Irene said. "I as Lady Sherlock; you and Nell as yourselves."

"What explains this sudden alliance?" he asked.

Irene blinked her daylight-gilded russet lashes until I thought she should swoon of supposed innocence. "We are all English."

"We are all *apparently* English," I put in, eating the plain bread and fruit I found the best items to order in Prague.

"I pass for such, do I not?" Irene asked. Her expression

brooked no disagreement; frankly, both Godfrey and I were too exhausted from our venture of the previous evening to argue.

That is how Irene always got her way: she exhausted any opposition.

"What do we do today?" Godfrey asked, most sensibly.

"Nothing." Irene seemed most pleased with herself. "I have some . . . archival investigations to pursue in town. Allegra will be well occupied when I explain her mission to the palace this afternoon. So you and Nell may . . . rest."

"Rest?" I demanded.

"You have had a trying night," she said, her flexible voice an arpeggio of soothing sounds, "both of you darlings. Simply think on how to look splendid tonight—Lady Sherlock would not care to associate with dowdy individuals—and I will do the rest."

"That," Godfrey said grimly, "is precisely what I am afraid of."

"And I," I added, "am not used to regarding myself as an ornamental object."

"Please do now, Nell," Irene beseeched me with a warm glance. "It is more important than you know."

"Nor am I an ornamental object," Godfrey put in, an unspoken growl underlining his protest.

"Dear man," Irene said, "sometimes we all must play such roles. Tonight is your grandest opportunity." She glanced from Godfrey to myself with the proud satisfaction of a puppetmaster eyeing her two most promising products. "Tonight will be a most memorable evening, count upon it."

That was the very difficulty, I thought as their conversation shifted into other matters. The previous night had already been memorable beyond belief, and Irene refused to enlighten us on what she had expected, or made of what we found. I thought back on these astounding events.

We did not find the Golem beneath the tomb of Rabbi Loew, but we did discover a subterranean network of crude tunnels that snaked into a dozen different directions under the Old Town. Our lone lantern was not sufficient for exploring such a maze. We could not separate, for which I was sublimely grateful, nor could we lay bread crumbs— for we had none, although that struck me as the most suitable deployment of the products of Bohemian bakeries.

"Interesting," Irene had commented when we had emerged again into the blessed fresh air surrounding the Jewish cemetery. She was always dispensing such annoyingly cryptic assessments. "What do you make of it, Nell?"

I sputtered for a moment before I spoke. "The tunnels were dark, dirty, damp. The air was both warm, and chill. I would not send an earthworm on an errand to such a place!"

Godfrey laughed as if I had made the greatest witticism on earth; such a treasure. No wonder even the odious Tatyana coveted him.

"The tunnels are obviously old," he speculated; "some defensive scheme of the ghetto against an attack. If the Golem was meant to hide in them, he would have to go bent double, for even I had to hunch over. An unwelcoming maze," he added, "as Nell says."

"Do you believe," Irene asked, "that we stumbled onto something long hidden, or in more modern use?"

I shuddered and thrust my gloved hands into the side pockets of the detested bloomers. "Ancient. Evil. To be avoided."

Godfrey extinguished the lantern and returned it to the black bag as he spoke. "Ancient, but useful in modern times. Impossible to say whether they have been used of late."

"Oh, if only I had a map to such a place!" In the dark, Irene's voice burst into a bright firework of passion.

"No map would exist—ever," Godfrey cautioned her. "That would be the entire reason for such a surreptitious network."

"That may have been the original reason," she said, "but—now . . . the possibilities are divinely unlimited."

"So are the possibilities of us contracting an ague," I reminded her. "May we return to the hotel and a bit of warmth?"

"Of course," she agreed too readily.

We were already picking our way through the dark, topsy-turvy graveyard and back within earshot of mirth, merriment and ardent liquors.

"The matters that await us tomorrow on Hradčany hill, my dear friends," she added in a deep, foreboding voice reminiscent of an ancient gypsy woman's, "are—may I say?—far more grave?"

I personally did not see how an expedition to Prague Castle could be any more ghastly than the previous evening's outing to the rabbi's tomb and its underlying secrets.

On Irene's orders, I attempted to dress as splendidly as I was capable of appearing.

"This is not a mere matter of vanity, Nell," she instructed me sternly in my chamber that afternoon. "When one mingles with the great and powerful, one must don whatever guise best suits."

"I am merely a secretary to Godfrey," I pointed out. "Surely no one will pay me any attention whatsoever, as is usual."

She shook an admonitory finger in front of my nose so urgently that I am sure my poor eyes crossed to regard it.

"Nell, you must listen and obey, as no doubt you expected your charges to do years ago. You can rest assured that a good many people will be paying you attention tonight, as you put it, merely for the fact of who your friends are. You must wear the cherry velvet gown I found for you at the Paris street fair. It is splendidly made and timeless in style."

"I do not think that I am a cherry-velvet person, Irene."

"Tonight you must be. Do not forget, I will be drawing

the vast majority of the attention to myself, but you still have a part to play."

"What of Godfrey?"

"I have advised him to wear simple black and white," she said impishly.

"Men's formal dress is always black and white. I meant, what part will he play?"

She sighed and stalked away. "One I do not like, but one that he has been cast in nevertheless."

"And that is?"

She turned in a whirl of skirts and scowling brows. "Target."

"Target? Of what? Not an air gun?"

"One can never be sure," she added glumly, pacing again. "But it is more as target of Tatyana. Oh, how tiresome that I must pause to deal with this unexpected issue, when so many other crucial events unfold!"

"What crucial events?"

She swooped close in a crackle of taffeta skirts as if to confide in me, but merely patted my cheek.

"You will see, Nell, you will see. *If*—you dress properly for me. There's a good girl. . . ."

Off she went, like a rather well dressed governess about her mysterious duties.

I had no one with whom to consult. Allegra was at the castle with the Queen. Why had I not been invited on such a mission? Godfrey was on the town, perhaps investigating the town's subterranean blueprints. Even such an uninspired errand would have been more profitable than regarding the cherry-velvet gown in my room and wondering what revelations awaited us at the castle that night.

Poor Godfrey! Caught between two formidable women. Poor Clotilde! Ignored by everyone but Allegra. Poor Irene! Forced to defend her husband while hampered by the guise of a fictitious person. Poor Penelope! Forced to gad about and know nothing. And lastly . . . poor Golem! The object of everyone's search and no one's sympathy. At least *I* would extend the poor hunted thing a modicum of pity. I had an absurd notion that the Golem was kept as much in the dark these days, as . . . as I was.

If I thought the cherry-velvet gown I wore that night a bit extravagant, the color faded to pearl pink next to the port-colored plush-velvet creation that floated down the hotel hall as Irene approached my door on Godfrey's arm.

I had been unable to wait meekly in my room, and—on hearing a grandiose swish in the passage—I opened my door to peep out.

Irene's gown had no sleeves, no neckline, merely a bodice as bare as a corset-top, like that of the notorious Madame X in Mr. Sargent's portrait of that name. A swath of rose-purple tulle swathed one bare shoulder and draped the full skirts. Sweeping designs in jet and a red stone that glimmered ruby-bright encrusted the hem and bodice. The Tiffany corsage slashed across this bloody ground in a glory of diamond-studded fire: snowflakes lit by an ever-passing comet of stars.

Despite her immodest elegance, Irene only had eyes for me.

"Nicely done, Nell! Quickly: I must have you inside for a small adjustment . . . here. And there!"

In front of my mirror I watched my long-labored-over curls prodded lower on my forehead, higher on my crown and looser over my neck and shoulders.

Irene tugged my neckline over the precipice of my shoulders.

I shrugged it back up.

She frowned and jerked it down, past repair.

"There! Do not fret. Hardly anyone will look at you with myself and Tatyana present, but it never hurts to be presentable . . . One never knows whom one might encounter."

"Irene!" Godfrey awaited discreetly in the hall, as he was

so expert at doing. "You behave as if you were going to a social duel with that woman, not unraveling the political conundrum the Rothschilds desire."

"You are right," she called out, then allowed herself to lean against the sofa back for a moment's rest. She lowered her voice so he could not hear us. "I have become diverted by another woman's artificial ploys. For this Tatyana can have no real regard for Godfrey, can she, Nell?"

I licked my lips, a cue for Irene to pull open her black velvet reticule and produce a pomade that both moistened and colored them.

"Irene . . . she is strange, this woman. I do believe that she is dangerous."

"Oh, I know that she is dangerous . . . but is Godfrey susceptible?"

"You ask me? You know these things far better than I."

Irene smiled, sadly. "I know these things in the abstract, down the street and across the wide world. As for my own neighborhood—we will see, Nell, what we see tonight. Much will be plain, and much still veiled. Keep watch, as I bid you before. Watch closely; much depends upon it."

"Can you not say more? Can you not be more specific? Irene, must you always play the sibyl?"

She shook her head, shaking her black-dyed curls into a gleaming torrent.

"I do not know more, Nell," she confessed, donning white velvet gloves. "I am a mere impresario. I have set the orchestra in motion, all its many sections and instruments of different voice; now I have no notion what tune it will play. I thrive on instinct, on panache, as does your despised acquaintance, Oscar Wilde. I throw bright balls into the air, in hopes that I will learn something from where they land. I am no Sherlock Holmes, my dear Nell; I am not so cold and calculating. So when circumstances conspire to threaten the center where my heart lies, I make a most unreliable compass. Watch for me tonight. Look for that which is not what it seems to be. See through the facades. Watch for the anomaly. Above all, protect Godfrey."

"I? Irene, you must speak more plainly—"

"No time," she said, pressing a white velvet fingertip to my lips.

I parted those lips to remind her of the colored pomade she had herself applied, but it was too late; a pale pink stain tinged the tip of her velvet-gloved finger.

The longer and farther abroad I traveled with Irene, the less I came to recognize myself. The figure I had glimpsed in my mirror tonight was a far cry from the timid dismissed drapery clerk Irene had rescued from the streets of London nearly a decade before.

Yet no matter how I evolved, Irene was always ahead of me, as a comet outruns its dissipating tail. I could never glory in my modest transformations, for they were pale imitations of Irene's mercurial self-manipulations.

Still, I set out that evening with Irene and Godfrey well satisfied that my new splendor should protect me from the moment I most dreaded, when the King of Bohemia would stare straight at me and declare: "It is she! The mousy woman who accompanied Irene Adler on her escape from Prague, Miss . . . What's-her-name?" Then he would frown and bellow, "That is such a patently ridiculous coiffure. Off with her head!"

At least Allegra was safe at the hotel; Irene had remained adamant to all her pleading.

Our carriage ride up Hradčany hill was silent. Godfrey brooded in the opposite corner, gently slapping his white kid evening gloves against one loose fist. I could understand the Russian woman's obsession; Godfrey gloomy was even more attractive than Godfrey at his charming best. His mental abstraction permitted one to admire the well-drawn lines of his dark hair and mustache, even his charcoal eyelashes over the dreamy pale silver eyes ordinarily so sharp and perceptive.

Irene, preening in the carriage until the last moment, shook her matching garnet bracelets down her gloves and admired the effect by the intermittent streetlights.

Yet she watched her husband, as I did, with an odd mix of fondness and fear. Nothing makes one more protective of one's possessions than the knowledge of another's obsession with them.

We all dreaded the next encounter with Tatyana, but it could not be helped. That was our mission in Bohemia: to face the facts, however fearsome, be it Golem or a more contemporary monster in a monstrous fair guise.

I felt that the evening would prove to be momentous. I resolved to make as many notes as I dared in my dance case; I hardly need worry about covering the sheet of thin white whalebone with the names of would-be escorts.

Once again we passed under the naked, straining bronze bodies of the gate's guardian statuary. A struggle as dire would soon transpire within, but the conflict would be far more subtle, and perhaps more deadly.

After we had bustled in and been relieved of our outer garments, we stood with a knot of other guests awaiting our turn to be announced.

"Together," Irene said softly, as if rehearsing fellow actors who were about to make a joint entrance. "We will be announced as one party. That should raise Tatyana's eyebrows."

"Irene," I protested. "You have become obsessed with this woman. What of the Rothschild commission?"

"Rothschilds come and go; one does not encounter an adversary as cunning and dangerous as Tatyana every day."

"I do not intend to allow that woman a moment's conversation," Godfrey put in, eyeing Irene sternly. "You wished my feeble attentions to make the King jealous, and all you have accomplished is setting that dreadful woman on me."

"I do not doubt that you will be most divinely surly to her this evening, Godfrey," she replied. "That will only encourage her, I assure you. Perhaps you should direct your attention elsewhere tonight."

"To you? That will enflame her further."

Irene assumed an innocently demure look that was irresistibly wicked. "I was thinking of someone less incendiary than myself: poor Clotilde, who has been publicly set aside in favor of another woman, one with no legal or moral claim to the King's affections. Surely no one can take offense if you pay polite attention to this neglected lady."

"Brava!" I put in. "An excellent suggestion, Irene. Tatyana will not dare venture too near Godfrey if he dances attendance on the Queen."

"Speaking of dancing," he added. "Must I?"

"You dance well!" she responded in surprise.

"But I do not like it."

Irene unfurled her fan of crimson feathers. "I do not see how you can command the Queen's time unless you offer to dance with her. I—or Lady Sherlock, rather—shall dance with those who ask me. No doubt even Nell will take a sedate gallop or two around the room with a respectable gentleman, should he ask. We must all appear as if we were mere merrymakers at a gay affair."

Godfrey donned an even more dour expression, now looking a most satisfactory and brooding Hamlet.

At that moment the footman leaned near him to ask for our identities. A half-minute later we heard our names, or what passed for them among some of us, shouted to all the world within earshot.

"Mr. Godfrey Norton. Lady Sherlock. Miss Penelope Puxleigh, of Paris, France, and London, England."

Into the bright lights and chatter we swept again to do battle. Irene suggested that we repair first to the supper table, as a good army marches on its stomach. How she could consider eating when laced until her waist seemed encompassable by a necklace I do not know; I can testify that her appetite never dwindled, no matter the circumstances.

I, of course, was too nervous to take more than a bite of cake. Godfrey had decided to brace himself with the punch, a vile lizard-green brew no doubt steeped in ardent liquors.

Around us people milled, the men in penguin perfection, the women a rainbow of rich color and fabric. Each of us unintentionally searched among the myriad shades of hair color, hunting the russet blond locks of the woman we all feared, each for his or her own reason.

"Oh!"

"Yes, Nell?" Irene swiftly turned away from making free with the goose-liver pâté.

"The King," I said.

Who could mistake his head shining in the candlelight of twenty chandeliers, rising above the common crowd like a sun-gilded alpine peak?

"Oh." Irene swallowed her disappointment with a last bit of pâté. "I thought you had noticed someone interesting."

"Such as the formidable Tatyana?" Godfrey suggested.

Irene's smile was secret and impudent. "Such as the Queen."

"Clotilde? Interesting?" I demanded. "Irene, it becomes you greatly to consider her welfare and self-regard, but I can think of no person in this entire assemblage who is more futilely present than that pathetic figurehead."

"Oh?" Irene answered skeptically. She stepped aside so that both Godfrey and I could have an unimpeded view, could in fact see past the glories of Irene's gown and person to something else.

That something else was Clotilde, abandoned by her husband after the obligatory joint entrance, moving into the room on a cloud of dazzling white silk-velvet and tulle, like a bride.

I can pay no greater tribute to my friend's skills and altruism than to say that Clotilde had blossomed from ugly yellow duckling into a showy white swan. Now that pale complexion and long feckless neck seemed possessed of felicitous grace. Now that pallid hair, piled away from the narrow face, seemed a gilt lace frame for a master sketch of sweetly underlined femininity.

Excitement burnished Clotilde's cheeks, but I recognized the inroads of the rouge pot and the hare's foot. Irene's hand lay in every blond silk curl, in every shimmering bead, in the very white-gold aura that radiated from the Queen's figure.

"By Jove," Godfrey said, standing to attention. "What has happened to her?"

"Allegra," Irene said happily. "That child has enormous potential. I tutored her a bit, of course, but the results are as spectacular as I had hoped." She glanced roguishly at Godfrey. "It will not be such punishment to avoid the importuning Tatyana by paying court at this Queen's side?"

"If the assignment involves dancing, it will be punishment," he said. "Not many women would reconstruct a former rival," he added in a teasing tone.

"Clotilde was never my rival; her only claim was aristocratic precedence."

"You are foolish to believe that the King will be swayed by a cosmetic improvement," he warned her. "From his past and present preferences, he craves more challenge than an ordinary woman can provide, and seems determined to find it one way or the other. Clotilde's transformation will not capture his regard."

"Perhaps not." Irene ducked her head like a schoolgirl caught out in a fond daydream. "Yet she will feel better about herself, and that is half the battle in any match, marital or royal."

He smiled ruefully. "You never needed to learn that skill."

Irene shrugged, a gesture that did wonders for the Tiffany diamonds, not to mention her poitrine. "Some are born knowing what is needed in life; some must be educated, even queens.''

"It will be a pleasure," Godfrey said, "to contribute to the Queen's more favorable view of herself. Your pardon, ladies."

He set down his glass on a tray, bowed and moved toward Clotilde. No one had yet dared approached her, and her eyes lit up as Godfrey's agreeable form came toward her.

Irene watched from the wings like a fond nanny. "She looks even more splendid than I could imagine. It is far from easy, Nell, to redesign a personage that is so opposite to one's own type. Women spend their lives learning their own best points; finding another's is most taxing. I am glad that I am not blond," she added, a new, stringent tone in her voice, and I knew she had spied Tatyana.

The object of our fears was regarding Godfrey, naturally, as he paid his respects to the Queen. The woman did nothing to disguise her avid interest. She watched like a hawk from near the doorway, awaiting her introduction.

We studied her, Irene and I, intently but with vastly different approaches, I imagine.

Tonight was one in which to be dazzled, and I admit that I was. How could the poor gentlemen withstand the separate but equal blandishments of such a trio of women? Clotilde in her new shimmering pale splendor carried the power of queenship like a scepter for the first time in her royal life. Irene, in regal red, with all her theatrical instincts and beauty polished into one apparently impervious resplendent facade, was like the fire that melts the snow of Clotilde's icy dignity.

And Tatyana. I loathed the woman, but that night I could no longer deny her personal power. She wore black, as Irene had on her debut as Lady Sherlock. For Tatyana to venture into any arena Irene had already declared her own was a bold move. That she was as successful as she was in a fashion sense, at least, said even more for the woman's personal power and ambition.

Where the subtle sheen of coq feathers had clothed Irene in a glamorous armor, Tatyana's gown was a cage of intricately beaded net and jet. It shifted around her as sensuously as a Liberty silk, glittering, glittering in tiny increments, like snowflakes of coal. I thought of Hans Christian Andersen's lethal yet seductive Snow Queen. Tatyana was the Cinders Queen: donning the dark as a contrast to her golden coloring; burning with the embers of emotions too black to bring into the light of day.

Was Godfrey poor Kay into whose heart the Cinder Queen would cast a lump of corrosive coal? Was Irene faithful Greta who would scour the world over to save his soul from that of the devouring woman who craved it?

Who was I in this drama? The knife-bearing robber girl who aided Greta? I hardly think so. The day I hefted a knife other than the table variety would be the day the Golem not only walked, but knocked politely and sat down to dinner at Prague Castle!

I studied Tatyana, that implacable, corrupt, wise and evil woman, who may even have caused Quentin ill luck in Afghanistan almost a decade before, and I shuddered to my soul, as I had not shuddered at the sight of the Golem. That had been a brute beast, if I indeed had seen what I thought. I saw before me now, in the guise of a woman of the world, a beast more terrifying than any creation of the Cabbala. I saw a creature who would have her will no matter who it hurt. Against that sort of selfishness, be it in a child in the nursery or in a head of state on his throne, an honest person, an ethical person is always in mortal danger.

Then I recalled the reported prediction of the gypsy woman. I do not believe in such nonsense, but I do not forget it, either. Three queens, she had said, would contend in Prague, to the death.

Three queens. One white, one red, one black. Who would win—and what would be the prize? Or the cost?

Chapter Thirty

A WICKED WOMAN

As so often happened when Irene set a Grand Plan in motion, she overlooked the obvious: myself.

If Godfrey was avoiding Tatyana by paying court to the Queen, and if Irene planned to keep an eye on the Russian woman, that left them occupied. I was left to play the usual wallflower.

On the other hand, I was also free to wander where I would and observe what I could. So I did.

Several points of interest struck me. While Irene watched Tatyana, the King's attention was all for Godfrey, who at the moment was sweeping the Queen around the dance floor in a most creditable waltz. Was fickle Willie becoming jealous of his neglected—and now newly magnificent—Queen?

Tatyana seemed aware of the supposed Lady Sherlock's keen regard, but ignored it in favor of keeping her eyes on Godfrey, even though she crossed the King's glowering glance whenever she did so. The Russian woman's attention was so fixed on my dear former employer, in fact, that I was able to study her as a entomologist might dissect some new species of loathsome bug.

I did not underestimate her. This woman was as compelling as Irene in her own way. Obviously accustomed to center stage, both the brunette Irene and the blond Tatyana circled each other at an apparently disinterested distance, all the while vying for position in their unspoken duel with one another.

Their gown colors that evening and current relationship to the King made Clotilde and Tatyana the most apparent rivals: White Queen and Black Queen dancing over the entire board to seize the King. Yet the gypsy woman had prattled of "three queens and two kings."

Including Tatyana, I saw before me the queens in question, only one of whom actually bore the title, and she was the least likely candidate. But what had the reference to "two kings" meant? Could one be Tatyana's "king"? Though Russians called their monarch by the title of czar, the function remained the same. Or did the cryptic comment mean that Wilhelm von Ormstein was of *two* minds? He had ever been so, pursuing Irene even while aware that he must marry Clotilde. Now he conducted an unsanctioned alliance with Tatyana, yet still publicly fretted over the neglected Queen's new popularity with Godfrey. Could Irene's clever transformation of Clotilde have fanned the marital fires?

What a spoiled boy he was—and tiresome to regard! I had to crick my neck to watch him, even across the vast ballroom. I directed my analysis back to my original object, the Black Queen, Tatyana One-name, also, perhaps, called "Sable" during spywork in Afghanistan.

Irene's inclinations toward fashion had trained me to examine others from the outside in, as superficial as such a method was. Clothes might not make the man, but they can often make sense of the woman.

By this standard, Tatyana was as enigmatic as ever. The unstructured flow of her gown might suggest the new Aesthetic Mode of female dress, but its roots lay in something other: the fragile draperies of the dancer.

Yet the long, black skirt she wore was weighted with

satin passementerie and beadwork, a bow to the venerable
tradition of elegant widowhood that Queen Victoria had
made so eminently imitable.

Knowing how Irene arranged to keep her throat unen-
cumbered by instinct, I could not understand why a former
dancer would wear diaphanous tissues over her shoulders,
yet anchor her lower limbs with bejeweled skirts.

Moreover, the designs decorating this cumbersome article seemed . . . familiar. In fact, I had seen something like
it in . . . at . . . on the occasion of— The precise memory
eluded me, just as I glimpsed but always lost sight of the
figures of Godfrey and the Queen threading among the
dancers.

I looked back to where Tatyana had been, and found her
gone. Then I glanced about for Irene. I could not see her,
either. Alarmed, I studied the crowd until at last I picked
her vibrant scarlet from among a pastel press of well-
gowned women.

I stared at her with the anxious reassurance of a nanny
who has found her favorite nursling. I expected danger
tonight, for no cause I could name, except perhaps the
gypsy's dire predictions.

"You are English, are you not?" a dry voice inquired
beside me.

Too startled to take proper offense at being addressed by
a strange man, I regarded my interrogator.

A strange man indeed, albeit not very dangerous-look-
ing. His salt-and-pepper hair and beard were seasoned with
the occasional wiry red strand. Indeed, his facial hair had
been trimmed like topiary into an intricate pattern, with no
apparent purpose save to underline his eccentric features,
the most striking of which was an overbearing nose that
could have competed with Cyrano de Bergerac's famous
but unfortunate appendage.

A monocle tinted slightly blue clung to one eye socket.
The silk ribbon that linked it to his lapel was of the color
purple, but otherwise nothing royal tinged his person. He

had a large wart on the back of one hand, and wore undistinguished evening dress, which could indicate that he was either rich and distinguished and did not care about appearances, or that he was an upstart nonentity who knew no better.

My head began to throb. Irene's system for character analysis by dress was highly ambiguous. I decided to answer his impertinent question in the interests of investigation.

"I am English, yes," I said coolly.

He nodded. "I as well. That enchanting lady who entered with you, she is English also?"

I abhor untruths, but committed one then. "Yes, but I cannot see what affair it is of yours."

"Pardon, dear lady." He bowed, running his wart-decorated hand over his springy hair. "I am not used to royal receptions. Lazarus Hampshire at your service, Madam." His smile exposed not very white teeth.

"I am not a Madam, but a Miss," I said sharply.

"Oh, indeed! Now that you mention it, I can see that it is so. Well, Miss—?"

"Huxleigh," I conceded in the interests of interrogation.

"Well, Miss Huxleigh, I am an itinerant banker abroad, and so hunger to see an English face and hear an English cast of phrase, that I have presumed to address a stranger. May I also presume to suggest that guests at such an elevated occasion must by nature be respectable?"

"You can suggest it, sir, but I am not convinced. Sometimes the most eminent persons behave in the least respectable way of all."

"How true, Miss Huxleigh. You have that English acerbity that I so miss among all these smiling people who bow and kiss hands and say everything but what they mean."

I couldn't help sighing agreement. "Yes, indeed . . . Mr Hampshire. What banking interests bring you to Prague? Pray do not be too specific; I do not understand financial matters in the slightest."

"An honest woman," he said with a low laugh that I quite detested. "A client in Leeds has inherited land from a distant connection in this city. Do you know it?"

"Prague?"

"Leeds."

"Dear me, no. I am from Shropshire originally."

"And now?"

"Paris," I replied shortly. Where another might take pride in residing in such a notorious place, I was annoyed to admit to it.

"Paris," he repeated, in the way of barristers and businessmen everywhere. Casanova owed his most irritating habits to human behavior, I fear. "And she—our fellow Englishwoman? Where does she live?"

I glanced, surprised, to Irene, who was sipping the bilious green punch with a tall gentleman wearing a much-outmoded long, flowing white beard, like that of an Old Testament prophet or a Lake poet of the last few decades, and tinted spectacles. When had she made the acquaintance of this unpromising fellow?

"I do not know," I replied. "I have not met Lady Sherlock until recently."

"Lady Sherlock," he repeated with a strange tone of satisfaction. "I am not familiar with such a title, and my work requires me to know Debrett's Peerage backward and forward."

When lost for words, I always follow Irene's dictum: ask a question. "Your work, sir?"

He nodded, retaining the unsettling monocle at his eye with the practice of long usage. "No one is more interested in the peerage than bankers. Do you know what county the lady calls home?"

"Why, sir? I told you that I hardly knew her."

The foolish face became sheepish. "I am a bachelor, Miss Huxleigh. In fact, I have never married, though I am long past the age for it. I must admit that your lovely acquaint-

ance caught my eye. I do not suppose you know if Lady
Sherlock is attached?"

"I most certainly do not! If I did, I would hardly tell any
gentleman forward enough to inquire."

He bent a suddenly intent gaze upon me. "We English
abroad must take care of each other, Miss Huxleigh. The
ordinary rules of parlor behavior do not apply."

"Ordinary rules of behavior apply everywhere, to everyone who is properly brought up," I answered with as much
hauteur as I could command.

My uninvited questioner backed away, bowing, his disconcerting monocle giving a last blue-white glint. "Then
accept my apologies, and farewells."

"Gladly, sir," I replied with indignant courtesy.

He moved into the crowd, becoming one with the many
other men wearing cutaway coat and striped trousers.

I unfurled my ornamental fan—an exceedingly silly affair
of tiny white plumes punctuated here and there with silk
rosebuds and cerise satin bows—and fanned my heated
cheeks.

Moments later another man was at my side: Godfrey,
slightly flushed from the dance floor.

"Irene is a cruel mistress," he announced, looking
winded.

"She is your wife," I admonished. "I do not wish to hear
talk of mistresses with that awful Tatyana about. How is
Clotilde doing?"

"Well. No one has asked her to dance since her wedding
and coronation months ago. Irene's scheme seems to be
working; once I deserted the Queen, a Moravian count
made so bold as to invite her to the next waltz. If the King
has a particle of sense, he will pay more attention to his
Queen."

"Then Clotilde is doomed to being ignored," I said
tartly, "although I admit that the King's gaze followed your
course around the ballroom."

"You see! Jealousy does wonders for the complacent spouse. Speaking of which, where is Irene?"

"Talking to a strange man near the supper table."

"The devil she is!"

"*Now* who has been complacent?"

Godfrey laughed with delighted surprise. "You are becoming quite the social critic, Nell; it becomes you."

"Better than this cherry-velvet gown."

"The gown is most attractive."

"But hardly subtle. If I am to be an efficient observer, I must not be too conspicuous."

"That has never stopped Irene."

"True," I said, my eyes wandering the room again in search of the various principals.

How many I needed to keep an eye on tonight: Tatyana, the King, Irene, Godfrey, the Queen, not to mention such minor figures as the gentleman who had spoken to me, and the one with the tinted spectacles to whom Irene had spoken, who was now standing alone by the wall, and Dr. Watson by the punch bowl and—and . . . *Dr. Watson* by the punch bowl!

"Nell, that is not ordinary wool broadcloth you are crushing on my sleeve, but a silk-weave coat made up by Baron Rothschild's tailor; it is worth a small fortune."

"Now is no time to be vain!" I retorted in a whisper, loosening my clutch on his coat sleeve nevertheless. "I have just seen Dr. Watson by the punch bowl."

"Punch bowl? Dr. Watson? What Dr. Watson?" Godfrey turned in the most annoyingly blatant way to peer here and there, looking for the object of my alarm.

I was forced to resort to his coat sleeve again, and a generous pinch of skin beneath. "*Our* Dr. Watson. Don't look! Not in that obvious way for which Irene always berates me."

Godfrey rubbed his injured sleeve, or arm, rather. I had not been a governess for several years for nothing. "Really,

Nell. We have more pressing problems than Dr. Watson, if it is indeed he."

The irritating man—Dr. Watson, I mean, not Godfrey—had ambled away from the supper table. Godfrey managed, by maneuvering around me as we spoke, to view the general area in a casual manner.

He froze for a moment, then turned to me to keep his back to Dr. Watson, who was now inspecting the crowd as if searching for someone.

"The very man indeed, Nell. He stands by the musicians now. Why is he here?"

"Why does it matter! Do you see what this means? If Dr. Watson is present, *the* man must be on the premises as well."

"Not necessarily. Dr. Watson may have a private life."

"Not if he resides—or used to—with an inveterate puzzle solver and busybody like Sherlock Holmes. Trust me, Godfrey; such a person has no private life, and certainly does not travel across all of Europe without there being deeds of a nefarious nature to investigate. What are we to do? He has seen us before, if not yet tonight."

Godfrey nodded, donning the thoughtful expression that so became him. I have never seen a man think with such flattering effect, but, then, I have never seen many men think.

"When we interviewed him in Paddington," Godfrey said, "you used your right name, though I did not. We can tell Dr. Watson—if he should approach us—that we visit Prague on further business involving your fiancé's affairs, I as barrister, you as loyal little woman."

"Oh, please, Godfrey! Explaining ourselves to Dr. Watson, should the occasion arise, is only half the problem. *Where* is Sherlock Holmes!"

"London?" Godfrey asked in vain hope. Then he shook his head. "You are right; he must be here. Why?"

"Barristers are obsessed with the interrogative in the motivational mood. The question is more direct: who? I have searched the chamber several times. Surely I would recognize Sherlock Holmes were he in a recognizable state. I have seen no one resembling him. Therefore, he is in disguise and could be anyone."

"Excellently argued, Nell. What can we do about it?"

"Nothing. We are both in our own guises, and helpless against him."

"Irene has never been helpless against him."

"Who is he?" I demanded again, wringing my gloved hands, which caused my fan and reticule, each suspended from a separate wrist, to sway around each other into a tangled knot. "The tinted spectacles are highly suspicious, but they were also worn by the Rothschild agent who passed you the travel guide," I muttered. "Then there was the rude man who spoke to me—his monocle was an obvious piece of disguise, and he was most interested in Irene's pseudotitle—"

Godfrey, I regret to say, was not paying proper attention to my speculations, but was smiling to himself and unspinning my tangled accoutrements so that I could move my hands again.

While we were involved in this minor enterprise, we neglected to note the arrival of a third person.

Suddenly aware of a presence, I looked up, braced for forthright English eyes and a demand for an explanation.

Tatyana stood beside us. I wondered how she had approached so softly on the hard marble floor.

She observed the end of Godfrey's rescue operation with amusement. "I had come to see if you were available for a turn around the room, Mr. Norton, but I see that you are occupied in more knotty matters."

He glanced up at her unmistakable voice, only I seeing how her presence had caused his hands to tighten momentarily. They fell away from my things just as the cords untwined.

Godfrey nodded slightly. "Madame Tatyana."

"You have not answered my proposal for a dance."

"The gentleman is usually the one who requests such things."

"I do not wait for gentlemen to request. Well?"

"I cannot desert Miss Huxleigh."

"Of course you can, and have already done so this evening. I saw you dancing with the Queen and found myself most eager for such an engagement with you."

She stood in a stance of court repose: head high, elbows in, her hands in their black lace gloves held before her waist with the fingers slightly steepled.

"You are a dancer, I understand, by profession," he said politely. "I do not care to dance unless politeness dictates; the Queen is our hostess. I fear I would disappoint you as a partner."

He bowed slightly again to put a period to the discussion.

"Then that would be interesting, Mr. Norton, for you have never disappointed me yet."

Godfrey's glance crossed mine. Would this woman refuse to take no for an answer?

We had our answer in an instant. Tatyana lifted a cynical blond eyebrow and looked at me. "Perhaps, Mr. Norton, you are more fearful of disappointing another lady of your acquaintance if you dance with me."

"Who?" he demanded recklessly. He obviously thought she was implying Irene, and betraying her knowledge of their true connection.

Her glance never left me, but her smile grew cruel. "Perhaps your so-called secretary . . ."

Godfrey stiffened, and I opened my mouth to voice loud objection, but the shameless hussy moved her knowing glance to Godfrey, and added, "Perhaps another . . . 'lady.' "

We both weighed the implication of that comment. She must know Irene was masquerading as Lady Sherlock.

"You need not fear any disappointed ladies, Mr. Norton," Tatyana purred. "Except for myself."

"If I feared anyone," he answered her implicit threat, "I should be a poor partner for a dance, or anything else."

"I find our deepest fears are not for ourselves, but for others close to us," she said. "So I wish to reassure you. I travel nowhere without bodyguards—an essential precaution in St. Petersburg."

"Bodyguards!" I burst out in disbelief.

She lifted a graceful arm. A lace-swathed forefinger indicated the directions of the compass.

"There. A broad man in striped coat." Near Queen Clotilde.

"There—" A man by the windows . . . near Irene.

"There—" The supper table.

"And there." Her last gesture was behind us.

We turned to the doorway to see the impassive-faced man in peasant tunic watching us with bored but brutal ice-blue eyes.

"A wise precaution," Tatyana added, "even in a city as safe as Prague, especially for the traveler far from home. Danger waits everywhere abroad." She smiled at us, and ran her fingers down the long, single strand of black pearls that anchored her filmy laces to her bosom like a chain. "You must take my word for it, dear friends. I knew a man once who sojourned in Paris and was bitten by a cobra outside of Notre Dame Cathedral."

Bitter, bitter was the knowledge of how she taunted us with her lethal role in our own past, virtually admitting to trying to poison Quentin in Paris for Colonel Moran. Irene had been correct. The woman had recognized us from the first, and had played with us ever since. What was her bewildering game with Godfrey?

"One dance, Mr. Norton, will not undo you," she said in her odiously suggestive voice. "Next you will be telling me that you cannot dance with me because you are married. *That* state can be altered, you know, by many means."

Godfrey had been a man of stone during all her blandishments. Some might mistake that poise for indecision, but I knew it hid a deep capacity for righteous anger. She had not noticed the white lines around his mouth, nor the tension in his entire frame; she was too busy toying with him, with us.

His eyes flicked to her indicated agents once again, perhaps gauging if she deceived us; perhaps deciding if they posed the threat she claimed.

Tatyana decided to cast a last insult my way.

"You mustn't worry about deserting Miss Huxleigh. I am sure that she is used to playing second fiddle in your life."

I gasped, staring at the woman's carnelian eyes. She believed her absurd charges; she saw all women as rivals.

Godfrey, suddenly decided, held out his right arm. "Shall we dance?"

He whisked her away, partly because his decision, once made, was swift; partly because he knew the lecture I was capable of giving the hussy. Although, in this instance, I found myself oddly incapable of motion or speech.

For all the times during my travels with Irene and Godfrey when I had worried about creating the wrong impression because of his escort, this was the first occasion that someone had actually accused me of impropriety. And, though I was innocent, the charge was so severe that I stood mired in shame, expecting every eye in the ballroom, every ear, every mouth, to be absorbing or passing on the slander.

How well I remembered the lessons of my youth: it is not enough for the decent woman to *be* free of blame; she must *appear* free of all blame, always, in all things.

Now I had been accused of vile midconduct, a disloyalty to my dearest friend as well as of behavior of the most humiliating and immoral sort, and I stood paralyzed. I hardly could muster the attention to watch Godfrey and the hateful woman take the dance floor.

How could even she think such a thing? That Godfrey

and Irene would tolerate such a situation? How could she—
but she could, and would. And had.

After what seemed minutes, I dragged my attention to
the dancers, a swirl of soft pastels among the sober black-
and-white evening dress of the men.

How easily visible Tatyana was in her mock-widow's
weeds. She and Godfrey sailed over the polished marble as
one to the lilting rhythm of a waltz. I glanced quickly to find
the supposed bodyguards still in place. The one near Irene
had moved, for the simple reason that Irene had noticed
Godfrey's new dancing partner, and had edged nearer,
along with the odd elderly gentleman in the tinted spectacles. If only this improbable person were our own body-
guard, for we sorely needed help of an outside nature!

I found myself wondering what Godfrey always did:
why. Why did Tatyana want so badly to dance with him?
To insult Irene and myself? To control us all, taunt us? Or
was it simpler than that? Was it something so simple and
basic that I seldom thought of such things? I recalled an
adage of my dear departed father when I was a child and
had trouble at school: children, he told me, oft accuse
others of the very wrongs they commit.

Hadn't Lizzie Cheek, the wicked thief at Whiteley's, my
first employment in London, tried to point false suspicion
on me, a total innocent? If Tatyana accused me of covet-
ing—of . . . wrongdoing with Godfrey, could not she herself be guilty of such a wish?

Now I had a reason to watch this dreadful charade for
signs that supported my theory. My first observation was
relief that Godfrey held her at a conventional social distance, a very proper twelve inches away. Although he did
not claim to be a gifted dancer, he was at least skillful. I
noticed a new stiffness in his posture, and deduced that
Godfrey was exerting considerable force to keep Tatyana at
arm's length; that this was more of a duel than a dance.

In that case, I trusted his superior strength to keep the
upper hand. They curved in a sweeping turn, and Tatyana

suddenly hesitated. This ploy drew Godfrey past her and allowed her to push close to him to continue the dance.

I am sure not only I noticed her triumphant smile as she whirled nearer on the turn. She took her hand from his left shoulder and fumbled at her gown. A moment later she had drawn up the long strand of pearls and looped them over his head, yoking them in artificial closeness.

Godfrey's steps stuttered, but she matched the roughness with perfect skill, laughing wildly as he swung her into a series of turns as if to whirl himself away from her odious vicinity.

They were not so much dancing now, as embracing. The music seemed to accelerate, reaching fever pitch. I realized that the piece was one of those novelty waltzes whose tempo goes faster and faster.

I glanced at the conductor, who was looking over his shoulder at Tatyana, nodding and smiling. No doubt Madame had requested—and paid for—this particular piece of music for this very particular partner.

Despite keeping up with the time and the wild woman in his arms, Godfrey's eyes darted around the room, no doubt seeking a plausible excuse for rescue.

But the other dancers, noticing the drama in their midst, now gave way. They drew back to the fringes of the dance floor, leaving the yoked couple a wide swath.

How diabolical that woman was! Godfrey was caught in a whirlpool of music and motion. Though his feet never faltered, he was like a mechanical man, like a Golem in evening dress, put through his unwilling paces.

Tatyana's right hand lifted from his shoulder again, despite the quickened turns, and thrust into her hair. She flung her hand back. Something small and bejeweled spun across the empty floor. A length of her fire-blond hair toppled, poured onto her shoulder like bleeding honey. Another turn, and it whipped loose behind her. Again and again her arm lifted, drawing out and discarding pins until her hair flew around in an ungoverned veil. Like Salome, she had more conventional veils to loose as well. The airy scarves upon her bodice drifted away one by one with the accelerating tempo.

I shall never forget that sight, a shocking symphony in black and white: Godfrey in his evening dress; Tatyana in her sober black gown except for her bare white arms, one lying along the black of Godfrey's guiding arm, the other snaking over his shoulder, behind his neck. The music, frantic by now, had them spinning in dizzying circles. Tatyana's blond hair whipped the air, her face and Godfrey's. She was laughing, laughing wildly, with utter exultation in the dance.

Her arm twisted tighter around his neck, forcing Godfrey's head toward hers. Her demonically laughing face drew nearer to his—she will kiss him . . . right here, before us all, before Irene. Oh, I cannot look—or . . . will she kill him?

Just when I thought that I must scream from sheer helplessness and horror, the music stopped. Godfrey, his face white though his cheeks were flushed, pulled the hateful pearls over his head and set Tatyana away from him. He did not push her, which would have been an act of violence that even such a woman did not merit of a gentleman.

He put his hands under her elbows, lifted her bodily, and set her a foot away from him, as one might move a mere mannequin.

I wanted to cheer. I had already seen Godfrey's unexpected strength: one night I had stayed late in his and Irene's rooms; he had lifted both myself and the chair I sat in from the table to indicate that I should leave—I still am not sure why, although I begin to glimpse such imperative motivations.

Then I held my breath, as did all in the vast chamber. No gesture of renunciation could be more plain. What would the prideful woman do now?

A expression of wild exhilaration suffused her dissolute face: she had *liked* his swift assertion of independence. I realized why in an instant: as a former ballerina, she expected partners to handle her.

Tatyana threw back her disordered head and laughed ecstatically, backing away from Godfrey, her hand fumbling at her breast. In an opera, she would have seized a concealed dagger from her garb and stabbed herself, or him. But Tatyana was a dancer, not a diva, and she had recently enjoyed a most exhilarating romp.

She seized the glorious pearls with which she had bound Godfrey so briefly, and ripped them from her neck.

A shocked silence struck the room and everyone in it. All eyes fixed on the scattering black beads. Even Tatyana's laughter died, and all that could be heard was the brittle clicks of falling pearls.

Only when the last one had stopped rolling did gentlemen rush to recover them, pecking about the floor like penguins turned to little red hens.

Godfrey and Tatyana stood frozen in the center of the floor, too fatigued to move, too exhausted and willful to end their dance-to-the-death. I finally thought to look for Irene, and found her, for once in her life, in the same state as I: too shocked to move.

We would not soon forget the evening's public and private humiliations at Tatyana's hands: Godfrey forced to dance to another woman's will . . . Irene seeing that even her nearest and dearest may suffer for the reckless life she leads . . .

I facing the wrong assumption that I have always most feared, that, no matter what I do, I will be suspected of being what I am not, a wicked woman.

Chapter Thirty-one

A SLAP IN THE FACE

Into the awful, awesome silence, came the sound of foot-steps.

Measured, inexorable, the fall of heavy feet upon marble echoed. The entire company heard, and still did not move, did not turn to stare.

Here, all was bright, yet frozen into a tableau, as if we were all Worth fashion mannequins posed in an elegant setting. Yet I recalled the ponderous advance of the Golem down the darkest streets in Prague.

These oncoming footsteps were as rhythmic as a clock's ticking, as mortality's dread tread through the Masque of the Red Death. I was also reminded of Mr. Poe's heedless aristocrats making merry while all around them the poor, the old and the ill succumbed to the plague that raged outside the castle until Death joined their noble, yet igno-ble, company in person.

As the steps drew nearer, drew even with me until I winced involuntarily at each firm footfall, I anticipated a tall, cadaverous figure bearing a scythe.

I was correct on one count only: the form that moved onto the deserted dance floor was tall, though far from emaciated, and wore a red military tunic blazing with decorations.

I had been so caught up in this closet drama that I had forgotten the fourth person whose pride Tatyana had recently cast to the ground, like pearls before swine, for the onlookers to judge and find wanting.

Wilhelm von Ormstein, his face the dull scarlet of utter rage, strode into the center of the floor, where Godfrey and Tatyana still stood.

He ignored the Russian woman (though one would think her disordered dress and hair would invite closer inspection) to pause before Godfrey. With the cessation of his steps, time resumed. The stirring of silks, satins and stiff shirtfronts agitated the air. I saw the scene in normal proportion again. We stand in Prague Castle, and its king is about to speak: what he says nearly unwinds time again and impresses new silence on the watchers.

"You, sir . . . banker." He addressed Godfrey with curled lip. "You have overstepped the bounds of even a king's hospitality. I would not ordinarily lower myself to deal with your ilk, but the offense is too deep to ignore. You have insulted my House; I will call you to account personally upon the field of honor."

"How have I offended, Your Majesty?" Godfrey inquired, quite reasonably.

"Your . . . dancing offends me."

Godfrey raised one eyebrow. "Is that not a trifling cause for a duel?"

"Not in this case." The King whirled impetuously to face his guests, swaying on his feet. "Witnesses abound. You have violated my hospitality by your overfamiliar attentions to—to . . ." He whirled back again, to glance at Tatyana, but his fury was for the man before him. "—the Queen."

A gasp shook the crowd, not because of the nature of the charge, but because of its incongruity.

"I danced a set or two with Her Majesty early in the

evening," Godfrey pointed out. "Surely this is not what has angered Your Majesty."

"That is exactly it! I take exception to your behavior. You have presumed beyond the limits of my endurance and I will have your h-h-hide for it."

King Willie swayed again after this pronouncement, a victim of two green and poisonous potions: jealousy and the evening's punch.

Or course the King's challenge was transparent: what had maddened him was not Godfrey's impeccable behavior toward Clotilde and even Tatyana, but the sight of his mistress's wanton public seduction of another. However, he could hardly challenge Tatyana to a duel, so poor Godfrey must pay the price.

"No!" cried a woman's voice.

I had no illusion's that it was Irene's, for the timbre was all wrong.

Queen Clotilde came rushing over to the trio, her slippers pattering across the burnished floor.

"No, Your Majesty! I assure you that Mr. Norton's attentions were not only innocent, but most kind. There is no wrong to right."

"I am the King," Willie roared. "I know when my honor has been besmirched. Would I dirty my own hands with such a nonentity were the matter not serious?"

Clotilde was not to be intimidated. She drew herself up, looking quite regal for once. "Sire, that is true, but I am your Queen. If you do not trust my assessment, you taint my own honor."

The King shook his head as if ridding himself of gnats. "Your honor will be restored when I have revenged it, as I will on the morrow." He turned to Godfrey again, all righteous outrage, this king who could not trouble himself to court his own wife. "My seconds will call upon you at dawn with news of the site for our meeting. The choice of weapon is yours."

"I cannot persuade Your Majesty that I have done nothing that merits offense?"

"No."

"I cannot convince Your Majesty that the dignity of your title will suffer from a duel with a commoner—?"

"No. That is true, but I do not care. All you can do is prove yourself the coward you are by leaving Prague before tomorrow's sun comes up."

Godfrey, as pale and composed as the King was florid and irate, nodded once. "Your seconds may call upon me at the Europa."

"And what is to be the weapon of your destruction?" the King demanded with a sneer that did not become him.

Godfrey hesitated. I could guess his quandary. The King's greater height and longer limbs would be to Godfrey's disadvantage with a sword, not to mention the likelihood of the King having studied this art since childhood. On the other hand, the King's heavier frame and thicker head from the night's drinking would benefit Godfrey in such a contest.

Before the King could cast another charge of cowardice at Godfrey, a new voice entered the fray, and this one I recognized instantly despite its uncustomary accents of the Queen's English.

"My fellow countryman," the bogus Lady Sherlock suggested smoothly, stepping into the vacant space around the three, "is not accustomed to fighting duels. He must have until morning to decide on his weapon."

"There is little to consider, Lady Sherlock." The King barely honored Irene with a second glance. (This alone spoke to his sad deterioration since our last encounter; he should at least have sensed some past connection between them, or been struck by her present beauty.) "It must be pistol or sword. I assure you that I am accomplished at both."

"Well, then—" Irene turned to Godfrey with a shrug.

"—make it pistols, Mr. Norton, and a bad business will be soon done."

I gasped, uncaring who heard me. Even a parson's daughter like myself knows that pistols are far more deadly in such meetings. True, a sword has many more chances to mutilate an opponent before the affair is done, while a single pistol shot may pass by, but a bullet that flies home is more often fatal than a cut or a stab.

Godfrey hesitated for an instant longer, no doubt thinking the same thing. Irene's expression was serene, calm, certain. She had spoken.

"Pistols," he said, the choice causing a ripple of consternation to shake the previously silent onlookers. This duel would risk the deaths of both men.

Clotilde wailed and fled the scene, but Tatyana stood her ground as she had for the entire time, watching the two men with the hungry eyes of a cat eyeing quarreling mice. One way or the other, her bloodlust or her ordinary lust would be satisfied.

"Will any stand up for you?" the King inquired in a tone that expected Godfrey to confess himself friendless.

I held my breath in anxiety that Irene would offer herself for the post, but she remained silent, for once.

"I, Your Majesty," said a man who stepped forward, "am not personally acquainted with Mr. Norton, but we are fellow Englishmen. I can do no less than serve as his second."

Worse and worse! This was the vile fellow who had queried me about Lady Sherlock. If he had an interest in Irene, could he be trusted to assist Godfrey in such a crucial role? Of course, he might be ignorant of their connection—unless he was a spy or the King's agent.

Or Sherlock Holmes!

"And I, Your Majesty," said another male voice, "am a physician and an Englishman. I will serve as both second to

Mr. Norton and doctor, should anyone require the latter services."

Of course the second second was that ubiquitous Dr. Watson! What a snarl.

"I have my own physicians," the King announced with a distasteful glance at Dr. Watson's honest face. He turned to Godfrey. "I suggest that you, sir, consult a physician of the soul before morning."

He spun on his heel, caught himself from reeling and stalked away.

Godfrey took advantage of the King's exit to approach his volunteers, leaving Tatyana bereft of both men with whom she had toyed so heartlessly.

She did not look in the least annoyed, especially since the hovering gentlemen who had retrieved her broken pearls came rushing over to return what they had recovered. No matter what happened to the men who currently caught her fancy, there would always be a fresh supply of new victims.

Tatyana opened her jet-covered reticule and, one by one, the eager gentlemen tumbled her lost pearls into it like heads into a basket. Madame DeFarge would have found a sister soul had Tatyana been alive during the Reign of Terror.

Godfrey, meanwhile, seemed relieved to be away from this siren and dealing with ordinary matters between men of goodwill, even if they were dangerous ventures.

"Thank you, sirs," he said to his new friends, shaking their hands heartily.

I could hear no more, for the people around me began to chatter of the events of the evening. I searched for Irene, but could not find her, which I thought rather odd. After a few more exchanges, the sinister stranger parted company with the other men, but Godfrey came toward me, bringing Dr. Watson with him!

"Is this not a fine coincidence?" he asked before they had quite arrived at my side. "An English doctor in Prague at just the right time to aid me in an affair of honor. May I present Dr. John H. Watson of Paddington. My secretary, Miss Huxleigh."

"Indeed. I am happy to assist a fellow citizen. How did you get into such a muddle, my dear sir? Your dances with the Queen were the soul of propriety, and you could hardly be blamed for the actions of that brazen hussy in black, though she is—" He glanced at Tatyana accepting tribute from her pearl-diving gentlemen. "—a fine figure of a woman, and no doubt. I have seen only one finer. . . ."

"Of course Mr. Norton was not at fault!" I interrupted the doctor's rather tiresome reminiscence before it strayed too close for comfort, for I knew of his and his associate's admiration for Mrs. Godfrey Norton. I also eschewed Godfrey's given name: Nortons were common enough, but Dr. Watson would have good reason to remember "Godfrey Norton," though he had never knowingly met him. Luckily, evening dress is a kind of disguise; no doubt the good doctor would not recall our odd interview in his Paddington consulting rooms. "Everything makes perfect sense when you understand that this Tatyana woman is the King's mistress. He could not publicly punish her for her unseemly behavior, so poor Godfrey must pay for it."

"You are most loyal, Miss Huxleigh," Dr. Watson said, smiling. "And that is a most fetching and ladylike gown that you wear. My wife Mary would be quite taken with it. I am sure that you would not under any circumstances engage in unseemly behavior. Indeed, I see that you can hardly bear to describe it. If I am not too bold, may I ask, have we met before? You and Mr. Norton strike me as vaguely familiar, yet I am embarrassed to say that I cannot tell why."

"All English people strike each other as familiar in a foreign clime," I said airily. "I was just thinking to myself that you do not seem a complete stranger. The effect is no doubt the sight of a good English face, especially when trouble has struck out of nowhere."

Dr. Watson frowned. "Who was that handsome lady

who advised you to use pistols, Norton? Another of these bloodthirsty femme fatales? Her coloring was Spanish, and a bit harsh to my taste, but her intonation was pure St. James."

"A new acquaintance," I put in again, as eager as Irene to direct the conversation. "Her name is Sarah—" There was no hope for it; I had to continue the charade Irene had begun. "—Lady . . . Sherlock."

"Sherlock?! You are certain?"

Godfrey and I exchanged a glance that could have been innocent inquiry, but was not.

"So she told us," Godfrey said. "Do you know her?"

"No, but I know the name." The good doctor laughed. "As a simple surname, not a title, however. I was unaware of such a title. . . . Still, I am ignorant on this subject. My former chambermate finds food for much thought in titles, though he is a bohemian fellow who bows before nobody, not even yonder King there. I shall have to ask him."

"Oh, he is with you?" I asked.

"Not here," Dr. Watson said shortly, oddly annoyed by my trite social inquiry.

I cannot blame him. I loathe small talk as well, but it works wonderfully well to disguise an interrogation.

"Mr. Norton," he added seriously. "I would advise you to leave Prague and forget this silly affair into which you have been drawn so unfairly, but you do not look a man who would do so. I will do all I can to assure fair play on the morrow. Now I must leave to get my rest. I recommend the same to you, with perhaps a tot of brandy before bed; but no more. The King has overdrunk tonight and will feel it in the morning. That is not much of an edge when one duels the member of a royal house, who has no doubt been schooled in such skills and shenanigans all his life, but it is something. Good night; and good night, Miss Huxleigh."

"A fine gentleman by nature," I commented as he walked away. "A pity that his association with Mr. Sherlock Holmes has led him so astray. Do not trust him,

Godfrey; he must know that his friend is indeed here, and in what guise. I suspect your first second."

"My first second? Of what?"

"Of being Sherlock Holmes in disguise."

Godfrey's eyes widened. "Then I'm done for," he proclaimed, melodrama in his voice. "No doubt that the gentlemen has cast a covetous eye on Irene and will endeavor to see me dead on the morrow. Be honest, Nell; you do not truly think that we are caught up in such amazing machinations, as in a French farce?"

"We are caught up in machinations," I told him sternly, "but I do not for a moment think that there is anything farcical about them, and, unfortunately in this case, nothing French."

"A duel?"

Allegra clasped her hands to the beruffled bodice of her combing gown and regarded my friends and myself with star-dusted eyes. She had expected us to regale her with tales of our evening at the castle, but she had not expected anything this exhilarating.

"How utterly thrilling! A duel is something I would expect Uncle Quentin to engage in at least weekly, but now you tell me that Mr. Norton—how many duels have you fought, Mr. Norton?"

Godfrey was at the sideboard of Irene and Allegra's suite, pouring Dr. Watson's prescribed tot of brandy—and then some.

"None," he said.

"None?" Allegra's elation turned to apprehension. She turned on Irene and myself. "How could you let him do this?"

"No one asked us." Irene sounded a bit sharp. She sat on the sofa in her crimson gown, inhaling one cigarette after another until she resembled a smudgepot.

"Are you proficient with the pistol, Mr. Norton?" Allegra asked delicately.

Godfrey took a long sip of a libation the color of dried blood. "More than I was a fortnight ago, but not as much as one would hope. I am not worried, however," he added. "After all, not a single barrister in the Temple could claim that he has been challenged to a duel by a King. I wish I had brought the dueling pistols given me by Baron Rothschild, though."

Irene suddenly spoke. "It is not your duel with the King that worries me."

"No?" I demanded indignantly. "And what should a proper wife worry about, if not her husband's very life and limb?"

"Not to mention his honor," Godfrey put in

Irene struck another lucifer, then shook the small flame out. "I worry about our joint duel with Tatyana more." She eyed her husband. "And that has taken a very nasty and unforeseen turn."

"Speaking of such nasty and unforeseen events," I added, eager to follow such a splendid opening, "what of the presence of Dr. Watson? Are you not worried that Mr. Holmes may be lurking about?"

Irene laughed, sounding relieved for the first time that evening. "That is the last thing on earth—and in Prague— that I do worry about, Nell. In fact, I should be glad if he were in the vicinity."

"Oh?" Godfrey approached her, cosseting his brandy.

She looked up, her smile limpid. "Sherlock Holmes is an old hand at such intrigues. He is English. If he has been engaged by one party or another to investigate this carnival of intrigue, his interests will not lay far from our own. I—we—could use an able ally."

"What of us?" Allegra inquired indignantly, sounding much like Irene during her more high-handed moments. "Are we worth nothing?"

"My dears, you are all worth everything; that is the entire difficulty!" Irene rose, took Godfrey's glass, and drained it. "Nell told me that Dr. Watson prescribed only a tot. You poured at least two-and-a-half 'tots.' Duelists must keep their hands steady and their heads clear. I will see you to your room."

"That sounds like a threat." His objection was so lightly stated that it was evident he did not dispute her plans in this instance at all.

"As in all threats, the promise is implicit." Irene threaded her arm through his. "Good night, sweet friends," she declaimed to Allegra and me in the manner of an exiting Shakespearian heroine. "May angels guide you to your rest. Sleep! And do not worry. We have more friends than you know, perhaps even Mr. Sherlock Holmes."

They left the suite, a handsome couple who seemed designed to occupy the top of a wedding cake in perfect, unblemished harmony for eternity.

The minute the door had closed behind them, Allegra turned to me. "Oh, Miss Huxleigh, you do not think that anything could happen to Mr. Norton?"

"He is to fight a duel. Usually such individuals are at risk of injury, if not death."

"Oh, but not Mr. Norton . . . he is so handsome, so clever, so much fun—"

"Those are not necessary qualifications for fighting duels, my dear."

"Oh. He said he was not unprepared."

I found myself rolling my eyes, a vulgar habit that Irene employed on occasion to better effect than I could, I am sure.

"A recent gift of dueling pistols has introduced him to the gentlemanly sports of fencing and shooting, I suspect. The King has spent a lifetime in such so-called disciplines."

"You are worried."

"I am . . . frantic, dear Allegra. Irene is uncharacteristically distracted—that she should ever welcome the interference of this Holmes person is most unlike her! I have seen poor Godfrey in the toils of a wanton woman—" I glanced at Allegra's wide and shining eyes. "—a most forward person, who recognizes none of the ordinary claims or loyalties. I am beside myself, Allegra, and there is nothing I can do! If there were . . . I would go to any length, risk any fate, face any danger to insure my friends' safety. But I can do nothing, save wait and watch."

I sighed and let my hands loosen on my cherry-velvet skirt, which now bore a double set of my fingerprints.

"I am sorry to have lost control of myself, Allegra. The situation is most trying to one of my temperament, who imagines that a well-ordered world is the goal of most sensible people. I am sorry that I ever met Baron Rothschild, that we ever returned to Prague. When we . . . return to Paris," I added with a lump in my throat, for it occurred to me that we might not all return, "I will give the Bible back!"

"Indeed, Miss Huxleigh, this is a serious matter. What can I do?"

"Only what I can do. Cause no trouble; be steadfast. Hope and pray for the best."

"Oh, I will, Miss Huxleigh!" The dear girl was about to melt into tears. "If only Uncle Quentin were alive and were here! He would help us."

Now I was on the verge of a rather moist indiscretion of my own. How I would like to consult Quentin about these events! A man of the wider world, as he had been, perhaps would have reassured me, at least, of Godfrey's chances of survival. Yet . . . he might live. To that hope I would hold, as I would to the hope that Godfrey, too, would survive the test that awaited him on the morrow.

Allegra and I wordlessly broke with our rather formal tradition and kissed each other good night, politely ignoring the other's tears.

As I returned to my solitary room, for the first time in my life I wished I possessed something like Irene's wicked black pistol. I might shoot someone with it without waiting for the formality of a duel—and her name began with the letter T.

Chapter Thirty-two

SUBTERRANEAN SCHEMES

I **cannot** speak for anyone else, from the King of Bohemia to Allegra, but I was unable to sleep for even half a wink that night.

I lay in my darkened room, staring at the faint light leaking through the drawn draperies. The light fell in slivers here and there, like scattered pins. I judged the night's progression by how these luminous barbs darkened and shortened as the moon made its bright journey across the sky.

Even when we had known Quentin to be in peril from Colonel Moran, the danger had not been so immediate, and definite. Dawn would bring not relief from this tension, but the ultimate exercise of it. Irene had not said that she would attend the duel, but I could not imagine her missing it, any more than I could imagine myself watching it.

So silent was the chamber, except for the ticks of the mantel clock, that when I heard a sound at the door, I thought I was dreaming, after all.

Again it came, that faint scratching. So Lucifer would demand admittance to my bedchamber in Neuilly. Could

the hotel cat be so bold as to presume upon guests? Or mice
. . . could the Europa have mice? Or even—rats!

I sat up in bed and listened.

When the scratching continued at regular intervals, and
rather impatient ones at that, I rose, found my slippers,
donned my robe and went to the door.

Turning the lock silenced the scratching. I eased the door
open and bent my gaze at the passage carpeting. Nothing
there, not even a small rat or a large mouse.

The door pushed open in one fell swoop, nearly knocking me off my feet.

"Nell, for goodness' sakes!" hissed a familiar contralto.
"I thought you would never answer."

"I thought you were a rat—or a mouse."

Irene turned to shut and lock the door behind her. "I
assure you that I am neither. If anything, I am a White
Rabbit, and I am late."

I stared at her in the dimness. Nothing about her was
white but her teeth, for she was clad all in black, clad in the
very slinking-about men's clothing she had donned on previous nocturnal forays. She had added another and unwel-
come adornment: the crepe hair mustache and Vandyke
she used on occasion when in male dress.

She thrust something equally impenetrable but soft as a
pillow at me. "Here. Wear these, and be quick about it!"

"What are these—?"

"Your walking-out clothes."

"They are not mine, and I am not walking out."

"Yes, you are, unless you wish to save wearing black to
Godfrey's funeral."

"Oh! Irene."

"Just dress."

"I must have a light."

"We can't risk light here. Let me help."

"Oh! Ow!! Irene, that was my eye!"

"Then keep your head up where it should be. There, the
bloomers are buttoned. It is chill out, but we dare not risk

wearing cloaks. Our progress will be less questioned if we look like men in trousers, not women in opera capes."

By now I had been infected with her urgency. "What progress?"

She sighed and fastened my black sailor blouse up the back. I could tell by the drawing of the fabric that it was buttoned awry, but would hardly dare mention that to Irene.

"Godfrey is in great danger, Nell."

"I know that!"

"There is only one way to save him."

"And we will accomplish that?"

"I . . . hope that we will accomplish that, if my theory is correct."

"And testing that theory requires—?"

"—you and I to venture again to the rabbi's tomb and into the catacombs beneath. Only one person can save Godfrey now, and that is the Golem of Prague."

"The Golem! It does not exist, and even if it did, how could it save Godfrey?"

"By attending the duel."

"Surely that would be a shocking sight, but I cannot see how the Golem would aid Godfrey in his affair of honor; he already has two seconds—"

"Believe me, the Golem is Godfrey's only hope—and Bohemia's as well, for a clever and nefarious plot is afoot to deliver the entire country and its people into the control of a sinister foreign power."

"Russia," I breathed.

"This is no time to be politically astute, Nell. We must hurry!"

Despite this imperative, at the door she drew me to a sudden stop. "You must carry this." She thrust something long and hard into my hands.

"What is this?"

"Godfrey's knife."

Only my long years of iron discipline learned as a

governess kept me from dropping the weapon I so well remembered. "That crude, vicious blade he carried in Monaco in the guise of Black Otto?"

"The same."

"Why can't you carry it?"

"I will have my hands full with the lantern and the pistol."

"Oh. Then why do we need a knife?"

"Because we will! And be silent when we leave the hotel; above all, don't drop it!"

"Do Godfrey and Allegra know of our mission?"

"No."

"How did you manage that?"

"I told Godfrey that I must not distract him on the eve of his duel and would spend the night with Allegra, and I told Allegra that a wife's place is at her husband's side at such a crucial time. They both sleep like lambs, thinking me safe in the other's room."

"I doubt they sleep."

"So do I; that was a figure of speech, Nell. Now may we be quiet and make our way out of this hotel with some discretion?"

"I am the soul of discretion," I managed to retort just as she opened the door and we went into the deserted hall.

Who can say what the hour was? Well past midnight, certainly. At such an hour in a hotel, not a creature was likely to be stirring, not even my imagined rats. Yet we went cautiously down the servants' stairs at the rear and only breathed freely when we passed through a nondescript door and found ourselves on the hotel's unprepossessing back stoop.

The scent of stale cabbage wafted from certain waste containers nearby, and a marmalade cat streaked down the alleyway.

Irene sighed her relief, despite having to inhale a vast attar of cabbage to do so. "Now is the simple part."

Some may regard moving surreptitiously through a convoluted foreign city late at night as mere child's play. I am not one of them. The moon was three-quarters full, and shed enough light to lead us, and worry us. We glimpsed citizens abroad, but none was so large and looming as the Golem, and none paid us any mind.

Still, I was surprisingly relieved to spy the jagged silhouettes of the cemetery when Irene's expert guidance led us to it. Moonlight gilded the crooked headstones; they seemed to shine, their engraved characters shivering in the night chill.

The smoke-darkened bulk of the rabbi's tomb was unaffected by this phenomenon. The pale notes attached to it gleamed like lichen or . . . maggots.

Irene went right to it, curiously confident that we would encounter no guards. She lit the lantern that directed its beam only forward and illuminated the dread structure. "You must find the mechanism that opens the crypt door, Nell."

"I may not be able to do so again."

"You must, for only you opened it before. Why do you think that I brought you along, instead of leaving you dreaming safely in your bed?"

"I was not dreaming! I was worrying like the rest of you."

"I know that you were. Stop worrying now, and concentrate on finding the place you pressed before."

My gloved fingers prodded the ungiving stone while I fretted about the theoretical guards Irene no longer regarded. Every irregularity seemed promising, but no touch produced any effect.

"Earlier you anticipated guards; now you do not. Earlier, you had us abandon the search below, Irene," I whispered. "Why are you so sure that you will find the Golem in those eerie tunnels now?"

"Because now I need him. Now I can use him." Her icy tone chilled my blood and boded no good for the Golem. "I told you before, Nell, that timing was all in this matter.

Our timetable has been forced by the King's foolish challenge, and Godfrey's even more foolish acceptance."

"You could have begged him to refuse."

"I do not beg, and Godfrey does not back down, in public or in private, or in any guise. Lady Sherlock does not beg either."

"Could the King . . . shoot him?"

"He will try his mightiest, Nell. His passion for this Tatyana is beyond reason; surely even you can see that."

"And Tatyana cares nothing for him? Doesn't she risk losing her royal road to influence?"

"Perhaps the road has grown rutted," Irene said. "Certainly she now has her eye on other, more attractive routes. Well—have you found anything? We do not have all night."

"I know; I know! Only . . . I do not know how I hit upon the secret in the first place."

"What you can do once with simple, idiot luck, you can do again. Try!"

Simple, idiot luck, indeed. Did she think me such a poor creature that I could not stumble onto the same secret twice? My hands pressed along the cold stone, stiffening with the contact. Finally a familiar swell was under my fingers. I noted the approximate distance from the ground, and pushed with all my might and main.

The dark stone before us darkened, then disappeared. Barely catching ourselves from falling, we followed the opening slab of stone into the same warm, earthy atmosphere that had greeted us before.

Irene brushed past me to hold the lantern high, illuminating the stone stairs that led below. The moonlight that still bathed my back slowly thinned to a single bar and vanished, leaving me as cold as someone who had lost a last shaft of sunlight.

Nothing in the ghostly atmosphere dissuaded Irene. She moved rapidly down the uneven steps and into the tunnels, retracing our earlier path. I followed her, clutching Godfrey's knife and suddenly glad of it.

She paused at the second juncture of another tunnel. "We stopped here before," she whispered. "You and Godfrey may have thought it whim on my part that I suggested we retreat, but I had a reason. Do you see this?" She held her lamp up to the side of the new tunnel.

In the raw limestone, a blue chalk mark had been laid as neatly as a direction on a dressmaker's pattern.

Irene pulled off her glove tips with her teeth—I cannot excuse such hoydenish behavior, except that she *was* holding the lantern in her other hand—and brushed her bare fingertips over the mark. She held them under the light.

"Blue. The mark is fresh."

"Why? We agreed that these tunnels were used long before the cemetery was closed in the seventeenth century. Who would be down here now?"

"Whoever would require marking the proper route."

"The Golem? Would such a creature pause to scratch a notation of its rampage?"

"No, but the *guardian* of the Golem might."

"Guardian? Do you mean to say that someone—something—accompanies this monster?"

"Why else would I have asked you to carry a knife, Nell?" she asked sardonically.

"If a knife will defend against it—and you have your pistol as well—you expect to meet . . . corporeal beings."

"What else are there?"

"Spirits, perhaps even that of the rabbi himself."

Her face, dramatically uplit by by lantern, relaxed into a slight smile. "If I could produce spirits at will, Nell, I would not need the Golem. Nothing prowls these elder byways, but you and I and some pawns in a political plot. These plotters may be dangerous enough to merit us bearing arms, but we need not fear for our souls."

"You omit the Golem," I added. "I have seen it, and I

can attest that it is far from a bodiless spirit. That does not mean that it is not supernatural.''

"Indeed it does not. We will proceed with the proper caution, physical and spiritual. I will rely upon you to supply the spiritual safeguards, but, I beg you, Nell—do not drop the knife!''

Irene led with the lantern and I followed. Our footfalls, however soft, seemed loud in the empty corridors. At another crossroads, Irene wordlessly pointed out another blue chalk mark. We followed the offshoot tunnel it indicated and came at last to a rough-hewn rock chamber. Distant subterranean water dripped, while a scratching like rats' feet echoed.

Irene put her bare hand on the rock—darkly gleaming with damp—and indicated that we would follow the wall around. She placed my hand on her shoulder, then doused the light.

I cannot adequately describe the utter, awful dark in which we then stood, our light-accustomed eyes blinding us to everything but blackness incarnate.

Irene began moving along the wall, drawing me with her. I clutched the knife in my left hand in such a way that I could use it if necessary. Our footsteps shuffled slowly forward.

What were we doing here, with Godfrey in such mortal straits? Playing Blind Man's Buff, as I had once before played it in Berkeley Square with a man whose own life later was in deadly danger?

Perhaps the sight of the foul Tatyana taking liberties with Godfrey, the strain of his forthcoming duel, had totally unhinged my rather melodramatic friend. I began to fear for something I had never before questioned: Irene's sanity.

Chapter Thirty-three

PRISONER OF PRAGUE

Ahead of us, as faint as fog, appeared a misty glow.

For once I dreaded that I had been right, and my friend tragically wrong. Ghosts did haunt these ancient tunnels, and we were about to encounter one of them.

Muted laughter drifted toward us on the stale scent of decay.

My hand seized Irene's shoulder in a spasmodic grip. I felt her wince at my warning; then her warm breath was tickling my ear.

"Almost there. Be of good heart."

We continued forward, our soft shuffles lost in the sound of someone talking ahead.

The glow intensified, indicating a merely human source of light: a lantern like our own.

Only one voice spoke; apparently it entertained itself. I recognized the German language, and even understood a few words.

"Eat," it suggested. "Drink." "Time goes." "You stay."

Did a Golem eat? I wondered. Did a Golem need an attendant to feed and water it, like a pet? What would keep such a creation alive once its makers were dead? A keeper as immortal as it was?

We had neared another opening into an adjoining tunnel. From this mouth the light and the odd, one-sided conversation both had issued.

Irene stopped at the very selvage edge of light, causing me to collide with her back. Only the prominences of her face and figure caught the light, including the revolver clutched in her right hand. She stooped to set down the lantern, then cocked the weapon.

The noise was louder than a snapped branch in a forest, for here the surrounding rock magnified sound. I shut my eyes, expecting I know not what, but at the least a rather disastrous discovery.

As I feared, the German voice paused. In the unnatural silence we could hear heavy, booted feet pacing in our direction. My only solace was that we likely would not live long enough to worry about Godfrey's survival. And if, perchance, our state of grace in our present lives saw us all to the same form of afterlife, we could meet again in some better world. I was not, however, sanguine.

Fee, fie, foe, fum. Thump, thump, thump, thump. Ponderous steps, as made by a walking monster. And what did a monster really eat and drink—besides bone and blood? Our triumph in finding the lair of the long-survived Golem would end in the fate of all flesh . . . dissolution, death—Closer. Closest! We are doomed, I thought, my eyes squeezed so painfully shut that fireflies curtsied on my inner lids.

"Halt!" Irene commanded in stern German.

I felt her back stiffen, and pictured her pistol-bearing arm thrusting forward into the light. What good were a few paltry gunshots against a monster of such height and girth and life span?

I waited to be caught up as a leaf in a stream, to be seized and smashed against the tunnel walls. Irene kept talking.

Her rapid German was unintelligible to me, but she seemed to be giving orders. What is more, I finally heard a sullen male voice muttering *ja wohl* like the tamest waiter at the Europa.

I dared flutter my eyes open enough to peek through my lashes.

A man stood before us. An . . . ordinary man. True, he was over five feet tall, rather rotund, and unabashedly untidy about his dress and grooming . . . but he looked quite an ordinary villain. Quite human. Quite mortal.

"Hold the pistol on our prisoner, Nell," she instructed, suddenly forcing the weapon into my hand, "while I bind him."

The metal was still warm from her flesh. Only that realization permitted me to hold the deadly instrument level. I clutched Godfrey's knife in the other hand, and must say that our prisoner regarded me with a look of unholy alarm.

Irene drew a length of rope from the side pocket of her man's jacket and swiftly approached the prisoner, binding his hands behind his back.

I doubted that she knew how to tie him securely, but did not want to inquire in front of him, even if he spoke only German. I am told that the German and English languages share many similarities, though I have never noticed many when in the presence of those who spoke German.

Once he was bound, she rejoined me to take charge of the pistol. Irene asked a series of short German questions, which he answered as briefly. Satisfied, she directed him toward the light with the pistol's barrel.

We followed, quickly discovering that the expected tunnel had been hollowed into a large chamber. The light came from a paraffin lamp set on a crude table, which was companioned by chairs as crude.

Irene motioned the man to one of the chairs, then put up her hand to stop him. Hurrying to the table, she extracted a formidable bread knife from a cut loaf before letting the man near.

I also noticed a glass water pitcher—full—and a wine

bottle—nearly empty, naturally—on the table, along with some newspapers.

"We did not need to bring our own," Irene noted, brandishing her bread knife. "You must take the revolver for another moment. We will be safer with our prisoner secured to the chair, rather than having him capable of lurching about."

"Yes," I said faintly, taking the incongruously warm grip again. "Lurching about is to be avoided at any cost." At that she handed me the bread knife as well.

Like a magician, Irene produced another coil of rope from her other side pocket. She knelt to bind the man's feet to the chair legs, an operation I watched with alarm, for he could have easily kicked out at her face.

However, he seemed most interested in keeping his eyes on me and my assortment of weapons, which I tried to hold with familiar aplomb while affecting an expression of utmost ferocity.

Once the poor fellow was bound before a simple meal that he could not touch, Irene reclaimed the pistol and lofted the lamp from the table.

"Now we must find our Golem. He cannot be far."

"He cannot?"

"I am relieved that we had only one keeper to disarm; at least this fellow claims that he is alone at his post, for now. Quick! What time is it?"

I at least had had the foresight to pin my lapel watch to my sailor collar. I lifted the up-facing dial, cleverly meant to be read only by the possessor, and strained to tell where the hands as fine as a spider's legs pointed.

"Almost three, Irene!"

She blew out a frustrated breath. "We must hurry, Nell, for we have other business to accomplish this night."

"More than finding the Golem?"

"Much more, but first we must find him, and enlist his aid."

"Really? The Golem will help us. Why?"

Irene's smile would have put Mona Lisa to shame. "He will have his reasons."

She held the lamp high above her shoulder and swept the cavern walls. They were bare, bereft of furnishings—then I saw a pale, shining gleam . . . the lamplight paused on this object. A humble porcelain chamber pot! Irene was indeed a White Rabbit tonight, leading me down a hare hole to curiouser and curiouser scenes.

Irene moved deeper into the dark, casting her light before her like the Americans' Statue of Liberty. It illuminated no huddled masses yearning to breathe free . . . but there—against the stony wall—a cot! A blanket.

We stood awestruck beside this sign of—not just human presence, for the guard had confirmed that, but of . . . habitation, perhaps inhuman habitation.

"Observe the extraordinary length of the cot, Nell."

"Irene, it must be . . . seven feet long. What does this mean?"

"That whoever has prepared this hidden nest equipped it for precisely what we seek."

"The Golem!" I was convinced beyond all doubt now. "Will a pistol and two knives be sufficient against it?"

Irene laughed. "No, but I will be."

"Irene, you overestimate yourself at critical times. Let us return to fetch reinforcements."

"I already have: you."

"We are but two women—"

"We are two determined women. Trust me, this Golem will be glad to see us."

"To . . . devour us, or worse."

"Nonsense; the Golem is a prisoner. He is no threat to us."

"You mean that, that man, and others, found the creature and turned him to their own uses against his will?"

"Yes, they re-created him, just as Rabbi Loew did centuries ago, albeit accidentally."

"How could anyone raise up such a monster accidentally?"

"Because they served a monstrous plot and would not stop at any means to accomplish it. But we will foil them, Nell, and lay the Golem to rest for good."

"Oh. We will not . . . kill it?"

"Now you are sympathetic? I thought you feared it."

"It may be as dumb as a beast of the field, used to evil purpose by bad men. Yet, when I saw it, I sensed some inner torment, however awe-inspiring its aspect."

"Your mercy becomes you." Irene's face hardened in the warm lamplight. "I, however, am not as inclined to that virtue as you. I confess that I would rather leave this creature penned up beneath Prague where it cannot repeat the ill it has done through the years."

"Then it is dangerous!"

Her look was fierce. "Only to those foolish enough to trust it. But, for Godfrey's sake, I will unleash it on Prague and Bohemia again, and God save them."

With that she moved farther along the wall, beyond the cot. Her small circle of hot light illuminated rock walls, rock floor, rocky emptiness.

Then, when our path was taking us almost back to the table with its silent prisoner, the lamplight glanced off cold metal—a length of black chain coiled like a cobra. One end was fastened to a great metal ring cemented into the rock wall.

Only a monster as massive and legendary as the Golem would require such brute containment! I felt my throat constrict.

"Irene, dare we risk releasing what this chain holds?"

She eyed me implacably. "It means Godfrey's life."

"Yes, and I would do anything—I am here, am I not? But there is a Greater Good; there is blasphemy that walks the earth and must be fought at all cost. There is Evil Incarnate."

"And, there, I think, is the Golem." Irene's lamplight followed the chain until it ended in a manacle.

I saw a massive foot in a crude shoe. Her inexorable light ran up the figure's long leg—in tattered trousers—past the huge rough-shirted torso—to a visage that would be unbearable even in a nightmare.

"Is this what you saw stalking the streets of Prague, Nell?" Irene asked in the biting tones of a prosecuting attorney.

I averted my face, though my eyes could not desert the creature. "Yes, yes! The face—the awful brown face, like broken crockery . . . I had not seen it so clearly before."

The creature, for all its size, cowered at the light, lifting an instinctive arm before its mockery of a face. Even from these manacled limbs chains clanked. Marley's Ghost could not have been as horrible to Scrooge as that debased yet mighty figure was to me.

It attempted to scrabble to its feet, using the wall to support itself, but the chains, the apparent dazzle of the lamp, made its movements futile.

Irene put the lamp on the ground and handed me the pistol again. I gripped it as if my . . . life depended on it.

Then Irene did the most astonishing thing. She pulled off her soft-brimmed man's hat and began pulling the hairpins out of her hair. In an odd way, the performance reminded me of Tatyana's display on the ballroom floor, save that Irene's movements held nothing of seduction, only grim, unrelenting purpose.

Her revelation of her sex had a remarkable effect on the Golem. Sounds—raw, guttural, unintelligible sounds—escaped that stiff earthenlike mouth. It pushed itself against the wall again, frantically, as if escaping a powerful vision.

Irene shook out her hair, jet-black in the strong light, but still gloriously shining along its waves. Could the Golem be a kind of reverse Samson, susceptible to the sight of a woman's long hair . . .?

The thing babbled piteously, so that my fear eased, especially when the chained hands—large and chapped red from cold—lifted in supplication. No doubt the sight of a bearded (and mustached) lady of great beauty had shattered the beast's last shred of sanity. Only a heart of stone could have resisted such mute appeal. Irene's at the moment was only soapstone, though harder than it usually was.

"Now is the time for your knife, Nell," she said, her voice still oddly brittle, as if torn between triumph and some other, less admirable but therefore more powerful emotion.

"My knife?" The squeak in my voice would hardly tame a mouse, much less the Golem. "Surely you don't expect me to—"

"I must keep the pistol on him. You must approach the beast and remove the thorn that torments it."

"Thorn? Irene, you make no sense."

"You must cut its bonds."

"But . . . it is chained. Steel will not cut iron."

She sighed. I sensed that it marked a change in her emotions. "It will cut leather."

I swallowed. "Leather? You mean . . . skin. Irene, what mad plan have you in mind, some sort of ungodly sacrifice—?"

"Approach the Golem of Prague, Nell. You will be safe, for it knows what a pistol is; moreover, it knows what I am. When you are nearer, you will see what must be done."

Never have I so imperiled myself, my soul, on faith. I had never known Irene to risk another when she stood by to take the lesser hazard, so, clasping both my knives, I edged nearer the pathetic but intimidatingly large figure.

With every step, the Horror That Was Its Face came clear. Only for Godfrey, I told myself. Only for Irene. Instead of flesh, I saw the stiff brown-orange of cheap pottery—what else should a clay man be made of? Only slits indicated eyes, mouth, nose. What else should a man-made man have but rudimentary senses? No wonder it had stumbled blindly, mutely through Prague—sheer power with only the crudest of features. Further, I could see, the closer I came, the *seams* that crisscrossed that awful man-made face like scars. I could see even—heaven help me!—the *stitches.*

Stitches? Seams?

The Golem held itself still, as if recognizing the necessity to control its impulses. Crouched as it was against the wall like Caliban, I could look down on its huge head.

I could see . . . the gleam of metal studs down the back of its bald head. Not studs . . . but rivets, in straps.

Not the face of a monster, but a monstrous . . . leather . . . mask literally bolted to a . . . human . . . head.

A wave of utter indignation enbolded me beyond my mettle. I slipped Godfrey's sharp and powerful knife under one rear strap, sawing desperately.

The tough material resisted the blade, but by now I was determined to unmask the phantom that had haunted my dreams. The Golem was someone's creature indeed; a prisoner used to terrify the ignorant; a prisoner subjected to a fearsome use.

The first strap broke on a raw tear. I attacked the next. The Golem was oddly quiet, hanging its head docilely while I performed my crude and arduous surgery.

Another strap sawed free! I applied myself to the next with a sense of fevered mission. I would not see even the maddest dog treated so, chained and masked.

At last the final strap gave before the sharp, shining point of my knife. I stepped back, panting.

The Golem's huge hands came up to the loosened leather. Slowly, as if it expected pain, the creature pulled the false face from its head.

I stepped back, prepared for greater horrors.

The skin beneath the ebbing mask looked patched, mottled red and white from the mask's pressure, the dirty brown hair and mustache were matted, the features so stiff they seemed unable to move, to see or speak.

I was unable to move, to see or speak, though an incredible realization dawned at a distance of perhaps—three feet.

Irene had no such inhibitions. Her vibrant voice declared into the utter silence, "Well, Willie, it's an unconventional crown you wear."

In answer, the Golem buried his face in his manacled hands, rubbing his roughened skin, digging into his matted scalp.

"Irene," he muttered in a voice as hoarse as a saw. "Irene! Irene?" with every intonation under the sun possible—amazement, shame, disbelief, regret, relief.

This litany to a single saint seemed to please her. She glanced at me. "The key to his bonds must be on the person of the guard. I will handle that task, if you will hold the pistol again. His Majesty is overcome, and may be unpredictable."

I took the dreadful object with experienced hands. His Majesty, Wilhelm von Ormstein, did not seem in a state to attempt anything but incoherence. However, I elected not to watch Irene perform the distasteful task of searching the guard.

In moments she was back with a large iron key in her possession; moments after that, the King's manacles fell away.

She had also brought the almost empty wine bottle and wordlessly offered it to him. He drank from it like a peasant, head thrown back, eyes shut. His mien was more ordinary when his face came level again. He dropped the empty bottle to the stony ground.

"How did you know?" he asked in English.

She shook her head. "That is not important now. I have come to give you your queen and kingdom back, but you must accommodate me for a while."

"Anything," he said flatly. "Anything. But I am . . . not myself."

A smile quirked the corners of her mouth. "Indeed, you would be surprised to what extent you are not yourself."

"I mean that I do not know if I can even stand. I have been chained here for so long."

"Save for your three escapes," she said.

"How did you know of that?"

"The people of the town took you for the Golem."

Anguish played across those features on which I had seen only arrogance before. "Is *that* why no one aided me? Why I was allowed to blunder blindly until my captors came and led me back to my prison? The people . . . feared me?"

"Once upon a time, not too distant, you relished your subjects' fear, Willie; when you would have made a woman the prisoner of your desire, your wishes, your royal blood and obligations."

He raised his hands to his face, shook his head. "Such a time is ancient history. Tell me what has happened while I have . . . slept here, like a prince in a fairy tale. Tell me what I must do. What you would have me do."

"That is simple. A dupe has ruled in your stead." She watched his giant frame shudder with shock. "A dupe has entered into a secret pact with Russia to cede Bohemia to its dreams of empire. A dupe has flaunted a foreign mistress in front of your queen—in this he is not so different, eh, Willie? Although your wrong was in intent rather than in execution."

The King's unbound hands lifted as if to shelter his now-naked face from such facts, from such truths.

"A dupe would duel my husband within three hours, and slay him."

"Your—husband. I recall . . ."

"You recall the truth. I will give you your life back. I will restore your queen and your throne, but you must be absolutely ruled by me for the next several hours. You must do as I say. You must be my subject."

He was silent for several moments, then looked up from red-rimmed eyes. "I have always been your subject, Irene; why do you think I tried to make you mine? And I do not want my queen back," he added with the old fierceness. "She is as nothing compared to you!"

"She is a queen," Irene said softly, unflattered, "and she has been treated abominably, both by you and your substitute. If you want your throne, you will have to win her; it is that simple."

"And, in the meantime, I must march to your tune."

"Yes," Irene said. "I do appreciate your putting that in musical terms, Willie."

"I have always been fond of music."

"You will become even fonder of it when you dance to my tune," she promised. Irene glanced at me. "The time, Nell!"

"Four o'clock."

"We have no time to waste! Back to the hotel."

"The Europa? Why?"

"We must install the King in a safe place." She eyed me steadily, her glance dropping to my hands, each of which still clutched a knife. "Then, Robber Girl, we must hasten to a very unsafe place and perform a miracle of politics, intimidation, blackmail and eleventh-hour salvation."

Chapter Thirty-four

BLACK RUSSIAN SABLE

During the long return trip to the hotel, I mused upon Irene's eerie reference to the same Hans Christian Andersen fairy tale that I had been contemplating, "The Snow Queen." I, the Robber Girl?

Certainly I carried the knives for the role; Irene had insisted that the guard's confederates would find him soon, and that we dare not leave even a bread knife with which he might sever his bonds.

The King, weakened by his confinement, was barely capable of carrying himself, much less pointed objects.

Such a sight we three must have made through the dim Prague streets: the King lurching between us, an arm thrown over our shoulders; we staggering forward despite the burden, Irene lustily singing a slurred tavern song in the deepest basso she could produce.

She instructed the King to "hum" along, and he complied meekly, adding a wandering but suprising tenor to the tune.

I remained silent, for my quavering soprano would have done nothing but attract suspicion—or thrown footwear.

Our guise was perfect. No one questions a tipsy trio about Prague at four in the morning. To do so would be unpatriotic, and would harm the business of the U Flecků and its ilk, and such establishments are national monuments to the renowned Bohemian fondness for fermented hops.

Once we reached the hotel, Irene and I battled the King up the back stairs. Our efforts were similar to shoving a sack of feed up a ladder into a loft. The walk had exhausted the King, and he was nearly drunk from confusion, elation and mystification.

Imagine the picture we presented when Irene scratched discreetly on Allegra's door, and the poor child finally heard and came to admit us.

Her eyes were already round as buttons when she edged the door open a crack: who would call at four in the morning but madmen and villains? When she saw us three, she immediate took us for the latter, and would have slammed the door shut, save that Irene thrust her booted foot in the way.

"Piano, Allegra, piano!" she begged, wincing from Allegra's sturdy attempt at door closing. "We have brought someone in need of tending."

Allegra eyed the figure slumped over our shoulders. "Oh, is it Godfrey? The duel was not to be fought until after six!"

Irene led us in and to the sofa, on which we let His Majesty collapse like the animated lead weight he resembled. His head fell against the sofa back so it basked in the light of the gasolier that Irene had turned on.

Allegra examined the King, not much impressed. "Not Godfrey, thank God! Where did you find this scoundrel?"

Irene looked both amused and satisfied as she sat down to extract her cigarette case from her apparently bottomless side pocket.

"Within desecrating distance of a graveyard, but he was not up to much mischief, being chained like the ghost he should be. Meet Wilhelm Gottsreich Sigismond von Ormstein, King of Bohemia."

"King?" Allegra came closer to peer into the King's exhausted face. "Another?"

"The first and only," Irene intoned on a breath of smug blue smoke. "You must tend him, Allegra, while Nell and I attend to other business. Godfrey must not know, for now, of his presence, so we three must hide the King in the bedroom."

"The bedroom?" Allegra paused. "My bedroom or your bedroom?"

"I doubt you will get much more sleep tonight, and I find it impolitic to store the King in my bedroom, for reasons that you might not fully appreciate, nor should you be expected to." Irene's turn of the room ended in her smashing her cigarette out in a tray. "So your bedroom, dear girl, will do nicely."

Allegra shrugged, a rude gesture that I feared she had acquired from Irene. "As you wish."

"I protest, Irene," said I. "Allegra is an unmarried young woman; such an arrangement is scandalous."

"No one will ever know, Nell; scandal does not exist without knowledge. Besides, the King is hardly in any condition to initiate any more scandals in his bucolic kingdom of Bohemia."

"And," said Allegra, "my friends in London will be thrilled to hear that I concealed a king in my bedchamber."

So much for averted scandal when the victim is eager to announce its existence to assorted friends and acquaintances.

Yet glad I was to have Allegra's young back help us hoist the King and propel him into the room in question, where he collapsed upon the bed in a semiunconscious state, like the commonest drunkard.

"What shall I do with him?" Allegra asked herself as much as us.

"Watch him," Irene instructed. "See that Godfrey does not see him, and that the King does not see anyone—not even a hotel maid. If he rouses, you could encourage him to clean up as much as possible—"

"—as far as is fit and proper for you to do so," I added swiftly.

Irene eyed me, then shook her head. "The times do not call for 'fit and proper,' Allegra. You must do what you can, as best you can. We will return to take custody of the King before dawn—"

This was news to me, and most unsettling.

"—for he must play the role of his life tomorrow. He must rise from the dead, and no one must notice."

"Yes, Madame Norton," Allegra answered meekly. "I will care for him as if he were my Uncle Quentin."

"Oh, you need not be *that* nice," Irene added. "Kings respond better to high-handed treatment; they recognize it from their own history. Whatever you do, you must not be intimidated by him; he is your charge, and his fealty is pledged to me. Remind him of that if he should become troublesome and insist on returning to Prague Castle prematurely."

"Indeed, Mrs. Norton, I will be as fierce a guardian to His Majesty as Miss Huxleigh was to me."

Irene glanced at the King. He lay, in his dull, crude clothes, like a dead moth on Allegra's delicate white linens, his limbs splayed and his mouth ajar, snoring softly.

"That should do nicely," she said, jerking her head to the door as a signal that I should accompany her away.

"Do I still need the knives?" I asked breathlessly as I trotted after her into the hotel passage.

"Of course. In fact, if you have a nail file that is sufficiently sharp, I suggest that we take it. We go now to beard the most dangerous beast of all."

Back into the streets. Back into the dark and the damp. Back into anxiety and mystery. I scuttled alongside Irene, barely keeping up with her unladylike long strides, unable to speak for the speed of our pace, my breath huffing onto the chill air like Red Indian smoke signals.

I could not discern the turnings of our route, and knew not if river or Old Town was on our right. Irene knew exactly where she was going, doubtless a result of her solitary expedition yesterday. When she paused before an old, sprawling structure, I knew it for our destination.

She headed directly for the rear. While I shivered at the danger of ignominious discovery, she forced the servants' door open and slipped up the stairs with the confidence of a practiced housebreaker.

Once we were upon the muffling carpet of an upstairs hall I tugged her sleeve. "Irene, how do you know where to go?"

"I have previously spied out the lay of the land. Be still now. I wish to catch our opponent unawares. Surprise is our most powerful weapon."

I doubt that she meant to include *my* surprise in this armament, but it certainly was included.

At a particular door she stopped. Why she chose this door of several along the passage, I cannot say. She reached into her pocket for the same implement that had opened the servants' door, and applied it to the lock. Such a small but telling clatter! I expected a mob of servants to descend upon us. No one came; in moments the door swung open on mute hinges.

Irene's hand on my arm dragged me into the dark beyond.

We stood for some time, listening to our own breathing while our eyes grew accustomed to the dark. At length the furniture showed itself as darker blots on the dim landscape before us, and we began treading carefully between these barriers.

Another door was unlocked. Irene turned the knob so slowly that it made no sound. We shortly after squeezed through the opening into another dark chamber.

"Stay." Irene's command was a hot whisper in my ear.

I felt rather than heard her move away. For a moment I heard nothing, then a rustle, a scratch of nails on cloth—the gasolier above us burst into light. In the violent glare a swath of bedroom furnishings leapt into being. I felt as if I watched a stage storm, or saw a photograph taken at the moment the powder flashes as bright as brimstone.

A figure moved in the ornate bed; another perched upon the upholstered foot like a leprechaun. . . .

"Not a centimer," Irene's voice ordered from the bed's foot. "Not a millimeter, Madame. Stay still, or my pistol shall speak out of turn and, I assure you, you will not like what it has to say."

"Who are you?" the figure demanded in the same language that Irene had used—English.

"Who do you think?" Irene asked.

A pause. "Lady Sherlock, I presume. A most innovative pseudonym, if a trifle obvious. But, then, the opera was your métier."

"The pseudonym was no worse than 'Sable,'" Irene answered.

"I was young then, and impressionable."

"Yes, I see that. That is no excuse now."

"And it was another country."

"Too bad the wench is not dead."

I knew not what they spoke of, save that the woman in the bed was Tatyana, and that the first duel of the new day was already well under way in this room.

"You trespass on my portion of the board, Madame," Tatyana noted.

"I have visited Bohemia before," Irene said blithely.

"Yes, I know."

"You know?"

"Of course. Do you think that we did not investigate the past of your tiresome king?"

"It is possible; you do not seem to have thought out your plan very well. And who is 'we'?"

Tatyana, who had gathered the covers to her shoulders at our lightning-like arrival, smiled and let the sheets slip away. She wore an unconventional nightdress of brunette lace against which her pale complexion shone like candle-wax, and her red-gold hair was the flame.

"I am not allowed to say."

"I imagine that you do much that you are not allowed."

"Always, but not in this instance."

"I care little for your tawdry conspiracy," Irene said. "In hours my husband fights a duel with your King. Godfrey must live."

"We are in utter harmony."

"He must not be so much as wounded."

"I concur completely, Madame. In fact, I have taken steps to insure that very outcome. Can you say as much?"

"I am still taking steps."

"Worry not." Tatyana piled a quantity of lace-covered pillows behind her and leaned back. "I have anticipated you, as usual. Your dramatic visit is only so much melodrama. Godfrey was always safe. I would not see a hair upon his head—or anyhere else—so much as shifted by the errant wind of a gunshot."

"How would you accomplish this?"

"Why did you advise your husband to choose pistol over sword?"

"Because a pistol can be tampered with when a sword cannot."

Tatyana shrugged, a gesture that set the lace on her strong shoulders ebbing.

"You planned to fill the King's pistol with blank shot?" Irene sounded unconvinced. "Why disarm your most potent weapon in the game to come?"

"Because the game is nearly over. I do not need him anymore and . . . he was growing tiresome." She eyed Irene slyly. "I do not think that Godfrey grows tiresome, does he?"

"You must ask someone other than I; someone who is not so biased, such as Miss Huxleigh there."

"There? That is Miss Huxleigh? Such an admirable assistant you and he have found. I have long searched for one who would blend so perfectly into the woodwork and have had little luck. No, I do not care for Miss Huxleigh's opinion on Godfrey's lack of tiresomeness. She is not an expert witness. I require personal testimony, and most often must . . . see for myself."

"A pity." Irene sounded not at all sorry. "I fear that we will not linger long enough in Prague for you to obtain any evidence of a personal sort. It is not sufficient that you plan to load the King's pistol with false shot. I too must see that for myself."

"If you wish to jeopardize the entire encounter—"

"I wish it. And I wish one other thing."

"You may express whatever you wish; that does not mean that you will get it."

"I wish the King to emerge unscathed as well."

"The King? Why should you care for this pawn who wears a false crown?"

"I do not," Irene said, "and him I leave to you and your confederates' tenderest mercies. It is the true King I would have walk away from that encounter—*after* the shots have been fired."

"A nice thought, but impractical. The King is missing."

"Yes, and now the King is missing from where he was when he was missing."

Tatyana scrambled upright among her pillows. "You have him? Where?"

"Where you will not get him. A subtle exchange of Kings suits my purpose, and ultimately yours. If you refuse to provide the occasion, I will be forced to produce the King publicly to renounce the conspirators. That will cause such a stir—St. Petersburg will buzz with it, as well as Vienna, Paris and London. That, I think, would not suit the great and glorious bear, your icy northern master."

Tatyana's handsome face curled into an expression of foiled rage. Her fingers curved like claws into the lace flouncing her pillows as she pummeled the feathers in a catlike rhythm. After just such bouts of purring and pummeling, the black Persian Lucifer would lash his tail and suddenly pounce, his fangs snapping at my arm.

Tatyana snapped with words, but they were fiercely spat.

"You have interfered with myself and my companions before, Madame, and know what a fatal outcome such meddling had on the Hammersmith Bridge. Do not mistake my personal interest in the admirable Godfrey for a sign of weakness. My associates would not hesitate to kill any who stood in our way."

"The bridge was as disastrous to your side as ours," Irene said calmly. "What I propose here is a truce. Come, I have captured the King. You have no choice. Withdraw peacefully, with an appearance of good grace, and you will live to fight another day. Resist, and you will be unmasked, along with the false King."

"And your price for permitting us this quiet withdrawal is Godfrey's life? You already had that, fool."

"Perhaps, but now I am sure of it."

"The true King betrayed you," Tatyana said with a snarl. (I hesitate to resort to such sensational description, but the woman was a wildcat, what can I say? I have never before seen such an uncivilized specimen, and indeed, she gives her entire sex an injurious name. Even Irene at her most bohemian is a mere amateur compared to the primal possessiveness of this willful wildwoman.)

"Why should you care to save him?" Tatyana demanded. "He is not worth either of us, or even your redoubtable Miss Huxleigh."

I was not enamored of that "even," either.

Irene considered the question with far more seriousness than I would have shown. "He is the true King; a certain nobility attaches to that alone. Even Willie, poor creature that he is, would not have behaved as abominably toward the Queen as your substitute. That is how I knew instantly that a dupe had taken his place, as well as by his most amazing indifference to myself, and even Miss Huxleigh.''

Another "even" applied to my humble self, which was growing less humble and more indignant by the minute!

"The real King knew me instantly," Irene went on without a pause, "despite my raven hair and our reunion in a most peculiar place, despite his own not-insubstantial privations these past months. You may have inadvertently made a better man of him, Madame Tatyana, perhaps even a finer King, despite your worst efforts.''

The woman threw back her head and laughed silently, then drew a deep breath. "A small improvement," she scoffed, "for King Will-he . . . will he what—amount to anything? He is beneath the both of us, no matter his stature or rank—and no matter the heights to which imprisonment and suffering might loft him. Such penances are always overestimated by the sentimental. I wonder that you bothered to claim such a pathetic conquest in the past.''

Irene's smile was as serene as her opponent's silent laugh had been stormy. "He is still better than his substitute, who was so besotted with you that he failed to lull my suspicions. Apparently you overlooked me.''

"Not at all. The fool was informed of the King's past alliances. He merely . . . forgot. And you are right about the reason for that. He is utterly, madly besotted with me. Unfortunately, I do not find that appealing.''

"You are perverse, Madame," Irene said. "I would rather stand accused of your charge, mere sentimentality. Let us say that if my innate beneficence does not explain my rescue of Willie, you forget another motive for my meddling in your political intrigues: I had grown fond of the Bohemian people during my previous stay. They may deserve better than a foreign satrapy, better than King Willie and the Austrians, but they do not deserve the domination of yet another foreign power, and one as devious as the master you serve. And," Irene finished, lifting the pistol as if she contemplated using it, "you forget that my mind might rest easier with you removed from the board. You are valuable to me only if you are able to perserve Godfrey and the true King from harm on the morrow. If you fail in either object, be assured that the next dawn will be your day of reckoning on quite another plane than this earthly vale of tears and woe."

Irene pointed the pistol at Tatyana's form, and sighted down the barrel. . . .

The woman exploded from her bed like a leopard springing for prey. I have never seen a human being move so quickly. Irene was off her perch in an instant, keeping her distance, while Tatyana crouched—I can only describe her feral posture thus—on the floor and watched her with predatory fury.

"I am dancer," Tatyana said, lifting her leonine head. "You are singer. We will see who survives."

"Not . . . now," Irene answered. "Not in Prague. Tomorrow we will arrange a quiet end to this charade. We will lie down together like the lion and the lamb, because it suits both our purposes. As for later—"

"You will not always be armed."

"You will not always be surrounded by fellow conspirators."

"You would kill, if you had to?" Tatyana said in her mocking voice. "I already have."

"I am close," Irene answered, so quietly that a chill sped down my arms.

. Yet I was glad for the knives I carried.

"I look forward to our meeting tomorrow," Tayana threatened.

"And tomorrow and tomorrow," Irene said sardonically. She backed to the door, where I waited.

When I opened it, we slipped through it like air eager to leave a noxious room. Only when we were safely back on the street did I speak.

"Can you trust her?"

"Not in the slightest, but she is better than her associates."

"Why?!"

"Because she has a weakness."

"Godfrey."

Irene nodded and drew me to a stop in the misty light of streetlamp. "What time is it, Nell? Rather, how much do we have?"

"Five o'clock. An hour."

"Much remains to be done. I have only you and Allegra. Godfrey must go to this duel knowing no more than he does now. If he loses that innocence, if he shows his unshakable alliance to us, she will destroy him as the lion does the lamb indeed. It is you and Allegra and I against her. Godfrey is the prize."

"And . . . the King?"

"He is . . . the price. And a high one at that."

Chapter Thirty-five

THE KING AND I

Weary, we scuttled back to the Europa Hotel, eager to outrun the dawn. Already Prague's many spires stood vaguely silhouetted against a subtly brightening eastern sky.

Irene and I were damp through, our unconventional clothes being no better barrier to night dew than our most delicate daily garb.

Servants and shopkeepers were stirring in the streets; as we neared the Europa's rear entrance, we had to duck into indiscriminate doorways to avoid being seen and questioned.

Irene led and I followed. We darted through the door in the interim between a greengrocer's delivery and an influx of coal. On the narrow rear stairs, voices drifted from nearby rooms where the hotel staff gathered to set the day in motion.

By nip and tuck—and the false hair on Irene's chinny-chin-chin—we arrived unchallenged at the door to her suite.

This time Allegra was alert to our slightest scratch, admitting us only an instant before a trio of maids bustled into the passage bound for the linen room.

"How is the King?" Irene inquired, tearing off her leather gloves and slouch-brimmed hat.

"See for yourselves." Allegra led us to her chamber.

There the King reclined on a heap of pillows, looking much restored and even a trifle annoyed.

"Wonderful!" Irene declared. "How did you accomplish this miracle of resuscitation, dear child?"

"The brandy decanter," Allegra said with a gesture to the vessel in question, which had sunk alarmingly low since I had last seen it.

"An excellent idea under the circumstances, but the King must not become too merry. Nell and I will have a small glass, if His Majesty has left any."

"I—" I began.

Irene eyed me sternly. "A small glass each. We have more work, of the most delicate sort."

Irene threw her hat and gloves down on a nearby table. "Well, Willie, we have just returned from an interview with your mistress."

"I have no mistress."

"You never knew this woman who calls herself Tatyana?"

"Tatyana . . . a woman of that name was attached to a party of Russian nobility who attended the wedding and coronation. I heard no other name, or if I did, I forgot it. These Russian surnames are interminable."

"No doubt why Madame Tatyana dispensed with hers," Irene murmured. "Ah, thank you, dear." She approvingly sipped the glass Allegra brought. "You may pour yourself a thimbleful or so—but only a bit. I will require your assistance as well as Nell's at the duel today."

The King was watching us with a wistful blue eye, while I choked down the prescribed liquor.

Irene answered his unspoken inquiry. "You have had enough, under the circumstances, and must keep your head about you for the difficult role you will play later."

"Which is—?" he asked.

She smiled. "Yourself. But you claim that you never knew this Tatyana in any . . . intimate fashion."

"In no fashion whatsoever!" he swore. A sly and self-satisfied look edged into his eyes. The King was definitely becoming his old self. "Are you . . . jealous, Irene?"

"I merely require the facts. You must understand that your queen, whom you wedded and never bedded, is somewhat estranged by your substitute's behavior."

"I wedded her, but never had an opportunity to bed her! I was given some drugged wine after the ceremony, and woke up where you found me. How much time has passed?"

Irene paused to calculate. "You were wed—"

"April the fourteenth."

"Then some six months has gone by."

"October? It is October!" He struggled to sit up in his abundant linens, but succeeded in merely flailing like a legless chicken.

Irene went to push him back down. "You must conserve your strength. When we accomplish the exchange today, you must seem as you ever were—the King, who has always been himself. Of course, you will have the excuse of your wound to explain any physical weakness or mental confusion. . . ."

"What wound?" he demanded.

"That dealt you by my dear husband Godfrey during your duel, naturally. How else would you be wounded today?"

"See here, Irene, I am not about to escape that foul dungeon only to be—what is the weapon?"

"Pistols."

"—only to be . . . shot. Good God, Irene, you would not have me wounded to teach me a lesson?"

She tilted her head of black hair to consider this new notion, then shook it regretfully. "I am afraid that is impossible to arrange, Willie. The impostor must fight the duel; he must be actually wounded. You will replace him, your arm bandaged most solicitously by the Misses Huxleigh and Stanhope here. Come, you must not look so shocked; could even a king have a lovelier set of Florence Nightingales?"

The King eyed us askance. "I believe your . . . loyal Miss Huxleigh loathes me. As for this infant virago, she has compelled me to take a most humiliating sponge bath, has confined me to my bed and forced brandy down my throat at a pace that does not allow for savoring."

"Savoring is not your role at the moment, Willie."

"And you do not address me in the proper manner."

"And shall not, until our business is done. You are my subject until your throne is yours again, remember, Willie?"

"Tell me your scheme."

"All you need know is this: the impostor and Godfrey are to meet with pistols this morning. I will accompany Godfrey. Nell and Allegra will come later with you in a separate carriage. This Tatyana will arrange for your substitute's wounding; she would have preferred death."

"So would I! This man must not be allowed to live to threaten my throne again."

"The conspirators are done with him. Enough people have died in this scheme, including an innocent girl in Paris. I will not have another corpse on my conscience."

The King's lips pursed in a royal pout, but he said nothing. He did not relish Irene reminding him who had the upper hand at the moment.

"Speaking of which," Irene added, "what became of the misguided maid who was persuaded to poison your father?"

The King frowned. "I do not know."

"You do not know? She was taken away in the custody of your guards."

"Then, if the captain of the guards did not have her killed, she languishes in some dungeon under Prague Castle."

"You do not *know?*" Irene repeated with an incredulity that did not quite conceal utter contempt.

He shrugged. "The family did not wish to make the assassination public. The girl must be buried one way or the other. I simply am not certain which method was used. She *did* murder my father."

"And I discovered that he *was* murdered!" Irene retorted. "Had I not done so, the entire family von Ormstein could have been picked off one by one, like rotten fruit from a tree."

"You were clever and successful," the King said. "I gave you my thanks. What more do you need?"

I had not often seen Irene speechless, but she was so before the King's impervious royal indifference to the feelings and well-being of others.

"We shall see, Willie," she said at last, so softly that he had to lean forward on his pillow to catch her words. "If you want your throne back, you must do as I say—now and in the immediate future."

"Will you remain in Bohemia, then, and rule through me?" he asked a bit bitterly—and with more than a modicum of interest.

Irene laughed as only she could, with total abandon to mirth. I have never seen one who embraced laughter as such utter, innocent emotional release. Her laughter was as lovely a thing as the sliding scales of an aria, only completely natural and unrehearsed.

"No . . . no, Willie; I have no wish to rule, through you or over your dead body. Can you not see the trouble the wish to rule has created in merely this handkerchief kingdom? Think of the evil it does worldwide! You wanted me as your mistress once, held helpless in a distant castle; now you would take me as a force to be reckoned with, and near at hand, as any power behind the throne must be. Neither role is worth a candle. Nor is your throne."

"Then why do you meddle in my affairs?"

"Because they affect far more—and more noble—persons than you, your Majesty, ranging from the peasant girl who killed your father to your queen."

"Clotilde? What has she to do with it? She is a mere marriage pawn, a young girl untried in the ways of the world."

"She has lived in a hostile castle for over half a year, Willie, humiliated before a court who saw her cast aside even before the marriage bed was warmed. She has no reason to love the name von Ormstein, or any who bear it. If she decides to flee to her father, the scandal would shake Europe."

He sobered as Irene described the situation with a surgeon's brutal analysis.

"I think that you can reclaim your queen," Irene added, "along with your throne—if you do as I say."

He frowned a regal frown, expecting servants to flee it. "She has not . . . disgraced herself with this impostor, you say? She has not been ruined?"

"No, Willie," Irene answered with admirable control, "she is the virginal bride you married, and most eager to do her duty and bear you children . . . sons."

"Hmmph. She was not an ugly girl, I recall . . . though I do not remember her clearly. I cannot say why. I remember you clearly enough."

"Perhaps Clotilde did not irritate you as much as I did."

"That is true. She seemed a docile, tractable girl from the first." He glanced at Irene from under his thick, blond brows. "She would serve her purpose and the state, but she was not . . . the kind of queen of whom plays are written."

"She will do her duty," Irene reminded him, "and that is all that you demand, but she has been abominably treated by your duplicate. She has reason to hate the name and face and facade of Wilhelm von Ormstein. You will have to woo her, Willie," she added slyly. "You will have to court your queen, as you would a mistress."

He frowned again. "Perhaps I would have been better off forgotten in that stinking dungeon, instead of bowing to the

whim of every woman whose path I cross." He glowered at
Irene, whose laughter was like tinkling bells.

"Perhaps, but it is too late, Willie. You have been rescued, and shall have to make the best of it. If you do, you
might even find that you like your life."

"Do you like yours?" he asked suddenly.

She hesitated for a moment. I saw her lost performing
career surface in the stormy seas of her tiger's bronze-
brown eyes, and sink again. "I like what I am making of it.
And I like this moment, Willie, very much."

He bowed his royal head and said nothing. He knew she
deserved her triumph at his expense, as he did not deserve
her mercy, her aid, her rescue. When he lifted his face
again, there was a slight, even a winning smile upon it.

"I do not like your hair black, Irene, but I would not
have failed to recognize you for an instant, even if you had
dyed your hair blue."

"I didn't think so, Willie," Irene answered with a half-
smile. She gave me an urgent look.

"Five-fifteen," I caroled on cue.

She nodded. "The King must don his duplicate's clothes
in the carriage, but he must be ready in every other respect.
He must shave."

"We have no straight razor," Allegra objected. "Can you
fetch Godfrey's?"

"Not without making him suspicious, and he is the one
person who must not be suspicious!"

Irene cast her eyes about the room, seeking improvisation. They ended on me.

"No!" I said, no matter what her solution was.

"Your knife, Nell, will do admirably."

"Which one?" I wailed.

"Godfrey's. It is sharp enough to shave a shark."

"My man always shaves me," the King objected.

"Your man shaves another's throat at this moment. You
will either have to submit to Miss Huxleigh's machinations, or to the sprightly Miss Stanhope's."

The King regarded us both with little confidence. Then he swallowed so his Adam's apple bobbed as if waterborne. "I will do it myself."

"Excellent." Irene was out of the chamber, we two behind her. "I must change clothes quickly, and consult with Godfrey. Remember, if he asks, you two are too . . . delicate, too . . . indisposed to attend the duel. He will nobly forbid you to go, in any case, although he will not expect compliance. And of course he will not get it from me. The moment we are gone, you must bundle the King in a cloak and follow."

"Where are we to go?" Allegra cried.

"Godfrey and I will stop at your rooms to tell you as soon as the false King's seconds have left his chamber. Now I must be quick—"

She dashed for her bedchamber, ripping the crepe hair from her chin as she went. Allegra turned to me.

"Where is this knife Mrs. Norton mentioned, Miss Huxleigh?"

I drew one from the right pocket of my bloomers; the other from the left.

Allegra's eyes grew as large as marbles; then she smiled wickedly. "I have never seen a king shave with a knife; in fact, I have never seen a king this close before. Let us go and let him think that we mean to practice our knife-honing skills on his jaws."

Tormenting kings is an amusement that quickly wanes, although many of the worst villains of history have not discovered this simple fact.

Some time later, Allegra held up her ivory hand mirror while the King scraped away at his own matted beard. I had never seen a man occupied in this ritual before, particularly when removing a six-month growth, and it was not a pretty or unpainful sight.

Wilhelm von Ormstein's season of penitence was well under way.

When at length his lower face was a reddened expanse of skin nicked here and there, Allegra completed his humiliation and discomfort by tilting a bottle of cologne onto an embroidered handkerchief and bidding him to wipe his abused skin with this bracing potion.

I had never seen a king wince before, but he bore it bravely with only a few moans.

A flutter in the outside chamber made us sternly admonish the King to remain out of sight and silent, and bolt for the outer room.

Despite the stressful events of the night, despite Allegra's and my perilous assignment to conduct the King to the duel and accomplish a secret substitution between himself and his impostor, the sight of Godfrey that morning was enough to strike us both motionless and mute.

He looked as ever, of course, although a bit sober. Yet we saw instantly the risk he was facing as if that Risk were the shadow of a dour black raven behind him.

While Irene and Allegra and I and the King fluttered at the edges of the scheme, Godfrey—innocent of all the manipulations—must take the only real Risk. He must face Death in the barrel of another man's pistol. No matter how Irene pulled her puppet strings from the sidelines, no matter how desperately the vile Tatyana maneuvered to save him, he stood four-square in the fatal path if any particle of all our plans went awry.

Irene seemed as deeply aware of his danger, of our desperation, as we did. She stage-managed this visit as she had every event in the past twelve hours since the false King's challenge. She kept her own fear from falling upon Godfrey like another fold of the dread Raven's heavy cloak. Her eyes eloquently admonished us to accomplish our roles even as she publicly approved our resolve to wait at the hotel until the deed was done.

"I had not anticipated your ready compliance with my wishes," Godfrey told us in some amazement. "Irene, of course—" He glanced at her then, with a tender certainty that wrung my heart. "—I had expected to be adamant. I had also expected objections from you two, and am delighted that you will follow the prudent course and remain here. The duel is a mere formality. Irene and I shall be back in time for breakfast."

We nodded meekly, through our tremulous tears, and wished Godfrey good luck and ardent prayers, and bid them goodbye like utterly docile ladies.

"We are not even venturing far afield," Irene said blithely on the way out of the door. "Only to Vrchlického Park near the Smetana Theater. We will see you shortly," she added with a significance neither Allegra nor I could ignore, though it skimmed above Godfrey's head.

No doubt his normal acuity was impaired by his forthcoming duel to the death. Yet his manner did not show this. He donned his top hat and gloves, and they left as though bound for the early races.

The moment they were gone, Allegra and I raced for her bedchamber and rushed through the door. We encountered a massive impediment—the King.

"Why were you lurking behind the door?" Allegra demanded with all the suavity of a fishwife. She was becoming as expert as Irene at taking royalty down a peg.

"You could have destroyed the entire scheme," I added in my sternest governess tone of outrage.

"I am sorry, ladies," the King said, shrugging. "I could not resist seeing . . . him."

"Him?" Allegra demanded.

Yet I understood, for I had witnessed Irene's fever to see "her."

"At least he is not ugly," the King conceded.

"Ugly?" Allegra was indignant. "Mr. Norton? Irene would never consort with someone ugly."

"That is some consolation," said the King, smiling over her head at mine.

I was appalled to find myself smiling back.

"I wonder if this English barrister can truly defend himself in a duel," the King ruminated. "There is only one way to find out, and I am most anxious to do so. Come, ladies; we must find me suitable disguise, then fetch a carriage. I know Vrchlického Park well, and know exactly where they go."

I eyed Allegra, as she eyed me. The King was beginning to show the regal quality of decisiveness. If curiosity had killed the cat, it now made the King eager to go where Irene led him—to the field of honor, where he could watch his own impostor try to shoot and kill his successful rival for Irene's affections and her very self.

Chapter Thirty-six

ROYAL DOUBLE CROSS

In the carriage on the way to Vrchlického Park, I attempted to instruct Allegra on the dramatis personae that we would find awaiting us. His Majesty, Wilhelm von Ormstein, assisted me in this process by drowsing with fitful snores beside me, wrapped in his borrowed cloak with such massive dignity that it was hard to believe he wore only underclothes beneath it. I tried not to think of what the King wore—or, rather, did not wear—nor of the sordid task ahead of Allegra and myself should Irene's scheme actually succeed. So I concentrated on telling Allegra who was who, though she seemed to have difficulty comprehending.

She clapped her hands to the ribbons of her enchanting blue silk bonnet and stopped me halfway through my recital.

"Please, Miss Huxleigh. I have been up all the night and cannot follow such convoluted affairs. You say that Godfrey's seconds include a Dr. Watson, who is associated with England's foremost consulting detective, Sherlock Holmes, and an obnoxious gentleman whom you met at the ball, who may be Sherlock Holmes himself in disguise—or who may an agent of Tatyana's, or who may be entirely innocent!"

"That is correct, Allegra. Also no doubt present in various guises will be several of the said Tatyana's henchmen, who had a hand in arranging the original substitution of the kings. I believe they expect the 'King' to be slain outright."

"What is to insure that this does not happen, thus destroying Irene's scheme to restore the real king to his rightful place?"

"Irene," I said promptly.

"But she must also insure that Godfrey is not killed."

"That is true."

"And what will we be doing during this critical time?"

I sighed. "We must lurk nearby, in the carriage, watching and waiting."

"You mean that we will be helpless to do anything."

"That is always true, Allegra, at such grand junctures in life, only most people are not so aware of their impotence."

Beside me, the King started awake, blinking his delft-blue eyes. "Impotence? You say the Pretender is impotent? I will slay him myself for ruining my reputation—"

I stared at him in horror for uttering this impropriety in front of ladies, even if he was half-asleep, but Allegra's nimble young brain leaped into the breach.

"No one is impotent, your Majesty," she said, patting his royal knee, "least of all you in a few hours when you regain your throne. You must rest now, and save yourself for the coming strain."

He nodded as if to agree, then nodded until his chin crashed to his chest, and slept.

Allegra sat back to draw her cloak closer against the morning chill. "We will have our hands full keeping King Willie quiet until he's needed."

"Indeed, but Irene depends upon us."

I had told our driver that we were going to a duel. Though this bald statement had elevated his hairy eye-

brows to the brim of his battered top hat, he slowed when
we reached the park and traveled the winding paths until he
found the party we sought.

I gestured to Allegra to lower her veil and stared out the
window through my own black tissue of netting. Though I
am not infected by Irene's inbred taste for the dramatic
(indeed, I shun it), I could not help feeling this morning that
I observed some vast and intricate operatic set, and that
Allegra and I were supernumeraries in the background,
with a secret mission to send one of the two principal
players into a startling new role, a major transformation, so
to speak.

A heavy fog haunted the park, weaving among the trees.
The grass was still emerald-green, glossy with dew and
damp, yet the sere gold of fallen leaves lay upon it like a
blight.

I was relieved to note several carriages drawn up among
the trees, all black as soot, with their horses blowing gey-
sers of steam into the autumn air.

Such a hellish scene it was! Those sinister vehicles poised
at the fringes of the wood, their restless dark chargers
puffing smoke like the very halitosis of Hades itself. The
gathered men added to the sober ambience, with their trou-
ser-clad legs as long as chimney pots and their tall plush-
velvet beaver top hats gleaming under a patina of dew. All
wore funereal black, save the women.

Until now I had not appreciated the morale-building
effect of Irene's choice of dress that morning. Now her full,
camel's-hair ivory cloak edged at wrist, hem, high neck and
cape in silver ostrich feathers shimmered like an Angel of
Mercy's robe in the misty air. Oxidized silver cord traced
elegant swirls over the cloak fabric, and her hat was as
angelic: gray felt trimmed with silver galloon and silver-
gray ostrich feathers tipped in black.

Of the three men in her group—two tall, one less so—I
could easily pick out Godfrey and his unlikely second, Dr.
Watson. Irene clung to his arm, tilting her captivating bon-

net to lean up and whisper, whisper in his ear for a long time. I wondered what endearments or encouragements she murmured, or if she only warned him of coming events.

The other woman present wore a full cloak of ruby velvet and brocade, caught close to define her formidable figure. Sable bordered her wrists, neck and hem and swathed her bonnet, turning it into a kind of bloated crown.

So now Irene was the White Queen, and Tatyana the Red. White was the color of Hope, I remembered, and also the shade of mourning chosen by the contrary French. And red? Red was passion and blood, with which Tatyana was well supplied.

I had predicted the personnel well. A small coterie surrounded the false king, who wore his most dazzling military uniform, a scarlet boast of broadcloth and wool braided and buttoned with constellations of brass.

Of the many men in his camp, I recognized not one, save that they all looked determined and dangerous.

Allegra crowded beside me at the carriage window as I peered past the velvet curtains—no wonder the entire affair seemed like a stage exercise!

We watched as Godfrey and the King marched to a middle meeting point, their seconds at their backs. The King's men presented a box that looked like it might hold the family silver. I knew its contents. In a moment, each man had lofted a gleaming pistol of polished wood and metal. The seconds stepped back from the field of fire.

One of the King's men lifted a gold pocket watch that glittered like a small sun through the wispy fog.

Godfrey and the King stood back to back—my, what a long back even the substitute King had; I was glad that Godfrey had not chosen swords.

At a command Allegra and I could not hear, they stepped away from one another, each with a pistol held upright in his hand. How unreal it was to watch such a scene with no sound! I felt that I could end it with one clap of my hands, but did not dare try, for fear I would distract Godfrey to his death.

Why would men do such a thing—try to kill one another over a trifle? For a moment I pitied the false King, who was soon to have a great fall. He had lived his role not wisely, but too well. He believed that Tatyana should live her role as his mistress also; that she loved him; that he could command or win her regard simply because he pretended to be King; that he was not a tool but an inevitability.

As for Godfrey, he was caught in a Great Game between fencing nations and meddling bankers, between two willful women who gave no quarter—to each other or to anyone else.

If Godfrey died—I should, I should . . .

Allegra clutched my shoulder. Clearly the duelists had strode a good seven or eight paces apart. Even one as sheltered as I knew that the call of "Ten" was the command to turn and fire, to find out who stood and who fell.

Neither man might be hit. Both might be mortally wounded. One might stand, wounded, while the other perished. Each might be wounded. The possibilities were agonizingly fluid.

I did not hear the call of the fatal number "Ten," but I saw the counter's mouth move.

I saw the King whirl a fraction of a second before the counter's mouth opened, and sight down his endless bloodred arm, his medals winking lewdly in the vague light.

Godfrey was turning swiftly, as if waltzing madly with the fog, in time with the counter's dropped mouth. Godfrey was playing fair, but the false King had not, he had turned before time, and now Godfrey's turning broad back was a black blot of target for his leveled pistol.

Smoke charged from the shining barrel. A sound shredded the silence as if a saw ripped through the rough-painted canvas of a backdrop.

I wish I could have torn the scene in half, like an artist's canvas, to keep the King's craven bullet from winging toward Godfrey. I could only watch, clutching Allegra's hands, while the true king snored softly in the corner of the carriage.

The smoke dissipated from the King's gun barrel. Godfrey, to his own apparent amazement, remained standing, remained unshaken. He stood in the classic duelist's posture, his side to his opponent, his arm extended with the death-dealing weapon at its farthest reach.

He had only to pull the trigger.

And did not.

No one had considered this, that Godfrey would choose not to shoot.

The King lowered his pistol arm, which trembled like an autumn leaf. He was helpless, no more than a target. His head turned for aid from his cohorts, from Tatyana, and met stiff silence and no motion.

And Godfrey did not shoot.

"Fire!" a woman's voice screamed.

I glanced at Irene, but she was a statue of silver ice, only her ostrich feathers trembling in the faint breeze.

"Fire!" Tatyana screamed from the opposite camp.

Godfrey's head recoiled from that bloodthirsty scream. His pistol began to lower, and the entire scheme, the exchange of Kings, the resolution of Clotilde's unhappiness, the plans of princes and plotters, was unraveling on his rightful repugnance for his opponent and his opponent's mistress.

I saw rather than heard Irene's mouth move, and she said but one word.

Sound and fury barked from the end of Godfrey's pistol, along with a clot of smoke.

The false King met it head-on, yet stood unshaken.

Then he clasped his shoulder and melted slowly to the ground like a large, bloody pool.

In the nearby woods, fog still performed a silent minuet among the trees. A small thick patch of it was fading like an apologetic cough. Behind it lurked a figure in an oxblood-colored tunic. I thought I glimpsed the dark shape of a pistol before the apparition merged into the convenient morning mist so obligatory for duels.

Men from both sides converged on the fallen King, only Irene and Tatyana keeping their places at opposite ends of the glade. White on green; red on green. They watched each other, not the dark clot of activity at the center of the board. They were armed with something other than pistols, and neither of them forgot it for a moment.

"I am a doctor!" a voice declared in English. "He must be taken out of the damp and off his feet."

Allegra sprang out of the carriage door to the ground before I could open my mouth. "Here, sir! My companion has been a nurse."

I suppose tending fevered charges as a governess qualifies as nursing of a sort. I would be loath to think Allegra so ready with an outright lie.

In moments the men had buoyed the stricken King and rushed him to our conveyance. They lifted him inside while I helped from within, easily hiding the real King behind my caped bulk.

"We will disrobe him, gentlemen, in privacy," Allegra insisted, leaping in after him and slamming the coach door while I snapped the curtains shut.

I heard them milling without, but was entirely too occupied to worry about what they thought.

Undressing an unconscious man in the semidark of a closed carriage and attiring another in his clothes, and vice versa, is an exercise whose difficulty beggars the imagination. That two men and two women utterly filled the carriage compartment was bad enough; that two of the men were of exceptional size was an addition burden.

The King, bestirring himself, actually deigned to remove his rival's boots, but this only resulted in more elbows being jammed into more ribs and eyes.

The desperate scuffles that emerged from the carriage

were truly enigmatic, and the poor vehicle swayed on its springs before we were through.

"Only a flesh wound," I shouted once to the supposed crowd outside, and continued wrestling with a phalanx of military buttons on the King's wretched uniform jacket.

No soldier suffered more in the performance of his duty. Perspiration actually streamed from my person, though luckily in places where it was not readily observable.

Allegra grunted like a navvy, and what the half-conscious false king muttered is not reprintable even in as private a medium as a diary. Allegra and I learned more of men's dress that day than unmarried ladies should know, but in the end we had our charges changed in their outer aspects.

"How is the King?" the doctor's voice demanded from outside the carriage. A German duet indicated the Doctors Sturm and Drang were also on the scene and eager to attend their royal patient.

"Ah . . . well," Allegra answered, stuffing a makeshift gag of pungent stockings down the poor wounded fellow's throat. "If you would like to see him, Doctor—" She nodded in the dim interior at Willie.

Clasping his left arm, he began to struggle through the welter of bodies to the door.

I caught him firmly by the ear (Oh, how many years I had longed to do such a thing!) and stopped his roar of protest by moving his hand from his right shoulder to his left, the true site of the wound, as indicated by a convenient bloodstain.

Looking horrified at his near gaffe, the King nodded his understanding and staggered out of the carriage.

"A mere crease," I heard him dismissing the wound in German as he hit the ground with the impact of a sack of potatoes. "No need of doctors. Get away. I wish peace and quiet, not idle fussing."

How quickly he sounded like a king again, I thought.

Allegra and I peeked out.

The crowd surrounded the King's tall head as he stalked back to the field of honor. We were forgotten as the main figure in the drama resumed his role.

The King marched up to Godfrey, who still stood his ground, and looked him up and down in a most thorough and arrogant manner.

"You have fought well, Englishman," he announced in our language. "I should have shot in your place too."

His next look was at Irene. He regarded her in silence for a long while, then turned on his heel, his entourage flowing into his wake, the German doctors still fussing at his fringes, and moved toward the gathered carriages.

The Red Queen did not move, only stared at Godfrey, who watched the wounded King depart in a kind of daze. I am certain that he had never shot a man before—or been led to believe that he had. Irene went to Godfrey, twined her arm through his, and they walked slowly to their carriage, ignoring Tatyana as if she were a phantom of the fog.

The woman turned in a swirl of red velvet and vanished into her carriage.

"It has worked!" Allegra embraced me in the shelter of our coach. "Dear Nell, you and I have accomplished a hidden miracle, but we shall get no credit, more's the pity."

"The best deeds go unnoticed," I said, removing her arms from my neck.

"Whatever shall we do with . . . him?" she asked next, eyeing the hapless man in the corner of the vehicle. His arm bore but a scratch, though his masquerade was mortally wounded and Tatyana was forever out of his grasp.

"Whatever Irene decides—" I began . . . and was rudely interrupted.

Our carriage door flew open. The unattractive face of the odious man from the ball leaned into our midst.

"Wilhelm von Ormstein the Second, I presume," he noted in perfect English, eyeing our captive. "We will relieve you of him."

"Who—" I began indignantly.

"What—?" Allegra demanded.

A second man leaned in to assist the first. Dr. Watson. In moments they had wrestled our charge from the carriage.

The man in the monocle tipped his top hat at us. "Most obliged, ladies," he said with a slight smile.

And they were gone.

Allegra and I regarded each other. We sat alone in a once-crowded carriage, with nothing to show for our labors—and our triumph—but . . . I leaned to the carriage floor and plucked up a single fallen brass button.

Chapter Thirty-seven

CZECH MATE

Two days later, we were all summoned to Prague Castle for an audience with the King.

Neither Allegra nor I had seen much of Godfrey or Irene during the interim. One would think they had been sequestered in his rooms, refusing to emerge.

We two had been forced to rely upon each other for entertainment, which was not a burden. Together, we had seen more of Prague than Irene and I had managed in our lengthy previous visit. Allegra was most impressed by my tales of Rabbi Loew's hidden crypt, but of course I dared not escort her below.

She begged and pleaded and finally prevailed upon me to visit the fortune-teller again, whom I recognized from Irene's and my previous consultation.

This wrinkled old woman seized upon my hand and predicted that I was about to go "on a long journey." (Not difficult to anticipate: I would return to Paris shortly.) She also predicted that I would "commune with my heart's desire." (Easy enough to do if one possesses sufficient imagination and few desires.)

Nevertheless, I enjoyed my holiday with Allegra, and

even continued to allow her to call me "Nell." That would teach Irene to leave us languishing while she was about her surreptitious business.

We four returned to Prague Castle in style, Godfrey looking positively Grand Operatic in his diplomatic morning suit via the Rothschild tailor; Irene a symphony in scintillating periwinkle blue; Allegra sweet in sincere lilac, and I the model of modernity in yellow-and-brown plaid.

The King wore his usual overelaborate uniform, and greeted us alone in his throne room.

"I owe you this rather ornate chair," he told Irene, gesturing to the rococo gilt affair that squatted on a dais at one end of the marble-floored chamber. "Before I resume it, I humbly beg your advice."

I would have suspected the King of a sense of humor, or even one of irony, had I not known better.

He led her to the chair in question, glanced at Godfrey, then seated her in it. "Tell me what you require."

Irene laid her gloved hands along those gilded arms and lifted her head on her swanlike neck. She looked every inch a queen.

"First," she said, "you must repair your damaged alliance with the Queen. Clotilde has been nobly faithful to your substitute, despite much provocation. You swim upstream with her, Willie, but you have the stamina, and it is worth your future."

He bowed his head.

"Second," she went on, "you will admit that I have been somewhat important to your current status."

He sighed and nodded, like a faithful servant.

"I believe," said Irene, examining her garnet bracelets, "that you owe me some small recompense."

"Which is—?" He no longer sounded so humble, for it had come down to common commerce.

"I had developed a . . . fancy for certain of the art works in your Long Gallery—oh, nothing relating to your family and forebears—merely some insignificant pictures I found pretty. I fear I am sentimental. I desire a souvenir of my last stay in Bohemia."

Irene with her head cast down, looking through her lashes, was a sight to beware of, but King Willie did not know that.

"If the works are obscure, you may have them, with my blessing," he said.

Obscure they were, for I then recalled Irene conducting me past them and identifying hidden Old Masters among the family portraiture. This alone was a coup to pale her capture of Queen Marie Antoinette's diamonds.

"Another matter," she said. "The . . . disposition of the misguided maid who aided in your father's death."

"I have inquired. She has been kept below these two-odd years."

"To forgive is the divine right of kings, Willie."

He balked. "She slew my sire! She was part of a foul plot by Bohemian patriots to ruin the von Ormstein rule."

"Which superseded the native Bohemian rule only in recent times. She was a mere tool, as was your recent replacement."

The King frowned. "What has become of him, by the way?"

"He has," Irene said airily with a wave of her gloved hand, "been wafted to a better world. Do you release the girl, or not?"

"She was a pawn," he said, grumbling. "She will try nothing like this again. I will release her."

Irene nodded.

"Is this all?" he asked, sounding impatient.

"Not . . . quite." Irene glanced at Godfrey and myself. "During my travels in Prague, I could not help but note that the National Theater mounts Mr. Dvořák's *Spectre's Bride*. You may recall, Willie, that I was . . . abruptly compelled to desert an earlier production of this enchanting cantata by . . . forces beyond my control."

"I remember," he growled.

Irene lifted her head, her voice, her entire aspect. "I wish to sing this role that was taken from me. Within the week. I wish an exclusive audience: Mr. Norton, and the Misses Huxleigh and Stanhope."

In the silence that followed this decree, only I had the temerity to speak.

"Irene! You are out of practice. Even you cannot sing such a taxing work with only a week's rehearsal. This is mad. Give it up."

"You will see for yourself, will you not, Nell?" she asked, as implacable as Cleopatra on her throne with an asp in her hand. "I wish a private performance of the work entire, for my friends."

"Of course," the King answered. "Mr. Dvořák will be ecstatic. And may . . . I attend?"

"No," Irene said, quite definite. "This is not a royal command performance, but a prima donna's command performance. I may have whom I wish attend, and you are not among my favored audience, nor even your admirable wife, Clotilde."

He bowed his head and said only, "Is that all?"

"For now," she responded, rising from his throne like a cat getting up after a long and profitable nap.

He stepped before her, barring her way, one foot upon the dais. "May not a humble king seek a boon?"

Irene's eyes glittered like her bracelets. "He may seek, but he may not find."

"I request . . . one last waltz."

At last Irene's composure chipped. "Is that all?" Then her eyes twinkled and sought mine. "My dear Nell did mention the unlikely possibility of my taking a gallop around the ballroom with the Golem of Prague." Her eyes next moved to Godfrey beside me, not so much seeking permission as requesting one last act of patience with her plunge into past business. "It would be most amusing to prove her wild surmise correct."

I could not restrain myself as I glanced around the elegant but empty chamber. "You have no music!"

"Ah," said the King, in a tone of nostalgia that I felt must grate on Godfrey. "Irene makes her own music."

"I would be happy," she told the King with another wicked glitter, "to have you dance to my tune." And she held out her arms in the proper position.

"Again," he amended; sweeping her down the dais and across the polished marble floor that mirrored their motions in foggy reflection.

Irene began to hum some lilting air in perfect pitch and time as they waltzed around the floor, the handsome couple that they had ever been.

In dawning horror, I recognized the tune as "The Emperor Waltz." Irene was providing music fit for even more than a mere king. I eyed Godfrey beside me. He stood as still as Irene had when the false king had challenged him to a duel, and when the equally false Tatyana had dared him to a dance. I could read nothing on his face or in his figure but iron control and a kind of concentrated yet hidden alertness.

At least the King held Irene a decent distance as he smiled down at her. She was not unaware of her partner, but lost in her own music, her own role, as if she were on stage.

And then her improvised melody ended, they stopped swaying and moved apart, and both broke suddenly into laughter at the ludicrous nature of the situation. Even Irene's laughter was operatic, an irresistible arpeggio that bubbled up from her diaphragm and chest and throat. She fanned her fingers to her mouth to contain it, to no avail.

The king stepped back from her, guffawing in his hearty German way, slapping his hands to his thighs, until tears pooled over his ice-blue eyes.

In that moment, self-delusion, prickly and pricked pride, and power and rivalry dissolved under the soothing balm of a finally achieved mutual respect.

Beside me, Godfrey's breath eased out in a not-quite-inaudible hiss. "It is over."

"It has been over for a very long time," I said. "Now, it is finished."

Irene moved to join us, among us commoners again and glad of it, from the expression on her face. She turned back to the King with one last imperial command.

"And next, I wish to see your Queen. Have you seen her since your durance?"

"No," he admitted with sudden sobriety, wiping away the last traces of his mirth. "She was . . . somewhat temperamental."

He promptly went to the door to direct a waiting lackey to invite the Queen to come and see "some old friends and, his Majesty hopes, a new one."

We waited in that room redolent of royalty; we waited for the one woman who held more sway over the King of Bohemia than even Irene did. We waited for the Queen.

She arrived, living up to her title, a vastly changed woman, one worn by fate into harder stuff than she was born for. She faced this man in the image of one who had humiliated her to the bone, and said nothing.

He eyed her, and indeed he now had something to eye.

Clotilde was nothing like the pale imitation of a woman Irene and I had met in Paris, nothing like the portrait over which we had ignobly sniggered in London months before. She had suffered, and she had been educated in the School of Irene Adler. She was a completely different woman, an utterly different Queen, than the false Willie had known and spurned. In addition, Irene's cosmetic magic had made her into a credible likeness of a lovely woman.

"My dear Queen." The King went to her. "My dear . . . wife. I must beg your pardon in front of these friendly witnesses—" He eyed us with a certain distaste. "I was . . . drugged. I have not been in my right mind for months, but the target of a foul plot. Only now am I myself again. The hazard to my own life this scheme cost me during that ill-advised duel has made me see the light. If you are willing to continue your role as my Queen, if you are willing to consider making that role a reality, I should be the happiest man on earth.''

He went down on one knee to her, most prettily.

Irene beamed upon the happy couple like a delighted, and demonic, duenna.

Clotilde eyed the repentant King. She clasped her gloved hands and lifted her milk-white chin, which suddenly seemed more determined than it ever had.

''That is for time to tell, your Majesty. Certainly I am inclined to do my duty, no matter the circumstance. If you wish something more . . . pleasant than that, you will have to earn my trust.''

The King gazed up at her. Perhaps he saw that she was indeed attractive enough when she was not miserable and mistreated. Certainly his eyes traveled the intricacies of her dress, à la Irene, and judged the assured self-confidence that was also due to Irene.

He was a king. But that did not mean that he required a subservient woman; indeed, he had shown tastes to the contrary in the past. Clotilde was wounded enough, and now woman enough, to give him the merry chase that he required to feel kingly.

He smiled at her, expecting ultimate concession.

She smiled at him, expecting to extract her long-overdue due. The Worth wardrobe was even now in the making. He would have little spending money for such fripperies as mistresses now.

They were a match made in heaven—and the separate hells to which they had been so recently subjected.

Irene beamed upon this marriage of true minds, not to mention bloodlines, then came to take Godfrey's arm and withdraw.

* * *

"Such a most extraordinary thing," Godfrey said, uncorking the champagne himself with the panache of a waiter to the white towel born.

We had returned to the suite I now occupied with Allegra. Irene and Godfrey had shared his cramped single chamber since the King's rescue, and had never complained of the accommodation, though Irene's trunks remained in the suite.

"During the duel," he went on, filling four glasses to the brim, "I had this astonishing sense that I could not fail. No fear, no anxiety, simply an uplifting conviction that I was invincible."

"As so you proved," Irene noted over the rim of her champagne flute. "To what do you attribute this surge of confidence?"

"To my brief time with the Rothschild fencing master," he said promptly, "and to some practice with some really first-rate weapons. I must resume these lessons on my return. Do you ladies realize how incredible the event was? I, a novice, struck my man with one shot, while he fired early and still went wide? I have an unsuspected talent for these affairs of honor."

"Still, we are not anxious for you to risk your life again soon," Irene purred, sipping champagne as delicately as Lucifer attacked his bowl of country cream.

"Risk? When a man has such phenomenal luck, combined with a modest skill, risk does not enter the picture." Godfrey froze, contemplating a less exuberant insight. "I could have killed him, I suppose; while that would not have been any loss to me, or you—poor Clotilde would have regarded herself a failure."

"Now she is a Queen indeed," Irene noted, "a Queen of Hearts, which is all the power most women covet. Had you not . . . preserved the King during the duel, you would never have seen that he is no threat to you, and never was."

"No, I would not have seen that for myself." Godfrey

went to link arms with her as they drank a toast from each other's glasses.

I did not know where to look. I cannot understand how two individuals can turn such a harmless convention into a most embarrassing moment for innocent onlookers, even though they are married—the toasters, I mean; not the onlookers.

Allegra linked arms with me and leaned close to whisper in my ear, "Oh, dear Nell, do not be embarrassed. Such moments are hard-won, as I believe that you will see for yourself in the not-too-distant future."

"What do you mean, you minx?"

She merely dimpled, which is a young woman's ploy for evading the question and soon wears thin, even on young men.

I ached for a moment alone with Irene, for I had many questions to ask her. Yet she was now involved in a flurry of rehearsals for her private performance of *The Spectre's Bride*.

When she was not billing and cooing with Godfrey, she was trilling and oohing with Mr. Dvořák at the National Theater. This gentleman was truly delighted to see her again; I had not missed the moisture that had sprung to his eyes when he had been told of her plan to sing in his cantata at last. Then he had grown stern and predicted an onslaught of practice and rehearsal.

Mr. Dvořák proved to be such a stern taskmaster that I was forced to confront Irene in her dressing room two days later, when Godfrey was escorting Allegra on a promised tour of the Prague beer gardens—I was given nothing to say about this departure from good form.

"You are not to peek, not to overhear a single note," Irene admonished when she found me there. "It will ruin the surprise."

"Irene, I can live with not knowing about your performance until it occurs; what I cannot tolerate is not knowing where the false king has gone. After all, Allegra and I were responsible for him, and I should be as loath to lose his life as you were the serving maid's who killed the King's father."

"Ah? Is that all, Nell?" Irene slapped her perfect features with a powder puff and beamed amid motes of flying dust, her eyes prudently closed. " 'Tis simplicity itself: Sherlock Holmes and Dr. Watson spirited the false king away for interrogation by the British Foreign Office, which is most interested in Russia's ambitions in Eastern Europe."

"Then the obnoxious gentleman *was* Sherlock Holmes?"

"That I cannot swear to, Nell," Irene said. "It depends upon which obnoxious gentleman you mean."

"The man with the monocle."

"I thought the Rothschild agent wore tinted glasses."

"He did. There was another man."

"There always is. Well, whoever . . . has made off with the false king, and he still lives, for what it is worth."

"Irene, don't you care? And why are you so certain that the British Foreign Office is involved in this affair?"

"Oh, I have contacts—" She powdered her face again, forcing me to close my eyes, a situation all too common between us.

"You are not in secret communication with Sherlock Holmes?" I asked suspiciously when I dared look around again.

"Certainly not! Though an instinct tells me that he was pleased to net the false king, I am sure that he has no idea that *I* am the one who permitted this to happen."

I was not so sure, but was not about to say so. "Who *was* the false king? And why—how?—did he bear such an amazing resemblance to King Willie?"

I finally had come up with a query worthy of Irene lowering her powder puff. "A splendid question, Nell." She eyed me humorously in the mirror. "You have heard that the Czar of Russia, Alexander the Third, is a massive man some six feet six inches tall, like the King of Bohemia?"

"Yes, of course; he is the husband of that petite little woman, the Empress Maria Feodorovna."

"He is also the father of more than the royal heirs and their sisters."

"You know that I do not understand these veiled references, Irene. You must make your meaning plain."

"Very well; you asked for it. The false king of Bohemia was Willie's very image because he was related to Willie, who is related to the Russian royal house. He is a by-blow of Czar Alexander."

"By-blow? What an odd expression."

"Not if one moves in royal circles." Irene set down her puff and eyed me frankly through the medium of her mirror. "This is one of those rare times when I can assert with utter propriety, Nell, that the substitute was a bastard. A quite genuine bastard," she intoned with unabashed relish, almost as if she were calling the true King of Bohemia by this shocking epithet. "His given name is Rudolf Something-Russian. Rudolf! Doesn't it sound like he escaped from the cast list of a Viennese operetta? Too delicious! This escapade ranks among my most intriguing, but I am glad to bow out of the denouement. Politics are so . . . fatiguing. No doubt Mr. Holmes and his Foreign Office cohorts are extracting reams of boring information about the czar's plans of empire from poor, betrayed Rudolf even now."

"I cannot imagine why you believe that you know so much of Mr. Holmes's movements."

Irene waved her arms in that carelessly encompassing manner that only a mistress of the stage can master. "I am an artist, Nell. I use my imagination. I highly recommend the exercise," she added pointedly.

I sat back on the little metal chair provided for guests, who were not expected to linger long. "Things have worked out quite to your advantage."

"Yes, they have," she answered with perfect satisfaction.

"The Queen is delighted by her new obsequious King."

"So she should be." A flicker of regret crossed Irene's face. "I never thought of imprisoning Willie for a few months to make him malleable. There the fair Tatyana outdoes me."

"She did not mean to make the King humble, but merely kept him alive as a leash on his duplicate, which she badly needed with the man so prone to jealousy."

"How astute of you, Nell! I never wondered why they didn't simply kill Willie from the first." She turned from her mirror with a surge of enthusiasm. "What an operetta the affair would make! It has everything—duplicate kings, a heartbroken queen, a jealous mistress, a duel, an interlude in a graveyard, foreign intrigue and a famous detective."

"Is the last element you refer to Sherlock Holmes—or yourself?"

"I have not decided yet," she said. "He may get credit for the capture of the dupe, but I resurrected the real king, which is what enabled Mr. Holmes to snag the substitute."

"You will get no more public acknowledgment of that than you did when you solved the murder of Willie's father," I warned her.

She allowed herself to pout, merely because the expression sat so well on her. "The kingdom of Bohemia is an utter ingrate, Nell, as kingdoms go. But, then, the brilliant in any field are all too often neglected."

"Taking home a king's ransom in undiscovered Old Masters is hardly neglect, Irene."

She shrugged. "They would have languished here, forgotten, as they have been for centuries already. By the way, I must commend you for your self-control in neglecting to blurt out that the paintings I requested were more than they seemed. I believe that you are making tremendous strides toward a practical view of the world."

"Toward larceny, you mean! At least you arranged for the release of that put-upon maid, though she was a murderer."

Irene smiled and applied the rouged white rabbit's foot to her cheeks. "Yes! I am quite content about that. Even murderers deserve the opportunity of a public hearing. Willie knew as well as I did that the girl only did what she was told, without realizing the consequences."

"A role you often expect me to play," I noted tartly. "I hope that means that I may expect a commuted sentence in heaven."

"I am sure that you will speed straight to the pearly gates, Nell, with no aid from me. I will wave from . . . below."

"I fear that the heavenly choir will be found one contralto short, and you will be let in on a technicality; you always elude disaster no matter how much you court it, Irene."

"Not always." Her face sobered. "Godfrey doesn't know how dangerous his duel really was, whom he really fought. Tatyana is capable of wounding and kidnapping him merely to have him to herself. She could destroy her heart's desire in the acquiring of it."

I moved uneasily on my chair. "I do not understand, Irene. You and Godfrey are wed; further, Godfrey has never responded to her approaches. Why would she persist?"

"Why would the King pursue me when it was obvious that I fled him? Such imperious personalities recognize sovereignty in no other being, not even—and perhaps especially not—in those they purport to love. The barbaric painting of Tatyana you described: do you know whom it represents? Salome, who so desired to possess that she devoured instead. Romantic love is not blind possession, Nell; love is liberation."

"Irene, that sentiment is quite profound, and most moral."

"Thank you." Her head bowed the tiniest bit.

"But you never saw the painting I described."

"I did not have to; I know where Madam Tatyana seeks

inspiration. She has no doubt danced the role, and will do so again."

"Not with . . . Godfrey in mind?"

Irene was silent for a moment. "She will not forget. Neither will I."

"How awful! I would like to think that love is noble and liberating, but so few practice that variety of it. I am content to remain a spinster, if that is the case."

Irene smiled a secret smile at the mirror and avoided looking at me. I shook out my skirts, preparing to withdraw, when a knock came on the dressing-room door.

"Yes?" Irene called, even that one word a melodious invitation.

"A token, Frau Norton," came a muffled voice from the other side.

Irene lifted her eyebrows at me and I rose to open the door.

In walked a huge spray of flowers in a vase, carried by what little of a man we could see behind the showy stalks.

"Gracious! There on the dressing table," she directed, moving makeup pots aside so the blossoming behemoth could rest there.

"Nell, have you—?"

Naturally I was expected to supply the change to reward the messenger for his labors. I fished through my worn leather coin purse and produced a few large, alien coins.

The man grinned and tipped his cap, so I must have given him a month's worth of beer money. Irene had turned her back to the door and was fussing with the flowers, searching for a card.

"Oh, Frau," he said from the threshold. "There is a box at the mouth of the vase."

Irene laid down the small white envelope she had found to search for the additional booty.

In moments, she had drawn a small, foil-wrapped oblong box from the arrangement. "How clever! I must open it."

"Who is it from?" I demanded. "Mr. Dvořák? Godfrey?"

She reluctantly laid the glittering box down to open the card; then her expression fell. "A mere florist's acknowledgment. Someone has written, 'By the grace of his Majesty, King Wilhelm.'"

"The King! He is indeed grateful to send you flowers for a performance you have forbidden him to see, but require him to pay for."

She tossed the card aside. "I suppose it is a nice gesture, but if Godfrey asks, you will say that the bouquet is from Mr. Dvořák."

"I will say no such thing! You must hope that Godfrey does not ask me."

"I hope that Willie's gift is a bit more kingly than the enclosure card." She picked up the box and began picking at the wrappings.

"Irene! You are not going to accept a gift from him?"

She regarded me with utter amazement. "Why not, Nell? I have blackmailed the man for a costly performance of a full cantata, not to mention stripped his ancestral walls of a fortune in paintings. Why can I not have one more little gift, a personal memento for the distress he gave me years ago? I hope his taste in jewelry is better than that of whoever concocted the Bohemian crown jewels—!"

"Irene! Set that foul package down at once! I will not sit here and watch you accept such a token. You are married, and now he is also married. Such an exchange is highly improper, no matter the King's gratitude—or your greed!"

"But I want to know what is in the package, Nell, even if I choose not to keep it, which I may, if it is uninteresting enough. You need not sit here and watch; you can wait in the hall."

I stood, as angry as I had been with Irene in . . . months. "I will, and you needn't bother showing it to me after; I am not interested."

"Good. Then leave."

"I will."

I marched to the door in a fearful temper, hearing foil crushing behind me. As I reached for the knob, it was turned out of my hand and the door flew open.

Chapter Thirty-eight

THE FABERGÉ FANG

I faced a tall, thin gentleman in a loose traveling cloak and soft cap, with very dark eyebrows and piercing gray eyes.

My mouth dropped.

He rushed past me, nay, *brushed* past me in the most rude manner possible.

"I am not too late?" he asked without pausing for an answer. "Madam!" he called in an urgent voice. He was not addressing me; he had, in fact, barely seen me.

Irene turned from the dressing table like an actress surprised by a premature entrance. "Mr. Holmes—" she breathed in a tone that defied description.

I will endeavor to characterize it anyway, as every instant of this encounter is emblazoned on my brain: her voice conveyed one part shock, one part awe and one part delight. "Mr. Sherlock Holmes," she repeated with more assurance. "Himself. As himself."

The man wasted no time on conventional greetings.

"What have you done with the flowers?" he demanded.

"Looked at them," she replied in a daze.

He did so as well, though not in the manner of one

appreciating nature's beauty. No, Mr. Sherlock Holmes bent down to study the vase and flowers as if they were alien deposits, his keen face moving around them in the obsessive manner of a bloodhound on a scent.

He unbent to fix his darting eye on the box in Irene's hand. "What is that?"

"A . . . present. From the King. It came with the flowers."

"Did it? I find that rather suggestive, do you not, Madam?"

"I find it rather . . . rewarding," she said, her tone ironic yet amused.

"Put it down." One long imperious finger pointed to the cluttered dressing-table top.

Irene complied, as if being asked to lay a loaded pistol aside. She delicately placed the gaily wrapped package on the wood and stepped away from it.

Mr. Holmes moved into the space she had vacated with the swiftness of a prizefighter. Then he went down on his knees—I tell the exact truth, I swear—braced his hands on the table edge and peered at and around the poor package.

"Do you have a buttonhook, Madam?"

Irene, untroubled by his barked orders, answered sweetly. "No, but I have a small dagger. Will that do?"

He glanced up at her, for the first time, and gave a snort of laughter. "Eminently."

The dagger was news to me. I watched while Irene bent to the floor, lifted her skirt and petticoats—lifted her skirt, I might add, with that man within immediate viewing distance—and reached into her laced leather boot top to extract what resembled a rather pointed letter opener.

I give the man credit. He seized the weapon without so much as glancing at its unconventional sheath, and thrust a hand into his cloak pocket to extract a magnifying glass.

Irene sat slowly, almost silently, on the chair I had vacated to watch him.

With the magnifying glass he examined the dressing-table top, the vase, the flowers and, most particularly, the package.

Then, focusing on the partly undone paper, he lifted it leaf by leaf from the package. Irene watched this procedure, at first with amusement, then with curiosity and finally with utter absorption, leaning her elbows on the dressing table and her head on her hands.

I remained by the door, observing this bizarre . . . dissection of an ordinary package. For Sherlock Holmes approached this commonplace act like a surgeon operating on some deathly contagious patient, as if any gesture might destroy a process that was precious and paramount.

So concentrated was his attention, so precise and delicate his movements, that I found myself holding my breath and almost forgetting to release it.

At last the crinkling paper had been prodded away.

A maroon leatherette jeweler's case sat before us, its gilt hinges gleaming in the gaslight.

Mr. Holmes eased the tip of Irene's dagger into the thin line of gilt, like a man opening a clam in search of a pearl.

"Stay back," he warned, glancing to Irene, and even to me in the mirror.

Hunched over this humble object like a miser, he lifted one hand to the lid and let his thumb and second finger poise on the lid's sides. His hand hung limp from above, the long, narrow fingers like a spider's legs.

"For heaven's sake," I breathed under my breath, so softly that no one heard me.

Irene did not move. She might have been a portrait of a woman rather than the real thing, and her face was utterly sober now.

With his fingertips bracing the box from the sides, he slid the dagger along the front opening, and down the left side to the back. Then it returned, a thin, sharp gold tongue almost tasting the gold-filled brass.

Something snakelike in this slow, calculated exploration repelled me, but, then, I had never liked Mr. Holmes. Still, I could not keep my eyes off his strange and silent performance; nor could Irene.

When the dagger ran lightly along the right side of the box, he suddenly held it still.

"Ah! Madam, if you will hold the box here—very carefully. . . ."

Irene rose and went to his left side. I did not like the way that she was forced to lean over his shoulder to follow his instructions.

"I will pull up—so, while depressing the dagger and . . . don't move, no matter what happens!"

I clutched a hand to my breast despite his orders. Clearly, some dread danger was about to be released into the room. I hoped that it was nothing venomous.

All I heard was a click, like Irene's pistol cocking. The lid sprang open, and I gave a small scream. Even Irene jumped back.

Mr. Holmes was as still as death. He finally stood and gazed down at the object now open to us all.

A magnificent blue enamel Fabergé cigarette case bearing the initial "I" in sinuous diamonds lay on the jeweler's white satin.

Irene's head drew slowly back from it as if it were indeed a serpent of sorts. "Poison?" she asked.

"A hidden prong on the right side of the lid, where you would rest the fingers of your left hand as you held the container in your right. The venom would have gone into your second finger and straight to your heart."

"Venom," I repeated weakly.

"I have seen this method before," Irene said, "but I was not expecting it."

"Perhaps," said Mr. Holmes, "you have had other things on your mind of late. I take it that you know the identity of the originator?"

She nodded slowly, then looked him in the face, the bare face. For the first time, no guise stood between them. "How did you—"

"Poor Rudolf is most disappointed in his erstwhile mistress. He resents her attempt to kill him, but before that he resented her showing that she had . . . other interests. That is why he challenged your husband to a duel. He knew that Madam Tatyana's obsession was serious, as she had plans to eliminate you."

"Eliminate Irene?" I squeaked from the door.

Mr. Holmes barely glanced my way. "I will take this tidy trap to England for further study now that it is disarmed—"

Irene's hand lifted involuntarily. "Do you need the contents?"

"I doubt that the cigarette case itself has been tampered with. You actually wish to keep this macabre souvenir?" He regarded Irene as if she were almost as worthy of his full attention as the deadly box had been.

She half-smiled, half-shrugged in that disarming way of hers. "It does bear my initial, and I am fond of Fabergé."

Mr. Holmes's thin lips folded, whether in exasperation or amusement I was not close enough to tell.

"I will have to study it before I let you have it."

She stepped aside, gesturing to the dressing table and light, and watched while he examined the inner case with the same exactitude that he had studied the outer one.

We waited, like maids upon a master, until at last he rose, picked up the glorious thing—like the deepest night sky studded with stars—and handed it to Irene with a bow.

"You will not let me convey my thanks later in more formal circumstances, I gather?" she said.

"I am here, dear lady, incognito, as are you, and return immediately to England."

He pushed aside the cloak to draw out a pocket watch and read the time. The golden sun of the sovereign Irene had given his disguised self at her wedding swung from his

watch chain. Only I knew of his associate's belief that Irene
was the lone woman who had won this strange man's admiration and . . . perhaps . . . touched his untouched heart.

If that was true, today he had enjoyed the sublime satisfaction of saving one who meant much to him. I knew too
well that exalted impulse, yet detected no sign of its ful-
fillment on that sharp, ascetic face. However, he did not
resemble a drug fiend, either, and I knew him to be that
sort, as well.

"How did you happen to come to Prague?" Irene asked.
No one was spared her ceaseless curiosity, not even a man
who only moments before had saved her life.

Mr. Holmes smiled then, an expression that humanized
his features if it did not soften them. "I was drawn here by
a matter you found expendable in the light of your own
larger affairs: the death of two Worth bead-girls in Paris."

"Two?" Irene's shock was palpable. "Perhaps if I had
stayed in Paris I could have prevented—"

He waved a dismissing hand. "You have done more than
your share of prevention in Bohemia, Madam. An investigating agent must not confuse himself with a prophet, or a
god, as I have more than one reason to know."

"Then the fashion mannequins' gowns were indeed
woven into a code between spies in the various courts of
Europe!" Irene said eagerly. "And the murdered bead-girls
must have realized the deception."

I stepped boldly away from the door. "That is why that
awful Madame Gallatin was so scathing when I dared to
improvise the pattern—"

Mr. Holmes regarded me with an unspoken question
that I found myself answering unbidden.

"I—I became a bead-girl for two days to learn more of
the murder just before we were diverted to Bohemia."

"Madame Gallatin was the chief conspirator at Maison
Worth," he declared. "If you meddled with the bead design, you are fortunate not to have made the closer acquaintance of a pair of scissors."

Irene blanched. "Then Nell left that establishment not a moment too soon; at least this Bohemian venture accomplished that."

He nodded.

"I did not have time to pursue the line of investigation at Maison Worth," she admitted, "but using the queens of Europe as unsuspecting carriers was a diabolically clever scheme for secret international communication. I gather that the Foreign Office now takes a greater interest in women's fashions than before?"

"As do I, Madam, as do I!" Mr. Holmes responded fervently.

Irene laughed. "I am not surprised that you on occasion become involved in Foreign Office matters, Mr. Holmes, but how on earth did you come upon poor Berthe's murder in Paris? Surely the affairs that draw you abroad usually involve far more elevated folk than bead-girls?"

"Allow me my secrets, Madam Norton, as I allow you yours," he said cryptically. "I cannot . . . relate every clue to my competitors."

Irene lifted her eyebrows. She had not missed his earlier advice that an investigator must not incur guilt in trying to play god; now he implied that he considered her a rival.

"This 'competitor' owes you her life," she said in a low tone.

"And I owe you the discovery of a counterfeit king. I confess that you were ahead of me on that score, but then you had a considerable head start, as well as a personal knowledge of the individuals involved. Rudolf will have much to say to us, and is more than willing. Your dagger, Madam."

She took it and restored it to its place of concealment. This time he watched, with admiration. I was unsure whether his admiration stemmed more from her audacity or his new appreciation of women's fashions, down to the underlayments.

"If you attempt to credit me with any heroics here," he

warned, "I will deny everything. I have sworn Dr. Watson to complete secrecy on the matter; now I require yours." He paused at the door for her assurance.

"Oh, I would not dream of doing such a thing, Mr. Holmes, especially when it makes me look such an innocent. Who would believe a dead woman, at any rate?"

"Not in certain quarters, Madam; not in certain quarters." He gazed at her for a long, odd moment, then bowed and brushed past me. He paused to look down his long nose directly into my face. "I have seen you before," he barked. "In London."

I swallowed, searching for my voice. "And you will see me again, no doubt," I managed to say stoutly, as a watchdog would warn a housebreaker against further incursions in the same neighborhood.

"I sincerely hope not" was his impolite reply, as he shouldered out into the deserted hall.

His footsteps died soon, but the silence he left in his wake outlasted them.

"Well." Irene's fingertips smoothed the cigarette case's gleaming enamel with its incised pattern of endless waves. "How fortunate that we leave Prague after my performance tonight."

"We leave tonight? I am not packed."

She smiled. "Not immediately after the performance, but tomorrow morning, first thing."

"I did not know that."

"I had not decided that."

"Perhaps you should not sing—"

"Impossible. Now, more than ever, I must sing. If I will not be silenced by the King of Bohemia, I will certainly not be silenced by a common Russian ballerina with no sense of borders!"

Chapter Thirty-nine

COMMAND PERFORMANCE

We sat in the royal box of the National Theater facing an architecture that resembled the interior of a gigantic Fabergé egg—vaulted, ornate white wood and plaster, red velvet curtains and garlands of shining gilt everywhere.

We sat alone—Allegra and Godfrey and I—gazing down on an empty luxuriance of crimson velvet seats toward a curtained stage draped in more velvet and gold fringe.

In the dark pit below the limelights, the orchestra in evening dress made a checkerboard of solemn black and white. The warm wooden and bright brass gleams of their oiled and polished instruments drew our eyes.

Besides we three, the members of the orchestra were the only visible humans in all that extravagant immensity. Not even the King and Queen of Bohemia were here to witness this strangely stirring occasion: Irene singing the role of which she had been defrauded more than two years before.

If ever revenge could be tailor-made in heaven, perhaps hers was the crowning design of some celestial Worth.

Then the world-famous composer, Antonín Dvořák himself, walked onto the stage, bowed to our paltry but heartfelt patter of clapping, and took his place in the pit.

The overture had the startling impact of apocalyptic

trumpets. Sound positively throbbed in that empty opera
house, with no rows of absorbing flesh and fabric to dull it.
We clutched new-bought opera glasses and—as the house-
lights dimmed and the huge curtain began to roll back like
some somnolent beast—we lifted them so as not to miss a
moment's sight.

No wonder Irene had dared to sing this role with little
preparation. *The Spectre's Bride* was a cantata consisting of
chorus, baritone, tenor and soprano. Rudimentary sets
sufficed, though stagehands drew pulleys and pulled strings
that made various curtains and set pieces lift and lower.

Yet, to us, the lone and attentive audience, music and not
stage illusions provided a dazzling, deft magic. When Irene
began to sing, mere magic became magnificence.

I had witnessed Irene in an operatic role, *Saint Ludmilla*,
only once, here in Prague. Godfrey and Allegra had never
seen her perform a major work. So we sat rapt as her voice
thrilled over the footlights to fill the entire empty house
until every surface reverberated with her presence, her
power, her voice.

I cannot convey the shock of a significant piece of music
to those who have witnessed only drawing-room recitals. I
knew that Irene sang like the proverbial angel, that her
voice had the deep, dark undercurrent of a cello, for all its
clarity and sweetness. I knew that she was an actress born
and could imply the heartbreak of a sob in a shimmering
glissando of sung syllables, but I had never truly *heard* her
before, until this night, until this performance, this cantata.

Godfrey did not move, nor seem to breathe. Allegra was
a frozen shadow on his other side, her eye-whites glistening
in the dark. Our only motions were the duel we fought
between employing our magnifying glasses, so we could see
Irene and her every expression close up, or using only
normal sight, so that we could view the entire spectacle,
with Irene a tiny figure below that yet rang like a bell to
inundate and overwhelm all our senses.

How little it mattered that we did not understand the

Bohemian language. Music and motion spoke a universal tongue. The subject matter was Gothic, even grisly. Irene played the young "bride" of the title, whose dead sweetheart comes to spirit her from her humble cottage to his lordly castle—a tomb in the nearby cemetery! How appropriate for our recent adventures in Bohemia.

What was inappropriate was Irene's "costume" throughout: a shimmering, flimsy nightgown as unanchored as the robe in which Tatyana had entertained Godfrey—and myself, of course. While we watched, listened, absorbed, time flew like flocks of swallows. I especially watched for the effective orchestration she had mentioned on the lines "Psi houfem ve vsi zavyli," which she had translated as "The dogs, awakened, howled and cried." Now that I saw the work's tone as the cantata reached its graveyard climax, I understood the reference. Though it was ironic that Irene sang *The Spectre's Bride*, given that she had once cherished the notion of becoming the King of Bohemia's bride, the gruesome story mattered little to the performance. All was sound and emotion and artistry. Triumph.

I glanced at Godfrey to see if his eyes glistened, as had the King of Bohemia's when he heard Irene sing. Only the normal moisture reflected from them, though he sat like a statue of stone; he was, after all, a British barrister.

Allegra and I were another story. On either side of the rapt but stoic Godfrey, we wrung our handkerchiefs, bit our lips, and tried to sniffle unnoticed during a swell of chorus.

In fact, I was often so overcome that I was forced to look away from the stage, lest my companions glimpse my distorted expression.

During such a face-saving interlude, I happened to glance to the side of the house, where I spied a still, dark figure lurking behind the curtain to the lobby.

I caught my breath, ready to complain that Irene's terms had been violated. The King should know better by now! Then I studied the man's figure—for it was surely male.

Tall . . . but as tall as the King of Bohemia? And this figure seemed . . . thinner.

I almost rose from my seat. Of all the impudence! *That* man had intruded where even kings would fear to tread. Imagine! Sherlock Holmes slinking into the National Theater to hear Irene sing! And he had said that he was returning to London immediately! What could one expect from a so-called consulting detective who stooped so easily to disguise except more prevarication?

I did indeed half rise in indignation, but Godfrey clasped my wrist. "You must not get so carried away, Nell," he whispered with a smile, "though it is stirring stuff."

I subsided, unwilling to direct his attention to yet another admirer of his wife; the King was bad enough. When I looked again, the figure had vanished, leaving me with the unpleasant thought that my imagination was at fault.

The cantata finished without incident, though the central chandelier swayed during the climactic scene, apparently a piece of elaborate stage business designed to enhance the audience's tension.

Irene sang on, oblivious to all but her role; oblivious to her audience even, as any good performer is, though she knew that she sang for us, and us only. Despite that, she always sang for herself, herself alone.

Afterward, and after applauding until our gloved palms burned, we went down to mingle with the performers and the musicians on the stage. The King's generosity had provided bottles of the finest French champagne, with which the company toasted and praised each other endlessly.

Mr. Dvořák roved from group to group, his broad brow sweat-dewed and tear tracks still visible upon his face.

"Splendid, splendid," he murmured in English, shaking hands with us all and adding to the injury the clapping had done them.

He found Irene, kissed her on both cheeks as a Frenchman would, then swept her into a most unconventional but rather endearing bear hug.

After receiving the maestro's tribute, she turned to God-frey, her face an unasked question. Godfrey went to her without a word, then lifted and swung her in a triumphant circle, refusing to return her to earth, despite her laughter and her pleas and orders, until someone came with over-flowing flutes of champagne for both of them.

Allegra had slipped my vigilant side and was proving the belle of the chorus members, particularly the young gentlemen, who endeavored to find some common lingual ground with her, with little success.

I watched and wandered, lost among a chatter of alien language, tired but happy and somehow satisfied. I eyed the edges of the various backdrops swaying above us, and the faint, starlike glimmer of a massive chandelier on high.

I was unaware of standing there, looking up, for very long, but a voice suddenly spoke in my ear.

"Pardon, Miss. English?"

I glanced at a man not dressed in costume, an ordinary-looking man in a jersey and trousers, then nodded.

"Beau-ti-ful setting," he said carefully, pridefully. "I pull." He pointed up, then to himself.

"Oh. You . . . pull the backdrops down and up. Up and down."

I loathe language barriers, for I found myself demonstrating my meaning as if playing a parlor game or ringing a bell.

He grinned. "She sing . . . beau-ti-ful."

I nodded and smiled, then glanced up again to the dimly glittering chandelier. I found myself frowning. When I looked at my companion, he was frowning, too.

"Big light—down," he said, glancing nervously to Irene at the center of a cluster of performers. He shook his head.

"Down . . . too soon, too fast?" I asked.

He shook his head. "Down . . . bad." He lifted a forefin-ger, smiled. "Man come . . . up."

"Man? What man?"

He looked around as if searching for a familiar form,

then shook his head. "All beau-ti-ful," he said. With a last nod, he moved on.

I remained, remembering the shuddering chandelier over Irene's head, remembering the tall, lean man in the shadows, later gone. I reconsidered the stage man's broken testimony.

Perhaps Sherlock Holmes—if it was indeed he—had another motive for braving tonight's private performance than eavesdropping on Irene's singing. Perhaps he had once again saved Irene from the implacable hand of an enemy.

I moved toward my friends, glancing up.

"Yes, Nell," Irene said regretfully as soon as she saw me. "You need not waggle your ever-present lapel watch at me. I know that the ball is over and we must go. I have just been telling Godfrey that I wish to depart first thing in the morning. My goal is accomplished; I cannot wait to leave Prague and go home."

At this news, Godfrey looked as happy as Peter Piper after his wife had retired to a pumpkin shell, but I was not deceived.

Irene suspected the deadly reach of her new foe, whether she realized another attempt had been made on her life or not, and she was eager to withdraw to a safer distance. I heartily, and silently, approved.

Chapter Forty

MY LIPS ARE SEALED

By dawn's early light we were all packing like fiends in our respective rooms when the door of mine shuddered to an urgent knock.

"Do you need help?" Irene asked without prelude when I admitted her.

"I can pack better than you," I replied with utter honesty and an unblinking stare.

If there is anything that Irene loathes more than my supposed tendency to "blurt," it is my unblinking stare.

"Do not look at me like that, Nell. We will soon be home."

"You call a four-day railway trip across most of Europe 'home'?"

"Soon is relative, as you well know." She dipped to adjust her black velvet bonnet in the mirror, and adjust her three-quarter-length black plush velvet mantle liberally decorated with soutache and jet beadwork. "It is vital to dress well for traveling," she noted, turning to eye my toilette. "Which outer garment do you wear?"

"The black silk rep jacket with lamb trim. I decided against the fur-trimmed cloak, as it may be warm once I am on the train."

"Most wise. You may even find it warmer than you think. One never knows what these European trains are like. As for your gown, the pink silk bodice is most . . . appealing, and I quite approve your choice of gray brocade skirt and jacket. A pity that you must pierce such splendid fabric with your lapel watch—"

"Thank you," I said firmly to end her incessant supervision of my wardrobe and appearance. "No one shall see much of me, at any rate, but you and Godfrey."

"Nell, I have some difficult news." Irene frowned so deeply that I trembled for her face.

"What?"

"You know that Allegra must meet her aunt and cousin in Vienna."

"Of course."

"You do not know that Godfrey and I, after all we have been through, desperately require . . . a holiday. I have always longed to see Vienna. Godfrey insists on taking me there forthwith. He is most . . . adamant," she said in a pleased tone. "And it is one thing that the King promised me that Godfrey can fulfill with ease."

"I see. So we are going to Vienna before we return to Paris. I suppose that I can put up with a detour, though I am most disappointed. Sophie has been unsupervised for far too long, and who knows what those beasts have been up to in our absence."

"You do not worry about the condition of those beasts of ours, do you, Nell?" Irene asked slyly.

"Of course not! I merely fear that they will eat each other up, and all we will find on our return will be a few bright feathers, an array of fallen whiskers and a sad tuft of fur."

Irene smiled. "Then you must go home straightaway and see to the little monsters! No—I will have no argument, Nell. Godfrey and I will see Allegra safely to her aunt in Vienna, then linger for a short . . . second honeymoon."

"I see," I said, seeing all too well.

What I also saw is that I would have to travel alone

across a string of foreign countries filled with foreign money and foreign . . . foreigners.

I did not even have Godfrey's cane-sword, or Irene's pistol. Or a dagger in my boot. I would mingle with . . . strangers and strange men. I would be alone, unescorted. I dared not tell Irene, however, how much the prospect terrified me.

"Godfrey will make all the arrangements when we reach the station, and—don't worry, Nell—we will see you safely aboard."

She hugged my shoulders, a gesture I most dislike. I do not care for clumsy attempts at physical affection, and I did not at all feel like being hugged at the moment, by anyone.

Of course I said nothing, but resumed my packing.

All too soon we bid the Hotel Europa goodbye. A carriage riding low on its springs due to our baggage—mostly Irene's infernal number of trunks; I shuddered to think how many more might return from a jaunt to Vienna—waited to take us to the train terminal.

Allegra, idiotically excited, bounced in her seat like a child of ten.

"Oh, dear Nell, I am so sorry that you will not see Vienna with us." Her merry manner did not lend her words a particle of sincerity.

"I am not sorry to miss Vienna," I said. "Another dissolute city, I understand."

"Really?" Allegra seemed delighted, but her face fell instantly. "I fear that I am to be returned to the shepherding of my aunt there, and will have not half so much fun as I have had in Prague."

"I should hope not."

Allegra eyed me critically. She had, I am sorry to say, developed some of Irene's exacting standards in dress. "That is a lovely bonnet, but why do you wear so much veiling? Are you in disguise?"

"Hardly, but a woman traveling alone," I said pointedly, "must do her best to avoid undue attention." I looked at

Godfrey and Irene across from us, but they were absorbed in a peculiarly low and intense conversation and utterly oblivious to my observation.

"Your best friend would not recognize you," Allegra complained with a charming pout. "Let me waft back at least one veil. There! Now you look mysterious, like a spy, instead of like a nun."

"You are too enamored of spies, young lady," I cautioned, but I did not restore my lifted veil. Her mention of resembling a nun had chilled my Anglican bones, and I confess that it was easier to see when less heavily draped.

Allegra smiled winningly. "Oh, dear Nell, you shall never know how much I wish I could be going back to Paris with you! Irene—Mrs. Norton and I had such a grand time on the way here; I am sure that you and I would have had an equally wonderful trip back. Mrs. Norton and I had an opportunity to commune on all the subjects of such great interest to a woman."

"Indeed. I fear I am not used to such communion and would have proved a dull companion, though I admit, Miss Minx, that I would dearly like your company on this return journey."

"Poor Nell!" Allegra announced in a touching tone of sympathy that was unfortunately not heard by our self-absorbed companions.

The dear child took my gloved hand, turned it over and began tracing the unseen lines.

"I see a long journey, English lady, but not a dull one. I see exotic men, romance, danger . . . daggers. An unexpected reunion. You must be on your guard—"

"Allegra," I protested, laughing despite myself. "That . . . tickles! What astonishing nonsense! You are a worse mimic than Irene. You 'see' nothing but your own vivid imagination, bless it. You must visit Neuilly again."

"I will, as soon as I can manage it," she promised with a wicked twinkle. "I adore animals, and you have so many. Kiss them for me."

Before I could respond to this odious request, our vehicle lurched to a stop, then shuddered as the coachman began heaving the baggage to porters below.

Even Irene and Godfrey were forced to pay attention to something other than each other as we all hurled through the crowds and confusion of the vast and busy Franz Josef station. In all too short a time, the tickets were purchased and I was delivered to my westward-bound train.

Steam hissed around us on the hard pavement, and made up for the absence of my second veil, which Allegra had brushed back over the top of my bonnet. I was suddenly as overwrought as I had been in the royal box at the opera, and was eager for my friends to leave so they should not see my distress.

"You will be late!" I warned them. "I will be fine."

"Indeed you will," Godfrey said, "as soon as I settle you in your compartment." He hefted the carpetbag that would accompany me and waited by the small stair to the train.

A steam-swathed cloud of rustling silk and violet perfume engulfed me. "Safe journey, Nell, and *do not worry!*" Irene urged.

"I never worry needlessly," I replied, just before another stream-borne force clasped me in a frivolous embrace.

"Dear Nell, I will miss you dreadfully," Allegra confessed, alarmingly close to tears. "Pray ignore my silly fortune-telling and have a dull, uninterrupted, ordinary journey."

"Thank you, Allegra," I said with dignity. "Of that I am sure."

Godfrey's arm on my elbow was guiding me into the narrow passage that led to my compartment. He eyed it expertly, then set my carpetbag on one of the facing seats.

"A first-class compartment, as ticketed," he noted with approval. "At least you will be undisturbed on your long journey." He doffed his hat to lean forward and enfold me in yet another embrace! One would think I was bound for the Black Hole of Calcutta. "Thank you for your usual invaluable assistance in Prague," he said softly. "We are lucky to have whisked Irene away from that muddle. And thank you for understanding that Irene and I require a recreational escape to Vienna."

What could I say? Very little, as I was consumed by a fit of choking for some reason. I merely nodded bravely. That seemed to satisfy Godfrey, who grinned at me, clapping my shoulders in a most comradely way, and left me to my large compartment.

I immediately sat and arranged myself at the window. Through boas of steam I saw Irene and Allegra standing side by side, waving and making all the idiotic motions one does to departing travelers who can see but cannot hear one. I pantomimed back. Soon Godfrey's tall form joined them. They looked a happy family there—he and she and young Allegra, almost like father, mother and daughter—though Irene would not have thanked me for that thought.

I felt—and likely looked—like the departing governess being granted a fond farewell while her erstwhile family goes on to new and separated adventures.

The comparison was unworthy of me. No doubt I was feeling some self-pity, for watching my friends slide away with the train's first jerking motions was like watching the pages of a photo album being irrevocably turned. We three would never be here again, in the same place and time, in the same fashion, in the same selves.

I watched until I could see only stream and strangers, all drawing behind me, then glanced around the compartment: green velvet upholstered seats with a net above each one to hold baggage. I glanced beyond the sliding door to the narrow passage. I would never get used to these modern foreign trains, whose compartments did not open on either side to the station itself. I disliked the fact that other passengers could glide along that passage and stare in at one.

I stared out to avoid that possibility. Despite the veil, I

doubted that my face was in good order to be seen at the moment. I certainly had no desire to see any of the other passengers on the train.

Prague, city of one hundred towers, was sliding away into the peaceful green Bohemian countryside. Our adventures here were over at last, once and for all. We left a grateful King and Queen behind—who would have thought that a mere two-odd years ago!

If Irene had not specifically solved the murder of the Paris bead-girls, she had seen the Bohemian maid and duped assassin freed from illicit incarceration. And she had sung her last encore in Bohemia, under her terms and in her own inimitable, often imperious style. Mr. Dvořák, the orchestra and cast would not soon forget her performance, nor would we three.

Nor would the woman who called herself Tatyana. She would not forget Irene . . . and she would not forget Godfrey.

I rubbed my gloved hands together, for the empty compartment was chill. No. I would not dwell on future fears for the entire four days. No sooner had I made this resolution than a noise at the compartment door made me turn.

The door was being drawn shut again, behind an intimidating figure in what I can only describe as cossack dress: full trousers, high boots, a gilt-swagged jacket, short cape edged in astrakhan fur; the face ruddy and bristling with brows and mustache and sideburns, topped by a cap of Persian lamb. All that was lacking was a curved sword.

This figure from an operetta braced himself against the motion, then stomped to the opposite seat and sat, pulling off heavy leather gloves with Persian lamb cuffs as though to stay for tea.

"Sir! This is a private compartment. You must leave."

His hearty smile bespoke utter incomprehension.

"Go!" I said, pointing like a villain in a melodrama. "This is MY compartment." The fact that the moving train made my arm jerk up and down like a rail signal did not lend authority to the gesture.

He frowned and leaned toward me, bracing his hands on his knees and smiling and nodding idiotically. Who knows what rude variety of language he spoke, perhaps even Russian, of which I knew no more than *"nyet."*

Not even beyond the outskirts of Prague, and already confronted with an importunate gentleman! What would Irene have done? I had no dagger, no pistol, and a carpetbag did not make a very portable weapon.

I relied on my commanding tones again, drawing myself up as Irene would. "I demand that you leave." This time I glowered as I pointed.

Alas, if I had mastered Irene's lines, I did not possess her convincing delivery, for the man just shook his shaggy head.

"This is not," he said—in English!—"the greeting that I expected."

While I digested these remarkable words from such a wildly unlikely source, he leaned back in his swaying seat to remove his hat and place his gloves in it, to remove his . . . sideburns, his eyebrows—

I looked into the remarkable hazel eyes emerging from the shrubbery of his false face, and knew them.

I stood without being aware of having moved, at one with the gently shuddering train. "Que-Quentin!"

The white scimitar of his smile emerged from the shadow of the false mustache as it peeled away. The revealed face was familiar, was alive, was smiling.

The train plunged into a tunnel. Motes of darkness swirled like bats at the edges of my eyes. A horrible vibrating buzz sounded in my brain. Everything was narrowing to a tiny dot of light at the end of a pitch-black tunnel. Then the light winked out.

I awoke as from a dream, swaying and rocking, like a

babe in arms. I *was* in arms. Or arm, at least, for such an encircling limb supported my back and shoulders.

I was in my seat again, or nearly so, for I was not quite upright.

Quentin's face hung over me, bare of disguise and quite . . . beautiful, looking very concerned and rewardingly contrite.

"My dear Nell," he was saying, "it was most inconsiderate of me to spring such a surprise on you, after all you have been through: I must still go disguised. The Nortons and I felt this would allow us the best reunion. Are you quite all right?"

I nodded, slowly. Doing so made his face seem to mirror my gesture. It was so near that I could see each tiny line the desert had etched around his wonderful hazel eyes. I could see every eyelash, every fleck of hazy sand within the shifting hourglass of his eyes.

"I have taken the liberty of lifting your veil," he said. No wonder I saw him so clearly. "Would you like me to find your pince-nez?"

Pince-nez. I seemed to remember some article of that name from a distant day. "No. I can see perfectly well . . . at this distance," I said in some wonder.

He smiled, and I watched his face fracture into yet another fascinating expression. I had never seen anyone so closely, nor so clearly.

"Are you still faint?" he asked. "I have some brandy."

Brandy. I did not require intoxicants now! "It is only . . . a bit hard to . . . breathe."

He glanced down, and the sight of his lowered eyelids almost undid me. "I also took the liberty of loosening the neck of your blouse. These Western clothes are unhealthily constricting."

I nodded. I did feel an uncustomary . . . lightness at my throat, and even as he spoke felt a stir of wind over my bare skin, warm wind. Oh. His breath.

"You look very pale," he said with a frown. "These

confounded corsets you women squeeze your innards into! Were we not on a public train I would wrest them apart.''

"Oh," I said, unaccountably thrilled at the idea, or at least by the definitive tone in which he had uttered it. "I am used to such constriction . . . but . . . I do have a Liberty silk dress in the . . . Eastern style that does not require corsets.''

"Do you?" he said, looking amused. "Where on earth did you get that?''

"Irene."

His eyes narrowed. "I fear that she is a very bad influence on you, Miss Huxleigh."

"But I am such a good one on her."

He laughed so heartily then that I felt it. He raised his left hand to—I can put it no other way—caress the edge of my loosened high collar.

"I am so very glad to see you again, Nell," he said softly but with such intensity that I blinked. He smiled. "And I should very much like to see you in your Liberty silk gown."

At that most interesting moment, the train truly plunged into a genuine tunnel. We were doused in instant black, like a conjoined candle that burns too hot, and I was very glad that he could not see my face.

Ten days later I was sitting in the parlor at Neuilly rolling up balls of yarn that Lucifer had clawed into a rainbow of entwined snarls.

The sound of a carriage outside brought my head up, but I waited for Sophie to open the door. I heard warm voices, eager greetings, the progress of two people who felt very much at home through the cottage to the threshold of my chamber.

Irene and Godfrey stood there, looking as polished as marble, beaming health and wealth and as much wisdom as two extremely handsome people can do.

"Nell! You are the picture of domesticity," Irene said,

rushing to kiss me. Her cheek was still chill from the cold, but glowed as if touched by rubies.

"Apparently Vienna has a few milliners," I observed.

Irene turned in a gay, laughing circle to display her latest gown: a traveling dress of sky-blue wool with dark blue velvet bodice and sleeves. Under a midnight-blue velvet hat shaded by silver ostrich plumes, Irene's rich mahogany-colored hair was gathered into a low-braided queue at her nape, a girlish style that suited her as grapes suited Casanova. "Monsieur Worth will disapprove, but I am not his exclusive mannequin yet. I must have him make up something splendid for when I sing at Alice's wedding at month's end. I owe her at least that for her introduction to the master of Maison Worth."

Godfrey handed hat and stick to Sophie, then came to sit on the stool beside me and roll yarn.

"How did your charges comport themselves while we were gone?" he inquired.

"Terrible. Casanova has been molting—feathers everywhere."

"Oh, I hope you saved them!" Irene put in. "They would look divine on a bonnet."

"Would Monsieur Worth approve?"

"He will probably want an entire gown of them."

"I have just the bird to recommend as his prime source," said I.

From his nearby cage, the bird in question raised a bit of Wagner's "Pilgrim's Chorus," which apt choice of a welcome-home anthem for Irene and Godfrey made me forgive his mottled head.

"And Lucifer has been shedding dreadfully."

"Ah," said Godfrey. "We can spin his unwanted fur into a shawl for Irene."

She shrugged at him good-humoredly and sat in the bergère. "What of your wild Messalina?"

I paused in my mechanical yarn winding. "That is Quentin's Messalina. I am a mere foster-owner. She is as mischievous as ever, but is leaving tufts of fur around the garden."

Godfrey eyed Irene. "You wish to claim that?"

"No, I leave fur to foreign women. So, Nell." She watched me as narrowly as Lucifer stalked Casanova. "How was your return journey?"

I sighed and lay the yarns on my lap. "As you expected and assured me: long, but uneventful, even dull."

"Uneventful?" Irene sat fully upright in her most queenly interrogating posture. "Nothing happened?"

"Of course not. Nothing happened."

I did not often have the pleasure of seeing Irene stupefied at my wit.

"*Nothing!*" she repeated, her eyes going wildly to Godfrey. "Did no one—?"

"Of course," I added idly, "I was most surprised and gratified to see Quentin Stanhope again, and appreciate your thoughtfulness in arranging an escort for me, after all. I completely understand the need for discretion, for Quentin told me that he is working as a spy again, for the Foreign Office. Being presumed dead is a great advantage in such work, he told me."

"Did he—tell you nothing else?"

"What else is there to tell, Irene? I was pleased to be informed of his involvement in the entire affair." I glanced at Godfrey. "Quentin was the man in the tinted glasses who left us the guidebook, can you imagine that?" I eyed Irene again. "And I was not *too* angry that you and Allegra had seen Quentin first and did not tell me of his presence; indeed, or even confirm that the poor man was truly alive."

Irene was speechless. Godfrey took that rare opportunity to excuse himself and leave the parlor.

"How was your and Godfrey's holiday?" I asked in my turn.

"Sublime! Vienna is as enchanting as her reputation. We drove, we walked, we ate, we talked, we walzed, we went out to the theater, we stayed in—everything was sublime." Her eyes rested knowingly on me. "Much truth pertains to the fact that one most treasures what one most is in danger of losing, or fears that one is."

"Indeed, danger as well as absence makes the heart grow fonder."

Irene leaned avidly forward on her chair. "Well?"

"Well, what?"

"Well, how did you learn the truth of that aphorism."

"From acute and constant observation, Irene. You know that I keep a diary."

"Of course I do! What is in it since your return from Prague?"

"I am shocked. My diary is private unless I choose to share it with you."

"And you do not choose to share your most recent . . . adventures alone, with me?"

I smiled and rolled yarn. "Just as you do not wish to share with Godfrey the information that Quentin's contact in the Foreign Office is a Mr. Mycroft Holmes—"

"I did not know that!" Irene interrupted in high dudgeon.

"Neither did I until Quentin told me, but I do not imagine that you will tell Godfrey that, nor that Sherlock Holmes was in contact with Quentin during the scheme to abstract the false king from Bohemia."

Irene sat back, deep in the upholstered chair. "No. Godfrey has enough to worry about."

"Tatyana," I said. "You must worry about her as well."

"What of Quentin, then?" Irene demanded with a trace of petulance.

"I will worry about Quentin."

Irene flounced up and regarded me like a woman who, had she the equipment, would twitch her tail. "I must find Sophie and see what her aunt has in mind for supper. I am famished, and if I cannot be fed news, I will have to make do with food."

I smiled as she left the room. I was still smiling when Godfrey peeked in a few minutes later.

"Where is Irene?" he asked.

"Sulking in the back garden, no doubt, and contemplating the leeks."

"You are not angry about our last, slight deception, Nell?"

I laid my work down and looked up at him. "How could I be angry at such a reunion; though I was a bit . . . distraught at the suddenness of it."

"Nothing that Stanhope couldn't handle, though?" Godfrey asked, a twinkle in his pewter eyes.

"You know that there is nothing that Quentin cannot handle, Godfrey."

"And nothing that our dear Miss Huxleigh cannot handle," he added, looking at me so carefully that I blushed.

I resumed my winding task. "We shall have to see about our dear Miss Huxleigh in due time."

Afterword

The alert and faithful reader will have realized by now that these excerpts from the diaries of Penelope Huxleigh are notable for their lack of corroboration with the assembled tales known as the Canon of Sherlock Holmes.

Except for the fact that Holmes himself stated his connection with the French family name of Vernet, not a particle of evidence in this document verifies the events Miss Huxleigh describes.

Holmes claimed Émile Jean Horace Vernet*, a painter of the martial scenes so popular with the French, who lived from 1789 to 1863. Since Vernet's sister was Holmes's grandmother, Émile would have been Holmes's great-uncle. His son, Émile Charles Hippolyte (1821–1900), was a landscape painter, but Holmes makes no mention of contact with any member of this artistic family. Marie Augus-

---

*The Vernet reference occurs in the memoir called "The Adventure of the Greek Interpreter," which is dated to the 1880s. "Art in the blood is liable to take the strangest forms," Holmes commented after mentioning his French connection to Dr. Watson.

tine Vernet (1825–98) could have been Émile's daughter or niece, but history has blurred the page that carried the specifics of that particular family tree, especially as regards its female members.

The whereabouts of Holmes and even Dr. Watson during the time of this escapade are also vague, and neither prove nor disprove the issue. Holmes dispensed with the case of "The Adventure of the Crooked Man" in mid-September of that year, and was not otherwise involved in a documented case until "The Adventure of Wisteria Lodge" at year's end. (The Ripper Case Holmes and Watson discuss in the current account was the sensational discovery of a slaughtered woman's trunk and arms in Pinchin Street on September 10, 1989. At first considered a final atrocity of Jack the Ripper, the case was later discounted as the work of the modern age's most infamous serial killer.)

Nor can any careful historian prove the substitution of the true King of Bohemia with a double for a period of months in 1889. (In fact, the entire point of the events described in this portion of the diaries is the successful accomplishment of a discreet restoration of the proper royal order.) Certainly the matters related here tally with what is known of Russian colonial ambitions both in the exotic East and in Eastern Europe.

As for the intriguing and shameless woman known only as Tatyana, the single name (as likely a pseudonym as "Sable") guarantees that she will remain a historical mystery.

Again, there is precedence. Russian ballerinas of the nineteenth century were often the mistresses of wealthy and noble men; even of the czar. Nor was it unknown for them to engage in spywork on their wide travels with various performing companies.

The age of the female dancer/choreographer was dawning in the 1890s, even as global unrest encouraged great nations to call upon unusual persons for supposedly patriotic purposes. Not many years later another dancer/spy would become notorious enough to remain a historical byword of both of her professions, although under a pseudonym: Mata Hari.

Fiona Witherspoon, PhD.,
AIA*
November 5, 1993

*Advocates of Irene Adler